KT-508-915

THE OXFORD LIBRARY OF
CLASSIC ENGLISH SHORT STORIES

VOLUME I

The two volumes of Classic English Short Stories have been compiled to reflect the excellence and variety of short fiction written in English during the twentieth century. This first volume covers the years from the turn of the century to 1956 and the stories included amply demonstrate the change in attitudes and aesthetics that occurred during that time, a period often restless and impatient and dominated by two world wars.

Roger Sharrock, who introduces this collection, is Emeritus Professor of English Language and Literature at the University of London. The selection of stories was originally made for the English Association by Dan Davin, himself a writer of short stories.

THE
OXFORD LIBRARY
OF
CLASSIC ENGLISH
SHORT STORIES

VOLUME I
1900–1956

With an Introduction by
ROGER SHARROCK

GUILD PUBLISHING LONDON

This edition published 1989 by
Guild Publishing
by arrangement with Oxford University Press

Selection © The English Association 1939 and 1958
Introduction © Roger Sharrock 1989

CN 6347

Set by CentraCet
Printed in Great Britain by
Richard Clay Ltd, Bungay, Suffolk

CONTENTS

INTRODUCTION

These volumes of twentieth-century short stories in English cover a wide range of human experience, comic and tragic, strange and everyday, life on both sides of the tracks; in styles of writing they are equally varied. Can we then speak of the art of the short story as if it is a clearly defined form like the sonnet or the ode? In English there is no single word for the form: we have to make do with two words, whereas German has *novelle* and *Erzählung* and French has *nouvelle* and *conte*. But the short story is far from being merely a truncated version of the novel. It may not have precise rules, but it aims at certain effects not usually attempted in longer fictions. Jorge Luis Borges has said that the short story 'has more of discovery about it than of deliberate invention'; Kipling held that it must have what he called 'economy of implication'; and most strikingly Chekhov declared that if an author describes a gun hanging on the wall on page one then that gun sooner or later must go off. These statements amount to a tentative programme for a form of writing bound to a principle of necessity working within a limited space of language with carefully proportioned inter-related parts. We are dealing with a single powerful impulse from a single impression (or discovery), something very different from the multi-form pattern and the large idea of the novel.

To look for a pedigree for the form leads to the uncovering of a misunderstanding. H. E. Bates, another master practitioner, writes of the short story's long history: the episode of Cain and Abel in Genesis is a short story and so is the New Testament parable of the prodigal son. But a little later he writes: 'The history of the English short story is very brief, for the simple reason that before the end of the nineteenth century it had no history.'

The apparent contradiction is due to a confusion between the modern short story and the traditional oral tale. The oral tale entertains, but it also conveys wisdom, religious or moral, or the mere good sense of folk tradition. It has been handed down in great repositories like the *Arabian Nights*, 'Chaucer's *Canterbury Tales* and Boccaccio's *Decameron*. It is found in the more romantic fictions of the Old Testament, the story of Samson in Judges, or that of Susanna and the elders in the Apocrypha. It does not have to be short since it can be told at several sittings; as the *Arabian Nights'* formula has it: 'Scheherazade saw the approach of dawn and discreetly fell silent.' Something of the wisdom and fascination of the folk-tale remain here in Frank O'Connor's 'The Majesty of the Law', V. S. Pritchett's 'The Scapegoat', and Chinua Achebe's 'Uncle Ben's Choice'.

The short story as represented by most of those in this collection evolved as a distinct, self-conscious form in the '80s and '90s of the last century. Stevenson, Kipling and Hardy established themselves with the English public, but some felt that the delicate skills of the new story were better managed elsewhere, by Chekhov in Russia and Maupassant in France. Henry James wrote, 'the little story is but scantily relished in England, where readers take their fiction rather by the volume than the page'. There is something in the view that the progress of the genuine short story was hindered by the dominance of the leisurely three-decker novel (what James called 'loose and baggy monsters'). Certainly there are short stories by Dickens and Thackeray which read like chunks from novels, slow-moving with expansive addresses to the reader and full descriptions of each character.

The new story aims at a goal wholly different from that of the novel; it attempts to capture the essence of an experience or a relationship, or the atmosphere of a place or time. Its economy produces intensity, it dispenses with full characterization, the luxury of minor characters, or even anything that can be called a plot. But if a *feeling* has been communicated, and our sensibility, however imperceptibly, changed by it, then the story has been successful. Every phrase, every word counts; a story may seem to share qualities of the lyric poem (Coleridge's 'the best words in the best order'). Another parallel is with impressionist paintings, attempts to record scenes in a manner that was optically faithful. The rise of the short story in France coincided with the rise of the impressionist movement.

At the time of its emergence about the turn of the century the new art short story profited from a new availability of outlets. A number of reviews and magazines sought to present several short stories rather than one or two long tales. Well known from the '90s are the *Yellow Book* and the *Savoy*, but there were many more popular ones, the *Strand* after 1900, and *The Wide World Magazine*. The writer's adaptation to the limits of length prescribed by editors went to mould the economy of the form. When Kipling began publishing in the *Civil and Military Gazette* of Lahore in 1886 he was tied to a 2000-word limit, not a clog but a stimulus to 'economy of implication'. Interestingly, the little sketches and essays of the *Spectator* and *Tatler* in the early eighteenth century were limited to 2000 words by the size of the single sheet which constituted the periodical; and such sketches, of Sir Roger De Coverly the Tory squire, of a Whig merchant or a man of fashion, have been regarded as the ancestors of the short story.

In our stories, first published in magazines like those of the '90s, detail is subordinated to a single or unique effect. This single effect is likely to be some complex of emotion reflected in a moment of an individual life. Often the strong evocation of a sense of place or of a particular time provides a poetic image, the 'objective correlative' to convey this unique emotion. In Elizabeth Bowen's 'Ivy Gripped the Steps' the controlling power of the past over the present in an individual life is what the central image conveys. In H. E. Bates' 'Great Uncle Crow' it is a child's recollection of a magical day spent with a charismatic grown-up which is evoked by a few sensuously realized details in half-understood scraps of conversation. Sometimes, when a unique concentrated emotion is absent, the method of the single effect can become calculated and mechanical. The extrovert humour of Saki's 'The Background' is all derived from the single premiss that a man's tattooed back might be classed as a national monument. A variation on this is the confidence trick on the reader exercised by William Sansom in 'The Girl on the Bus' through which unrequited love is suddenly transformed into requited.

Economy and aesthetic unity are accompanied by impersonality and objectivity. The great primitive exemplar of the latter is Flaubert's 'Un Coeur Simple'. Impersonal detachment affects the whole moral character of the story, not just its technique. The wish to shed dogmatism entails scepticism about the possibility of any easy solution to human or religious problems. It is significant that Graham Greene has written Catholic novels but not Catholic short stories. His 'When Greek Meets Greek' in this collection is a cheerfully amoral description of the encounter of two criminal families. 'Everything in this world is relative and approximate', wrote Chekhov in 1887; the tentative and impressionistic short story excels in treating relative and approximate versions of a fleeting reality. Modern stories of the supernatural do not seem to deal with another realm or dimension; rather they are concerned with the doubtful and ambiguous borders of human experience; as in Walter De La Mare's superb 'Seaton's Aunt', a sensation of unreality is encountered but the problem always left unresolved. In another story by an early twentieth-century master, H. G. Wells' 'The Door in the Wall', a visionary experience is used as an image of the ideal integrated life opposed to convention, Wells' perpetual theme.

The spare form of the short story cannot concern itself with the vast complexity of the modern social world; its is a form for the pre-social and the post-social, the child and the old man, before the intense circle of natural experience widens and after it narrows again into memory and obsession. The peculiar, the eccentric, the lonely, the downright mad; these, with children and old people, make up a great part of the population of the modern short story. This world of mild alienation is not as morbid as it sounds: even the failure of people to communicate can produce high comedy, as in Olivia Manning's 'A Spot of Leave' and John Updike's 'Should Wizard Hit Mommy?'

If the well-made story, the story of single effect and fleeting impression, the legacy of Poe, Maupassant and Chekhov, is of such recent growth, will it pass away or be sucked back into the main current of the tale, that anecdotage of the race stretching back through millennia? To answer we have to think why in the twentieth century the tale declined and the new short story flourished. The best answer has been offered by Walter Benjamin in his brilliant essay on Leskov, the nineteenth-century Russian who could still draw on the sustenance of the folk-tale tradition. Writing only after the First World War Benjamin seems to anticipate the moral consequences of a dozen other terrible wars, the nuclear age, and the new technological revolution. The old story-teller dealt in shared experience, but now men and women return from the battlefields or the alienated inner cities, not richer, but poorer in communicable experience. 'A generation that had gone to school on a horse-drawn street-car now stood under an open sky in a countryside in which nothing remained unchanged but the clouds, and beneath these clouds . . . the tiny, fragile human body.' The world of the short story is the world of these fragile individuals, their sensibilities driven in on themselves in reaction against incommunicable experience.

What of the future? This can only depend on changes within that individual with his withdrawn, highly perceptive consciousness. Clearly at some time we must regain that common public experience which gave the old teller of tales his authority. In this connection, while sensibility has contracted, the area of the language has expanded, and there is untold hope for the story in the new literatures of English: in later stories here, America, the West Indies, India, Australia, New Zealand, and Canada are represented. In such linguistic movement and response to new challenge anything can happen.

Roger Sharrock

MONTAGUE JAMES
Casting the Runes

April 15th, 190–.

DEAR SIR,—I am requested by the Council of the —— Association to return to you the draft of a paper on *The Truth of Alchemy*, which you have been good enough to offer to read at our forthcoming meeting, and to inform you that the Council do not see their way to including it in the programme.

I am,
Yours faithfully,
——Secretary

April 18th.

DEAR SIR,—I am sorry to say that my engagements do not permit of my affording you an interview on the subject of your proposed paper. Nor do our laws allow of your discussing the matter with a Committee of our Council, as you suggest. Please allow me to assure you that the fullest consideration was given to the draft which you submitted, and that it was not declined without having been referred to the judgement of a most competent authority. No personal question (it can hardly be necessary for me to add) can have had the slightest influence on the decision of the Council.

Believe me (ut supra).

April 20th.

The Secretary of the —— Association begs respectfully to inform Mr. Karswell that it is impossible for him to communicate the name of any person or persons to whom the draft of Mr. Karswell's paper may have been submitted; and further desires to intimate that he cannot undertake to reply to any further letters on this subject.

'And who *is* Mr. Karswell?' inquired the Secretary's wife. She had called at his office, and (perhaps unwarrantably) had picked up the last of these three letters, which the typist had just brought in.

'Why, my dear, just at present Mr. Karswell is a very angry man.

But I don't know much about him otherwise, except that he is a person of wealth, his address is Lufford Abbey, Warwickshire, and he's an alchemist, apparently, and wants to tell us all about it; and that's about all—except that I don't want to meet him for the next week or two. Now, if you're ready to leave this place, I am.'

'What have you been doing to make him angry?' asked Mrs. Secretary.

'The usual thing, my dear, the usual thing: he sent in a draft of a paper he wanted to read at the next meeting, and we referred it to Edward Dunning—almost the only man in England who knows about these things—and he said it was perfectly hopeless, so we declined it. So Karswell has been pelting me with letters ever since. The last thing he wanted was the name of the man we referred his nonsense to; you saw my answer to that. But don't you say anything about it, for goodness' sake.'

'I should think not, indeed. Did I ever do such a thing? I do hope, though, he won't get to know that it was poor Mr. Dunning.'

'Poor Mr. Dunning? I don't know why you call him that; he's a very happy man, is Dunning. Lots of hobbies and a comfortable home, and all his time to himself.'

'I only meant I should be sorry for him if this man got hold of his name, and came and bothered him.'

'Oh, ah! yes. I dare say he would be poor Mr. Dunning then.'

The Secretary and his wife were lunching out, and the friends to whose house they were bound were Warwickshire people. So Mrs. Secretary had already settled it in her own mind that she would question them judiciously about Mr. Karswell. But she was saved the trouble of leading up to the subject, for the hostess said to the host, before many minutes had passed, 'I saw the Abbot of Lufford this morning.' The host whistled. '*Did* you? What in the world brings him up to town?' 'Goodness knows; he was coming out of the British Museum gate as I drove past.' It was not unnatural that Mrs. Secretary should inquire whether this was a real Abbot who was being spoken of. 'Oh no, my dear: only a neighbour of ours in the country who bought Lufford Abbey a few years ago. His real name is Karswell.' 'Is he a friend of yours?' asked Mr. Secretary, with a private wink to his wife. The question let loose a torrent of declamation. There was really nothing to be said for Mr. Karswell. Nobody knew what he did with himself: his servants were a horrible set of people; he had invented a new religion for himself, and practised no one could tell what appalling rites; he was very easily offended, and never forgave anybody; he had a dreadful face (so the lady insisted, her husband somewhat demurring); he never did a kind action, and whatever influence he did exert was mischievous. 'Do the poor man justice, dear,' the husband interrupted. 'You forget the treat he gave the school children.' 'Forget it, indeed! But I'm glad you mentioned it, because it gives an idea of the man. Now, Florence, listen to this. The first winter he was at Lufford this delightful neighbour of ours wrote to the clergyman of his parish (he's not ours, but we know him very well) and offered to show the school children some magic-lantern slides. He said he had some new kinds, which he thought would interest them. Well, the clergyman was rather surprised, because Mr. Karswell had shown himself inclined to be unpleasant to the children—complaining of their trespassing, or something of the sort; but of course he accepted, and the evening was fixed, and our friend went himself to see that everything went right. He said he never had been so thankful for anything as that his own children were all prevented from being there: they were at a children's party at our house, as a matter of fact. Because this Mr. Karswell had evidently set out with the intention of frightening these poor village children out of their wits, and I do believe, if he had been allowed to go on, he would actually have done so. He began with some comparatively mild things. Red Riding Hood was one, and even then, Mr. Farrer said, the wolf was so dreadful that several of the smaller children had to be taken out: and he said Mr. Karswell began the story by producing a noise like a wolf howling in the distance, which was the most gruesome thing he had ever heard. All the slides he showed, Mr. Farrer said, were most clever; they were absolutely realistic, and where he had got them or how he worked them he could not imagine. Well, the show went on, and the stories kept on becoming a little more terrifying each time, and the children were mesmerized into complete silence. At last he produced a series which represented a little boy passing through his own park—Lufford, I mean—in the evening. Every child in the room could recognize the place from the pictures. And this poor boy was followed, and at last pursued and overtaken, and either torn in pieces or somehow made away with, by a horrible hopping creature in white, which you saw first dodging about among the trees, and gradually it appeared more and more plainly.

Mr. Farrer said it gave him one of the worst nightmares he ever remembered, and what it must have meant to the children doesn't bear thinking of. Of course this was too much, and he spoke very sharply indeed to Mr. Karswell, and said it couldn't go on. All *he* said was: "Oh, you think it's time to bring our little show to an end and send them home to their beds. *Very* well!" And then, if you please, he switched on another slide, which showed a great mass of snakes, centipedes, and disgusting creatures with wings, and somehow or other he made it seem as if they were climbing out of the picture and getting in amongst the audience; and this was accompanied by a sort of dry rustling noise which sent the children nearly mad, and of course they stampeded. A good many of them were rather hurt in getting out of the room, and I don't suppose one of them closed an eye that night. There was the most dreadful trouble in the village afterwards. Of course the mothers threw a good part of the blame on poor Mr. Farrer, and, if they could have got past the gates, I believe the fathers would have broken every window in the Abbey. Well, now, that's Mr. Karswell: that's the Abbot of Lufford, my dear, and you can imagine how we covet *his* society.'

'Yes, I think he has all the possibilities of a distinguished criminal, has Karswell,' said the host. 'I should be sorry for any one who got into his bad books.'

'Is he the man, or am I mixing him up with some one else?' asked the Secretary (who for some minutes had been wearing the frown of the man who is trying to recollect something). 'Is he the man who brought out a *History of Witchcraft* some time back—ten years or more?'

'That's the man; do you remember the reviews of it?'

'Certainly I do; and what's equally to the point, I knew the author of the most incisive of the lot. So did you: you must remember John Harrington; he was at John's in our time.'

'Oh, very well indeed, though I don't think I saw or heard anything of him between the time I went down and the day I read the account of the inquest on him.'

'Inquest?' said one of the ladies. 'What has happened to him?'

'Why, what happened was that he fell out of a tree and broke his neck. But the puzzle was, what could have induced him to get up there. It was a mysterious business, I must say. Here was this man—not an athletic fellow, was he? and with no eccentric twist about him that was ever noticed—walking home along a country road late in the evening—no tramps about—well known and liked in the place—and he suddenly begins to run like mad, loses his hat and stick, and finally shins up a tree—quite a difficult tree— growing in the hedgerow: a dead branch gives way, and he comes down with it and breaks his neck, and there he's found next morning with the most dreadful face of fear on him that could be imagined. It was pretty evident, of course, that he had been chased by something, and people talked of savage dogs, and beasts escaped out of menageries; but there was nothing to be made of that. That was in '89, and I believe his brother Henry (whom I remember as well at Cambridge, but *you* probably don't) has been trying to get on the track of an explanation ever since. He, of course, insists there was malice in it, but I don't know. It's difficult to see how it could have come in.'

After a time the talk reverted to the *History of Witchcraft*. 'Did you ever look into it?' asked the host.

'Yes, I did,' said the Secretary. 'I went so far as to read it.'

'Was it as bad as it was made out to be?'

'Oh, in point of style and form, quite hopeless. It deserved all the pulverizing it got. But, besides that, it was an evil book. The man believed every word of what he was saying, and I'm very much mistaken if he hadn't tried the greater part of his receipts.'

'Well, I only remember Harrington's review of it, and I must say if I'd been the author it would have quenched my literary ambition for good. I should never have held up my head again.'

'It hasn't had that effect in the present case. But come, it's half-past three; I must be off.'

On the way home the Secretary's wife said, 'I do hope that horrible man won't find out that Mr. Dunning had anything to do with the rejection of his paper.' 'I don't think there's much chance of that,' said the Secretary. 'Dunning won't mention it himself, for these matters are confidential, and none of us will for the same reason. Karswell won't know his name, for Dunning hasn't pub-lished anything on the same subject yet. The only danger is that Karswell might find out, if he was to ask the British Museum people who was in the habit of consulting alchemical manuscripts: I can't very well tell them not to mention Dunning, can I? It would set them talking at once. Let's hope it won't occur to him.'

However, Mr. Karswell was an astute man.

* * *

This much is in the way of prologue. On an evening rather later in the same week, Mr. Edward Dunning was returning from the British Museum, where he had been engaged in Research, to the comfortable house in a suburb where he lived alone, tended by two excellent women who had been long with him. There is nothing to be added by way of description of him to what we have heard already. Let us follow him as he takes his sober course homewards.

A train took him to within a mile or two of his house, and an electric tram a stage farther. The line ended at a point some three hundred yards from his front door. He had had enough of reading when he got into the car, and indeed the light was not such as to allow him to do more than study the advertisements on the panes of glass that faced him as he sat. As was not unnatural, the advertisements in this particular line of cars were objects of his frequent contemplation, and, with the possible exception of the brilliant and convincing dialogue between Mr. Lamplough and an eminent K.C. on the subject of Pyretic Saline, none of them afforded much scope to his imagination. I am wrong: there was one at the corner of the car farthest from him which did not seem familiar. It was in blue letters on a yellow ground, and all that he could read of it was a name— John Harrington—and something like a date. It could be of no interest to him to know more; but for all that, as the car emptied, he was just curious enough to move along the seat until he could read it well. He felt to a slight extent repaid for his trouble; the advertisement was *not* of the usual type. It ran thus: 'In memory of John Harrington, F.S.A., of The Laurels, Ashbrooke. Died Sept. 18th, 1889. Three months were allowed.'

The car stopped. Mr. Dunning, still contemplating the blue letters on the yellow ground, had to be stimulated to rise by a word from the conductor. 'I beg your pardon,' he said, 'I was looking at that advertisement; it's a very odd one, isn't it?' The conductor read it slowly. 'Well, my word,' he said, 'I never see that one before. Well, that is a cure, ain't it? Some one bin up to their jokes 'ere, I should think.' He got out a duster and applied it, not without saliva, to the pane and then to the outside. 'No,' he said, returning, 'that ain't no transfer; seems to me as if it was reg'lar *in* the glass, what I mean in the substance, as you may say. Don't you think so, sir?' Mr. Dunning examined it and rubbed it with his glove, and agreed. 'Who looks after these advertisements, and gives leave for them to be put up? I wish you would inquire. I will just take a note of the words.' At this moment there came a call from the driver: 'Look alive, George, time's up.' 'All right, all right; there's somethink else what's up at this end. You come and look at this 'ere glass.' 'What's gorn with the glass?' said the driver, approaching. 'Well, and oo's 'Arrington? What's it all about?' 'I was just asking who was responsible for putting the advertisements up in your cars, and saying it would be as well to make some inquiry about this one.' 'Well, sir, that's all done at the Company's orfice, that work is: it's our Mr. Timms, I believe, looks into that. When we put up to-night, I'll leave word, and per'aps I'll be able to tell you to-morrer if you 'appen to be coming this way.'

This was all that passed that evening. Mr. Dunning did just go to the trouble of looking up Ashbrooke, and found that it was in Warwickshire.

Next day he went to town again. The car (it was the same car) was too full in the morning to allow of his getting a word with the conductor: he could only be sure that the curious advertisement had been made away with. The close of the day brought a further element of mystery into the transaction. He had missed the tram, or else preferred walking home, but at a rather late hour, while he was at work in his study, one of the maids came to say that two men from the tramways were very anxious to speak to him. This was a reminder of the advertisement, which he had, he says, nearly forgotten. He had the men in—they were the conductor and driver of the car—and when the matter of refreshment had been attended to, asked what Mr. Timms had had to say about the advertisement. 'Well, sir, that's what we took the liberty to step round about,' said the conductor. 'Mr. Timms 'e give William 'ere the rough side of his tongue about that: 'cordin' to 'im there warn't no advertisement of that description sent in, nor ordered, nor paid for, nor put up, nor nothink, let alone not bein' there, and we was playing the fool takin' up his time. "Well," I says, "if that's the case, all I ask of you, Mr. Timms," I says, "is to take and look at it for yourself," I says. "Of course if it ain't there," I says, "you may take and call me what you like." "Right," he says, "I will": and we went straight off. Now, I leave it to you, sir, if that ad., as we term 'em, with 'Arrington on it warn't as plain as ever you see anythink—blue letters on yeller glass, and as I says at the time, and you borne me out, reg'lar *in* the glass, because, if you remember, you recollect of me swabbing it with my duster.' 'To be sure I do, quite clearly—well?' 'You may say well, I don't think. Mr. Timms he gets in that car with a light—no, he told William to 'old the light outside. "Now," he says, "where's your precious ad. what we've 'eard so much about?" "'Ere it is," I says, "Mr. Timms," and I laid my 'and on it.' The conductor paused.

'Well, said Mr. Dunning, 'it was gone, I suppose. Broken?'

'Broke!—not it. There warn't, if you'll believe me, no more trace of them letters—blue letters they was—on that piece o' glass, than—well, it's no good *me* talkin'. *I* never see such a thing. I leave it to William here if—but there, as I says, where's the benefit in me going on about it?'

'And what did Mr. Timms say?'

'Why 'e did what I give 'im leave to—called us pretty much anythink he liked, and I don't know as I blame him so much neither. But what we thought, William and me did, was as we seen you take down a bit of a note about that—well, that letterin'——'

'I certainly did that, and I have it now. Did you wish me to speak to Mr. Timms myself, and show it to him? Was that what you came in about?'

'There, didn't I say as much?' said William. 'Deal with a gent if you can get on the track of one, that's my word. Now perhaps, George, you'll allow as I ain't took you very far wrong to-night.'

'Very well, William, very well; no need for you to go on as if you'd 'ad to frog's-march me 'ere. I come quiet, didn't I? All the same for that, we 'adn't ought to take up your time this way, sir; but if it so 'appened you could find time to step round to the Company's orfice in the morning and tell Mr. Timms what you seen for yourself, we should lay under a very 'igh obligation to you for the trouble. You see it ain't bein' called—well, one thing and another, as we mind, but if they got it into their 'ead at the orfice as we seen things as warn't there, why, one thing leads to another, and where we should be a twelve-munce 'ence—well, you can understand what I mean.'

Amid further elucidations of the proposition, George, conducted by William, left the room.

The incredulity of Mr. Timms (who had a nodding acquaintance with Mr. Dunning) was greatly modified on the following day by what the latter could tell and show him; and any bad mark that might have been attached to the names of William and George was not suffered to remain on the Company's books; but explanation there was none.

Mr. Dunning's interest in the matter was kept alive by an incident of the following afternoon. He was walking from his club to the train, and he noticed some way ahead a man with a handful of leaflets such as are distributed to passers-by by agents of enterprising firms. This agent had not chosen a very crowded street for his operations: in fact, Mr. Dunning did not see him get rid of a single leaflet before he himself reached the spot. One was thrust into his hand as he passed: the hand that gave it touched his, and he experienced a sort of little shock as it did so. It seemed unnaturally rough and hot. He looked in passing at the giver, but the impression he got was so unclear that, however much he tried to reckon it up subsequently, nothing would come. He was walking quickly, and as he went on glanced at the paper. It was a blue one. The name of Harrington in large capitals caught his eye. He stopped, startled, and felt for his glasses. The next instant the leaflet was twitched out of his hand by a man who hurried past, and was irrecoverably gone. He ran back a few paces, but where was the passer-by? and where the distributor?

It was in a somewhat pensive frame of mind that Mr. Dunning passed on the following day into the Select Manuscript Room of the British Museum, and filled up tickets for Harley 3586, and some other volumes. After a few minutes they were brought to him, and he was settling the one he wanted first upon the desk, when he thought he heard his own name whispered behind him. He turned round hastily, and in doing so, brushed his little portfolio of loose papers on to the floor. He saw no one he recognized except one of the staff in charge of the room, who nodded to him, and he proceeded to pick up his papers. He thought he had them all, and was turning to begin work, when a stout gentleman at the table behind him, who was just rising to leave, and had collected his own belongings, touched him on the shoulder, saying, 'May I give you this? I think it should be yours,' and handed him a missing quire. 'It is mine, thank you,' said Mr. Dunning. In another moment the man had left the room. Upon finishing his work for the afternoon, Mr. Dunning had some conversation with the assistant in charge, and took occasion to ask who the stout gentleman was. 'Oh, he's a man named Karswell,' said the assistant; 'he was asking me a week ago who were the great authorities on alchemy, and of course I told him you were the only one in the country. I'll see if I can't catch him: he'd like to meet you, I'm sure.'

'For heaven's sake don't dream of it!' said Mr. Dunning, 'I'm particularly anxious to avoid him.'

'Oh! very well,' said the assistant, 'he doesn't come here often: I dare say you won't meet him.'

More than once on the way home that day Mr. Dunning confessed to himself that he did not look forward with his usual cheerfulness to a solitary evening. It seemed to him that something ill defined and impalpable had stepped in between him and his fellow men—had taken him in charge, as it were. He wanted to sit close up to his neighbours in the train and in the tram, but as luck would have it both train and car were markedly empty. The conductor George was thoughtful, and appeared to be absorbed in calculations as to the number of passengers. On arriving at his house he found Dr. Watson, his medical man, on his doorstep. 'I've had to upset your household arrangements, I'm sorry to say, Dunning. Both your servants *hors de combat*. In fact, I've had to send them to the Nursing Home.'

'Good heavens! what's the matter?'

'It's something like ptomaine poisoning, I should think: you've not suffered yourself, I can see, or you wouldn't be walking about. I think they'll pull through all right.'

'Dear, dear! Have you any idea what brought it on?'

'Well, they tell me they bought some shell-fish from a hawker at their dinner-time. It's odd. I've made inquiries, but I can't find that any hawker has been to other houses in the street. I couldn't send word to you; they won't be back for a bit yet. You come and dine with me to-night, anyhow, and we can make arrangements for going on. Eight o'clock. Don't be too anxious.'

The solitary evening was thus obviated; at the expense of some distress and inconvenience, it is true. Mr. Dunning spent the time pleasantly enough with the doctor (a rather recent settler), and returned to his lonely home at about 11.30. The night he passed is not one on which he looks back with any satisfaction. He was in bed and the light was out. He was wondering if the charwoman would come early enough to get him hot water next morning, when he heard the unmistakable sound of his study door opening. No step followed it on the passage floor, but the sound must mean mischief, for he knew that he had shut the door that evening after putting his papers away in his desk. It was rather shame than courage that induced him to slip out into the passage and lean over the banister in his nightgown, listening. No light was visible; no further sound came: only a gust of warm, or even hot air played for an instant round his shins. He went back and decided to lock himself into his room. There was more unpleasantness, however. Either an economical suburban company had decided that their light would not be required in the small hours, and had stopped working, or else something was wrong with the meter; the effect was in any case that the electric light was off. The obvious course was to find a match, and also to consult his watch: he might as well know how many hours of discomfort awaited him. So he put his hand into the well-known nook under the pillow: only, it did not get so far. What he touched was, according to his account, a mouth, with teeth, and with hair about it, and, he declares, not the mouth of a human being. I do not think it is any use to guess what he said or did; but he was in a spare room with the door locked and his ear to it before he was clearly conscious again. And there he spent the rest of a most miserable night, looking every moment for some fumbling at the door: but nothing came.

The venturing back to his own room in the morning was attended with many listenings and quiverings. The door stood open, fortunately, and the blinds were up (the servants had been out of the house before the hour of drawing them down); there was, to be short, no trace of an inhabitant. The watch, too, was in its usual place; nothing was disturbed, only the wardrobe door had swung open, in accordance with its confirmed habit. A ring at the back door now announced the charwoman, who had been ordered the night before, and nerved Mr. Dunning, after letting her in, to continue his search in other parts of the house. It was equally fruitless.

The day thus begun went on dismally enough. He dared not go to the Museum: in spite of what the assistant had said, Karswell might turn up there, and Dunning felt he could not cope with a probably hostile stranger. His own house was odious; he hated sponging on the doctor. He spent some little time in a call at the Nursing Home, where he was slightly cheered by a good report of his housekeeper and maid. Towards lunchtime he betook himself to his club, again experiencing a gleam of satisfaction at seeing the Secretary of the Association. At luncheon Dunning told his friend the more material of his woes, but could not bring himself to speak of those that weighed most heavily on his spirits. 'My poor dear man,' said the Secretary, 'what an upset! Look here: we're alone at home, absolutely. You must put up with us. Yes! no excuse: send your things in this afternoon.' Dunning was unable to stand out: he was, in truth, becoming acutely anxious, as the hours went on, as to what that night might have waiting for him. He was almost happy as he hurried home to pack up.

His friends, when they had time to take stock of him, were rather shocked at his lorn appearance, and did their best to keep him up to the mark. Not altogether without success: but, when the two men were smoking alone later, Dunning became dull again. Suddenly he said, 'Gayton, I believe that alchemist man knows it was I who got his paper rejected.' Gayton whistled. 'What makes you think that?' he said. Dunning told of his conversation with the Museum assistant, and Gayton could only agree that the guess seemed likely to be correct. 'Not that I care much,' Dunning went on, 'only it might be a nuisance if we were to meet. He's a bad-tempered party, I imagine.' Conversation dropped again; Gayton became more and more strongly impressed with the desolateness that came over Dunning's face and bearing, and finally—though with a considerable effort—he asked him point-blank whether something serious was not bothering him. Dunning gave an exclamation of relief. 'I was perishing to get it off my mind,' he said. 'Do you know anything about a man named John Harrington?' Gayton was thoroughly startled, and at the moment could only ask why. Then the complete story of Dunning's experiences came out—what had happened in the tramcar, in his own house, and in the street, the troubling of spirit that had crept over him, and still held him; and he ended with the question he had begun with. Gayton was at a loss how to answer him. To tell the story of Harrington's end would perhaps be right; only, Dunning was in a nervous state, the story was a grim one, and he could not help asking himself whether there were not a connecting link between these two cases, in the person of Karswell. It was a difficult concession for a scientific man, but it could be eased by the phrase 'hypnotic suggestion'. In the end he decided that his answer to-night should be guarded; he would talk the situation over with his wife. So he said that he had known Harrington at Cambridge, and believed he had died suddenly in 1889, adding a few details about the man and his published work.

He did talk over the matter with Mrs. Gayton, and, as he had anticipated, she leapt at once to the conclusion which had been hovering before him. It was she who reminded him of the surviving brother, Henry Harrington, and she also who suggested that he might be got hold of by means of their hosts of the day before. 'He might be a hopeless crank,' objected Gayton. 'That could be ascertained from the Bennetts, who knew him,' Mrs. Gayton retorted; and she undertook to see the Bennetts the very next day.

It is not necessary to tell in further detail the steps by which Henry Harrington and Dunning were brought together.

The next scene that does require to be narrated is a conversation that took place between the two. Dunning had told Harrington of the strange ways in which the dead man's name had been brought before him, and had said something, besides, of his own subsequent experiences. Then he had asked if Harrington was disposed, in return, to recall any of the circumstances connected with his brother's death. Harrington's surprise at what he heard can be imagined: but his reply was readily given.

'John,' he said, 'was in a very odd state, undeniably, from time to time, during some weeks before, though not immediately before, the catastrophe. There were several things; the principal notion he had was that he thought he was being followed. No doubt he was an impressionable man, but he never had had such fancies as this before. I cannot get it out of my mind that there was ill-will at work, and what you tell me about yourself reminds me very much of my brother. Can you think of any possible connecting link?'

'There is just one that has been taking shape vaguely in my mind. I've been told that your brother reviewed a book very severely not long before he died, and just lately I have happened to cross the path of the man who wrote that book in a way he would resent.'

'Don't tell me the man was called Karswell.'

'Why not? that is exactly his name.'

Henry Harrington leant back. 'That is final to my mind. Now I must explain further. From something he said, I feel sure that my brother John was beginning to believe—very much against his will—that Karswell was at the bottom of his trouble. I want to tell you what seems to me to have a bearing on the situation. My brother was a great musician, and used to run up to concerts in

town. He came back, three months before he died, from one of
these, and gave me his programme to look at—an analytical
programme: he always kept them. "I nearly missed this one," he
said. "I suppose I must have dropped it: anyhow, I was looking for
it under my seat and in my pockets and so on, and my neighbour
offered me his: said 'might he give it me, he had no further use for
it,' and he went away just afterwards. I don't know who he was—a
stout, clean-shaven man. I should have been sorry to miss it; of
course I could have bought another, but this cost me nothing." At
another time he told me that he had been very uncomfortable both
on the way to his hotel and during the night. I piece things together
now in thinking it over. Then, not very long after, he was going
over these programmes, putting them in order to have them bound
up, and in this particular one (which by the way I had hardly
glanced at), he found quite near the beginning a strip of paper with
some very odd writing on it in red and black—most carefully
done—it looked to me more like Runic letters than anything else.
"Why," he said, "this must belong to my fat neighbour. It looks as
if it might be worth returning to him; it may be a copy of something;
evidently some one has taken trouble over it. How can I find his
address?" We talked it over for a little and agreed that it wasn't
worth advertising about, and that my brother had better look out
for the man at the next concert, to which he was going very soon.
The paper was lying on the book and we were both by the fire; it
was a cold, windy summer evening. I suppose the door blew open,
though I didn't notice it: at any rate a gust—a warm gust it was—
came quite suddenly between us, took the paper and blew it straight
into the fire: it was light, thin paper, and flared and went up the
chimney in a single ash. "Well," I said, "you can't give it back
now." He said nothing for a minute: then rather crossly, "No, I
can't; but why you should keep on saying so I don't know." I
remarked that I didn't say it more than once. "Not more than four
times, you mean," was all he said. I remember all that very clearly,
without any good reason; and now to come to the point. I don't
know if you looked at that book of Karswell's which my unfortunate
brother reviewed. It's not likely that you should: but I did, both
before his death and after it. The first time we made game of it
together. It was written in no style at all—split infinitives, and
every sort of thing that makes an Oxford gorge rise. Then there was
nothing that the man didn't swallow: mixing up classical myths,

and stories out of the *Golden Legend* with reports of savage customs of to-day—all very proper, no doubt, if you know how to use them, but he didn't: he seemed to put the *Golden Legend* and the *Golden Bough* exactly on a par, and to believe both: a pitiable exhibition, in short. Well, after the misfortune, I looked over the book again. It was no better than before, but the impression which it left this time on my mind was different. I suspected—as I told you—that Karswell had borne ill will to my brother, even that he was in some way responsible for what had happened; and now his book seemed to me to be a very sinister performance indeed. One chapter in particular struck me, in which he spoke of "casting the Runes" on people, either for the purpose of gaining their affection or of getting them out of the way—perhaps more especially the latter: he spoke of all this in a way that really seemed to me to imply actual knowledge. I've not time to go into details, but the upshot is that I am pretty sure from information received that the civil man at the concert was Karswell: I suspect—I more than suspect—that the paper was of importance: and I do believe that if my brother had been able to give it back, he might have been alive now. Therefore, it occurs to me to ask you whether you have anything to put beside what I have told you.'

By way of answer, Dunning had the episode in the Manuscript Room at the British Museum to relate. 'Then he did actually hand you some papers; have you examined them? No? because we must, if you'll allow it, look at them at once, and very carefully.'

They went to the still-empty house—empty, for the two servants were not yet able to return to work. Dunning's portfolio of papers was gathering dust on the writing-table. In it were the quires of small-sized scribbling paper which he used for his transcripts: and from one of these, as he took it up, there slipped and fluttered out into the room with uncanny quickness, a strip of thin light paper. The window was open, but Harrington slammed it to, just in time to intercept the paper, which he caught. 'I thought so,' he said; 'it might be the identical thing that was given to my brother. You'll have to look out, Dunning; this may mean something quite serious for you.'

A long consultation took place. The paper was narrowly examined. As Harrington had said, the characters on it were more like Runes than anything else, but not decipherable by either man, and both hesitated to copy them, for fear, as they confessed, of perpetuating whatever evil purpose they might conceal. So it has remained impossible (if I may anticipate a little) to ascertain what was

conveyed in this curious message or commission. Both Dunning and
Harrington are firmly convinced that it had the effect of bringing its
possessors into very undesirable company. That it must be returned
to the source whence it came they were agreed, and further, that
the only safe and certain way was that of personal service; and here
contrivance would be necessary, for Dunning was known by sight
to Karswell. He must, for one thing, alter his appearance by shaving
his beard. But then might not the blow fall first? Harrington thought
they could time it. He knew the date of the concert at which the
'black spot' had been put on his brother: it was June 18th. The
death had followed on September 18th. Dunning reminded him that
three months had been mentioned on the inscription on the car-
window. 'Perhaps,' he added, with a cheerless laugh, 'mine may be
a bill at three months too. I believe I can fix it by my diary. Yes,
April 23rd was the day at the Museum; that brings us to July 23rd.
Now, you know, it becomes extremely important to me to know
anything you will tell me about the progress of your brother's
trouble, if it is possible for you to speak of it.' 'Of course. Well, the
sense of being watched whenever he was alone was the most
distressing thing to him. After a time I took to sleeping in his room,
and he was the better for that: still, he talked a great deal in his
sleep. What about? Is it wise to dwell on that, at least before things
are straightened out? I think not, but I can tell you this: two things
came for him by post during those weeks, both with a London
postmark, and addressed in a commercial hand. One was a woodcut
of Bewick's roughly torn out of the page: one which shows a moonlit
road and a man walking along it, followed by an awful demon
creature. Under it were written the lines out of the "Ancient
Mariner" (which I suppose the cut illustrates) about one who,
having once looked round—

> walks on,
> And turns no more his head,
> Because he knows a frightful fiend
> Doth close behind him tread.

The other was a calendar, such as tradesmen often send. My
brother paid no attention to this, but I looked at it after his death,
and found that everything after September 18 had been torn out.
You may be surprised at his having gone out alone the evening he

was killed, but the fact is that during the last ten days or so of his life he had been quite free from the sense of being followed or watched.'

The end of the consultation was this. Harrington, who knew a neighbour of Karswell's, thought he saw a way of keeping a watch on his movements. It would be Dunning's part to be in readiness to try to cross Karswell's path at any moment, to keep the paper safe and in a place of ready access.

They parted. The next weeks were no doubt a severe strain upon Dunning's nerves: the intangible barrier which had seemed to rise about him on the day when he received the paper, gradually developed into a brooding blackness that cut him off from the means of escape to which one might have thought he might resort. No one was at hand who was likely to suggest them to him, and he seemed robbed of all initiative. He waited with inexpressible anxiety as May, June, and early July passed on, for a mandate from Harrington. But all this time Karswell remained immovable at Lufford.

At last, in less than a week before the date he had come to look upon as the end of his earthly activities, came a telegram: 'Leaves Victoria by boat train Thursday night. Do not miss. I come to you to-night. Harrington.'

He arrived accordingly, and they concocted plans. The train left Victoria at nine and its last stop before Dover was Croydon West. Harrington would mark down Karswell at Victoria, and look out for Dunning at Croydon, calling to him if need were by a name agreed upon. Dunning, disguised as far as might be, was to have no label or initials on any hand luggage, and must at all costs have the paper with him.

Dunning's suspense as he waited on the Croydon platform I need not attempt to describe. His sense of danger during the last days had only been sharpened by the fact that the cloud about him had perceptibly been lighter; but relief was an ominous symptom, and, if Karswell eluded him now, hope was gone: and there were so many chances of that. The rumour of the journey might be itself a device. The twenty minutes in which he paced the platform and persecuted every porter with inquiries as to the boat train were as bitter as any he had spent. Still, the train came, and Harrington was at the window. It was important, of course, that there should be no recognition: so Dunning got in at the farther end of the

corridor carriage, and only gradually made his way to the compartment where Harrington and Karswell were. He was pleased, on the
whole, to see that the train was far from full.

Karswell was on the alert, but gave no sign of recognition.
Dunning took the seat not immediately facing him, and attempted,
vainly at first, then with increasing command of his faculties, to
reckon the possibilities of making the desired transfer. Opposite to
Karswell, and next to Dunning, was a heap of Karswell's coats on
the seat. It would be of no use to slip the paper into these—he
would not be safe, or would not feel so, unless in some way it could
be proffered by him and accepted by the other. There was a
handbag, open, and with papers in it. Could he manage to conceal
this (so that perhaps Karswell might leave the carriage without it),
and then find and give it to him? This was the plan that suggested
itself. If he could only have counselled with Harrington! but that
could not be. The minutes went on. More than once Karswell rose
and went out into the corridor. The second time Dunning was on
the point of attempting to make the bag fall off the seat, but he
caught Harrington's eye, and read in it a warning. Karswell, from
the corridor, was watching: probably to see if the two men recognized each other. He returned, but was evidently restless: and, when
he rose the third time, hope dawned, for something did slip off his
seat and fall with hardly a sound to the floor. Karswell went out
once more, and passed out of range of the corridor window. Dunning
picked up what had fallen, and saw that the key was in his hands in
the form of one of Cook's ticket-cases, with tickets in it. These cases
have a pocket in the cover, and within very few seconds the paper
of which we have heard was in the pocket of this one. To make the
operation more secure, Harrington stood in the doorway of the
compartment and fiddled with the blind. It was done, and done at
the right time, for the train was now slowing down towards Dover.

In a moment more Karswell re-entered the compartment. As he
did so, Dunning, managing, he knew not how, to suppress the
tremble in his voice, handed him the ticket-case, saying, 'May I
give you this, sir? I believe it is yours.' After a brief glance at the
ticket inside, Karswell uttered the hoped-for response, 'Yes, it is;
much obliged to you, sir,' and he placed it in his breast pocket.

Even in the few moments that remained—moments of tense
anxiety, for they knew not to what a premature finding of the paper
might lead—both men noticed that the carriage seemed to darken

about them and to grow warmer; that Karswell was fidgety and oppressed; that he drew the heap of loose coats near to him and cast it back as if it repelled him; and that he then sat upright and glanced anxiously at both. They, with sickening anxiety, busied themselves in collecting their belongings; but they both thought that Karswell was on the point of speaking when the train stopped at Dover Town. It was natural that in the short space between town and pier they should both go into the corridor.

At the pier they got out, but so empty was the train that they were forced to linger on the platform until Karswell should have passed ahead of them with his porter on the way to the boat, and only then was it safe for them to exchange a pressure of the hand and a word of concentrated congratulation. The effect upon Dunning was to make him almost faint. Harrington made him lean up against the wall, while he himself went forward a few yards within sight of the gangway to the boat, at which Karswell had now arrived. The man at the head of it examined his ticket, and, laden with coats, he passed down into the boat. Suddenly the official called after him. 'You, sir, beg pardon, did the other gentleman show his ticket?' 'What the devil do you mean by the other gentleman?' Karswell's snarling voice called back from the deck. The man bent over and looked at him. 'The devil? Well, I don't know, I'm sure,' Harrington heard him say to himself, and then aloud, 'My mistake, sir; must have been your rugs! ask your pardon.' And then, to a subordinate near him, ''Ad he got a dog with him, or what? Funny thing: I could 'a' swore 'e wasn't alone. Well, whatever it was, they'll 'ave to see to it aboard. She's off now. Another week and we shall be gettin' the 'oliday customers.' In five minutes more there was nothing but the lessening lights of the boat, the long line of the Dover lamps, the night breeze, and the moon.

Long and long the two sat in their room at the 'Lord Warden'. In spite of the removal of their greatest anxiety, they were oppressed with a doubt, not of the lightest. Had they been justified in sending a man to his death, as they believed they had? Ought they not to warn him, at least? 'No,' said Harrington; 'if he is the murderer I think him, we have done no more than is just. Still, if you think it better—but how and where can you warn him?' 'He was booked to Abbeville only,' said Dunning. 'I saw that. If I wired to the hotels there in Joanne's Guide, "Examine your ticket-case, Dunning", I should feel happier. This is the 21st: he will have a day. But I am afraid he has gone into the dark.' So telegrams were left at the hotel office.

It is not clear whether these reached their destination, or whether, if they did, they were understood. All that is known is that, on the afternoon of the 23rd, an English traveller, examining the front of St. Wulfram's Church at Abbeville, then under extensive repair, was struck on the head and instantly killed by a stone falling from the scaffold erected round the north-western tower, there being, as was clearly proved, no workman on the scaffold at that moment: and the traveller's papers identified him as Mr. Karswell.

Only one detail shall be added. At Karswell's sale a set of Bewick, sold with all faults, was acquired by Harrington. The page with the woodcut of the traveller and the demon was, as he had expected, mutilated. Also, after a judicious interval, Harrington repeated to Dunning something of what he had heard his brother say in his sleep: but it was not long before Dunning stopped him.

'SAKI' (H. H. MUNRO)
The Background

'THAT woman's art-jargon tires me,' said Clovis to his journalist friend. 'She's so fond of talking of certain pictures as "growing on one", as though they were a sort of fungus.'

'That reminds me,' said the journalist, 'of the story of Henri Deplis. Have I ever told it you?'

Clovis shook his head.

'Henri Deplis was by birth a native of the Grand Duchy of Luxemburg. On maturer reflection he became a commercial traveller. His business activities frequently took him beyond the limits of the Grand Duchy, and he was stopping in a small town of Northern Italy when news reached him from home that a legacy from a distant and deceased relative had fallen to his share.

'It was not a large legacy, even from the modest standpoint of Henri Deplis, but it impelled him towards some seemingly harmless extravagances. In particular it led him to patronize local art as represented by the tattoo-needles of Signor Andreas Pincini. Signor Pincini was, perhaps, the most brilliant master of tattoo craft that Italy had ever known, but his circumstances were decidedly impoverished, and for the sum of six hundred francs he gladly undertook to cover his client's back, from the collar-bone down to the waistline, with a glowing representation of the Fall of Icarus. The design, when finally developed, was a slight disappointment to Monsieur Deplis, who had suspected Icarus of being a fortress taken by Wallenstein in the Thirty Years' War, but he was more than satisfied with the execution of the work, which was acclaimed by all who had the privilege of seeing it as Pincini's masterpiece.

'It was his greatest effort, and his last. Without even waiting to be paid, the illustrious craftsman departed this life, and was buried under an ornate tombstone, whose winged cherubs would have afforded singularly little scope for the exercise of his favourite art. There remained, however, the widow Pincini, to whom the six hundred francs were due. And thereupon arose the great crisis in the life of Henri Deplis, traveller of commerce. The legacy, under the stress of numerous little calls on its substance, had dwindled to very insignificant proportions, and when a pressing wine bill and sundry other current accounts had been paid, there remained little more than 430 francs to offer to the widow. The lady was properly indignant, not wholly, as she volubly explained, on account of the suggested writing-off of 170 francs, but also at the attempt to depreciate the value of her late husband's acknowledged master-piece. In a week's time Deplis was obliged to reduce his offer to 405 francs, which circumstance fanned the widow's indignation into a fury. She cancelled the sale of the work of art, and a few days later Deplis learned with a sense of consternation that she had presented it to the municipality of Bergamo, which had gratefully accepted it. He left the neighbourhood as unobtrusively as possible, and was genuinely relieved when his business commands took him to Rome, where he hoped his identity and that of the famous picture might be lost sight of.

'But he bore on his back the burden of the dead man's genius. On presenting himself one day in the steaming corridor of a vapour bath, he was at once hustled back into his clothes by the proprietor, who was a North Italian, and who emphatically refused to allow the celebrated Fall of Icarus to be publicly on view without the permission of the municipality of Bergamo. Public interest and official vigilance increased as the matter became more widely known, and Deplis was unable to take a simple dip in the sea or river on the hottest afternoon unless clothed up to the collar-bone in a substantial bathing garment. Later on the authorities of Bergamo conceived the idea that salt water might be injurious to the masterpiece, and a perpetual injunction was obtained which debarred the muchly harassed commercial traveller from sea bathing under any circumstances. Altogether, he was fervently thankful when his firm of employers found him a new range of activities in the neighbourhood of Bordeaux. His thankfulness, however, ceased abruptly at the Franco-Italian frontier. An impos-ing array of official force barred his departure, and he was sternly reminded of the stringent law which forbids the exportation of Italian works of art.

'A diplomatic parley ensued between the Luxemburgian and Italian Governments, and at one time the European situation became overcast with the possibilities of trouble. But the Italian Government stood firm; it declined to concern itself in the least with the fortunes or even the existence of Henri Deplis, commercial traveller, but was immovable in its decision that the Fall of Icarus (by the late Pincini, Andreas), at present the property of the municipality of Bergamo, should not leave the country.

'The excitement died down in time, but the unfortunate Deplis, who was of a constitutionally retiring disposition, found himself a few months later once more the storm-centre of a furious controversy. A certain German art expert, who had obtained from the municipality of Bergamo permission to inspect the famous masterpiece, declared it to be a spurious Pincini, probably the work of some pupil whom he had employed in his declining years. The evidence of Deplis on the subject was obviously worthless, as he had been under the influence of the customary narcotics during the long process of pricking in the design. The editor of an Italian art journal refuted the contentions of the German expert and undertook to prove that his private life did not conform to any modern standard of decency. The whole of Italy and Germany were drawn into the dispute, and the rest of Europe was soon involved in the quarrel. There were stormy scenes in the Spanish Parliament, and the University of Copenhagen bestowed a gold medal on the German expert (afterwards sending a commission to examine his proofs on the spot), while two Polish schoolboys in Paris committed suicide to show what *they* thought of the matter.

'Meanwhile, the unhappy human background fared no better than before, and it was not surprising that he drifted into the ranks of Italian anarchists. Four times at least he was escorted to the frontier as a dangerous and undesirable foreigner, but he was always brought back as the Fall of Icarus (attributed to Pincini, Andreas, early Twentieth Century). And then one day, at an anarchist congress at Genoa, a fellow-worker, in the heat of debate, broke a phial full of corrosive liquid over his back. The red shirt that he was wearing mitigated the effects, but the Icarus was ruined beyond recognition. His assailant was severely reprimanded for assaulting a fellow-anarchist and received seven years' imprisonment for defacing a national art treasure. As soon as he was able to leave the hospital Henri Deplis was put across the frontier as an undesirable alien.

'In the quieter streets of Paris, especially in the neighbourhood of the Ministry of Fine Arts, you may sometimes meet a depressed, anxious-looking man, who, if you pass him the time of day, will answer you with a slight Luxemburgian accent. He nurses the illusion that he is one of the lost arms of the Venus de Milo, and hopes that the French Government may be persuaded to buy him. On all other subjects I believe he is tolerably sane.'

H. G. WELLS
The Door in the Wall

ONE confidential evening, not three months ago, Lionel Wallace told me this story of the Door in the Wall. And at the time I thought that so far as he was concerned it was a true story.

He told it me with such a direct simplicity of conviction that I could not do otherwise than believe in him. But in the morning, in my own flat, I woke to a different atmosphere; and as I lay in bed and recalled the things he had told me, stripped of the glamour of his earnest slow voice, denuded of the focused, shaded table light, the shadowy atmosphere that wrapped about him and me, and the pleasant bright things, the dessert and glasses and napery of the dinner we had shared, making them for the time a bright little world quite cut off from everyday realities, I saw it all as frankly incredible. 'He was mystifying!' I said, and then: 'How well he did it! ... It isn't quite the thing I should have expected him, of all people, to do well.'

Afterwards as I sat up in bed and sipped my morning tea, I found myself trying to account for the flavour of reality that perplexed me in his impossible reminiscences, by supposing they did in some way suggest, present, convey—I hardly know which word to use—experiences it was otherwise impossible to tell.

Well, I don't resort to that explanation now. I have got over my intervening doubts. I believe now, as I believed at the moment of telling, that Wallace did to the very best of his ability strip the truth of his secret for me. But whether he himself saw, or only thought he saw, whether he himself was the possessor of an inestimable privilege or the victim of a fantastic dream, I cannot pretend to guess. Even the facts of his death, which ended my doubts for ever, throw no light on that.

That much the reader must judge for himself.

I forget now what chance comment or criticism of mine moved so reticent a man to confide in me. He was, I think, defending himself against an imputation of slackness and unreliability I had made in relation to a great public movement, in which he had disappointed me. But he plunged suddenly. 'I have,' he said, 'a preoccupation——

'I know,' he went on, after a pause, 'I have been negligent. The fact is—it isn't a case of ghosts or apparitions—but—it's an odd thing to tell of, Redmond—I am haunted. I am haunted by something—that rather takes the light out of things, that fills me with longings . . .'

He paused, checked by that English shyness that so often overcomes us when we would speak of moving or grave or beautiful things. 'You were at Saint Althelstan's all through,' he said, and for a moment that seemed to me quite irrelevant. 'Well'—and he paused. Then very haltingly at first, but afterwards more easily, he began to tell of the thing that was hidden in his life, the haunting memory of a beauty and a happiness that filled his heart with insatiable longings, that made all the interests and spectacle of worldly life seem dull and tedious and vain to him.

Now that I have the clue to it, the thing seems written visibly in his face. I have a photograph in which that look of detachment has been caught and intensified. It reminds me of what a woman once said of him—a woman who had loved him greatly. 'Suddenly,' she said, 'the interest goes out of him. He forgets you. He doesn't care a rap for you—under his very nose . . .'

Yet the interest was not always out of him, and when he was holding his attention to a thing Wallace could contrive to be an extremely successful man. His career, indeed, is set with success. He left me behind him long ago; he soared up over my head, and cut a figure in the world that I couldn't cut—anyhow. He was still a year short of forty, and they say now that he would have been in office and very probably in the new Cabinet if he had lived. At school he always beat me without effort—as it were by nature. We were at school together at Saint Althelstan's College in West Kensington for almost all our school-time. He came into the school as my co-equal, but he left far above me, in a blaze of scholarships and brilliant performance. Yet I think I made a fair average running. And it was at school I heard first of the 'Door in the Wall'—that I was to hear of a second time only a month before his death.

To him at least the Door in the Wall was a real door, leading through a real wall to immortal realities. Of that I am now quite assured.

And it came into his life quite early, when he was a little fellow between five and six. I remember how, as he sat making his confession to me with a slow gravity, he reasoned and reckoned the date of it. 'There was,' he said, 'a crimson Virginia creeper in it—all one bright uniform crimson, in a clear amber sunshine against a white wall. That came into the impression somehow, though I don't clearly remember how, and there were horse-chestnut leaves upon the clean pavement outside the green door. They were blotched yellow and green, you know, not brown nor dirty, so that they must have been new fallen. I take it that means October. I look out for horse-chestnut leaves every year and I ought to know.

'If I'm right in that, I was about five years and four months old.'

He was, he said, rather a precocious little boy—he learned to talk at an abnormally early age, and he was so sane and 'old-fashioned', as people say, that he was permitted an amount of initiative that most children scarcely attain by seven or eight. His mother died when he was two, and he was under the less vigilant and authoritative care of a nursery governess. His father was a stern, preoccupied lawyer, who gave him little attention and expected great things of him. For all his brightness he found life grey and dull, I think. And one day he wandered.

He could not recall the particular neglect that enabled him to get away, nor the course he took among the West Kensington roads. All that had faded among the incurable blurs of memory. But the white wall and the green door stood out quite distinctly.

As his memory of that childish experience ran, he did at the very first sight of that door experience a peculiar emotion, an attraction, a desire to get to the door and open it and walk in. And at the same time he had the clearest conviction that either it was unwise or it was wrong of him—he could not tell which—to yield to this attraction. He insisted upon it as a curious thing that he knew from the very beginning—unless memory has played him the queerest trick—that the door was unfastened, and that he could go in as he chose.

I seem to see the figure of that little boy, drawn and repelled. And it was very clear in his mind, too, though why it should be so was never explained, that his father would be very angry if he went in through that door.

Wallace described all these moments of hesitation to me with the utmost particularity. He went right past the door, and then, with his hands in his pockets and making an infantile attempt to whistle, strolled right along beyond the end of the wall. There he recalls a number of mean dirty shops, and particularly that of a plumber and decorator with a dusty disorder of earthenware pipes, sheet lead, ball taps, pattern books of wall-paper, and tins of enamel. He stood pretending to examine these things, and *coveting*, passionately desiring, the green door.

Then, he said, he had a gust of emotion. He made a run for it, lest hesitation should grip him again; he went plump with outstretched hand through the green door and let it slam behind him. And so, in a trice, he came into the garden that has haunted all his life.

It was very difficult for Wallace to give me his full sense of that garden into which he came.

There was something in the very air of it that exhilarated, that gave one a sense of lightness and good happening and well-being; there was something in the sight of it that made all its colour clean and perfect and subtly luminous. In the instant of coming into it one was exquisitely glad—as only in rare moments, and when one is young and joyful one can be glad in this world. And everything was beautiful there. . . .

Wallace mused before he went on telling me. 'You see,' he said, with the doubtful inflexion of a man who pauses at incredible things, 'there were two great panthers there. . . . Yes, spotted panthers. And I was not afraid. There was a long wide path with marble-edged flower borders on either side, and these two huge velvety beasts were playing there with a ball. One looked up and came towards me, a little curious as it seemed. It came right up to me, rubbed its soft round ear very gently against the small hand I held out, and purred. It was, I tell you, an enchanted garden. I know. And the size? Oh! it stretched far and wide, this way and that. I believe there were hills far away. Heaven knows where West Kensington had suddenly got to. And somehow it was just like coming home.

'You know, in the very moment the door swung to behind me, I forgot the road with its fallen chestnut leaves, its cabs and tradesmen's carts, I forgot the sort of gravitational pull back to the discipline and obedience of home, I forgot all hesitations and fear,

forgot descretion, forgot all the intimate realities of this life. I
became in a moment a very glad and wonder-happy little boy—in
another world. It was a world with a different quality, a warmer,
more penetrating and mellower light, with a faint clear gladness in
its air, and wisps of sun-touched cloud in the blueness of its sky.
And before me ran this long wide path, invitingly, with weedless
beds on either side, rich with untended flowers, and these two great
panthers. I put my little hands fearlessly on their soft fur, and
caressed their round ears and the sensitive corners under their ears,
and played with them, and it was as though they welcomed me
home. There was a keen sense of home-coming in my mind, and
when presently a tall, fair girl appeared in the pathway and came
to meet me, smiling, and said "Well?" to me, and lifted me and
kissed me, and put me down and led me by the hand, there was no
amazement, but only an impression of delightful rightness, of being
reminded of happy things that had in some strange way been
overlooked. There were broad red steps, I remember, that came
into view between spikes of delphinium, and up these we went to a
great avenue between very old and shady dark trees. All down this
avenue, you know, between the red chapped stems, were marble
seats of honour and statuary, and very tame and friendly white
doves. . . .

'Along this cool avenue my girl-friend led me, looking down—I
recall the pleasant lines, the finely modelled chin of her sweet kind
face—asking me questions in a soft, agreeable voice, and telling me
things, pleasant things I know, though what they were I was never
able to recall. . . . Presently a Capuchin monkey, very clean, with a
fur of ruddy brown and kindly hazel eyes, came down a tree to us
and ran beside me, looking up at me and grinning, and presently
leaped to my shoulder. So we two went on our way in great
happiness.'

He paused.

'Go on,' I said.

'I remember little things. We passed an old man musing among
laurels, I remember, and a place gay with paroquets, and came
through a broad shaded colonnade to a spacious cool palace, full of
pleasant fountains, full of beautiful things, full of the quality and
promise of heart's desire. And there were many things and many
people, some that still seem to stand out clearly and some that are
vaguer; but all these people were beautiful and kind. In some way—

I don't know how—it was conveyed to me that they all were kind to me, glad to have me there, and filling me with gladness by their gestures, by the touch of their hands, by the welcome and love in their eyes. Yes——'

He mused for a while. 'Playmates I found there. That was very much to me, because I was a lonely little boy. They played delightful games in a grass-covered court where there was a sun-dial set about with flowers. And as one played one loved. . . .

'But—it's odd—there's a gap in my memory. I don't remember the games we played. I never remembered. Afterwards, as a child, I spent long hours trying, even with tears, to recall the form of that happiness. I wanted to play it all over again—in my nursery—by myself. No! All I remember is the happiness and two dear playfellows who were most with me. . . . Then presently came a sombre dark woman, with a grave, pale face and dreamy eyes, a sombre woman, wearing a soft long robe of pale purple, who carried a book, and beckoned and took me aside with her into a gallery above a hall—though my playmates were loth to have me go, and ceased their game and stood watching as I was carried away. "Come back to us!" they cried. "Come back to us soon!" I looked up at her face, but she heeded them not at all. Her face was very gentle and grave. She took me to a seat in the gallery, and I stood beside her, ready to look at her book as she opened it upon her knee. The pages fell open. She pointed, and I looked, marvelling, for in the living pages of that book I saw myself; it was a story about myself, and in it were all the things that had happened to me since ever I was born. . . .

'It was wonderful to me, because the pages of that book were not pictures, you understand, but realities.'

Wallace paused gravely—looked at me doubtfully.

'Go on,' I said. 'I understand.'

'They were realities—yes, they must have been; people moved and things came and went in them; my dear mother, whom I had near forgotten; then my father, stern and upright, the servants, the nursery, all the familiar things of home. Then the front door and the busy streets, with traffic to and fro. I looked and marvelled, and looked half doubtfully again into the woman's face and turned the pages over, skipping this and that, to see more of this book and more, and so at last I came to myself hovering and hesitating outside the green door in the long white wall, and felt again the conflict and the fear.

'"And next?" I cried, and would have turned on, but the cool hand of the grave woman delayed me.

'"Next?" I insisted, and struggled gently with her hand, pulling up her fingers with all my childish strength, and as she yielded and the page came over she bent down upon me like a shadow and kissed my brow.

'But the page did not show the enchanted garden, nor the panthers, nor the girl who had led me by the hand, nor the playfellows who had been so loth to let me go. It showed a long grey street in West Kensington, in that chill hour of afternoon before the lamps are lit; and I was there, a wretched little figure, weeping aloud, for all that I could do to restrain myself, and I was weeping because I could not return to my dear playfellows who had called after me, "Come back to us! Come back to us soon!" I was there. This was no page in a book, but harsh reality; that enchanted place and the restraining hand of the grave mother at whose knee I stood had gone—whither had they gone?'

He halted again, and remained for a time staring into the fire.

'Oh! the woefulness of that return!' he murmured.

'Well?' I said, after a minute or so.

'Poor little wretch I was!—brought back to this grey world again! As I realized the fullness of what had happened to me, I gave way to quite ungovernable grief. And the shame and humiliation of that public weeping and my disgraceful home-coming remain with me still. I see again the benevolent-looking old gentleman in gold spectacles who stopped and spoke to me—prodding me first with his umbrella. "Poor little chap," said he; "and are you lost then?"— and me a London boy of five and more! And he must needs bring in a kindly young policeman and make a crowd of me, and so march me home. Sobbing, conspicuous, and frightened, I came back from the enchanted garden to the steps of my father's house.

'That is as well as I can remember my vision of that garden—the garden that haunts me still. Of course, I can convey nothing of that indescribable quality of translucent unreality, that *difference* from the common things of experience that hung about it all; but that— that is what happened. If it was a dream, I am sure it was a day-time and altogether extraordinary dream. . . . H'm!—naturally there followed a terrible questioning, by my aunt, my father, the nurse, the governess—every one. . . .

'I tried to tell them, and my father gave me my first thrashing for telling lies. When afterwards I tried to tell my aunt, she punished me again for my wicked persistence. Then, as I said, every one was forbidden to listen to me, to hear a word about it. Even my fairy-tale books were taken away from me for a time—because I was too "imaginative". Eh? Yes, they did that! My father belonged to the old school. . . . And my story was driven back upon myself. I whispered it to my pillow—my pillow that was often damp and salt to my whispering lips with childish tears. And I added always to my official and less fervent prayers this one heart-felt request: "Please God I may dream of the garden. Oh! take me back to my garden!" Take me back to my garden! I dreamt often of the garden. I may have added to it, I may have changed it; I do not know. . . . All this, you understand, is an attempt to reconstruct from fragmentary memories a very early experience. Between that and the other consecutive memories of my boyhood there is a gulf. A time came when it seemed impossible I should ever speak of that wonder glimpse again.'

I asked an obvious question.

'No,' he said. 'I don't remember that I ever attempted to find my way back to the garden in those early years. This seems odd to me now, but I think that very probably a closer watch was kept on my movements after this misadventure to prevent my going astray. No, it wasn't till you knew me that I tried for the garden again. And I believe there was a period—incredible as it seems now—when I forgot the garden altogether—when I was about eight or nine it may have been. Do you remember me as a kid at Saint Althelstan's?'

'Rather!'

'I didn't show any signs, did I, in those days of having a secret dream?'

§ 2

He looked up with a sudden smile.

'Did you ever play North-West Passage with me? . . . No, of course you didn't come my way!'

'It was the sort of game,' he went on, 'that every imaginative child plays all day. The idea was the discovery of a North-West

Passage to school. The way to school was plain enough; the game consisted in finding some way that wasn't plain, starting off ten minutes early in some almost hopeless direction, and working my way round through unaccustomed streets to my goal. And one day I got entangled among some rather low-class streets on the other side of Campden Hill, and I began to think that for once the game would be against me and that I should get to school late. I tried rather desperately a street that seemed a cul-de-sac, and found a passage at the end. I hurried through that with renewed hope. "I shall do it yet," I said, and passed a row of frowsy little shops that were inexplicably familiar to me, and behold! there was my long white wall and the green door that led to the enchanted garden!

'The thing whacked upon me suddenly. Then, after all that garden, that wonderful garden, wasn't a dream!'

He paused.

'I suppose my second experience with the green door marks the world of difference there is between the busy life of a schoolboy and the infinite leisure of a child. Anyhow, this second time I didn't for a moment think of going in straight away. You see———. For one thing, my mind was full of the idea of getting to school in time—set on not breaking my record for punctuality. I must surely have felt *some* little desire at least to try the door—yes. I must have felt that. . . . But I seem to remember the attraction of the door mainly as another obstacle to my overmastering determination to get to school. I was immensely interested by this discovery I had made, of course—I went on with my mind full of it—but I went on. It didn't check me. I ran past, tugging out my watch, found I had ten minutes still to spare, and then I was going downhill into familiar surroundings. I got to school, breathless, it is true, and wet with perspiration, but in time. I can remember hanging up my coat and hat. . . . Went right by it and left it behind me. Odd, eh?'

He looked at me thoughtfully. 'Of course I didn't know then that it wouldn't always be there. Schoolboys have limited imaginations. I suppose I thought it was an awfully jolly thing to have it there, to know my way back to it; but there was the school tugging at me. I expect I was a good deal distraught and inattentive that morning, recalling what I could of the beautiful strange people I should presently see again. Oddly enough I had no doubt in my mind that they would be glad to see me. . . . Yes, I must have thought of the garden that morning just as a jolly sort of place to which one might resort in the interludes of a strenuous scholastic career.

'I didn't go that day at all. The next day was a half-holiday, and that may have weighed with me. Perhaps, too, my state of inattention brought down impositions upon me, and docked the margin of time necessary for the *détour*. I don't know. What I do know is that in the meantime the enchanted garden was so much upon my mind that I could not keep it to myself.

'I told—what was his name?—a ferrety-looking youngster we used to call Squiff.'

'Young Hopkins,' said I.

'Hopkins it was. I did not like telling him. I had a feeling that in some way it was against the rules to tell him, but I did. He was walking part of the way home with me; he was talkative, and if we had not talked about the enchanted garden we should have talked of something else, and it was intolerable to me to think about any other subject. So I blabbed.

'Well, he told my secret. The next day in the play interval I found myself surrounded by half a dozen bigger boys, half teasing, and wholly curious to hear more of the enchanted garden. There was that big Fawcett—you remember him?—and Carnaby and Morley Reynolds. You weren't there by any chance? No, I think I should have remembered if you were. . . .

'A boy is a creature of odd feelings. I was, I really believe, in spite of my secret self-disgust, a little flattered to have the attention of these big fellows. I remember particularly a moment of pleasure caused by the praise of Crawshaw—you remember Crawshaw major, the son of Crawshaw the composer?—who said it was the best lie he had ever heard. But at the same time there was a really painful undertow of shame at telling what I felt was indeed a sacred secret. That beast Fawcett made a joke about the girl in green——'

Wallace's voice sank with the keen memory of that shame. 'I pretended not to hear,' he said. 'Well, then Carnaby suddenly called me a young liar, and disputed with me when I said the thing was true. I said I knew where to find the green door, could lead them all there in ten minutes. Carnaby became outrageously virtuous, and said I'd have to—and bear out my words or suffer. Did you ever have Carnaby twist your arm? Then perhaps you'll understand how it went with me. I swore my story was true. There was nobody in the school then to save a chap from Carnaby, though Crawshaw

put in a word or so. Carnaby had got his game. I grew excited and
red-eared, and a little frightened. I behaved altogether like a silly
little chap, and the outcome of it all was that instead of starting
alone for my enchanted garden, I led the way presently—cheeks
flushed, ears hot, eyes smarting, and my soul one burning misery
and shame—for a party of six mocking, curious, and threatening
schoolfellows.

'We never found the white wall and the green door. . . .'

'You mean——?'

'I mean I couldn't find it. I would have found it if I could.

'And afterwards when I could go alone I couldn't find it. I never
found it. I seem now to have been always looking for it through my
schoolboy days, but I never came upon it—never.'

'Did the fellows—make it disagreeable?'

'Beastly. . . . Carnaby held a council over me for wanton lying. I
remember how I sneaked home and upstairs to hide the marks of
my blubbering. But when I cried myself to sleep at last it wasn't for
Carnaby, but for the garden, for the beautiful afternoon I had
hoped for, for the sweet friendly women and the waiting playfellows,
and the game I had hoped to learn again, that beautiful forgotten
game. . . .

'I believed firmly that if I had not told—— . . . I had bad times
after that—crying at night and wool-gathering by day. For two
terms I slacked and had bad reports. Do you remember? Of course
you would! It was *you*—your beating me in mathematics that
brought me back to the grind again.'

§ 3

For a time my friend stared silently into the red heart of the fire.
Then he said: 'I never saw it again until I was seventeen.

'It leaped upon me for the third time—as I was driving to
Paddington on my way to Oxford and a scholarship. I had just one
momentary glimpse. I was leaning over the apron of my hansom
smoking a cigarette, and no doubt thinking myself no end of a man
of the world, and suddenly there was the door, the wall, the dear
sense of unforgettable and still attainable things.

'We clattered by—I too taken by surprise to stop my cab until
we were well past and round a corner. Then I had a queer moment,
a double and divergent movement of my will: I tapped the little
door in the roof of the cab, and brought my arm down to pull out

my watch. "Yes, sir!" said the cabman, smartly. "Er—well—it's nothing," I cried. "*My* mistake! We haven't much time! Go on!" And he went on. . . .

'I got my scholarship. And the night after I was told of that I sat over my fire in my little upper room, my study, in my father's house, with his praise—his rare praise—and his sound counsels ringing in my ears, and I smoked my favourite pipe—the formidable bulldog of adolescence—and thought of that door in the long white wall. "If I had stopped," I thought, "I should have missed my scholarship, I should have missed Oxford—muddled all the fine career before me! I begin to see things better!" I fell musing deeply, but I did not doubt then this career of mine was a thing that merited sacrifice.

'Those dear friends and that clear atmosphere seemed very sweet to me, very fine but remote. My grip was fixing now upon the world. I saw another door opening—the door of my career.'

He stared again into the fire. Its red light picked out a stubborn strength in his face for just one flickering moment, and then it vanished again.

'Well,' he said and sighed, 'I have served that career. I have done—much work, much hard work. But I have dreamt of the enchanted garden a thousand dreams, and seen its door or at least glimpsed its door, four times since then. Yes—four times. For a while this world was so bright and interesting, seemed so full of meaning and opportunity, that the half-effaced charm of the garden was by comparison gentle and remote. Who wants to pat panthers on the way to dinner with pretty women and distinguished men? I came down to London from Oxford, a man of bold promise that I have done something to redeem. Something—and yet there have been disappointments. . . .

'Twice I have been in love—I will not dwell on that—but once, as I went to some one who, I knew, doubted whether I dared to come, I took a short cut at a venture through an unfrequented road near Earl's Court, and so happened on a white wall and a familiar green door. "Odd!" said I to myself, "but I thought this place was on Campden Hill. It's the place I never could find somehow—like counting Stonehenge—the place of that queer daydream of mine." And I went by it intent upon my purpose. It had no appeal to me that afternoon.

'I had just a moment's impulse to try the door, three steps aside were needed at the most—though I was sure enough in my heart that it would open to me—and then I thought that doing so might delay me on the way to that appointment in which my honour was involved. Afterwards I was sorry for my punctuality—I might at least have peeped in and waved a hand to those panthers, but I knew enough by this time not to seek again belatedly that which is not found by seeking. Yes, that time made me very sorry. . . .

'Years of hard work after that, and never a sight of the door. It's only recently it has come back to me. With it there has come a sense as though some thin tarnish had spread itself over my world. I began to think of it as a sorrowful and bitter thing that I should never see that door again. Perhaps I was suffering a little from overwork—perhaps it was what I've heard spoken of as the feeling of forty. I don't know. But certainly the keen brightness that makes effort easy has gone out of things recently, and that just at a time— with all these new political developments—when I ought to be working. Odd, isn't it? But I do begin to find life toilsome, its rewards, as I come near them, cheap. I began a little while ago to want the garden quite badly. Yes—and I've seen it three times.'

'The garden?'

'No—the door! And I haven't gone in!'

He leaned over the table to me, with an enormous sorrow in his voice as he spoke. 'Thrice I have had my chance—*thrice!* If ever that door offers itself to me again, I swore, I will go in, out of this dust and heat, out of this dry glitter of vanity, out of these toilsome futilities. I will go and never return. This time I will stay. . . . I swore it, and when the time came—*I didn't go.*

'Three times in one year have I passed that door and failed to enter. Three times in the last year.

'The first time was on the night of the snatch division on the Tenant's Redemption Bill, on which the Government was saved by a majority of three. You remember? No one on our side—perhaps very few on the opposite side—expected the end that night. Then the debate collapsed like eggshells. I and Hotchkiss were dining with his cousin at Brentford; we were both unpaired, and we were called up by telephone, and set off at once in his cousin's motor. We got in barely in time, and on the way we passed my wall and door— livid in the moonlight, blotched with hot yellow as the glare of our lamps lit it, but unmistakable. "My God!" cried I. "What?" said Hotchkiss. "Nothing!" I answered, and the moment passed.

'"I've made a great sacrifice," I told the whip as I got in. "They all have," he said, and hurried by.

'I do not see how I could have done otherwise then. And the next occasion was as I rushed to my father's bedside to bid that stern old man farewell. Then, too, the claims of life were imperative. But the third time was different; it happened a week ago. It fills me with hot remorse to recall it. I was with Gurker and Ralphs—it's no secret now, you know, that I've had my talk with Gurker. We had been dining at Frobisher's, and the talk had become intimate between us. The question of my place in the reconstructed Ministry lay always just over the boundary of the discussion. Yes—yes. That's all settled. It needn't be talked about yet, but there's no reason to keep a secret from you. . . . Yes—thanks! thanks! But let me tell you my story.

'Then, on that night things were very much in the air. My position was a very delicate one. I was keenly anxious to get some definite word from Gurker, but was hampered by Ralphs' presence. I was using the best power of my brain to keep that light and careless talk not too obviously directed to the point that concerned me. I had to. Ralphs' behaviour since has more than justified my caution. . . . Ralphs, I knew, would leave us beyond the Kensington High Street, and then I could surprise Gurker by a sudden frankness. One has sometimes to resort to these little devices. . . . And then it was that in the margin of my field of vision I became aware once more of the white wall, the green door before us down the road.

'We passed it talking. I passed it. I can still see the shadow of Gurker's marked profile, his opera hat tilted forward over his prominent nose, the many folds of his neck wrap going before my shadow and Ralphs' as we sauntered past.

'I passed within twenty inches of the door. "If I say good-night to them, and go in," I asked myself, "what will happen?" And I was all a-tingle for that word with Gurker.

'I could not answer that question in the tangle of my other problems. "They will think me mad," I thought. "And suppose I vanish now!—Amazing disappearance of a prominent politician!" That weighed with me. A thousand inconceivably petty worldlinesses weighed with me in that crisis.'

Then he turned on me with a sorrowful smile, and, speaking slowly, 'Here I am!' he said.

'Here I am!' he repeated, 'and my chance has gone from me. Three times in one year the door has been offered me—the door that goes into peace, into delight, into a beauty beyond dreaming, a kindness no man on earth can know. And I have rejected it, Redmond, and it has gone——'

'How do you know?'

'I know. I know. I am left now to work it out, to stick to the tasks that held me so strongly when my moments came. You say I have success—this vulgar, tawdry, irksome, envied thing. I have it.' He had a walnut in his big hand. 'If that was my success,' he said, and crushed it, and held it out for me to see.

'Let me tell you something, Redmond. This loss is destroying me. For two months, for ten weeks nearly now, I have done no work at all, except the most necessary and urgent duties. My soul is full of inappeasable regrets. At nights—when it is less likely I shall be recognized—I go out. I wander. Yes. I wonder what people would think of that if they knew. A Cabinet Minister, the responsible head of that most vital of all departments, wandering alone—grieving—sometimes near audibly lamenting—for a door, for a garden!'

§ 4

I can see now his rather pallid face, and the unfamiliar sombre fire that had come into his eyes. I see him very vividly to-night. I sit recalling his words, his tones, and last evening's *Westminster Gazette* still lies on my sofa, containing the notice of his death. At lunch to-day the club was busy with his death. We talked of nothing else.

They found his body very early yesterday morning in a deep excavation near East Kensington Station. It is one of two shafts that have been made in connexion with an extension of the railway southward. It is protected from the intrusion of the public by a hoarding upon the high road, in which a small doorway has been cut for the convenience of some of the workmen who live in that direction. The doorway was left unfastened through a misunderstanding between two gangers, and through it he made his way.

My mind is darkened with questions and riddles.

It would seem he walked all the way from the House that night—he has frequently walked home during the past Session—and so it is I figure his dark form coming along the late and empty streets, wrapped up, intent. And then did the pale electric lights near the station cheat the rough planking into a semblance of white? Did that fatal unfastened door awaken some memory?

Was there, after all, ever any green door in the wall at all?

I do not know. I have told his story as he told it to me. There are times when I believe that Wallace was no more than the victim of the coincidence between a rare but not unprecedented type of hallucination and a careless trap, but that indeed is not my profoundest belief. You may think me superstitious, if you will, and foolish; but, indeed, I am more than half convinced that he had, in truth, an abnormal gift, and a sense, something—I know not what—that in the guise of wall and door offered him an outlet, a secret and peculiar passage of escape into another and altogether more beautiful world. At any rate, you will say, it betrayed him in the end. But did it betray him? There you touch the inmost mystery of these dreamers, these men of vision and the imagination. We see our world fair and common, the hoarding and the pit. By our daylight standard he walked out of security into darkness, danger, and death.

But did he see like that?

JOHN GALSWORTHY
Spindleberries

THE celebrated painter, Scudamore—whose studies of Nature had been hung on the line for so many years that he had forgotten the days when, not yet in the Scudamore manner, they depended from the sky—stood where his cousin had left him so abruptly. His lips, between comely grey moustache and comely pointed beard, wore a mortified smile, and he gazed rather dazedly at the spindleberries fallen on to the flagged courtyard from the branch she had brought to show him. Why had she thrown up her head as if he had struck her, and whisked round so that those dull-pink berries quivered and lost their rain-drops, and four had fallen? He had but said: 'Charming! I'd like to use them!' And she had answered: 'God!' and rushed away. Alicia really was crazed; who would have thought that once she had been so adorable? He stooped and picked up the four berries—a beautiful colour, that dull pink! And from below the coatings of success and the Scudamore manner a little thrill came up; the stir of emotional vision. Paint! What good? How express? He went across to the low wall which divided the courtyard of his expensively restored and beautiful old house from the first flood of the River Arun wandering silvery in pale winter sunlight. Yes, indeed! How express Nature, its translucence and mysterious unities, its mood never the same from hour to hour? Those brown-tufted rushes over there against the gold grey of light and water—those restless, hovering, white gulls. A kind of disgust at his own celebrated manner welled up within him—the disgust expressed in Alicia's 'God!' Beauty! What use—how express it? Had she been thinking the same thing?

He looked at the four pink berries glistening on the grey stone of the wall and memory stirred. What a lovely girl she had been, with her grey-green eyes shining under long lashes, the rose-petal colour in her cheeks, and the too-fine dark hair—now so very grey—always blowing a little wild. An enchanting, enthusiastic creature! He remembered, as if it had been but last week, that day when they started from Arundel Station by the road to Burpham, when he was twenty-nine and she twenty-five, both of them painters and neither

of them famed—a day of showers and sunlight in the middle of
March, and Nature preparing for full spring! How they had
chattered at first and when their arms touched, how he had thrilled,
and the colour had deepened in her rain-wet cheeks; and then,
gradually, they had grown silent; a wonderful walk, which seemed
leading so surely to a more wonderful end. They had wandered
round through the village and down past the chalk-pit and Jacob's
ladder, into the field path and so to the river bank. And he had
taken her ever so gently round the waist, still silent, waiting for that
moment when his heart would leap out of him in words and hers—
he was sure—would leap to meet it. The path entered a thicket of
blackthorn with a few primroses close to the little river running full
and gentle. The last drops of a shower were falling, but the sun had
burst through, and the sky above the thicket was cleared to the blue
of speedwell flowers. Suddenly she had stopped and cried: 'Look,
Dick! Oh, look! It's heaven!' A high bush of blackthorn was lifted
there, starry white against the blue and that bright cloud. It seemed
to sing, it was so lovely; the whole of spring was in it. But the sight
of her ecstatic face had broken down all his restraint, and tightening
his arm round her he had kissed her lips. He remembered still the
expression of her face, like a child's startled out of sleep. She had
gone rigid, gasped, started away from him, quivered and gulped,
and broken suddenly into sobs. Then, slipping from his arm, she
had fled. He had stood at first, amazed and hurt, utterly bewildered;
then, recovering a little, had hunted for her full half an hour before
at last he found her sitting on wet grass, with a stony look on her
face. He had said nothing, and she nothing, except to murmur:
'Let's go on; we shall miss our train!' And all the rest of that day
and the day after, until they parted, he had suffered from the feeling
of having tumbled down off some high perch in her estimation. He
had not liked it at all; it had made him very angry. Never from that
day to this had he thought of it as anything but a piece of wanton
prudery. Had it—had it been something else?

He looked at the four pink berries, and, as if they had uncanny
power to turn the wheel of memory, he saw another vision of his
cousin five years later. He was married by then, and already hung
on the line. With his wife he had gone down to Alicia's country
cottage. A summer night, just dark and very warm. After many
exhortations she had brought into the little drawing-room her last
finished picture. He could see her now placing it where the light

fell, her tall, slight form already rather sharp and meagre, as the
figures of some women grow at thirty, if they are not married; the
nervous, fluttering look on her charming face, as though she could
hardly bear this inspection; the way she raised her shoulder just a
little as if to ward off an expected blow of condemnation. No need!
It had been a beautiful thing, a quite surprisingly beautiful study of
night. He remembered with what a really jealous ache he had gazed
at it—a better thing than he had ever done himself. And, frankly,
he had said so. Her eyes had shone with pleasure.

'Do you really like it? I tried so hard!'

'The day you show that, my dear,' he had said, 'your name's
made!' She had clasped her hands and simply sighed: 'Oh, Dick!'
He had felt quite happy in her happiness, and presently the three of
them had taken their chairs out, beyond the curtains, on to the dark
veranda, had talked a little, then somehow fallen silent. A wonderful
warm, black, grape-bloom night, exquisitely gracious and inviting;
the stars very high and white, the flowers glimmering in the garden-
beds, and against the deep, dark blue, roses hanging, unearthly,
stained with beauty. There was a scent of honeysuckle, he remembered, and many moths came fluttering by towards the tall, narrow
chink of light between the curtains. Alicia had sat leaning forward,
elbows on knees, ears buried in her hands. Probably they were
silent because she sat like that. Once he heard her whisper to
herself: 'Lovely, lovely! Oh, God! How lovely!' His wife, feeling the
dew, had gone in, and he had followed; Alicia had not seemed to
notice. But when she too came in, her eyes were glistening with
tears. She said something about bed in a queer voice; they had
taken candles and gone up. Next morning, going to her little studio
to give her advice about that picture, he had been literally horrified
to see it streaked with lines of white—Alicia, standing before it, was
dashing her brush in broad smears across and across. She heard
him and turned round. There was a hard red spot in either cheek,
and she said in a quivering voice: 'It was blasphemy. That's all!'
And turning her back on him she had gone on smearing it with
white. Without a word, he had turned tail in simple disgust. Indeed,
so deep had been his vexation at that wanton destruction of the best
thing she had ever done or was ever likely to do, that he had
avoided her for years. He had always had a horror of eccentricity.
To have planted her foot firmly on the ladder of fame and then
deliberately kicked it away; to have wantonly foregone this chance

of making money—for she had but a mere pittance! It had seemed
to him really too exasperating, a thing only to be explained by
tapping one's forehead. Every now and then he still heard of her,
living down there, spending her days out in the woods and fields,
and sometimes even her nights, they said, and steadily growing
poorer and thinner and more eccentric; becoming, in short, impos-
sibly difficult, as only Englishwomen can. People would speak of
her as 'such a dear', and talk of her charm, but always with that
shrug which is hard to bear when applied to one's relations. What
she did with the productions of her brush he never inquired, too
disillusioned by that experience. Poor Alicia!

The pink berries glowed on the grey stone, and he had yet another
memory. A family occasion when Uncle Martin Scudamore
departed this life, and they all went up to bury him and hear his
will. The old chap, whom they had looked on as a bit of a disgrace,
money-grubbing up in the little grey Yorkshire town which owed its
rise to his factory, was expected to make amends by his death, for
he had never married—too sunk in industry, apparently, to have
the time. By tacit agreement, his nephews and nieces had selected
the Inn at Bolton Abbey, nearest beauty spot, for their stay. They
had driven six miles to the funeral, in three carriages. Alicia had
gone with him and his brother, the solicitor. In her plain black
clothes she looked quite charming, in spite of the silver threads
already thick in her fine dark hair, loosened by the moor wind. She
had talked of painting to him with all her old enthusiasm, and her
eyes had seemed to linger on his face as if she still had a little
weakness for him. He had quite enjoyed that drive. They had come
rather abruptly on the small grimy town clinging to the river banks,
with old Martin's long, yellow-brick house dominating it, about two
hundred yards above the mills. Suddenly, under the rug, he felt
Alicia's hand seize his with a sort of desperation, for all the world
as if she were clinging to something to support her. Indeed, he was
sure she did not know it was his hand she squeezed. The cobbled
streets, the muddy-looking water, the dingy, staring factories, the
yellow, staring house, the little dark-clothed, dreadfully plain work-
people, all turned out to do a last honour to their creator; the
hideous new grey church, the dismal service, the brand-new tomb-
stones—and all of a glorious autumn day! It was inexpressibly
sordid—too ugly for words! Afterwards the will was read to them
seated decorously on bright mahogany chairs in the yellow mansion,

a very satisfactory will, distributing in perfectly adjusted portions, to his own kinsfolk and nobody else, a very considerable wealth. Scudamore had listened to it dreamily, with his eyes fixed on an oily picture, thinking, 'My God! What a thing!' and longing to be back in the carriage smoking a cigar to take the reek of black clothes and sherry—sherry!—out of his nostrils. He happened to look at Alicia. Her eyes were closed; her lips, always sweet-looking, quivered amusedly. And at that very moment the will came to her name. He saw those eyes open wide, and marked a beautiful pink flush, quite like that of old days, come into her thin cheeks. 'Splendid!' he had thought; 'it's really jolly for her. I *am* glad! Now she won't have to pinch. Splendid!' He shared with her to the full the surprised relief showing in her still beautiful face.

All the way home in the carriage he felt at least as happy over her good fortune as over his own, which had been substantial. He took her hand under the rug and squeezed it, and she answered with a long, gentle pressure, quite unlike the clutch when they were driving in. That same evening he strolled out to where the river curved below the Abbey. The sun had not quite set, and its last smoky radiance slanted into the burnished autumn woods. Some white-faced Herefords were grazing in lush grass, the river rippled and gleamed all over golden scales. About that scene was the magic which has so often startled the hearts of painters, the wistful gold— the enchantment of a dream. For some minutes he had gazed with delight which had in it a sort of despair. A little crisp rustle ran along the bushes; the leaves fluttered, then hung quite still. And he heard a voice—Alicia's—speaking. 'The lovely, lovely world!' And moving forward a step, he saw her standing on the river bank, braced against the trunk of a birch tree, her head thrown back, and her arms stretched wide apart as though to clasp the lovely world she had apostrophized. To have gone up to her would have been like breaking up a lovers' interview, and he turned round instead and went away.

A week later he heard from his brother that Alicia had refused her legacy. 'I don't want it,' her letter had said simply; 'I couldn't bear to take it. Give it to those poor people who live in that awful place.' Really eccentricity could go no farther! They decided to go down and see her. Such mad neglect of her own good must not be permitted without some effort to prevent it. They found her very thin and charming; humble, but quite obstinate in her refusal. 'Oh!

I couldn't really! I should be so unhappy. Those poor little stunted people who made it all for him! That little, awful town! I simply couldn't be reminded. Don't talk about it, please. I'm quite all right as I am.' They had threatened her with lurid pictures of the workhouse and a destitute old age. To no purpose; she would not take the money. She had been forty when she refused that aid from heaven—forty, and already past any hope of marriage. For though Scudamore had never known for certain that she had ever wished or hoped for marriage, he had his theory—that all her eccentricity came from wasted sexual instinct. This last folly had seemed to him monstrous enough to be pathetic, and he no longer avoided her. Indeed, he would often walk over to tea in her little hermitage. With Uncle Martin's money he had bought and restored the beautiful old house over the River Arun, and was now only five miles from Alicia's, across country. She, too, would come tramping over at all hours, floating in with wild flowers or ferns, which she would put into water the moment she arrived. She had ceased to wear hats, and had by now a very doubtful reputation for sanity about the country-side. This was the period when Watts was on every painter's tongue, and he seldom saw Alicia without a disputation concerning that famous symbolist. Personally, he had no use for Watts, resenting his faulty drawing and crude allegories, but Alicia always maintained with her extravagant fervour that he was great because he tried to paint the soul of things. She especially loved a painting called 'Iris'—a female symbol of the rainbow, which indeed, in its floating eccentricity, had a certain resemblance to herself. 'Of course he failed,' she would say; 'he tried for the impossible and went on trying all his life. Oh! I can't bear your rules and catchwords, Dick; what's the good of them! Beauty's too big, too deep!' Poor Alicia! She was sometimes very wearing.

He never knew quite how it came about that she went abroad with them to Dauphiné in the autumn of 1904—a rather disastrous business. Never again would he take any one travelling who did not know how to come in out of the cold. It was a painter's country, and he had hired a little *château* in front of the Glandaz mountain— himself, his wife, their eldest girl, and Alicia. The adaptation of his famous manner to that strange scenery, its browns and French greys and filmy blues, so preoccupied him that he had scant time for becoming intimate with these hills and valleys. From the little gravelled terrace in front of the annexe, out of which he had made a studio, there was an absorbing view over the pantiled old town of Die. It glistened below in the early or late sunlight, flat-roofed and of pinkish yellow, with the dim, blue River Drôme circling one side, and cut, dark cypress trees dotting the vineyarded slopes. And he painted it continually. What Alicia did with herself they none of them very much knew, except that she would come in and talk ecstatically of things and beasts and people she had seen. One favourite haunt of hers they did visit—a ruined monastery high up in the amphitheatre of the Glandaz mountain. They had their lunch up there, a very charming and remote spot, where the watercourses and ponds and chapel of the old monks were still visible, though converted by the farmer to his use. Alicia left them abruptly in the middle of their praises, and they had not seen her again till they found her at home when they got back. It was almost as if she had resented laudation of her favourite haunt. She had brought in with her a great bunch of golden berries, of which none of them knew the name; berries almost as beautiful as these spindleberries glowing on the stone of the wall. And a fourth memory of Alicia came.

Christmas Eve, a sparkling frost, and every tree round the little *château* rimed so that they shone in the starlight as though dowered with cherry blossom. Never were more stars in clear black sky above the whitened earth. Down in the little town a few faint points of yellow light twinkled in the mountain wind keen as a razor's edge. A fantastically lovely night—quite 'Japanese', but cruelly cold. Five minutes on the terrace had been enough for all of them except Alicia. She—unaccountable, crazy creature—would not come in. Twice he had gone out to her, with commands, entreaties, and extra wraps; the third time he could not find her. She had deliberately avoided his onslaught and slid off somewhere to keep this mad vigil by frozen starlight. When at last she did come in she reeled as if drunk. They tried to make her really drunk, to put warmth back into her. No good! In two days she was down with double pneumonia; it was two months before she was up again—a very shadow of herself. There had never been much health in her since then. She floated like a ghost through life, a crazy ghost, who would steal away, goodness knew where, and come in with a flush in her withered cheeks, and her grey hair wild blown, carrying her spoil— some flower, some leaf, some tiny bird, or little soft rabbit. She never painted now, never even talked of it. They had made her give up her cottage and come to live with them, literally afraid that she would starve herself to death in her forgetfulness of everything. These spindleberries even! Why, probably, she had been right up this morning to that sunny chalk-pit in the lew of the Downs to get them, seven miles there and back, when you wouldn't think she could walk seven hundred yards, and as likely as not had lain there on the dewy grass looking up at the sky, as he had come on her sometimes. Poor Alicia! And once he had been within an ace of marrying her! A life spoiled! By what, if not by love of beauty? But who would have ever thought that the intangible could wreck a woman, deprive her of love, marriage, motherhood, of fame, of wealth, of health? And yet—by George!—it had!

Scudamore flipped the four pink berries off the wall. The radiance and the meandering milky waters; that swan against the brown tufted rushes; those far, filmy Downs—there was beauty! *Beauty!* But, damn it all—moderation! Moderation! And, turning his back on that prospect, which he had painted so many times in his celebrated manner, he went in, and up the expensively restored staircase to his studio. It had great windows on three sides, and perfect means for regulating light. Unfinished studies melted into walls so subdued that they looked like atmosphere. There were no completed pictures—they sold too fast. As he walked over to his easel his eye was caught by a spray of colour—the branch of spindleberries set in water, ready for him to use, just where the pale sunlight fell so that their delicate colour might glow and the few tiny drops of moisture still clinging to them shine. For a second he saw Alicia herself as she must have looked, setting them there, her transparent hands hovering, her eyes shining, that grey hair of hers all fine and loose. The vision vanished! But what had made her bring them after that horrified 'God!' when he spoke of using them? Was it her way of saying: 'Forgive me for being rude'? Really she was pathetic, that poor devotee! The spindleberries glowed in their silver-lustre jug, sprayed up against the sunlight. They looked triumphant—as well they might, who stood for that which had ruined—or was it saved?—a life! Alicia! She had made a pretty mess of it, and yet who knew what secret raptures she had felt with her subtle lover, Beauty, by starlight and sunlight and moonlight, in the fields and woods, on the hilltops, and by riverside? Flowers, and the flight of birds, and the ripple of the wind, and all the shifting play of light and colour which made a man despair when he wanted to use them; she had taken them, hugged them to her with no afterthought, and been happy! Who could say that she had missed the prize of life? Who could say it? . . . Spindleberries! A bunch of spindleberries to set such doubts astir in him! Why, what was beauty but just the extra value which certain forms and colours, blended, gave to things—just the extra value in the human market! Nothing else on earth, nothing! And the spindleberries glowed against the sunlight, delicate, remote!

Taking his palette, he mixed crimson lake, white, and ultramarine. What was that? Who sighed, away out there behind him? Nothing!

'Damn it all!' he thought; 'this is childish. This is as bad as Alicia!' And he set to work to paint in his celebrated manner—spindleberries.

LEONARD MERRICK
The Judgement of Paris

In the summer of the memorable year ——, but the date doesn't matter, Robichon and Quinquart both paid court to Mademoiselle Brouette. Mademoiselle Brouette was a captivating actress, Robichon and Quinquart were the most comic of comedians, and all three were members of the Théâtre Suprême.

Robichon was such an idol of the public's that they used to laugh before he uttered the first word of his role; and Quinquart was so vastly popular that his silence threw the audience into convulsions.

Professional rivalry apart, the two were good friends, although they were suitors for the same lady, and this was doubtless due to the fact that the lady favoured the robust Robichon no more than she favoured the skinny Quinquart. She flirted with them equally, she approved them equally—and at last, when each of them had plagued her beyond endurance, she promised in a pet that she would marry the one that was the better actor.

Tiens! Not a player on the stage, not a critic on the Press could quite make up his mind which the better actor was. Only Suzanne Brouette could have said anything so tantalizing.

'But how shall we decide the point, Suzanne?' stammered Robichon helplessly. 'Whose pronouncement will you accept?'

'How can the question be settled?' queried Quinquart, dismayed. 'Who shall be the judge?'

'Paris shall be the judge,' affirmed Suzanne. 'We are the servants of the public—I will take the public's word!'

Of course she was as pretty as a picture, or she couldn't have done these things.

Then poor Quinquart withdrew, plunged in reverie. So did Robichon. Quinquart reflected that she had been talking through her expensive hat. Robichon was of the same opinion. The public lauded them both, was no less generous to one than to the other—to wait for the judgement of Paris appeared equivalent to postponing the matter *sine die*. No way out presented itself to Quinquart. None occurred to Robichon.

'Mon vieux, said the latter, as they sat on the terrace of their favourite café a day or two before the annual vacation, 'let us discuss this amicably. Have a cigarette! You are an actor, therefore you consider yourself more talented than I. I, too, am an actor, therefore I regard you as less gifted than myself. So much for our artistic standpoints! But we are also men of the world, and it must be obvious to both of us that we might go on being funny until we reached our death-beds without demonstrating the supremacy of either. Enfin, our only hope lies in versatility—the conqueror must distinguish himself in a solemn part!' He viewed the other with complacence, for the quaint Quinquart had been designed for a droll by Nature.

'Right!' said Quinquart. He contemplated his colleague with satisfaction, for it was impossible to fancy the fat Robichon in tragedy.

'I perceive only one drawback to the plan,' continued Robichon, 'the Management will never consent to accord us a chance. Is it not always so in the theatre? One succeeds in a certain line of business and one must be resigned to play that line as long as one lives. If my earliest success had been scored as a villain of melodrama, it would be believed that I was competent to enact nothing but villains of melodrama; it happened that I made a hit as a comedian, wherefore nobody will credit that I am capable of anything but being comic.'

'Same here!' concurred Quinquart. 'Well, then, what do you propose?'

Robichon mused. 'Since we shall not be allowed to do ourselves justice on the stage, we must find an opportunity off it!'

'A private performance? Good! Yet, if it is a private performance, how is Paris to be the judge?'

'Ah,' murmured Robichon, 'that is certainly a stumbling-block.'

They sipped their apéritifs moodily. Many heads were turned towards the little table where they sat. 'There are Quinquart and Robichon, how amusing they always are!' said passers-by, little guessing the anxiety at the laughter-makers' hearts.

'What's to be done?' sighed Quinquart at last.

Robichon shrugged his fat shoulders, with a frown.

Both were too absorbed to notice that, after a glance of recognition, one of the pedestrians had paused, and was still regarding them irresolutely. He was a tall, burly man, habited in rusty black, and the next moment, as if finding courage, he stepped forward and spoke:

'Gentlemen, I ask pardon for the liberty I take—impulse urges me to seek your professional advice! I am in a position to pay a moderate fee. Will you permit me to explain myself?'

'Monsieur,' returned Robichon, 'we are in deep consideration of our latest parts. We shall be pleased to give you our attention at some other time.'

'Alas!' persisted the new-comer, 'with me time presses. I, too, am considering my latest part—and it will be the only speaking part I have ever played, though I have been "appearing" for twenty years.'

'What? You have been a super for twenty years?' said Quinquart, with a grimace.

'No, monsieur,' replied the stranger grimly. 'I have been the Public Executioner; and I am going to lecture on the horrors of the post I have resigned.'

The two comedians stared at him aghast. Across the sunlit terrace seemed to have fallen the black shadow of the guillotine.

'I am Jacques Roux,' the man went on. 'I am "trying it on the dog" at Appeville-sous-Bois next week, and I have what you gentlemen call "stage fright"—I, who never knew what nervousness meant before! Is it not queer? As often as I rehearse walking on to the platform, I feel myself to be all arms and legs—I don't know what to do with them. Formerly, I scarcely remembered my arms and legs; but, of course, my attention used to be engaged by the other fellow's head. Well, it struck me that you might consent to give me a few hints in deportment. Probably one lesson would suffice.'

'Sit down,' said Robichon. 'Why did you abandon your official position?'

'Because I awakened to the truth,' Roux answered. 'I no longer agree with capital punishment; it is a crime that should be abolished.'

'The scruples of conscience, hein?'

'That is it.'

'Fine!' said Robichon. 'What dramatic lines such a lecture might contain! And of what is it to consist?'

'It is to consist of the history of my life—my youth, my poverty, my experiences as Executioner, and my remorse.'

'Magnificent!' said Robichon. 'The spectres of your victims

pursue you even to the platform. Your voice fails you, your eyes start from your head in terror. You gasp for mercy—and imagination splashes your outstretched hands with gore. The audiece thrill, women swoon, strong men are breathless with emotion.' Suddenly he smote the table with his big fist, and little Quinquart nearly fell off his chair, for he divined the inspiration of his rival. 'Listen!' cried Robichon, 'are you known at Appeville-sous-Bois?'

'My name is known, yes.'

'Bah! I mean are you known personally, have you acquaintances there?'

'Oh, no. But why?'

'There will be nobody to recognize you?'

'It is very unlikely in such a place.'

'What do you estimate that your profits will amount to?'

'It is only a small hall, and the prices are cheap. Perhaps two hundred and fifty francs.'

'And you are nervous, you would like to postpone your début?'

'I should not be sorry, I admit. But, again, why?'

'I will tell you why—I offer you five hundred francs to let me take your place!'

'Monsieur!'

'Is it a bargain?'

'I do not understand!'

'I have a whim to figure in a solemn part. You can explain next day that you missed your train—that you were ill, there are a dozen explanations that can be made; you will not be supposed to know that I personated you—the responsibility for that is mine. What do you say?'

'It is worth double the money,' demurred the man.

'Not a bit of it! All the Press will shout the story of my practical joke—Paris will be astounded that I, Robichon, lectured as Jacques Roux and curdled an audience's blood. Millions will speak of your intended lecture tour who otherwise would never have heard of it. I am giving you the grandest advertisement, and paying you for it, besides. Enfin, I will throw a deportment lesson in! Is it agreed?'

'Agreed, monsieur!' said Roux.

Oh, the trepidation of Quinquart! Who could eclipse Robichon if his performance of the part equalled his conception of it? At the theatre that evening Quinquart followed Suzanne about the wings pathetically. He was garbed like a buffoon, but he felt like Romeo.

The throng that applauded his capers were far from suspecting the romantic longings under his magenta wig. For the first time in his life he was thankful that the author hadn't given him more to do.

And, oh, the excitement of Robichon! He was to put his powers to a tremendous test, and if he made the effect that he anticipated he had no fear of Quinquart's going one better. Suzanne, to whom he whispered his project proudly, announced an intention of being present to 'see the fun'. Quinquart also promised to be there. Robichon sat up all night preparing his lecture.

If you wish to know whether Suzanne rejoiced at the prospect of his winning her, history is not definite on the point; but some chroniclers assert that at this period she made more than usual of Quinquart, who had developed a hump as big as the Panthéon.

And they all went to Appeville-sous-Bois.

Though no one in the town was likely to know the features of the Executioner, it was to be remembered that people there might know the actor's, and Robichon had made up to resemble Roux as closely as possible. Arriving at the humble hall, he was greeted by the lessee, heard that a 'good house' was expected, and smoked a cigarette in the retiring-room while the audience assembled.

At eight o'clock the lessee reappeared.

'All is ready, Monsieur Roux, he said.

Robichon rose.

He saw Suzanne and Quinquart in the third row, and was tempted to wink at them.

'Ladies and gentlemen——'

All eyes were riveted on him as he began; even the voice of the 'Executioner' exercised a morbid fascination over the crowd. The men nudged their neighbours appreciatively, and women gazed at him, half horrified, half charmed.

The opening of his address was quiet enough—there was even a humorous element in it, as he narrated imaginary experiences of his boyhood. People tittered, and then glanced at one another with an apologetic air, as if shocked at such a monster's daring to amuse them. Suzanne whispered to Quinquart: 'Too cheerful; he hasn't struck the right note.' Quinquart whispered back gloomily: 'Wait; he may be playing for the contrast!'

And Quinquart's assumption was correct. Gradually the cheerfulness faded from the speaker's voice, the humorous incidents were past. Gruesome, hideous, grew the anecdotes. The hall shivered.

Necks were craned, and white faces twitched suspensively. He dwelt on the agonies of the Condemned, he recited crimes in detail, he mirrored the last moments before the blade fell. He shrieked his remorse, his lacerating remorse. 'I am a murderer,' he sobbed; and in the hall one might have heard a pin drop.

There was no applause when he finished—that set the seal on his success; he bowed and withdrew amid tense silence. Still none moved in the hall, until, with a rush, the representatives of the Press sped forth to proclaim Jacques Roux an unparalleled sensation.

The triumph of Robichon! How generous were the congratulations of Quinquart, and how sweet the admiring tributes of Suzanne! And there was another compliment to come—nothing less than a card from the Marquis de Thevenin, requesting an interview at his home.

'Ah!' exclaimed Robichon, enravished, 'an invitation from a noble! That proves the effect I made, hein?'

'Who may he be?' inquired Quinquart. 'I never heard of the Marquis de Thevenin!'

'It is immaterial whether you have heard of him,' replied Robichon. 'He is a marquis, and he desires to converse with me! It is an honour that one must appreciate. I shall assuredly go.'

And, being a bit of a snob, he sought a fiacre in high feather.

The drive was short, and when the cab stopped he was distinctly taken aback to perceive the unpretentious aspect of the nobleman's abode. It was, indeed, nothing better than a lodging. A peasant admitted him, and the room to which he was ushered boasted no warmer hospitality than a couple of candles and a decanter of wine. However, the sconces were massive silver. Monsieur le marquis, he was informed, had been suddenly compelled to summon his physician, and begged that Monsieur Roux would allow him a few minutes' grace.

Robichon ardently admired the candlesticks, but began to think he might have supped more cosily with Suzanne.

It was a long time before the door opened.

The Marquis de Thevenin was old—so old that he seemed to be falling to pieces as he tottered forward. His skin was yellow and shrivelled, his mouth sunken, his hair sparse and grey; and from this weird face peered strange eyes—the eyes of a fanatic.

'Monsieur, I owe you many apologies for my delay,' he wheezed. 'My unaccustomed exertion this evening fatigued me, and on my

return from the hall I found it necessary to see my doctor. Your
lecture was wonderful, Monsieur Roux—most interesting and
instructive; I shall never forget it.'

Robichon bowed his acknowledgements.

'Sit down, Monsieur Roux, do not stand! Let me offer you some
wine. I am forbidden to touch it myself. I am a poor host, but my
age must be my excuse.'

'To be the guest of monsieur le marquis,' murmured Robichon,
'is a privilege, an honour, which—er——'

'Ah,' sighed the marquis. 'I shall very soon be in the Republic
where all men are really equals and the only masters are the worms.
My reason for requesting you to come was to speak of your
unfortunate experiences—of a certain unfortunate experience in
particular. You referred in your lecture to the execution of one
called "Victor Lesueur". He died game, hein?'

'As plucky a soul as I ever dispatched!' said Robichon, savouring
the burgundy.

'Ah! Not a tremor? He strode to the guillotine like a man?'

'Like a hero!' said Robichon, who knew nothing about him.

'That was fine,' said the marquis; 'that was as it should be! You
have never known a prisoner to die more bravely?' There was a
note of pride in his voice that was unmistakable.

'I shall always recall his courage with respect,' declared Robichon, mystified.

'Did you respect it at the time?'

'Pardon, monsieur le marquis?'

'I inquire if you respected it at the time; did you spare him all
needless suffering?'

'There is no suffering,' said Robichon. 'So swift is the knife
that——'

The host made a gesture of impatience. 'I refer to mental
suffering. Cannot you realize the emotions of an innocent man
condemned to a shameful death?'

'Innocent! As for that, they all say that they are innocent.'

'I do not doubt it. Victor, however, spoke the truth. I know it.
He was my son.'

'Your son?' faltered Robichon, aghast.

'My only son—the only soul I loved on earth. Yes; he was
innocent, Monsieur Roux. And it was you who butchered him—he
died by your hands.'

'I—I was but the instrument of the law,' stammered Robichon. 'I was not responsible for his fate, myself.'

'You have given a masterly lecture, Monsieur Roux,' said the marquis musingly; 'I find myself in agreement with all that you said in it—"you are his murderer". I hope the wine is to your taste, Monsieur Roux? Do not spare it!'

'The wine?' gasped the actor. He started to his feet, trembling—he understood.

'It is poisoned,' said the old man calmly. 'In an hour you will be dead.'

'Great Heavens!' moaned Robichon. Already he was conscious of a strange sensation—his blood was chilled, his limbs were weighted, there were shadows before his eyes.

'Ah, I have no fear of you!' continued the other; 'I am feeble, I could not defend myself; but your violence would avail you nothing. Fight, or faint, as you please—you are doomed.'

For some seconds they stared at each other dumbly—the actor paralysed by terror, the host wearing the smile of a lunatic. And then the 'lunatic' slowly peeled court-plaster from his teeth, and removed features, and lifted a wig.

And when the whole story was published, a delighted Paris awarded the palm to Quinquart without a dissentient voice, for while Robichon had duped an audience, Quinquart had duped Robichon himself.

Robichon bought the silver candlesticks, which had been hired for the occasion, and he presented them to Quinquart and Suzanne on their wedding-day.

GEOFFREY MOSS
Defeat

THIS sister of Hasso von Koekritz has asked me to write this story.

My qualifications to do so are these. Twelve years ago, when he was assistant military attaché in Brussels, I knew him well. After that, it is true, I saw him only for a few days; still, he then discussed with me his position and its difficulties. Besides that, as I understood his mentality, I can interpret his motives, and can guess what his thoughts must have been. In any case, I was an eyewitness of what I am going to relate.

The race of Koekritz is an ancient one, and in the Middle Ages, when the Hohenzollerns were still unknown in those parts, and when Berlin was not yet even a village, this family with a few others dominated the Mark of Brandenburg. 'From Koekritz and Luderitz, from Krachten and from Itzenplitz, may the Good God deliver us.' This doggerel, dating from those times, gives a vivid enough suggestion of Hasso's ancestry. The lands of the family lay amidst those sandy wastes and endless reedy meres about the Spree, where, because of the extreme poverty of the soil, none but a hardy race could have lived at all, and where any adventure must have tempted. From the first they were fighters. A Koekritz served Carlos Quinto in Italy: one fought under Marlborough, several under Frederick the Great. A Koekritz fell at Austerlitz, another at Waterloo. The father of my friend led a charge at Gravelotte.

When I knew Hasso von Koekritz in Brussels he was well off, and, to all appearances, more interested in sport, in social life, and in having a good time generally, than in the not too strenuous duties at his Legation. In the mornings we often rode together (for neither of us did work begin till the gentlemanly hour of eleven), and in the evenings we often dined *à deux* at Leymann's or at the Filet de Sole. Koekritz was fond of a good Bordeaux, I remember. 'A devilish good wine, I find this: a devilish good wine! Well! well!' and his long-sighted grey eyes would twinkle and his lean sailor-like face would twist into that tight, crooked smile which was so characteristic of him. He was barely thirty then, but of an uncommonly hard-bitten type.

One way and another I saw a lot of him. We went to the same dances: once we made a trip to Paris together: I mounted him for a few days' hunting in England: he gave me some duck-shooting at his home. I don't think that in those days I thought of him as being of any particular nationality. He was a jolly fellow to go about with: he spoke perfect English: we had tastes in common. Then came the war, and for ten years I heard nothing of him.

I

'If you are really determined on going there, I can give you an introduction,' said some one I met in Berlin. 'It's to a major in the Green Police, a Graf Koekritz.'

'Koekritz!' I answered. 'I knew a Graf Koekritz in Brussels once. Hasso his name was. But he was a soldier—in the Guard Hussars.'

It was the same, the man told me. An explanation followed.

After the war, the army being reduced to practically nothing, Koekritz, it appeared, had found himself a civilian. But soldiering had been his career, and his property had long been let to a farmer. The post-war rent, still the same and still paid in marks, brought him in yearly only the price of a single meal. He had, therefore, the alternative of living on his brother, who was head of the family, or of finding a way of keeping himself. So, when the Security Police had been raised, he had joined it.

'Look him up,' my informant in Berlin said to me. 'He'll be glad to see you. He isn't likely to find an industrial town on the Rhine too congenial. I'm afraid we Brandenburgers rather tend to look down on Rhine folk. They're a bit too modern, and a bit too soft to our way of thinking. You remember his *appartement* in the Boulevard du Régent? *Himmel!* He knew how to make himself comfortable. It must be rough on him now. Remember me to him, if you do see him.'

II

As soon as I had unpacked my boxes, I left the hotel and went in search of Koekritz. At the police barracks they gave me the address of his lodgings. Eventually I found the house, which was in a good part of the town. His rooms were at the top of it, on the fifth floor. There was, of course, no lift: and on account of my lameness I took some time to climb the stairs, and arrived breathless. I rang the bell and waited. Nothing happened, so I rang again. I was just going away when I heard some one moving about within the flat. Two women held a muffled discussion, some one lifted the shutter of the circular peep-hole which was matched by a medallion on the other half of the door, and peered at me through it. Then, rather distrustfully, one door was opened by a thin old lady. She wore a purple dress bound with black cloth; her grey hair was drawn rigidly back. She had high cheek-bones and sour lips.

'What do you want?' she asked uninvitingly, blinking at me, for the hall within was very dark, while the landing on which I stood was light.

'Can I see Graf Koekritz, please?'

She looked me over, her thin hands clasped each other. 'Come in.'

I did so, and she shut the door behind me, bolted, locked, and chained it. Then, without a word, she turned and shuffled away into the chill unventilated twilight leaving me to follow her.

Pieces of large sepulchral furniture loomed around us. A confusion of stags' heads and Oriental swords crowded the dim walls. A joss-house lantern, surrounded by glass beads and baubles, hung so low that I almost touched it as I passed.

We went through a crowded drawing-room, thence through a dining-room, which had the air of never being used, but which had a table large enough for a dozen people. At the farther end of it were more double doors. The old lady tapped with thin knuckles.

'Come in,' said a voice.

I should have known it was Koekritz, even if I had expected some one else to be there. Indeed, I was surprised to find how unmistakably I recognized his voice after so long.

The old lady did not open the door, but continued rapping until it was opened from within. Then she slid away.

III

'Why! My dear fellow! My dear fellow! . . . what on earth . . .? Come in! come in!'

He took me by the arm, drew me into the room, and shut the door.

'You haven't changed a bit. Why, it must be . . . it must be twelve years. . . . But come along and sit down. This is nice!'

He led me, still by the elbow, towards the window. 'Which do

you prefer—the rocking-chair or this?' I chose 'this', which had a
castor missing.

What bit of good luck had brought me there? Why hadn't I let
him know I was coming? He was obviously delighted to see me.
'Well! Well!' He looked me up and down, and his lips twisted into
his tight, crooked smile. 'My dear fellow, this is nice!'

Though his voice was just the same as of old, his appearance had
changed a good deal. He was very spare, almost angular. At the
temples his brown hair was turning to grey. It was still brushed in
the English way, and he wore it longer than is usual in Germany.
The lines about his mouth were far more pronounced, and he looked
more hard-bitten than ever. At the moment he was dressed in the
faded grey-green of the Security Police.

'You came through it all right, then,' he asked.

I could still ride, I told him. We gave each other news of old
friends. How was he getting on?

'Oh, not so bad,' he answered. 'Not so bad! I'm lucky to have a
job. Lots of our officers have gone under altogether, you know.'

'Come for a walk. I've only just arrived, and I want to see the
town,' I said.

The room chilled me. A comfortless-looking bed had been made
up on a divan, and his brushes and toilet things were ranged along
the top of a bookcase, but the room was one of those indeterminable
chambers which large German flats possess. It might have been
called a boudoir, but one felt that it had always been used as an
ante-room to the kitchen; a place where a bicycle would be kept and
polished, and where an informal evening meal would be eaten with
the cook within convenient calling distance. It had been transformed
into a bedroom with a minimum of trouble and forethought.

'Right,' he said. 'Wait! I'll change my togs. We wear plain clothes
when we're off duty now—the army also. Democracy! It suits me,
as a matter of fact. That was one thing I liked about the Brussels
job. I never cared for hanging about in uniform all day. Have a
cigarette?'

He shed his tunic on to the big central table. 'I'm going along to
the bathroom. I wash there, you know. Messy having a basin and
things here!'

I offered to come and watch him.

'I'd sooner——Well——It's better if you wait here. This *appartement* belongs to two old ladies. One of them let you in just now.

Father was a General. They're pretty badly hit. No servant and that sort of thing. And the washing is done at home, and it gets dried in the bathroom.'

'Ash-tray!' He pushed one to my side, largely, I fancied, to avoid further explanations.

'Wait here, like a good chap, won't you? Shan't be a minute. Always a bit of a mess in the bathroom, you know,' he added, with confidential cheerfulness, as he went out.

When my cigarette was finished, I got up to help myself to another from the big dining-table, and having done so I took stock of the room.

The walls were covered with paper in which light brown, muddy green, and mauves predominated. The room was large, but there was only one window, the lower panes of which were of stained glass, depicting scenes from Æsop's Fables: the upper panes were frosted. This made the room even dingier. There was the divan that had been made into a bed, which was heaped high with some quilted *Bett decke*, and covered with a lace spread. Around another angle of the wall was a built-in cosy-corner, with family photographs let into the panels above. It would have held five or six, but could not be reached, because of a hammered brass table. There were some pictures, mostly engravings. One, I remember, was of Blücher, with a raised sword: another of some German philosopher or musician—I knew his face, but could not place him—standing bareheaded in a terrific thunderstorm. There was rather a nice old print of Sans Souci, with a dedication plate, showing that it had been given by Frederick himself. The glass-doored bookcase had been emptied, and served Koekritz for a chest of drawers and wardrobe. One the top of it were two or three old paper-covered novels. There was no bedroom furniture.

I had returned to my chair, and was just wondering how my friend amused himself in this place, when he came in again, rubbing the back of his thin neck with a towel.

'It's nice seeing you again, old man. You're not married or anything?' he asked, as he struggled into a clean shirt. I reassured him.

He brought from the bookcase a blue serge jacket, and slipped it over the back of a chair. Its seams and elbows were rather shiny: I recognized the cut of it. On the central table lay the brass-bound trouser-press which I remembered.

'I'm really quite comfortable here,' he said, as if he had guessed my thoughts. 'They're quite decent old bodies, though not very cheerful. As there isn't a servant, one doesn't have to lock things up, which is a blessing. People aren't as honest here as they used to be before the war, you know. I suppose that's so everywhere. Really quite comfortable here, you know, and they get me some hot fodder, no matter what time I get back. And my job often keeps me pretty late. And even if they've gone to bed, there's a gas-stove in the kitchen. I've the use of the dining-room as well, if I need it. Besides, I don't know what the old things would do if I moved on. I don't fancy they've anything at all else left to live on now. Well! Well! I'm ready. . . . Come on! Where shall we go?'

We stole out through the dining-room, through the empty drawing-room, and the dark, chilly hall. Koekritz unlocked the door, and we went out.

'Cheer up! Cheer up!' he said, taking my elbow with a laugh which reminded me of the old Brussels days.

IV

The town proved a disappointment to me. The public buildings were in various styles of the last eighty years. None was interesting. Some had been requisitioned, and flew a tricolour. There were the usual wide boulevards with half-grown trees, the trams, prosperous villas in their gardens: clean, tall workmen's dwellings with red bed-quilts airing over the verandas and gay window-boxes: and all around the city stretched the usual model factories, by which it lived. In the ugly barracks there were French troops, and two reasonably smart sentries guarded the gate. A small detachment escorting a wagon passed us. No one took any notice of it, for this was in the old occupied territory, and there had been a French garrison in the town for more than four years.

'How do you get on with them?' I asked. 'Do they give a lot of trouble?'

'Oh! I . . . I've nothing to complain of. No army of occupation can be perfect. I expect, if it were our turn this time, we'd be just the same. A little friction here and there: nothing that amounts to much. Temperaments of the two races so different, you see. We're always carrying out everything to the very letter: we're unadaptable: we don't shrug our shoulders and make the best of things. Our burgomasters, and people like that, are always on their dignity.

Even when we want to be pleasant, we're clumsy. And the French—you know what they are! They're always worrying about abstract ideas, *la gloire, l'honneur*, and always talking about being the victors; and looking for insults. But when one makes allowances for all that, things might be a lot worse. There are grievances, here and there, and some are pretty real. I come across most of them, unfortunately, because, when some one thinks he's been done down, he comes trotting round to us to complain. He might as well put his grievance in a bottle and float it down the Rhine in hopes the Dutch would open it, and get things put right for him. But when one thinks of what our occupation of their territory would mean, I don't suppose there's much to choose one way or another.'

We talked mostly of such matters, for in twelve years so much had happened to both of us, that most of the old points of our contact had been obliterated. There were so many subjects upon which I should not have cared to venture. I would not have been the first to speak of horses, one of his chief interests in the past. Obviously he could afford none now. Dancing—I doubted if there was any social life for him in this industrial town. The society of it even before the war must have been chiefly commercial, and the very real differences between the classes in Germany had always made the mixing of them difficult. When I thought of his old life in the Boulevard du Régent, I could not imagine how Koekritz now spent his leisure. So I kept as much as possible off personal matters, and our talk during those first hours together was largely of war and peace.

Inevitably we discussed the Treaties, and the like. Koekritz was temperate, with a detachment which somehow suggested to me that he had felt too deeply and too long about these things, and that he had kept his thoughts to himself till his bitterness had burnt itself away, and that there remained in its place an emptiness which it was not pleasant to contemplate. Perhaps all this was my fancy, for he spoke with his old dry cheerfulness. It was only sometimes, in a pause, while he skirted some subject, that this feeling came to me.

It was a mess! Of course, it was a mess! There it was! That was that! The war had lasted too long: too much had been destroyed: too many lives had been lost.

One couldn't have expected the people who came out on top to have been very moderate.

That night we dined together.

V

'You've been back in Brussels since the war?' Koekritz asked.

It was two nights later, and we were sitting over our dinner-table in the restaurant of my hotel.

I had been in Brussels for a few days. I gave him news of people we had known. We explored the past. What had happened to Miette? She had bought a little cabaret and was doing well, I told him.

'Miette! I can't fancy her in that role.' He smiled at me over his glass. 'But here's to her!'

He himself had been in Brussels during the war, but he had never stayed longer than he could help. There had been no social life. Most of his old Belgian friends had kept away from the capital. In any case, those had been difficult times. Did I know who had his *appartement* now?'

'Good days those!' he said. 'Good days! Do you remember the night we raced old Villainquatorze's new Delauney back from Ostend? Or that fancy dress ball at the Monnaie? Good days! They'll never come again. Well! Well!'

Koekritz seemed very happy that evening. I had discovered some Bordeaux—really first-rate stuff. Even a *Flamand* cellar need not have been ashamed of it. I don't suppose he had tasted any for a long while. His twisted smile was less taut. No one watching him would have guessed that life was not still easy for him as it had been in the Boulevard du Régent.

His manner was just the same as it had been in those days. He still spoke excellent English, but the turning of his phrases gave a curious suggestion of being out of date. Then I realized what produced this impression. He was using the slang of twelve years before. That was all it was! His English had been anchored while the speech of the rest of us had flowed on. He was still saying the 'some wine', 'some night', which we had borrowed, but had long since discarded. And words I needed to express our changed conditions puzzled him. 'Axed' needed explanation: the ramifications of 'stunt' were not easy.

We talked of dead men and of past customs. England had changed, I told him.

'Not as this country has,' he said, with the slightest nod towards a table near us, where, as at most of the others, sat French officers.

Things had changed in Germany, fundamentally, and so quickly, too, he added. While he spoke, Koekritz watched one with his long-sighted grey eyes. Then sometimes he would look down at his hands and would turn his loose signet ring round and round, and smile to himself. And sitting there that evening, the recollection of these forgotten tricks came back to me. He was thinking of these changes.

'For example?' For a while he sat silent.

'Do you really care to hear, I wonder?'

He looked up suddenly. His glance was almost distrustful. I felt that we were approaching a subject seldom mentioned.

'Of course I do.'

'All right. . . . Well. . . . I dare say you won't understand when I do tell you! . . . Here the changes all came in a matter of days. They were obvious enough, God knows, but how we . . . say myself—felt about them you very likely won't understand. The thing that struck me most, and which, I suppose, I shall never forget——' He broke away from his subject and caught another. 'It's all over now, and there's a new generation growing up, and things will begin to improve soon—they must. . . . It's *some* wine, this you're giving me! A devilish good wine!'

'Go on! What was it?'

'All right! But it isn't worth hearing, I promise you: still, if you want to know, it was our arrival—what's the word? Oh, thank you—our home-coming. You see, when I'd ridden out with my squadron at my heels in new service dress, we'd passed the Emperor, as he took our salute, and we thought—I suppose every one did, both sides—that it was going to be a walk-over, just a few charges, and then in a month or two we'd be back, hung round with orders and putty medals. There were bands, of course, and flags and people shouting and Heaven knows what more of all that. I saw the look the Emperor gave us—he knew most of us personally, you see—and that was one of the remembrances we took away with us. Well, those four years went somehow. It was odd that feeling how the thing would drag on for ever. I suppose it was the same thing on both sides. But even till quite the end, though everything was—well—falling to bits, to us at the Front things were really still the same. We'd got a country. We'd got homes to go to. We'd been beaten before. A nation that does much scrapping must get a hiding sometimes. The French had been in Berlin before, but equally we'd been in Paris. My father was luckier. Six months' war and a victory.

Still, one can't grumble. I'd jogged my old charger through three
enemy capitals in as many years, and I'm still on top of the turf!
Well, to go on, we couldn't hold out much longer. The knowledge
came slowly: it was bad watching the men. We were losing: we'd
get bad peace terms, but it would be over.

'I hadn't seen the Emperor for the best part of a year, but my
brother was with him at the end. Only two days before he said to
my brother that, if things got worse, he could count on those who
were by him to ride in with him and get finished. And then, after
all—— Well! you guess what a knock what actually happened must
have been! It was nearer to us in the Guards Corps, for we knew
him, but for the whole nation it was much the same. We're a people
that had been used to being ridden on a pretty tight rein: we were
used to it, and we liked it. You see us to-day. No policy. Like a
loose horse that's badly hit, and scared to death. That's this country!
We'd staked such a lot on one selection! But people don't always
run to what one thought was their form. Things don't always turn
out as one expects. Do you remember the money I dropped on that
cert. you gave me in Brussels?'

'Yes, go on!'

'You really want all this? All right! . . . Well, when we got back,
I hadn't any squadron. We'd been broken up, and I came in leading
a company of God knows what foot regiment. And the welcome we
got! There was the President of the week-old Republic, all in black,
looking like a Karl Strasse undertaker. Not a cheer! Well, perhaps
half a dozen. None of the old black, white, and red we'd been
fighting under: but a lot of half-starved boys waving their red flags.
There were decent people, too, but naturally the men were old 'uns,
and the women were mostly crying—always a bore! Some of the
Bolsheviki people were for hooting us, but they hadn't the pluck.
Not much of a meeting, was it? The worst part was thinking of the
under-officers. There was nothing in front of them, you see; and
they knew it. We were a glum lot, I don't mind telling you! For
most of us it was just the end of everything. Odd the things that
come into one's head sometimes, isn't it?'

Koekritz stopped.

'Yes?'

'Well, I've never troubled much over poetry, and that sort of
stuff, but as we came to it and one saw the Brandenburger Torr
rising up above one like a cliff, I thought of that bit about "All hope

abandon". It was a dull day, and with those little red rags being fluttered about all round the foot of it, and the winter sky showing through its five arches, the Torr looked bigger and greyer than ever. God knows how many times I've ridden through it with my squadron, but I felt that day as if I'd never seen it before. We came level with it: the column wheeled round: it got bigger and bigger: and there we were, under the centre arch. Then the men's march sounded all loud and echoing—you know the way it does when troops go under a hollow place—and then I saw the little red flags fluttering under the bare trees all the way down the Linden, as far as the eye could see. It sounds silly, but coming through the Brandenburger Torr that day, one seemed to have left everything one had ever known behind one.'

Koekritz paused.

'Well, I'm a lucky fellow, and I've no business to have bored you with all this. I'm in clover, really. Quite an interesting job I've got. Come round one morning and look me up at the police barracks. You'll be interested to see my men. I don't suppose there is anything quite the same anywhere in the world. We keep them pretty fit— well fed—trained to the last ounce. They are mostly the younger under-officers of the old army. They've got sport and boxing. They're as hard as hell. They'll interest you.'

The manager of the hotel came to our table and whispered to me. 'It's nearly ten o'clock sir. After that no one is allowed in the streets or in the public rooms in here: but if you and the gentleman with you would like to stay longer, I will speak to the French colonel. He is very amiable and usually makes exceptions for guests here.'

I asked Koekritz what he wanted to do.

'I'll be going back,' he said. 'I can't very well take favours in my position, even when I'm in plain clothes. There isn't very much give-and-take between us and the garrison just now. I'll stay a minute or two till the rest go, and then I'll follow suit.'

The waiter came, and I paid the bill. How long was I staying? Over Sunday, at any rate, I told him.

Koekritz played with his ring for a minute of two. 'I shouldn't, if I were you,' he said, looking up suddenly. 'There's something on here next Sunday and . . . well, there may be trouble.'

'Yes, I know.'

Our eyes met. Koekritz tapped a soft tattoo upon the table.

'Are you watching it for some one in particular?'

I let the reflected light flutter on the knife I held.

'All right,' said Koekritz. 'But it's only fair to warn you there may be hell to pay.'

VI

During the next two days I saw nothing of Koekritz. He was busy making ready for what might happen, he said, when we spoke over the telephone. Indeed, the preparations of both sides were visible enough. Notices were posted at every street corner, announcing that on Sunday a great demonstration would be held in favour of forming the Rhinelands and the Ruhr Gebeit into a republic under French protection, and to prevent the proclamations from being destroyed by the townspeople, armed sentries were mounted near many of them. The strength of the garrison was displayed in other ways: patrols of cavalry and infantry moved about the streets, and a detachment of light tanks took up their positions before the railway station and remained there for some hours. Examining posts were established at several important cross-roads in the city, and at these passports had to be shown and carts were searched. Indeed, traffic in the main streets was rendered almost impossible.

From the outside world we were completely cut off, for all the local newspapers were suspended, and either the postal service of the *Régie* trains had broken down, as usual, or mails were being deliberately held up. A military descent was made upon the Rathaus, and the money destined for the unemployed confiscated so that the number of 'discontents' should be increased. The burgomaster protested and was thrown into prison.

The townspeople on their side, profiting by the experience with Separatists in other places, were taking all manner of precautions. Barbed wire entanglements were erected by voluntary workers on Thursday, in front of the Town Hall, the post office, banks, and other public buildings, but had to be removed next morning by order of the French garrison. The shopkeepers could be seen overhauling their iron shutters, or barricading windows which had none. Front doors were boarded up and shored with timber. Everything of value disappeared from the shops.

The food queues grew longer, for the transport services became daily worse. The supplies of bread were exhausted before every one could be satisfied, and those unable to buy hung about the shops till dusk. On Friday the unemployed, for whom there was now no dole, made a demonstration and did some small damage in the town; but the police, attempting to disperse them, were driven from the streets by the military and were confined to barracks. Eventually some money was obtained and distributed, and thus order was restored.

VII

It was Saturday morning that I went to the barracks of the Security Police. Koekritz must have left word at the gate, for I was at once conducted through chilly stone-flagged corridors to the exercising ground behind the building. There I found him watching the training of his men. He nodded to me abstractedly and said nothing, so I remained near him in silence.

In various parts of the Square squads were being exercised in musketry drill, gymnastics, running, and boxing. Some were in shorts, some in shirt-sleeves, some in full marching order. The men were clean-shaven and seemed all much of an age—thirty, per-haps—and though they were hollow-cheeked and rather colourless, obviously they were extremely fit.

Koekritz stood very still, his feet apart, his hands clasped behind him. Whether he was intent upon the work going on around him, or whether his thoughts were elsewhere, I could not tell. His expression was not a happy one. His grey eyes did not move. He looked older, I thought.

'What do you make of 'em?' he asked suddenly, and without turning towards me. They were certainly in fine condition, I said. But there was about them something which made the Green Police different from any other body of men I had seen, but which it was difficult to define. One associates physical fitness with a certain stolidity, with perhaps even a phlegmatic bearing, but these men had a sort of uneasy alertness. One might have fancied that they had always to fend for themselves, lived outnumbered, and were ever on their guard. To watch them long produced uncomfortable suggestions. All this I tried to explain to Koekritz.

'I know what you mean,' he said. 'You see, they've been on active service, or something devilish like it, for nine years now. It's a longish time: and in the end it tells.'

Most of them had been under-officers in the war, he added. And short rations and the growing certainty of defeat had acted on them, both directly and also through the difficulty they had had in heartening their men.

'As a matter of fact, their job here is pretty heavy going, too!'

'Like yesterday?' I threw in.

'Let's talk of something pleasant,' said Koekritz as we moved off across the Square.

The boxing was earnest rather than skilful, but some locks and trips I saw being practised by another party were neatly done. The movements of the drilling squads were impressively, even jerkily, sudden, but too individual for parade smartness. One was conscious of personalities working together, where one would have expected, especially in that country, a machine. About the skirmishing there was a forcefulness which made practice very like stark reality. Few words of command were to be heard. In all that was done there was a grimness not easy to describe.

'You said something about the trouble the police had yesterday,' said Koekritz. 'Things like that are inevitable when you get a weak force trying to carry on the duties of its Government and another force, much stronger, doing its damnedest to upset it. And all that in the same town at the same time! I don't think the garrison here are much to blame. It can't be fun for them either. But anyhow, things like yesterday's show can't be helped, and my men realize it, thank God! They've had to do some pretty hard thinking in their time, you see, and they're not affected by checks the way younger troops would be. What's the worst for them is having to stand, as they do, between the French and the civil population. There are always—what's the word! Yes, thanks!—there are always pin-pricks. People get a grievance and they come to our fellows and hand in their protest. Then, because we can't do anything, they think we don't really care. It's that that touches the raw! I've felt it myself, so I know. Right on the raw!'

Did he have much to do with the inhabitants of the place? I asked; for I was in the town largely to discover their views. His work kept him in constant touch with the city authorities, he told me, but socially he had no more to do with them than he could help. It was not easy to fancy the Graf Koekritz of the old Brussels days without a social background, but I realized how utterly his life had changed. No, he didn't miss it, he said. For one thing he was too busy. But in any case, the more people he met outside his duties, the more people would come to him with grievances that he had no means of righting.

'I can give you an instance,' he said, as we watched some squads being formed up. 'No one's allowed to leave his house at night, as you know; well, there's a fellow who's got an *appartement* below where I live. His wife was expecting a child—the first. So off he goes to the occupation authorities and asks permission for the doctor to come that night, after some other place he'd got to be at. He couldn't get the permit. The rule was the rule and that was that! But the officer he saw couldn't leave it alone. "Haven't you Bosches got enough children as it is?" he says. They are always worrying about their own falling birth-rate, and I'm sure he only meant it as a joke. Well, it wouldn't have mattered, only the man's wife had a bad time and the child was born dead. That's how things happen. No one was particularly to blame. Still, every time I meet him on the stairs I've got to hear it all over again. What can I do? No one's particularly to blame, but the fellow thinks I could do something if I wanted to.'

The squads re-formed, the parade was dismissed, and the men trooped briskly but cheerlessly into the barracks, leaving Koekritz and myself alone in the empty Square.

'Well! Well!' he said. The hardness faded out of his eyes, the fixity of his lips relaxed into his twisted smile.

'They're a pretty good pack, aren't they?' he added, with a nod at the now empty doorways.

VIII

I had arranged with Koekritz that he should dine with me that night, but in the evening a telephone message was sent to say that he was too busy and could not come. So, resigned to a solitary meal, I was choosing my wine, when an English journalist, whom I had met in the hall, asked if he might share my table.

He had arrived by motor that afternoon, and had come to see what the Sunday demonstration would produce. We exchanged my local news for his of the world outside, for I had seen no paper for several days. Many thought, he said, that a *coup d'état* would be attempted in the town next day. The French, so his information went, were bringing some two thousand Separatists in their *Régie* trains from all parts of the Rhineland: their flying column, he called it. We discussed to what extent the movement was spontaneous, and I told him that the adherents in the town were said to number twenty to thirty.

Presently the manager stopped at our table and talked with us. He was, like so many of his profession, a devout internationalist. All this was a foolishness, he said. Times were bad enough. Look at the prices! We had been considering them—if from a different angle, we explained—but he passed quickly to another subject. These Separatists were mostly professional criminals, he said, and many were not Germans at all. This, in some cases at least, was true, I knew; for I had seen their dossiers and lists of convictions in the police barracks that morning. Why, he wanted to know, should the French Army, which was now the chief support of his hotel, arm such people and import them into a town where no one was allowed weapons for their own defence? It would only mean more work for the French themselves. What was the sense in that! The Separatists wouldn't bring money to the town or his hotel. They'd either steal what they wanted or they'd pay in notes of their own manufacture. Of course, if the French did not prevent them, the Security Police would arrest them, armed or not, in the ordinary way. But the Garrison would never have that! And would we believe it, the procession was even to pass the doors of his hotel. He, at any rate, was going to take no chances. He was going to have every door barricaded, and every window shuttered. So, if we wished to see the procession, we must do it from the balconies of our rooms. But why should it be allowed at all! It was all a foolishness!

'*Das ist nicht le business*, gentlemen!' was his polyglot complaint, as he bowed himself away.

The journalist and I discussed the chances of-trouble. He had, since his arrival, paid a visit to the Rathaus and had heard much there. At a meeting of all parties it had been arranged that, as there was no way of preventing this influx of 'undesirables', every one else should remain at home: and, as the only protest which could be made, every street should be empty, every blind down.

Except the Communists, all had voted for this: and they, who were as opposed as the rest were to the Separatists, had only refused because on principle they never worked with other parties! They had ways of their own, they had proclaimed, to prevent their country from being broken up. It was in this possibility of conflict that the real danger lay, said the journalist as we sipped our coffee.

The restaurant, although it was Saturday, was almost empty that night. The blue uniform of the French showed vivid amongst the bare white table-cloths. There were scarcely any other guests. A sense of impending events hung in the air. There were times when no one was speaking and when the waiters, scurrying along with loose covered dishes, seemed strangely noisy. Once some one laughed and, surprised by his own voice, looked awkwardly about him. Once the lights flickered and went out, but only for a moment. The manager even forgot to ask us if we wished to remain after the prohibited hour: and not having noticed the time, we were surprised, when the Colonel rose as usual and walked down the restaurant pointing with his whip to the various tables. 'These can stay: and these! Outside, the rest!'

'The fat will be in the fire if the Communists really have a go at the other fellows,' said the journalist as we moved towards the door. 'The French are only waiting for an excuse to disarm the police. Then there'll be battle, murder—and the rest of it!'

On the first landing our ways parted, and, as I went along the deserted corridor to my room, the words of Koekritz came back to me with leaden insistence. 'There may be hell to pay. There may be hell to pay.'

IX

Soon after nine next morning I was on the balcony of my room: by ten o'clock the manager and a porter insisted on lowering the heavy roller shutters behind me: at half-past ten the Green Policeman on point duty before the hotel was withdrawn, and thereafter the wide Platz was utterly deserted.

Time passed, but the procession, which should have started its march at ten-thirty, did not appear. No one stirred in the streets: the stillness grew almost oppressive. For a while I watched some sparrows, and in doing so I let my cigarette burn out. Then, to my annoyance, I found that not only had I no matches, but also that the shutter behind me was so heavy that to raise it from outside was impossible.

Presently I heard on the still air the whistle of an engine. I concluded that one of the *Régie* special trains had arrived, but an hour went by and nothing happened. To kill time I had just begun to make sketches in my pocket-book, when in a side-street to the right of the Square a dog barked, and then all at once I heard the shuffle of disordered feet. Another delay. Presumably the head of the column had halted to let the rest of it catch up lost distance. Then the march was begun again: a few voices took up a weak-hearted song, and the procession hove into sight around the corner.

At the head two youths carried a double-poled banner. Behind them a large man in a belted trench-coat marched with a defiant demeanour, a heavy pistol in his hand. After him struggled the rest. Most were boys of, say, from sixteen to twenty-two, beardless, poorly dressed, with mufflers, or with their shirts open. The more dashing affected caps, the more abject, spiritless felt hats. I observed, besides, a few older men, mostly unshaved. There did not appear to be any particular formation, but five abreast was perhaps the average. Their song almost died out, was revived by some one in comparative authority, thrived for a little, and wilted again. No attempt was being made to keep step. Those in rear checked and then hurried uncomfortably.

Passing below the hotel, some of the procession noticed me with jocular remarks. The man in the trench-coat looked up, and our eyes met. He was of a swarthy, bull-necked, and dangerous type. He was an immense fellow, and I wondered if he were a man of whom the journalist had spoken. If he were, he had been a gun-man in Ireland, and afterwards a French secret agent and terrorist in the Upper Silesian plebiscite area, where he had been employed to prevent the population from voting.

I had intended to count the number of the Separatists, but I started too late, became confused, and fell back on mere estimation. When the tail of the column had passed, I did not think that there had been more than three hundred of them. I was wondering why so few had been brought, when a second body appeared from the same direction. This detachment was better organized, and indeed some sort of step was being kept. There was no singing, but two or three of the elder men called the pace in some dialect. This company wore boots of what I took to be the French Army pattern. Close behind it followed another, less disciplined but much larger. More banners, several little hand-carts, and a small rear party ended the procession.

These last files were just level with the hotel, when suddenly I heard shouts, some cheers, an increasing clamour, and then the rap-rap of revolver shots. I leant over the railings and looked down the main street into which the leading detachment had passed. The middle of the procession was swaying this way and that and was apparently being attacked from a side-street.

The threatened collision between the Separatists and the local Communists was, I imagined, taking place. Those who were still in the Square came to a standstill, looked anxiously about them and grasped their weapons. As far as I could tell, only a few of them had pistols. The remainder was armed with rusty and obsolete sabres or lengths of leaden gas piping. All had on their sleeves green, white, and red brassards.

Suddenly from almost below my balcony came a roar of cheers, and looking down I saw a mob of men breaking out from the concealment of a little alley. Some of them wore red badges, and one waved a red flag. These were evidently the Communists, who, profiting by their knowledge of the town, had made a feint against the head of the procession and were now taking it in rear. The surprise was complete, or complete enough to stampede the least disciplined of the Separatists, who broke ranks and scattered across the Square, pursued by their assailants. Sticks and stones flew in the air: some shots cracked out, but by whom they were fired it was impossible to tell. The two mobs, intermingling, drifted in confusion to the farther side of the Platz, leaving the space before the hotel strewn with missiles and caps, but otherwise clear. Then from my balcony the fight was hidden by the tree-tops.

In the street to the left, where the larger part of the procession still remained, a counter-attack was being prepared. The leaders formed up their men with unexpected promptitude, and small parties were dribbled one after another along the side of the Square and out of my sight. From behind the trees came more cheers and the report of an occasional shot. The fighting spread over the Square and groups drove each other backwards and forwards.

There was little shooting, and that was wild. Presumably no one had much ammunition. Which side was winning I could not tell. From the left the leading detachment of the procession was still ebbing spasmodically back into the Platz; while from the streets on the right the Communists were still being reinforced. Some of the combatants, badly hurt, were helped away by their comrades. One man I saw limping out of the battle to a tree, to which he clung for a while, till his grasp slackened, and he slid to the ground.

The energy of the fighters was waning, and both sides were drawing back, the Separatists to the left, and the Communists to the right, when from the farthest corner of the Square came cries, but this time of a new sort. Soon these became distinct:

Polizei! Grüne Polizei! Polizei! Polizei! Polizei! And all at once every one in sight began running towards the hotel. The mobs, again thoroughly mixed but still carrying on some sort of warfare, surged into the main street through which the procession had originally been moving; while some small parties vanished in other directions. At the exit from the Platz a few Separatists halted and started to fire at groups of police advancing under the trees. Then the tap-tap-tap-tap of machine pistols spluttered out. The Green Police had opened fire, but obviously they were aiming high, for bursts of plaster flaked from the upper stories of a house. The rear-guard of the Separatists waited for no more, and followed the rest in its retreat. Then from under the low trees men of the Green Police swept into the open, moving in diamond-shaped groups of four. Some of these parties followed the retreating mob to the left along the main street and, a little way down it, established themselves across the roadway. In the same manner all other approaches to the Platz were blocked. Some ambulance men arrived and took charge of the injured. Within five minutes order had been re-established.

Then for the first time I noticed Koekritz, scarcely distinguishable from his men, walking, pistol in hand, from one group to another. He passed by the hotel, visited the picquet blocking the main street to the left, and then returned to the Square. There he stopped and looked about him. From my balcony on the first floor he was only a few yards distant.

'Hullo!' I called to him.

He spun round quickly.

'It's you, is it?'

'It's over now?'

'I hope so. Farther down there,' he nodded towards the left, 'our next detachment has taken charge and is rounding the visitors into their hall. They can hold their blessed meeting and then, now we've got the streets clear, they can go back to their trains in comfort. They'll have earned their francs to-day. We've got the Communists on the trot. They're quite sensible really. And, now they've had their show, they'll go home.'

Had there been many casualties? He didn't know. Some of the injured must have been helped away. In his area there were two dead, one a local Communist, and the other 'some poor devil' not yet identified. Seven or eight others were badly hurt. There would be no more trouble, he thought, except perhaps from a few stray bands of Separatists who had turned to the right in the Square, instead of following the rest of the procession. These were loose somewhere in the town. All considered, it had gone off better than he'd expected; and that was that! And all he wanted was a smoke! I waved a cigarette to him, but he refused. He couldn't smoke on duty.

'Will you dine with me to-night?' I called to him.

'Delighted! Thanks awfully! Same time?'

He looked younger, I thought, more like *Hasso le Beau* of Boulevard du Régent days. Anxieties had told on him during the past week, but now that the trouble was past, a little of his old jauntiness had returned.

When would he be off duty? That depended! The Separatists would have to be sheep-dogged?—No, of course not. Shepherded back to the station, and those of them who had not followed the rest would have to be rounded up and taken to their trains. His men would have to get their dinners, he'd have to visit the hospital to see about the injured, he'd have to write up his official report, perhaps he'd have to see the new burgomaster, and then he'd be free.

'Would eight-thirty suit you better than eight?' I asked. But before he could reply the attention of us both was drawn elsewhere. For from my right came a familiar rumble, and looking down the street I saw a French light tank rounding the corner into the Platz. It completed its turn, faced us, squared itself, and covered with its machine-gun the blocking picquet of Security Police through which it had forced its way.

'What's up now?' I called to Koekritz: and, as I did so, a troop of cavalry clattered out of the same side-street. It passed behind the tank: its sections wheeled in our direction and presented a solid front, as the slats of a Venetian blind do, when they are turned. Then in an unbroken line, stretching from kerb to kerb, they swept towards us. Alone in the middle of the empty roadway, Koekritz awaited them. I do not think he knew any more than I did what was about to happen. He faced their onrush, holding his pistol at his side. I thought for an instant they would ride him down, and I wondered if he would fire. But a few lengths short of him the leader of the troop shouted a command, and his men reined up suddenly.

For a moment he and Koekritz regarded each other. Then Koekritz relaxed his pose.

'It's all right now,' he said, with at any rate an appearance of ease, and in excellent French.

'Order is established,' he went on. '*Messieurs les Separatists* are already in the hall which you have requisitioned for them. What do you want beyond that?'

They were only a few yards from me, and from my low balcony I could see and hear as well as if I had been watching a piece of acting from a stage box. This thought came to me, as I stood there, with my friend before me in I knew not what danger: and in this clash of reality with unreality I felt at once that irony which mocks us and will not let us be.

The leader of the troop did not answer Koekritz. Perhaps the expression of his face hardened. Behind him sat his men, impass-able, silent, watching; and solitary before them stood Koekritz in his worn grey-green; a rather faded figure against the rich brown background of the horses, the chilling glitter of swords, and the riders' airy blue.

I had a feeling that more was to follow, that the troopers were waiting for something. Then suddenly I knew what that something was, for behind them I saw a thin stream of armed Separatists trickling round the corner, from the street by which the French themselves had come. In all there must have been eighteen or twenty of them. Once in the Platz they broke into three groups. One crept to a place behind the heels of the horses: another moved round the farther flank of the troop and took up a position opposite the hotel, and the remaining party was led along the pavement, past the fronts of the houses to a spot just below my balcony. Alone in the middle of the roadway stood Koekritz, now surrounded on three sides, the nearest of his men out of hail. All round him was the silence of suspense. He turned his head, and for a moment our eyes met: his lips twisted, but the smile failed: he nodded and looked away. I felt the French were about to humble him before those Separatists of theirs. It was not a thing I wished to watch. I retired to the window behind me and tried once more to lift the shutter, but I could not. I turned to the street again. Koekritz was still standing there, his hand on his hip, waiting. I had seen him in that attitude once before, years ago in Brussels. It had been at a *concours hippique*, and he had stood so, chatting, just before he mounted for his turn at the jumps. In a lightning flash of memory there came back to me the picture of that forgotten afternoon, of him in his scarlet and silver, beside his big roan. Then the throw-back faded under the present.

The leader of the troop moved forward a yard to two.

'Surrender your arms!' he called to Koekritz in a loud, clear voice.

Koekritz looked to right and to left where the Separatists waited, gripping their lengths of leaden pipe.

'I am on duty here. My men have restored order. If we are disarmed, do I understand that you will then accept the responsibility of . . . of keeping order?'

The leader of the troop looked full into his face. I saw the man's elbows close to his side, the pull on his reins tighten.

'Surrender your arms, I tell you!'

Koekritz raised his pistol. He swayed a little and raised his chin.

'If you disarm my men, will you guarantee to protect them against these?'

The Frenchman bent a little towards him. I had no idea what was going to happen.

'We French do not interfere in purely German affairs.'

The words came low, spiteful, and distinct.

Koekritz stood rigid, his pistol raised. Whether it was covering the other I could not tell. Then he turned and, in that meeting of our eyes, I understood the full meaning of what lay before him. It was a fate he had always dreaded: he had discussed it with me: and I knew the alternatives that faced him. He could surrender and be thrown unarmed to the mercy of that mob: he could refuse and be shot down out of hand: he could sell his life as dear as he might. But if, under whatever provocation, he should fire upon troops of the French Occupation, his own country would pay.

The silence grew tenser. I knew what I must do. I gripped the railing before me and shouted to the leader of the troop. I have no idea what I said. For perhaps half a minute I continued shouting at him. I suppose every one turned towards me, but I saw only that one man. Then for a second I paused, and he looked away.

I had failed, and I realized that nothing could save Hasso Koekritz: that every one was helpless in that land where only vengeance ruled.

The leader of the troop leant back in his saddle.

'For the last time! Surrender your arms!'

I gripped the railing more tightly and waited.

'*Bien!*' said Koekritz suddenly, and changing his grip upon it, he handed over his pistol, with an extreme restraint of gesture.

The leader of the troop turned a little and shouted a word of command. The line of horsemen reined back a few yards. On either side of the roadway the Separatists shifted this way and that. In the middle Hasso Koekritz waited for them. A gruff voice shouted a command, and from both sides the Separatists began a slow, disjointed advance. They crept forward with their lengths of piping raised, ready to strike. Some guarded themselves with a crooked arm. Foot by foot they slid forward over the asphalt and closed in on Koekritz.

They were almost within reach of him. Again I called to the French, and as I did so, I saw Koekritz spin round suddenly and throw himself furiously upon one of his assailants. The man went down. Koekritz got under the guard of a second and felled him. He was turning on another when the first blow fell. It struck him between his left elbow and shoulder. The broken arm dropped to his side. For a moment he checked. Another struck at him and reached his head. He wheeled round, his face gushing blood.

I looked over the railing and measured the drop, but my lameness held me where I stood. Perhaps I went on shouting: I do not know. Afterwards the journalist told me that a French trooper had tried to intervene, but had been ordered back. I saw the next blow bring Koekritz to his knees, but he struggled up and fought on. Some injured man roared in his pain: the clamour increased. The Separatists must have been hindered by their very numbers: they had no room to swing their weapons. One of them who had fallen and was trying to rise, protected Koekritz from that quarter. He turned and charged for a gap in the ring. For an instant I saw him clearly, bare-headed, desperate. Then a blow struck him squarely, and he went down. The attack closed in and hid him.

Presently the noise decreased: the rain of blows slackened and ceased. The circle widened. Some of the troopers who had now dismounted drew near and joined it. In the centre at their feet lay a limp form in a faded green jacket. For a moment they stood silent. Then the tension slackened, congratulations were exchanged, and the French and their agents shook hands over the body which they had vanquished.

I leant back against the wall and caught my breath. Koekritz was dead. There was nothing that I could do.

All at once, from the farther side of the Platz, came the sound of firing. Below my balcony a sharp command was shouted. The soldiers doubled to their horses and swung into their saddles: the sections wheeled to the right: the troop trotted off towards the new conflict: the Separatists in their gangs followed. Then, while the cavalry were still crossing the Square, the fight at the other end of it swung into my view. By a corner house I saw three grey-green figures battling against a mob. Another shot rang out: one of them fell: and suddenly the fight dissolved into a side-street. The French reached the same corner: they and their Separatists turned it and disappeared.

A wounded dog, yelping horribly, limped across the Square and out of sight. In the distance the sounds of fighting rose and fell. Presently all was still. Below me on the smeared and trodden asphalt lay Hasso von Koekritz, torn and broken, but at last beyond defeat.

RICHARD HUGHES
A Night at a Cottage

ON the evening that I am considering I passed by some ten or twenty cosy barns and sheds without finding one to my liking: for Worcestershire lanes are devious and muddy, and it was nearly dark when I found an empty cottage set back from the road in a little bedraggled garden. There had been heavy rain earlier in the day, and the straggling fruit-trees still wept over it.

But the roof looked sound, there seemed no reason why it should not be fairly dry inside—as dry, at any rate, as I was likely to find anywhere.

I decided: and with a long look up the road, and a long look down the road, I drew an iron bar from the lining of my coat and forced the door, which was only held by a padlock and two staples. Inside, the darkness was damp and heavy: I struck a match, and with its haloed light I saw the black mouth of a passage somewhere ahead of me: and then it spluttered out. So I closed the door carefully, though I had little reason to fear passers-by at such a dismal hour in so remote a lane: and lighting another match, I crept down this passage to a little room at the far end, where the air was a bit clearer, for all that the window was boarded across. Moreover, there was a little rusted stove in this room: and thinking it too dark for any to see the smoke, I ripped up part of the wainscot with my knife, and soon was boiling my tea over a bright, small fire, and drying some of the day's rain out of my steamy clothes. Presently I piled the stove with wood to its top bar, and setting my boots where they would best dry, I stretched my body out to sleep.

I cannot have slept very long, for when I woke the fire was still burning brightly. It is not easy to sleep for long together on the level boards of a floor, for the limbs grow numb, and any movement wakes. I turned over, and was about to go again to sleep when I was startled to hear steps in the passage. As I have said, the window was boarded, and there was no other door from the little room—no cupboard even—in which to hide. It occurred to me rather grimly that there was nothing to do but to sit up and face the music, and that would probably mean being haled back to Worcester jail, which I had left two bare days before, and where, for various reasons, I had no anxiety to be seen again.

The stranger did not hurry himself, but presently walked slowly down the passage, attracted by the light of the fire: and when he came in he did not seem to notice me where I lay huddled in a corner, but walked straight over to the stove and warmed his hands at it. He was dripping wet; wetter than I should have thought it possible for a man to get, even on such a rainy night: and his clothes were old and worn. The water dripped from him on to the floor: he wore no hat, and the straight hair over his eyes dripped water that sizzled spitefully on the embers.

It occurred to me at once that he was no lawful citizen, but another wanderer like myself; a gentleman of the Road; so I gave him some sort of greeting, and we were presently in conversation. He complained much of the cold and the wet, and huddled himself over the fire, his teeth chattering and his face an ill white.

'No,' I said, 'it is no decent weather for the Road, this. But I wonder this cottage isn't more frequented, for it's a tidy little bit of a cottage.'

Outside the pale dead sunflowers and giant weeds stirred in the rain.

'Time was,' he answered, 'there wasn't a tighter little cot in the co-anty, nor a purtier garden. A regular little parlour, she was. But now no folk'll live in it, and there's very few tramps will stop here either.'

There were none of the rags and tins and broken food about that you find in a place where many beggars are used to stay.

'Why's that?' I asked.

He gave a very troubled sigh before answering.

'Gho-asts,' he said; 'gho-asts. Him that lived here. It is a mighty sad tale, and I'll not tell it you: but the upshot of it was that he drowned himself, down to the mill-pond. All slimy, he was, and floating, when they pulled him out of it. There are fo-aks have seen un floating on the pond, and fo-aks have seen un set round the corner of the school, waiting for his childer. Seems as if he had forgotten, like, how they were all gone dead, and the why he drowned hisself. But there are some say he walks up and down this cottage, up and down; like when the small-pox had 'em, and they couldn't sleep but if they heard his feet going up and down by their do-ars. Drownded hisself down to the pond, he did: and now he Walks.'

The stranger sighed again, and I could hear the water squelch in his boots as he moved himself.

'But it doesn't do for the like of us to get superstitious,' I answered. 'It wouldn't do for us to get seeing ghosts, or many's the wet night we'd be lying in the roadway.'

'No,' he said; 'no, it wouldn't do at all. I never had belief in Walks myself.'

I laughed.

'Nor I that,' I said. 'I never see ghosts, whoever may.'

He looked at me again in his queer melancholy fashion.

'No,' he said. ''Spect you don't ever. Some folk doan't. It's hard enough for poor fellows to have no money to their lodging, apart from gho-asts sceering them.'

'It's the coppers, not spooks, make me sleep uneasy,' said I. 'What with coppers, and meddlesome-minded folk, it isn't easy to get a night's rest nowadays.'

The water was still oozing from his clothes all about the floor, and a dank smell went up from him.

'God! man,' I cried, 'can't you *never* get dry?'

'Dry?' He made a little coughing laughter. 'Dry? I shan't never be dry . . . 'tisn't the likes of us that ever get dry, be it wet *or* fine, winter *or* summer. See that!'

He thrust his muddy hands up to the wrist in the fire, glowering over it fiercely and madly. But I caught up my two boots and ran crying out into the night.

DOROTHY L. SAYERS
The Dragon's Head

'UNCLE Peter!'

'Half a jiff, Gherkins. No, I don't think I'll take the Catullus, Mr. Ffolliott. After all, thirteen guineas is a bit steep without either the title or the last folio, what? But you might send me round the Vitruvius and the Satyricon when they come in; I'd like to have a look at them, anyhow. Well, old man, what is it?'

'Do come and look at these pictures, Uncle Peter. I'm sure it's an awfully old book.'

Lord Peter Wimsey sighed as he picked his way out of Mr. Ffolliott's dark back shop, strewn with the flotsam and jetsam of many libraries. An unexpected outbreak of measles at Mr. Bultridge's excellent preparatory school, coinciding with the absence of the Duke and Duchess of Denver on the Continent, had saddled his lordship with his ten-year-old nephew, Viscount St. George, more commonly known as Young Jerry, Jerrykins, or Pickled Gherkins. Lord Peter was not one of those born uncles who delight old nurses by their fascinating 'way with' children. He succeeded, however, in earning tolerance on honourable terms by treating the young with the same scrupulous politeness which he extended to their elders. He therefore prepared to receive Gherkins's discovery with respect, though a child's taste was not to be trusted, and the book might quite well be some horror of woolly mezzotints or an inferior modern reprint adorned with leprous electros. Nothing much better was really to be expected from the 'cheap shelf' exposed to the dust of the street.

'Uncle! there's such a funny man here, with a great long nose and ears and a tail and dogs' heads all over his body. *Monstrum hoc Cracoviæ*—that's a monster, isn't it? I should jolly well think it was. What's *Cracoviæ*, Uncle Peter?'

'Oh,' said Lord Peter, greatly relieved, 'the Cracow monster?' A portrait of that distressing infant certainly argued a respectable antiquity. 'Let's have a look. Quite right, it's a very old book—Munster's *Cosmographia Universalis*. I'm glad you know good stuff when you see it, Gherkins. What's the *Cosmographia* doing out here, Mr. Ffolliott, at five bob?'

'Well, my lord,' said the bookseller, who had followed his customers to the door, 'it's in a very bad state, you see; covers loose and nearly all the double-page maps missing. It came in a few weeks ago—dumped in with a collection we bought from a gentleman in Norfolk—you'll find his name in it—Dr. Conyers of Yelsall Manor. Of course, we might keep it and try to make up a complete copy when we get another example. But it's rather out of our line, as you know, classical authors being our speciality. So we just put it out to go for what it would fetch in the *status quo*, as you might say.'

'Oh, look!' broke in Gherkins. 'Here's a picture of a man being chopped up in little bits. What does it say about it?'

'I thought you could read Latin.'

'Well, but it's all full of sort of pothooks. What do they mean?'

'They're just contractions,' said Lord Peter patiently.

'"*Solent quoque hujus insulæ cultores*"—It is the custom of the dwellers in this island, when they see their parents stricken in years and of no further use, to take them down into the market-place and sell them to the cannibals, who kill them and eat them for food. This they do also with younger persons when they fall into any desperate sickness.'

'Ha, ha!' said Mr. Ffolliott. 'Rather sharp practice on the poor cannibals. They never got anything but tough old joints or diseased meat, eh?'

'The inhabitants seem to have had thoroughly advanced notions of business,' agreed his lordship.

The viscount was enthralled.

'I *do* like this book,' he said; 'could I buy it out of my pocket-money, please?'

'Another problem for uncles,' thought Lord Peter, rapidly ransacking his recollections of the *Cosmographia* to determine whether any of its illustrations were indelicate; for he knew the duchess to be strait-laced. On consideration, he could only remember one that was dubious, and there was a sporting chance that the duchess might fail to light upon it.

'Well,' he said judicially, 'in your place, Gherkins, I should be inclined to buy it. It's in a bad state, as Mr. Ffolliott has honourably told you—otherwise, of course, it would be exceedingly valuable;

but, apart from the lost pages, it's a very nice clean copy, and certainly worth five shillings to you, if you think of starting a collection.'

Till that moment, the viscount had obviously been more impressed by the cannibals than by the state of the margins, but the idea of figuring next term at Mr. Bultridge's as a collector of rare editions had undeniable charm.

'None of the other fellows collect books,' he said; 'they collect stamps, mostly. I think stamps are rather ordinary, don't you, Uncle Peter? I was rather thinking of giving up stamps. Mr. Porter, who takes us for history, has got a lot of books like yours, and he is a splendid man at footer.'

Rightly interpreting this reference to Mr. Porter, Lord Peter gave it as his opinion that book-collecting could be a perfectly manly pursuit. Girls, he said, practically never took it up, because it meant so much learning about dates and type-faces and other technicalities which called for a masculine brain.

'Besides,' he added, 'it's a very interesting book in itself, you know. Well worth dipping into.'

'I'll take it, please,' said the viscount, blushing a little at transacting so important and expensive a piece of business; for the duchess did not encourage lavish spending by little boys, and was strict in the matter of allowances.

Mr. Ffolliott bowed, and took the *Cosmographia* away to wrap it up.

'Are you all right for cash?' inquired Lord Peter discreetly. 'Or can I be of temporary assistance?'

'No, thank you, uncle; I've got Aunt Mary's half-crown and four shillings of my pocket-money, because, you see, with the measles happening, we didn't have our dormitory spread, and I was saving up for that.'

The business being settled in this gentlemanly manner, and the budding bibliophile taking personal and immediate charge of the stout, square volume, a taxi was chartered which, in due course of traffic delays, brought the *Cosmographia* to 110A Piccadilly.

'And who, Bunter, is Mr. Wilberforce Pope?'

'I do not think we know the gentleman, my lord. He is asking to see your lordship for a few minutes on business.'

'He probably wants me to find a lost dog for his maiden aunt.

What it is to have acquired a reputation as a sleuth! Show him in. Gherkins, if this good gentleman's business turns out to be private, you'd better retire into the dining-room.'

'Yes, Uncle Peter,' said the viscount dutifully. He was extended on his stomach on the library hearthrug, laboriously picking his way through the more exciting-looking bits of the *Cosmographia*, with the aid of Messrs. Lewis & Short, whose monumental compilation he had hitherto looked upon as a barbarous invention for the annoyance of upper forms.

Mr. Wilberforce Pope turned out to be a rather plump, fair gentleman in the late thirties, with a prematurely bald forehead, horn-rimmed spectacles, and an engaging manner.

'You will excuse my intrusion, won't you?' he began. 'I'm sure you must think me a terrible nuisance. But I wormed your name and address out of Mr. Ffolliott. Not his fault, really. You won't blame him, will you? I positively badgered the poor man. Sat down on his doorstep and refused to go, though the boy was putting up the shutters. I'm afraid you will think me very silly when you know what it's all about. But you really mustn't hold poor Mr. Ffolliott responsible, now, will you?'

'Not at all,' said his lordship. 'I mean, I'm charmed and all that sort of thing. Something I can do for you about books? You're a collector, perhaps? Will you have a drink or anything?'

'Well, no,' said Mr. Pope, with a faint giggle. 'No, not exactly a collector. Thank you very much, just a spot—no, no, literally a spot. Thank you; no'—he glanced round the bookshelves, with their rows of rich old leather bindings—'certainly not a collector. But I happen to be—er, interested—sentimentally interested—in a purchase you made yesterday. Really, such a very small matter. You will think it foolish. But I am told you are the present owner of a copy of Munster's *Cosmographia*, which used to belong to my uncle, Dr. Conyers.'

Gherkins looked up suddenly, seeing that the conversation had a personal interest for him.

'Well, that's not quite correct,' said Wimsey. 'I was there at the time, but the actual purchaser is my nephew. Gerald, Mr. Pope is interested in your *Cosmographia*. My nephew, Lord St. George.'

'How do you do, young man,' said Mr. Pope affably. 'I see that the collecting spirit runs in the family. A great Latin scholar, too, I expect, eh? Ready to decline *jus-jurandum* with the best of us? Ha,

ha! And what are you going to do when you grow up? Be Lord
Chancellor, eh? Now, I bet you think you'd rather be an engine-
driver, what, what?'

'No, thank you,' said the viscount, with aloofness.

'What, not an engine-driver? Well, now, I want you to be a real
business man this time. Put through a book deal, you know. Your
uncle will see I offer you a fair price, what? Ha, ha! Now, you see,
that picture-book of yours has a great value for me that it wouldn't
have for anybody else. When *I* was a little boy of your age it was
one of my very greatest joys. I used to have it to look at on Sundays.
Ah, dear! the happy hours I used to spend with those quaint old
engravings, and the funny old maps with the ships and salamanders
and "*Hicdracones*"—you know what *that* means, I dare say. What
does it mean?'

'Here are dragons,' said the viscount, unwillingly but still
politely.

'Quite right. I *knew* you were a scholar.'

'It's a very attractive book,' said Lord Peter. 'My nephew was
quite entranced by the famous Cracow monster.'

'Ah yes—a glorious monster, isn't it?' agreed Mr. Pope, with
enthusiasm. 'Many's the time I've fancied myself as Sir Lancelot or
somebody on a white war horse, charging that monster, lance in
rest, with the captive princess cheering me on. Ah! childhood!
You're living the happiest days of your life, young man. You won't
believe me, but you are.'

'Now what is it exactly you want my nephew to do?' inquired
Lord Peter a little sharply.

'Quite right, quite right. Well now, you know, my uncle, Dr.
Conyers, sold his library a few months ago. I was abroad at the
time, and it was only yesterday, when I went down to Yelsall on a
visit, that I learnt the dear old book had gone with the rest. I can't
tell you how distressed I was. I know it's not valuable—a great
many pages missing and all that—but I can't bear to think of its
being gone. So, purely from sentimental reasons, as I said, I hurried
off to Ffolliott's to see if I could get it back. I was quite upset to find
I was too late, and gave poor Mr. Ffolliott no peace till he told me
the name of the purchaser. Now, you see, Lord St. George, I'm here
to make you an offer for the book. Come, now, double what you
gave for it. That's a good offer, isn't it, Lord Peter? Ha, ha! And
you will be doing me a very great kindness as well.'

Viscount St. George looked rather distressed, and turned appealingly to his uncle.

'Well, Gerald,' said Lord Peter, 'it's your affair, you know. What do you say?'

The viscount stood first on one leg and then on the other. The career of a book-collector evidently had its problems, like other careers.

'If you please, Uncle Peter,' he said, with embarrassment, 'may I whisper?'

'It's not usually considered the thing to whisper, Gherkins, but you could ask Mr. Pope for time to consider his offer. Or you could say you would prefer to consult me first. That would be quite in order.'

'Then, if you don't mind, Mr. Pope, I should like to consult my uncle first.'

'Certainly, certainly; ha, ha!' said Mr. Pope. 'Very prudent to consult a collector of greater experience, what? Ah! the younger generation, eh, Lord Peter? Regular little business men already.'

'Excuse us, then, for one moment,' said Lord Peter, and drew his nephew into the dining-room.

'I say, Uncle Peter,' said the collector breathlessly, when the door was shut, '*need* I give him my book? I don't think he's a very nice man. I *hate* people who ask you to decline nouns for them.'

'Certainly you needn't, Gherkins, if you don't want to. The book is yours, and you've a right to it.'

'What would *you* do, uncle?'

Before replying, Lord Peter, in the most surprising manner, tiptoed gently to the door which communicated with the library and flung it suddenly open, in time to catch Mr. Pope kneeling on the hearthrug intently turning over the pages of the coveted volume, which lay as the owner had left it. He started to his feet in a flurried manner as the door opened.

'Do help yourself, Mr. Pope, won't you?' cried Lord Peter hospitably, and closed the door again.

'What is it, Uncle Peter?'

'If you want my advice, Gherkins, I should be rather careful how you had any dealings with Mr. Pope. I don't think he's telling the truth. He called those woodcuts engravings—though, of course, that may be just his ignorance. But I can't believe that he spent all his childhood's Sunday afternoons studying those maps and picking out the dragons in them, because, as you may have noticed for yourself, old Munster put very few dragons into his maps. They're mostly just plain maps—a bit queer to our ideas of geography, but perfectly straightforward. That was why I brought in the Cracow monster, and, you see, he thought it was some sort of dragon.'

'Oh, I say, uncle! So you said that on purpose!'

'If Mr. Pope wants the *Cosmographia*, it's for some reason he doesn't want to tell us about. And, that being so, I wouldn't be in too big a hurry to sell, if the book were mine. See?'

'Do you mean there's something frightfully valuable about the book, which we don't know?'

'Possibly.'

'How exciting! It's just like a story in the *Boys' Friend Library*. What am I to say to him, uncle.'

'Well, in your place I wouldn't be dramatic or anything. I'd just say you've considered the matter, and you've taken a fancy to the book and have decided not to sell. You thank him for his offer, of course.'

'Yes—er, won't you say it for me, uncle?'

'I think it would look better if you did it yourself.'

'Yes, perhaps it would. Will he be very cross?'

'Possibly,' said Lord Peter, 'but, if he is, he won't let on. Ready?'

The consulting committee accordingly returned to the library. Mr. Pope had prudently retired from the hearthrug and was examining a distant bookcase.

'Thank you very much for your offer, Mr. Pope,' said the viscount, striding stoutly up to him, 'but I have considered it, and I have taken a—a—a fancy for the book and decided not to sell.'

'Sorry and all that,' put in Lord Peter, 'but my nephew's adamant about it. No, it isn't the price; he wants the book. Wish I could oblige you, but it isn't in my hands. Won't you take something else before you go? Really? Ring the bell, Gherkins. My man will see you to the lift. *Good* evening.'

When the visitor had gone, Lord Peter returned and thoughtfully picked up the book.

'We were awful idiots to leave him with it, Gherkins, even for a moment. Luckily, there's no harm done.'

'You don't think he found out anything while we were away, do you, uncle?' gasped Gherkins, open-eyed.

'I'm sure he didn't.'

'Why?'

'He offered me fifty pounds for it on the way to the door. Gave the game away. H'm! Bunter.'

'My lord?'

'Put this book in the safe and bring me back the keys. And you'd better set all the burglar alarms when you lock up.'

'Oo—er!' said Viscount St. George.

On the third morning after the visit of Mr. Wilberforce Pope, the viscount was seated at a very late breakfast in his uncle's flat, after the most glorious and soul-satisfying night that ever boy experienced. He was almost too excited to eat the kidneys and bacon placed before him by Bunter, whose usual impeccable manner was not in the least impaired by a rapidly swelling and blackening eye.

It was about two in the morning that Gherkins—who had not slept very well, owing to too lavish and grown-up a dinner and theatre the evening before—became aware of a stealthy sound somewhere in the direction of the fire-escape. He had got out of bed and crept very softly into Lord Peter's room and woken him up. He had said: 'Uncle Peter, I'm sure there's burglars on the fire-escape.' And Uncle Peter, instead of saying, 'Nonsense, Gherkins, hurry up and get back to bed,' had sat up and listened and said: 'By Jove, Gherkins, I believe you're right.' And had sent Gherkins to call Bunter. And on his return, Gherkins, who had always regarded his uncle as a very top-hatted sort of person, actually saw him take from his handkerchief-drawer an undeniable automatic pistol.

It was at this point that Lord Peter was apotheosed from the state of Quite Decent Uncle to that of Glorified Uncle. He said:

'Look here, Gherkins, we don't know how many of these blighters there'll be, so you must be jolly smart and do anything I say sharp, on the word of command—even if I have to say "Scoot". Promise?'

Gherkins promised, with his heart thumping, and they sat waiting in the dark, till suddenly a little electric bell rang sharply just over the head of Lord Peter's bed and a green light shone out.

'The library window,' said his lordship, promptly silencing the bell by turning a switch. 'If they heard, they may think better of it. We'll give them a few minutes.'

They gave them five minutes, and then crept very quietly down the passage.

'Go round by the dining-room, Bunter,' said his lordship; 'they may bolt that way.'

With infinite precaution, he unlocked and opened the library door, and Gherkins noticed how silently the locks moved.

A circle of light from an electric torch was moving slowly along the bookshelves. The burglars had obviously heard nothing of the counter-attack. Indeed, they seemed to have troubles enough of their own to keep their attention occupied. As his eyes grew accustomed to the dim light, Gherkins made out that one man was standing holding the torch, while the other took down and examined the books. It was fascinating to watch his apparently disembodied hands move along the shelves in the torch-light.

The men muttered discontentedly. Obviously the job was proving a harder one than they had bargained for. The habit of ancient authors of abbreviating the titles on the backs of their volumes, or leaving them completely untitled, made things extremely awkward. From time to time the man with the torch extended his hand into the light. It held a piece of paper, which they anxiously compared with the title-page of a book. Then the volume was replaced and the tedious search went on.

Suddenly some slight noise—Gherkins was sure *he* did not make it; it may have been Bunter in the dining-room—seemed to catch the ear of the kneeling man.

'Wot's that?' he gasped, and his startled face swung round into view.

'Hands up!' said Lord Peter, and switched the light on.

The second man made one leap for the dining-room door, where a smash and an oath proclaimed that he had encountered Bunter. The kneeling man shot his hands up like a marionette.

'Gherkins,' said Lord Peter, 'do you think you can go across to that gentleman by the bookcase and relieve him of the article which is so inelegantly distending the right-hand pocket of his coat? Wait a minute. Don't on any account get between him and my pistol, and mind you take the thing out *very* carefully. There's no hurry. That's splendid. Just point it at the floor while you bring it across, would you? Thanks. Bunter has managed for himself, I see. Now run into my bedroom, and in the bottom of my wardrobe you will find a bundle of stout cord. Oh! I beg your pardon; yes, put your hands down by all means. It must be very tiring exercise.'

The arms of the intruders being secured behind their backs with a neatness which Gherkins felt to be worthy of the best traditions of Sexton Blake, Lord Peter motioned his captives to sit down and dispatched Bunter for whisky-and-soda.

'Before we send for the police,' said Lord Peter, 'you would do me a great personal favour by telling me what you were looking for, and who sent you. Ah! thanks, Bunter. As our guests are not at liberty to use their hands, perhaps you would be kind enough to assist them to a drink. Now then, say when.'

'Well, you're a gentleman, guv'nor,' said the First Burglar, wiping his mouth politely on his shoulder, the back of his hand not being available. 'If we'd a known wot a job this wos going' ter be, blow me if we'd a touched it. The bloke said, ses 'e, "It's takin' candy from a baby," 'e ses. "The gentleman's a reg'lar softie," 'e ses, "one o' these 'ere sersiety toffs wiv a maggot fer old books," that's wot 'e ses, "an' ef yer can find this 'ere old book fer me," 'e ses, "there's a pony for yer." Well! Sech a job! 'E didn't mention as 'ow there'd be five 'undred fousand bleedin' ole books all as alike as a regiment o' bleedin' dragoons. Nor as 'ow yer kept a nice little machine-gun like that 'andy by the bedside, *nor* yet as 'ow yer was so bleedin' good at tyin' knots in a bit o' string. No—'e didn't think ter mention them things.'

'Deuced unsporting of him,' said his lordship. 'Do you happen to know the gentleman's name?'

'No—that was another o' them things wot 'e didn't mention. 'E's a stout, fair party, wiv 'orn rims to 'is goggles and a bald 'ead. One o' these 'ere philanthropists, I reckon. A friend o' mine, wot got inter trouble onct, got work froo 'im, and the gentleman comes round and ses to 'im, 'e ses, "Could yer find me a couple o' lads ter do a little job?" 'E ses, an' my friend, finkin' no 'arm, you see, guv'nor, but wot it might be a bit of a joke like, 'e gets 'old of my pal an' me, an' we meets the gentleman in a pub dahn Whitechapel way. W'ich we was ter meet 'im there again Friday night, us 'avin' allowed that time fer ter git 'old of the book.'

'The book being, if I may hazard a guess, the *Cosmographia Universalis?*'

'Sumfink like that, guv'nor. I got its jaw-breakin' name wrote down on a bit o' paper, wot my pal 'ad in 'is 'and. Wot did yer do wiv that 'ere bit o' paper, Bill?'

'Well, look here,' said Lord Peter, 'I'm afraid I must send for the police, but I think it likely, if you give us your assistance to get hold of your gentleman, whose name I strongly suspect to be Wilberforce Pope, that you will get off pretty easily. Telephone the police, Bunter, and then go and put something on that eye of yours. Gherkins, we'll give these gentlemen another drink, and then I think perhaps you'd better hop back to bed; the fun's over. No? Well, put a good thick coat on, there's a good fellow, because what your mother will say to me if you catch a cold I don't like to think.'

So the police had come and taken the burglars away, and now Detective-Inspector Parker, of Scotland Yard, a great personal friend of Lord Peter's, sat toying with a cup of coffee and listening to the story.

'But what's the matter with the jolly old book, anyhow, to make it so popular?' he demanded.

'I don't know,' replied Wimsey, 'but after Mr. Pope's little visit the other day I got kind of intrigued about it and had a look through it. I've got a hunch it may turn out rather valuable, after all. Unsuspected beauties and all that sort of thing. If only Mr. Pope had been a trifle more accurate in his facts, he might have got away with something to which I feel pretty sure he isn't entitled. Anyway, when I'd seen—what I saw, I wrote off to Dr. Conyers of Yelsall Manor, the late owner——'

'Conyers, the cancer man?'

'Yes. He's done some pretty important research in his time, I fancy. Getting on now, though; about seventy-eight, I fancy. I hope he's more honest than his nephew, with one foot in the grave like that. Anyway, I wrote (with Gherkins's permission, naturally) to say we had the book and had been specially interested by something we found there, and would he be so obliging as to tell us something of its history. I also——'

'But what did you find in it?'

'I don't think we'll tell him yet, Gherkins, shall we? I like to keep policemen guessing. As I was saying, when you so rudely interrupted me, I also asked him whether he knew anything about his good nephew's offer to buy it back. His answer has just arrived. He says he knows of nothing specially interesting about the book. It has been in the library untold years, and the tearing out of the maps must have been done a long time ago by some family vandal. He can't think why his nephew should be so keen on it, as he certainly never pored over it as a boy. In fact, the old man declares the engaging Wilberforce has never even set foot in Yelsall Manor to his knowledge. So much for the fire-breathing monsters and the pleasant Sunday afternoons.'

'Naughty Wilberforce!'

'M'm. Yes. So, after last night's little dust-up, I wired the old boy we were tootling down to Yelsall to have a heart-to-heart talk with him about his picture-book and his nephew.'

'Are you taking the book down with you?' asked Parker. 'I can give you a police escort for it if you like.'

'That's not a bad idea,' said Wimsey. 'We don't know where the insinuating Mr. Pope may be hanging out, and I wouldn't put it past him to make another attempt.'

'Better be on the safe side,' said Parker. 'I can't come myself, but I'll send down a couple of men with you.'

'Good egg,' said Lord Peter. 'Call up your myrmidons. We'll get a car round at once. You're coming, Gherkins, I suppose? God knows what your mother would say. Don't ever be an uncle, Charles; it's frightfully difficult to be fair to all parties.'

Yelsall Manor was one of those large, decaying country mansions which speak eloquently of times more spacious than our own. The original late Tudor construction had been masked by the addition of a wide frontage in the Italian manner, with a kind of classical portico surmounted by a pediment and approached by a semicircular flight of steps. The grounds had originally been laid out in that formal manner in which grove nods to grove and each half duly reflects the other. A late owner, however, had burst out into the more eccentric sort of landscape gardening which is associated with the name of Capability Brown. A Chinese pagoda, somewhat resembling Sir William Chambers's erection in Kew Gardens, but smaller, rose out of a grove of laurustinus towards the eastern extremity of the house, while at the rear appeared a large artificial lake, dotted with numerous islands, on which odd little temples, grottoes, tea-houses, and bridges peeped out from among clumps of shrubs, once ornamental, but now sadly overgrown. A boat-house, with wide eaves like the designs on a willow-pattern plate, stood at one corner, its landing-stage fallen into decay and wreathed with melancholy weeds.

'My disreputable old ancestor, Cuthbert Conyers, settled down here when he retired from the sea in 1732,' said Dr. Conyers, smiling faintly. 'His elder brother died childless, so the black sheep returned to the fold with the determination to become respectable and found a family. I fear he did not succeed altogether. There were very queer tales as to where his money came from. He is said to have been a pirate, and to have sailed with the notorious Captain Blackbeard. In the village, to this day, he is remembered and spoken of as Cut-throat Conyers. It used to make the old man very angry, and there is an unpleasant story of his slicing the ears off a groom who had been heard to call him "Old Cut-throat". He was not an uncultivated person, though. It was he who did the land-scape-gardening round at the back, and he built the pagoda for his telescope. He was reputed to study the Black Art, and there were certainly a number of astrological works in the library with his name on the fly-leaf, but probably the telescope was only a remembrance of his seafaring days.

'Anyhow, towards the end of his life he became more and more odd and morose. He quarrelled with his family, and turned his younger son out of doors with his wife and children. An unpleasant old fellow.

'On his deathbed he was attended by the parson—a good, earnest, God-fearing sort of man, who must have put up with a deal of insult in carrying out what he firmly believed to be the sacred duty of reconciling the old man to this shamefully treated son. Eventually, "Old Cut-throat" relented so far as to make a will, leaving to the younger son "My treasure which I have buried in Munster". The parson represented to him that it was useless to bequeath a treasure unless he also bequeathed the information where to find it, but the horrid old pirate only chuckled spitefully, and said that, as he had been at the pains to collect the treasure, his son might well be at the pains of looking for it. Further than that he would not go, and so he died, and I dare say went to a very bad place.

'Since then the family has died out, and I am the sole represent-ative of the Conyers, and heir to the treasure, whatever and wherever it is, for it was never discovered. I do not suppose it was very honestly come by, but, since it would be useless now to try and find the original owners, I imagine I have a better right to it than anybody living.

'You may think it very unseemly, Lord Peter, that an old, lonely man like myself should be greedy for a hoard of pirate's gold. But my whole life has been devoted to studying the disease of cancer, and I believe myself to be very close to a solution of one part at least of the terrible problem. Research costs money, and my limited means are very nearly exhausted. The property is mortgaged up to the hilt, and I do most urgently desire to complete my experiments before I die, and to leave a sufficient sum to found a clinic where the work can be carried on.

'During the last year I have made very great efforts to solve the mystery of "Old Cut-throat's" treasure. I have been able to leave much of my experimental work in the most capable hands of my assistant, Dr. Forbes, while I pursued my researches with the very slender clue I had to go upon. It was the more expensive and difficult that Cuthbert had left no indication in his will whether Münster in Germany or Munster in Ireland was the hiding-place of the treasure. My journeys and my search in both places cost money and brought me no farther on my quest. I returned, disheartened, in August, and found myself obliged to sell my library, in order to defray my expenses and obtain a little money with which to struggle on with my sadly delayed experiments.'

'Ah!' said Lord Peter. 'I begin to see light.'

The old physician looked at him inquiringly. They had finished tea, and were seated around the great fireplace in the study. Lord Peter's interested questions about the beautiful, dilapidated old house and estate had led the conversation naturally to Dr. Conyers's family, shelving for the time the problem of the *Cosmographia*, which lay on a table beside them.

'Everything you say fits into the puzzle,' went on Wimsey, 'and I think there's not the smallest doubt what Mr. Wilberforce Pope was after, though how he knew that you had the *Cosmographia* here I couldn't say.'

'When I disposed of the library, I sent him a catalogue,' said Dr. Conyers. 'As a relative, I thought he ought to have the right to buy anything he fancied. I can't think why he didn't secure the book then, instead of behaving in this most shocking fashion.'

Lord Peter hooted with laughter.

'Why, because he never tumbled to it till afterwards,' he said. 'And oh, dear, how wild he must have been! I forgive him everything. Although,' he added, 'I don't want to raise your hopes too high, sir, for, even when we've solved old Cuthbert's riddle, I don't know that we're very much nearer to the treasure.'

'To the *treasure*?'

'Well, now, sir. I want you first to look at this page, where there's a name scrawled in the margin. Our ancestors had an untidy way of signing their possessions higgledy-piggledy in margins instead of in a decent, Christian way in the fly-leaf. This is a handwriting of somewhere about Charles I's reign: "Jac: Coniers". I take it that goes to prove that the book was in the possession of your family at any rate as early as the first half of the seventeenth century, and has remained there ever since. Right. Now we turn to page 1099, where we find a description of the discoveries of Christopher Columbus. It's headed, you see, by a kind of map, with some of Mr. Pope's monsters swimming about in it, and apparently representing the Canaries, or, as they used to be called, the Fortunate Isles. It doesn't look much more accurate than old maps usually are, but I take it the big island on the right is meant for Lanzarote, and the two nearest to it may be Teneriffe and Gran Canaria.'

'But what's that writing in the middle?'

'That's just the point. The writing is later than "Jac: Coniers's" signature; I should put it about 1700—but, of course, it may have been written a good deal later still. I mean, a man who was elderly in 1730 would still use the style of writing he adopted as a young man, especially if, like your ancestor the pirate, he had spent the early part of his life in outdoor pursuits and hadn't done much writing.'

'Do you mean to say, Uncle Peter,' broke in the viscount excitedly, 'that that's "Old Cut-throat's" writing?'

'I'd be ready to lay a sporting bet it is. Look here, sir, you've been scouring round Münster in Germany and Munster in Ire-land—but how about good old Sebastian Munster here in the library at home?'

'God bless my soul! Is it possible?'

'It's pretty nearly certain, sir. Here's what he says, written, you see, round the head of that sort of sea-dragon:

> Hic in capite draconis ardet perpetuo Sol.
> Here the sun shines perpetually upon the Dragon's Head.

Rather doggy Latin—sea-dog Latin, you might say, in fact.'

'I'm afraid,' said Dr. Conyers, 'I must be very stupid, but I can't see where that leads us.'

'No; "Old Cut-throat" was rather clever. No doubt he thought

Liber V.
DE NOVIS INSVLIS, 1099
quomodo, quando, & per quem
illæ inuentæ sint.

Hriſtophorus Columbus natione Genuenſis, cùm diu in aula regis Hiſpan⸗
rum deuerſatus fuiſſet, animum induxit, ut hactenus inacceſſas orbis partes p
aorarer. Petiit præterea à rege ut uoto ſuo non deeſſet ſuturi ſibi & toti Hiſ.

that, if anybody read it, they'd think it was just an allusion to where it says, farther down, that "the islands were called *Fortunatæ* because of the wonderful temperature of the air and the clemency of the skies". But the cunning old astrologer up in his pagoda had a meaning of his own. Here's a little book published in 1678— Middleton's *Practical Astrology*—just the sort of popular handbook an amateur like "Old Cut-throat" would use. Here you are: "If in your figure you find Jupiter or Venus or *Dragon's head*, you may be confident there is Treasure in the place supposed. . . . If you find *Sol* to be the Significator of the hidden Treasure, you may conclude there is Gold, or some jewels." You know, sir, I think we may conclude it.'

'Dear me!' said Dr. Conyers. 'I believe, indeed, you must be right. And I am ashamed to think that if anybody had suggested to me that it could ever be profitable to me to learn the terms of astrology, I should have replied in my vanity that my time was too valuable to waste on such foolishness. I am deeply indebted to you.'

'Yes,' said Gherkins, 'but where *is* the treasure, uncle?'

'That's just it,' said Lord Peter. 'The map is very vague; there is no latitude or longitude given; and the directions, such as they are, seem not even to refer to any spot on the islands, but to some place in the middle of the sea. Besides, it is nearly two hundred years since the treasure was hidden, and it may already have been found by somebody or other.'

Dr. Conyers stood up.

'I am an old man,' he said, 'but I still have some strength. If I can by any means get together the money for an expedition, I will not rest till I have made every possible effort to find the treasure and to endow my clinic.'

'Then, sir, I hope you'll let me give a hand to the good work,' said Lord Peter.

Dr. Conyers had invited his guests to stay the night, and, after the excited viscount had been packed off to bed, Wimsey and the old man sat late, consulting maps and diligently reading Munster's chapter *'De Novis Insulis'*, in the hope of discovering some further clue. At length, however, they separated, and Lord Peter went upstairs, the book under his arm. He was restless, however, and, instead of going to bed, sat for a long time at his window, which looked out upon the lake. The moon, a few days past the full, was riding high among small, windy clouds, and picked out the sharp eaves of the Chinese tea-houses and the straggling tops of the unpruned shrubs. 'Old Cut-throat' and his landscape-gardening! Wimsey could have fancied that the old pirate was sitting now beside his telescope in the preposterous pagoda, chuckling over his riddling testament and counting the craters of the moon. 'If *Luna*, there is silver.' The water of the lake was silver enough; there was a great smooth path across it, broken by the sinister wedge of the boat-house, the black shadows of the islands, and, almost in the middle of the lake, a decayed fountain, a writhing Celestial dragon-shape, spiny-backed and ridiculous.

Wimsey rubbed his eyes. There was something strangely familiar about the lake; from moment to moment it assumed the queer unreality of a place which one recognizes without having ever known it. It was like one's first sight of the Leaning Tower of Pisa too like its picture to be quite believable. Surely, thought Wimsey, he knew that elongated island on the right, shaped rather like a winged monster, with its two little clumps of buildings. And the island to the left of it, like the British Isles, but warped out of shape. And the third island, between the others, and nearer. The three formed a triangle, with the Chinese fountain in the centre, the moon shining steadily upon its dragon head. '*Hic in capite draconis ardet perpetuo*——'

Lord Peter sprang up with a loud exclamation, and flung open the door into the dressing-room. A small figure wrapped in an eiderdown hurriedly uncoiled itself from the window-seat.

'I'm sorry, Uncle Peter,' said Gherkins. 'I was so *dreadfully* wide awake, it wasn't any good staying in bed.'

'Come here,' said Lord Peter, 'and tell me if I'm mad or dreaming. Look out of the window and compare it with the map— Old Cut-throat's "New Islands". He made 'em, Gherkins; he put 'em here. Aren't they laid out just like the Canaries? Those three islands in a triangle, and the fourth down here in the corner? And the boat-house where the big ship is in the picture? And the dragon fountain where the dragon's head is? Well, my son, that's where your hidden treasure's gone to. Get your things on, Gherkins, and damn the time when all good little boys should be in bed! We're going for a row on the lake, if there's a tub in that boat-house that'll float.'

'Oh, Uncle Peter! This is a *real* adventure!'

'All right,' said Wimsey. 'Fifteen men on the dead man's chest, and all that! Yo-ho-ho, and a bottle of Johnny Walker! Pirate expedition fitted out in dead of night to seek hidden treasure and explore the Fortunate Isles! Come on, crew!'

Lord Peter hitched the leaky dinghy to the dragon's knobbly tail and climbed out carefully, for the base of the fountain was green and weedy.

'I'm afraid it's your job to sit there and bail, Gherkins,' he said. 'All the best captains bag the really interesting jobs for themselves. We'd better start with the head. If the old blighter said head, he probably meant it.' He passed an arm affectionately round the creature's neck for support, while he methodically pressed and pulled the various knobs and bumps of its anatomy. 'It seems beastly solid, but I'm sure there's a spring somewhere. You won't forget to bail, will you? I'd simply hate to turn round and find the boat gone. Pirate chief marooned on island and all that. Well, it isn't its back hair, anyhow. We'll try its eyes. I say, Gherkins, I'm sure I felt something move, only it's frightfully stiff. We might have thought to bring some oil. Never mind; it's dogged as does it. It's coming. It's coming. Booh! Pah!'

A fierce effort thrust the rusted knob inwards, releasing a huge spout of water into his face from the dragon's gaping throat. The fountain, dry for many years, soared rejoicingly heavenwards, drenching the treasure-hunters, and making rainbows in the moonlight.

'I suppose this is "Old Cut-throat's" idea of humour,' grumbled Wimsey, retreating cautiously round the dragon's neck. 'And now I can't turn it off again. Well, dash it all, let's try the other eye.'

He pressed for a few moments in vain. Then, with a grinding clang, the bronze wings of the monster clapped down to its sides, revealing a deep square hole, and the fountain ceased to play.

'Gherkins!' said Lord Peter, 'we've done it. (But don't neglect bailing on that account!) There's a box here. And it's beastly heavy. No; all right, I can manage. Gimme the boat-hook. Now I do hope the old sinner really did have a treasure. What a bore if it's only one of his little jokes. Never mind—hold the boat steady. There. Always remember, Gherkins, that you can make quite an effective crane with a boat-hook and a stout pair of braces. Got it? That's right. Now for home and beauty. . . . Hullo! what's all that?'

As he paddled the boat round, it was evident that something was happening down by the boat-house. Lights were moving about, and a sound of voices came across the lake.

'They think we're burglars, Gherkins. Always misunderstood. Give way, my hearties—

'A-roving, a-roving, since roving's been my ru-i-in,
I'll go no more a-roving with you, fair maid.'

'Is that you, my lord?' said a man's voice as they drew in to the boat-house.

'Why, it's our faithful sleuths!' cried his lordship. 'What's the excitement?'

'We found this fellow sneaking round the boat-house,' said the man from Scotland Yard. 'He says he's the old gentleman's nephew. Do you know him, my lord?'

'I rather fancy I do,' said Wimsey. 'Mr. Pope, I think. Good evening. Were you looking for anything? Not a treasure, by any chance? Because we've just found one. Oh! don't say that. *Maxima reverentia*, you know. Lord St. George is of tender years. And, by the way, thank you so much for sending your delightful friends to call on me last night. Oh, yes, Thompson, I'll charge him all right. You there, doctor? Splendid. Now, if anybody's got a spanner or anything handy, we'll have a look at Great-grandpapa Cuthbert. And if he turns out to be old iron, Mr. Pope, you'll have had an uncommonly good joke for your money.'

An iron bar was produced from the boat-house and thrust under the hasp of the chest. It creaked and burst. Dr. Conyers knelt down tremulously and threw open the lid.

There was a little pause.

'The drinks are on you, Mr. Pope,' said Lord Peter. 'I think, doctor, it ought to be a jolly good hospital when it's finished.'

NAOMI MITCHISON
The Hostages

THERE were only three of us left now; the others had been hung
over the ramparts, one every morning. Elxsente was still sick and
we didn't know what to do with him; he was only a child, and cried
for his mother at nights; some of the others had done that, and I
would have too, but I was fifteen and had to set a good example.
They used to take us out on to the walls, and whip us where the
men from our own cities could see us; of course they had the right
to do it, but some of us weren't very old, and used to cry even at the
thought of it, which was bad for every one. But we could look out
when we were taken up, and there was our camp, spread and
shining below us; once there was an attack while we were there and
we all cheered, but the Romans paid us back in kicks for that. I saw
the banner of Mireto from time to time, and thought I could make
out my father at the head of the spearmen, and my big brother with
him; and once I saw a herald whom I knew, and called out to him,
but he didn't hear me. Every day we hoped the town would fall,
though we should very likely have been killed before any one could
get to us; still, it was a chance, and better than being dragged out
and choked like dogs at the end of a rope. We knew our people were
pressing hard and might soon starve the town out; for the last week
they had given us nothing but water and a very little bread; the one
who was chosen to be hung every morning used to leave his share
of the bread to any one he liked. There wasn't too much water,
either; the last day Teffre and I had given it all to Elxsente; we
thought we should be able to eat his bread—he wouldn't touch it—
but we were too thirsty.

I was awake all that night, though Teffre slept for a little. I leant
up against the wall at the back, with Elxsente's head on my
shoulder; he seemed easier that way. I thought about home, and
tried to imagine I was in my own room; I wondered if they were
looking after my pony properly, and I tried to remember whether
I'd mended the bridle before I was sent away as a hostage to the
Romans; I couldn't be sure, and it worried me.

When it was just light Teffre woke up and said he heard shouting;

we both listened and I heard it too. He went over to the slit, but of course he could see nothing; he used always to think he might see something some time. But certainly there was cheering, and Teffre said he was sure we'd taken the town; but it wasn't the first time he'd thought that, and I wasn't hopeful, particularly as nothing else happened for hours. My back was very sore from the beating, and we'd had no chance of a wash for weeks. Elxsente was better after his sleep, and thirsty, but the water was all gone.

Then the door opened, and the man we called the Boar—we all hated him—came in. I wondered which of us he was going to take, and rather hoped it would be Teffre, because I was much better at looking after Elxsente—I didn't want it to be *him* anyhow. Teffre asked him what had happened—he never could learn not to—and the man hit his hand with the iron key, and then said, 'The General's come, and your people have all run away.' That was hard hearing for us; we knew it wasn't true about our army having run, but we supposed they'd withdrawn, and we were very unhappy, but we said nothing and waited. He went on: 'You dogs, you ought to be hung, but the General's begged your lives and you've been given to him.'

We didn't quite understand at once, and then a great tall man came in, all in armour, with a golden helmet plumed with a black horse-tail; he could only stand upright in the middle of the arch; he looked at us and asked, 'Are these all that are left?' The Boar stood at attention as he said, 'Yes, sir,' and then to us: 'Down on your knees before your master!' I don't remember what Teffre did, but I simply sat and stared at the General; one can't think very quickly after one hasn't slept all night. The Boar came over and hit me and I was afraid he was going to hit Elxsente; so I knelt, and Elxsente knelt, leaning against me, and Teffre knelt in the other corner. The light came in through the doorway, behind the General, and he looked very big, as if he could tread us into the ground; a little wind came in too and I heard the horse-hairs rustling against the bronze.

He was speaking to us, but I didn't hear it all; I was thinking that we were going to live, and I was glad and thankful, and then I thought that our army was beaten, and perhaps my father and brother were killed; I felt that I loved Mireto, my city, terribly, and that it would be awful if the Romans were to take her; and then I thought it might be better to die after all. I heard the General saying that our lives were forfeit, but that he had asked that we should be spared, and then about how wicked it was of the League of the Cities to have broken the treaty; I was wondering if it was any use my telling him that bad treaties ought to be broken, but just then Elxsente slipped forward and I had to catch him; he felt very hot and was breathing fast. The General came up to us and stooped over him; Elxsente threw his arms round my neck and held on tight with his face pressed into my shoulder; the General said, 'Don't be frightened,' and lifted his head quite gently; he asked how long he'd been like this, and I told him ten days, and said could we have some water for him. He asked if we had not had any, and I said yes, but that Elxsente had had his share and our share too, but he was all burnt up and always wanted more. He turned round to the Boar and the metal plates on his kilt swung against my face; he told him to get us water, and then felt Elxsente's head and hands, and told me he thought he would live. When the water came Elxsente let go of me with one hand and drank and looked up at the General, and Teffre drank, and then I drank; I've never tasted anything as good as that water; I felt quite different at once, and I would have spoken to the General to justify our cities, only he went out.

That day we had dried figs with our bread, and in the evening they brought some milk for Elxsente. We heard how the General had marched up secretly and surprised and scattered our camp and relieved the town; a few days afterwards the Boar told us peace had been made; some of the cities were given up to Rome, and the walls of Mireto had to be pulled down. Teffre and I talked it over; we wondered whether we ought to outlive the disgrace—*his* city was to pay tribute and have Rome for overlord—but finally we made up our minds to go on living for a little longer at least; we didn't quite know how to kill ourselves, and besides there was Elxsente; his city had to pay tribute too, but he didn't understand the shame of it, like we did.

By the time they let us out, Elxsente was much better, but we were none of us very strong. They tied us into a wagon; we sat on the bottom, out of the sun, and saw the tops of the trees that we passed under along the road, but not much else. The journey took three days, and then we stopped outside the walls of Rome. There was dust all over everything, dust in our hair and ears and eyelashes, dust caked on our hands and feet, white dust on the bread and fruit we ate. The wagon was drawn up on the inside of a square, and we

sat on the edge trying to see what was happening; prisoners—our
own men—were brought in under guard, formed up, and chained,
of course we all looked hard to see if there was any one we knew
among them; often we thought we saw faces of friends, but they
never were. Then one of my father's men was marched past and I
shouted to him; he turned and called to me that my father had
escaped, but he didn't know about my brother; still, that was
something. There were women prisoners too, from the towns that
had been taken, and armour and horses and gold cups from the
altars of the Gods. Teffre saw one cartload from his own city and
raged at being so helpless. And then Elxsente cried out and said he
saw his cousin among the women, a white-faced girl with eyes
swollen from tears and dust; we all called, but she didn't hear or
heed, and Elxsente was terribly disappointed.

Then we were taken out of the wagon over to a heap of chains
and one of the soldiers found light ones for us. Then we waited at
the edge of the road till our turn came. The Roman soldiers went
by first, crowned and singing; after them our prisoners, chained
together; and more Romans; and trophies of swords and spears, and
the pick of the cattle that had been taken; and more Romans; and a
great line of women and children, and pictures of the battles, and
ox-carts full of gold and silver, well guarded; and more Romans
still, and more prisoners; and we were bitterly angry and sad. Then
there was a place for us, and we joined the march with Roman
soldiers in front of us and at each side. At first there was nothing
but choking dust, until we got to the suburbs, where the streets had
been watered, which kept the dust down and was pleasant to the
feet. But then the crowds began, crowds of shouting enemies at the
two edges of the road; they frightened me more than anything; we
were so helpless and alone in the middle of them, and sometimes
the noise would suddenly swell up into a roar all round us, and
Elxsente would shrink up close to me; once or twice they threw
things at us, but nothing sharp enough to cut. A man who walked
in front of us kept on repeating in a shout that we were the hostages
from the cities who were spared by order of the General and that
the rest were hung. He said it over and over again like a corncrake:
I would have given a lot to kill that man. We must have had seven
or eight miles to walk in the sun at the pace of the slowest oxen; at
first I looked about me and whispered to the others from time to
time and sang our marching song under my breath, but later I was

too tired to do anything but stumble along with my head down. My
hands were chained behind my back so that I couldn't even wipe
the sweat off my forehead or the dust out of my eyes. About half-
way Teffre cut his foot on a sharp stone and fell, but one of the
guards picked him up and helped him along. I was miserable about
Elxsente; he wasn't well yet and the sun was burning on our heads;
he knew he must go through the day without whimpering for the
honour of his city, and he did it well, but I could feel how much it
was costing him and I could do nothing to help him; I was thankful
when the soldier on his side said, 'I've a child of my own,' and took
him on to his shoulder for part of the way. The day seemed endless,
but suddenly we were halted in a great square place where some
one was speaking from the top of a flight of steps. I saw the General
a long way off, wearing a laurel wreath and a purple robe, but I
was too tired to see much; all those great white buildings were
swimming in the heat and there wasn't a breath of wind to blow
away the smell, that seemed everywhere, of leather and onions, and
the hot crowd.

When the Triumph was over and our chains were taken off, we
were locked up in a little barred room, a prison of some sort, with
straw on the flag-stones. We lay there, thankful for the dark and
quiet, and slept like the dead all night. The first day a woman, who
seemed too dazed to speak, brought us food; the second day another
woman brought it; she was Elxsente's cousin. He rushed up to her
with, 'Where's mother?' and she burst into tears and put her arms
round him. She had seen his father dead of wounds and knew his
mother and the baby sister were burned in a house with some other
women who'd tried to escape from the soldiers. But she could hardly
speak about it; something terrible must have happened to her too;
and she mightn't stay with us. Elxsente cried all that day, and even
while he slept he was sobbing and calling, 'Mother, mother'; I
couldn't bear it, I put my hands over my ears so as not to hear, but
I knew it was going on all the time and I couldn't sleep at all. Teffre
was very much upset; he seemed to have thought that when it was
all over he could go back to the old life, but this showed him that
he couldn't; perhaps it was lucky for him that his mother was dead
years before. Mireto had not been sacked, so my mother and sisters
should have been safe, and I knew my father had escaped, but my
brother might be killed or anything; and besides, I was the oldest
and I realized it all better: how this was the end of the League of

the Cities, our Gods were powerless, and our hope and honour in ashes.

The next morning we were taken away again; we were used to obeying orders now. An old soldier with a black beard was in charge of us; he wouldn't answer questions or let us talk among ourselves much. As we went through the streets a woman recognized us and threw a dead rat: it hit Elxsente; but I was glad it wasn't a brick. We had a long way to walk (though we got a lift for a few miles on a wagon that was leaving the town empty), first along one of the big main ways that went out between gardened houses and under arches, right into the country, and then along a lane with deep ruts, beside vineyards and cornfields; it was past noon when we came to a long low house with a walled garden where there were pomegranate trees. There was no one to be seen, and the soldier stopped, sat down on the bottom step of the ones that led up to the house door, and ate bread and onions. We sat on the ground beside him and waited, and the afternoon got hotter and hotter; we were all very tired. We'd had nothing to eat since early that morning—we hoped the soldier would give us something, but he didn't, and of course we couldn't ask. Teffre was complaining of his foot, which was badly swollen: I tied it up with fresh grass and a strip torn from my own tunic. Elxsente was crying all the time, quite hopelessly; his face was streaked with dirt and tears, and his hair was tangled into grey knots all over his head. I was unhappy enough myself; I tried to tell them stories, but that reminded us of home and made it all worse. Elxsente put his head down on my knee, and I felt his hot little face, wet against my skin. Teffre cried every time he moved his foot, and I was near it myself, but I thought of our being among the enemy and that we must show we were men. Still nobody came; sometimes we heard a cock crowing behind the house, and once a reaper passed through the trees in front of us with a sickle under his arm, but he never looked our way.

Then we heard voices inside the house and a lady came out on to the steps, with a maid carrying a basket behind her. The soldier saluted and spoke to her; she was all in blue, with the western sun on her face and hair. She ran down the steps and saw us. 'Oh,' she said, 'oh—you children! You poor children!' and in a moment she was beside me and had gathered Elxsente up into her arms; he lay there limp with his eyes half-shut, still crying. 'Have you been here all day,' she asked, 'with nothing to eat?' I nodded and she called up to the maid to bring food and drink quickly. I was glad to see how angry she was with the soldier; she sent him away and sat down on the steps with Elxsente on her knee, sobbing a little less. The maid brought milk and barley cakes and pears and grapes; we ate everything, and she fed Elxsente herself. Then the General came round from the other side of the garden; I knew him at once, though he was wearing a woollen tunic and sandals instead of armour; the bailiff (though we didn't know who he was till afterwards) was at his side. I stood up, and his wife stood up holding Elxsente to her breast.

He looked at us kindly enough and told the bailiff to take Teffre and me down to the pool to wash. We went with him, Teffre limping badly; it was a broad, shallow, stone basin, with sunflowers growing round it. We stripped and went in and washed off layers and layers of dust and sweat, and swam among the lily-pads till he told us to come out. They brought us clean clothes and we put them on with our hair dripping; he took us back to the house, to a clean, light room with blankets spread on the floor for us, and Teffre sat on a table while some one bandaged his foot properly. Then Elxsente came in and told us how the women of the house had washed him and dressed him and been kind to him, and he lay down on the blankets and I covered him, and he went to sleep almost at once. Then the General sent for me; he was sitting alone in a tall chair, with candles behind him. He asked me if I thought we should be ransomed; I said I believed Teffre and I would be, but that Elxsente's father and mother were killed, so I couldn't tell about him. He sent me away, and the mistress met me in the hall and asked if Elxsente was asleep.

The next day we were left alone most of the time, to eat and rest, but after that, when Teffre's foot was better, we were given work to do about the farm and garden, under the bailiff; it wasn't hard— getting in the grapes and apples, feeding the geese, driving the cows home, and so on. Elxsente got well wonderfully quickly, and forgot about his mother for hours together; the mistress petted him a lot and the General spoke to him whenever he saw him.

But the weeks went on and the autumn was going; there were frosts at night; once round the pond and out was as far as we cared to swim. But none of us heard anything from our homes. And then one day the General sent for Teffre to tell him he'd been ransomed, and his uncle was waiting to take him away. In an hour he'd said

good-bye to us and was gone; I've never seen him since. Of course
Elxsente and I were glad for his sake, but it made me wonder what
was going to happen to me; I thought of all sorts of things; perhaps
the soldier might have been wrong about my father; perhaps he was
dead and my brother was dead, and all our money was gone;
perhaps I should never see Mireto and my mother and our house
again. Every one was good to us, but of course we were no more
free than any of the slaves, and I didn't like to think of all my life
being like that. At one time I thought of running away, but I should
probably have been caught, and anyhow I should have had to leave
Elxsente; I had a plan that my father should ransom him too and
he should come back and live with us and be my little brother, now
that he had no one of his own kin left. We used to talk about that in
the evenings.

But it was winter now. We were busy pruning the vines and fruit
trees; Elxsente worked with me, but of course I had longer hours
and did more. After it was dark the mistress used often to have us
in and we sat with them, making withy plaits, while the General
talked about farming and wild beasts and told us all his adventures.
Sometimes he talked about Rome, things she had done in the past,
things he said she would do in the future. I thought about Mireto
and said nothing, but Elxsente seemed to believe it. We worshipped
with them too: the country Gods are the same all the world over.
Sometimes we went out after wolves and once I was in the thick of
it, when either a hound or the wolf bit me in the arm. Looking back
on it all now it seems such a waste of time that I didn't really enjoy
it; but then I didn't know what had happened at home.

One day I was coming up to the house with my pruning knife
and a great bundle of prunings to burn; Elxsente had gone in, but I
had stayed to finish the row, and it was nearly dark; I heard hoofs
behind me, turned, and there was my father! I threw down the
bundle and ran to him, and he was off his horse and had me in his
arms, all in a moment. The horse grazed by the roadside and we
talked. Of course I asked first about mother and every one. 'My
little son,' he said, 'you didn't hear all this long time! All's well at
home, but you know I'd spent all the money we had in arming my
men. There was nothing left, and I had all I could do to raise
enough to buy you both back. Did you know your brother was taken
prisoner during the siege? I couldn't find him for months; he had
been sold as a slave in the Roman market, and I bought him back

first: he was having a bad time. But I thought you would be well treated here—they've not been unkind to you, son?' He looked at the bundle of wood, and then at the bound place on my arm where I'd had the wolf-bite. I told him they'd all been kind and what sort of life it was; he put me up on his horse—it was fine to be in the saddle again—with the prunings behind, and we went up to the house. The General met my father and took him in, and I led the horse round to the stables and bedded him down.

When I came in they'd settled my ransom, and father said we should go home the next day. I was so happy I could hardly think, and then, with a jump, I remembered Elxsente. 'Oh, father,' I said, 'can't you buy back my friend too? He's got no one left, and I told him I'd take him home with me.' Father looked miserable and said he couldn't—I found out afterwards how hard the ransom money had been to come by—but that he'd try to later, for the honour of the cities. But the General said, 'I don't want to have Elxsente ransomed; I've another plan for him; call him and we'll see.' He came in, and the mistress with him; he ran over to me and took my hands: 'Oh, you're going,' he said, 'you're going back to your mother and I shall be left all alone!' But the General leaned forward, saying, 'Elxsente, you know I've no children of my own. Will you come and live with me always, and be my son?' and the mistress spoke softly to him: 'Stay with us, dear.' And Elxsente looked at them and looked at me and then looked down on the floor, wondering. And I said, 'Think of your City, Elxsente! Don't put yourself into the hands of the enemy!' and he said to me, 'Would it be very wrong to stay? I think I'd like to stay.' I would have spoken, but my father stopped me and spoke himself: 'You know that I'm of the Cities, child, on your side; so you can trust me; and I advise you to stay.' Then Elxsente went over to the mistress and put his arms round her neck, and she and the General kissed him, and called him son. And the General gave back the ransom money to my father and said to me that while there was peace I should always be welcome in his house.

The next day father and I set out for home. Elxsente came with us as far as the main road, and there we said our good-byes. Elxsente went back to the house, and father and I struck out over the hills for Mireto. We were back within the week and everything was right again. I found I hadn't mended my pony's bridle, but my brother had done it for me after he came home.

FRANK O'CONNOR
The Majesty of the Law

OLD Dan Bride was breaking brosna for the fire when he heard a step up the path. He paused, a bundle of saplings on his knee.

Dan had looked after his mother while the spark of life was in her, and after her death no other woman had crossed the threshold. Signs on it, his house had that look. Almost everything in it he had made with his own hands in his own way. The seats of the chairs were only slices of log, rough and round and thick as the saw had left them. And with the rings still plainly visible through the grime and polish that coarse trouser-bottoms had in the course of long years imparted. Into these Dan had rammed stout knotted ash boughs which served alike for legs and back. The deal table, bought in a shop, was an inheritance from his mother, and a great pride and joy to him, though it rocked forward and back whenever he touched it. On the wall, unglazed and flyspotted, hung in mysterious isolation a Marcus Stone print and beside the door was a calendar representing a racehorse. Over the door hung a gun, old but good and in excellent condition, and before the fire was stretched an old setter who raised his head expectantly whenever Dan rose or even stirred.

He raised it now as the steps came nearer, and when Dan, laying down the bundle of saplings, cleaned his hands thoughtfully in the seat of his trousers, he gave a loud bark, but this expressed no more than a desire to display his own watchfulness. He was half human and knew that people thought he was old and past his prime.

A man's shadow fell across the oblong of dusty light thrown over the half-door before Dan looked round.

'Are you alone, Dan?' asked an apologetic voice.

'Oh, come in, come in, sergeant, come in and welcome,' exclaimed the old man, hurrying on rather uncertain feet to the door, which the tall policeman opened and pushed in. He stood there, half in sunlight, half in shadow, and seeing him so, you would have realized how dark was the interior of Dan's house. One side of his red face was turned so as to catch the light, and behind it an ash tree raised its boughs of airy green against the sky. Green fields, broken here and there by clumps of red-brown rock, flowed down-hill, and beyond them, stretched all across the horizon, was the sea, flooded and almost transparent with light. The sergeant's face was fat and fresh, the old man's face, emerging from the twilight of the kitchen, had the colour of wind and sun, while the features had been so shaped by the struggle with time and the elements that they might as easily have been found impressed upon the surface of a rock.

'Begor, Dan,' said the sergeant, ''tis younger you're getting.'

'Middling I am, sergeant, middling,' agreed the old man in a voice which seemed to accept the remark as a compliment of which politeness would not allow him to take too much advantage. 'No complaints.'

'Faix, and 'tis as well. No wan but a born idiot would believe them. And th' ould dog don't look a day older.'

The dog gave a low growl as though to show the sergeant that he would remember this unmannerly reference to his age, but indeed he growled every time he was mentioned, under the impression that people could have nothing but ill to say of him.

'And how's yourself, sergeant?'

'Well, now, like that in the story, Dan, neither on the pig's back or at the horse's tail. We have our own little worries, but, thanks be to God, we have our compensations.'

'And the wife and care?'

'Good, glory and praise be to God, good. They were away from me with a month, the lot of them, at the mother-in-law's place in Clare.'

'Ah, do you tell me so?'

'I had a fine, quiet time.'

The old man looked about him, and then retired to the near-by bedroom from which he emerged a moment later with an old shirt. With this he solemnly wiped the seat and back of the log-chair nearest the fire.

'Take your ease, now, take your ease. 'Tis tired you must be after the journey. How did you come?'

'Teigue Leary it was that gave me a lift. Wisha, now Dan, don't you be putting yourself about. I won't be stopping. I promised them I'd be back inside an hour.'

'What hurry is on you?' asked the old man. 'Look now, your foot was on the path when I rose from putting kindling on the fire.'

'Now! Now! You're not making tea for me.'

'I am not then, but for myself, and very bad I'll take it if you won't join me.'

'Dan, Dan, that I mightn't stir, but 'tisn't an hour since I had a cup at the barracks.'

'Ah, *Dhe*, whisht, now! Whisht, will you! I have something that'll put an appetite on you.'

The old man swung the heavy kettle on to the chain over the open fire, and the dog sat up, shaking his ears with an expression of the deepest interest. The policeman unbuttoned his tunic, opened his belt, took a pipe and a plug of tobacco from his breast-pocket, and crossing his legs in easy posture, began to cut the tobacco slowly and carefully with his pocket-knife. The old man went to the dresser, and took down two handsomely decorated cups, the only cups he had, which, though chipped and handleless, were used at all only on very rare occasions: for himself, he preferred tea from a basin. Happening to glance into them, he noticed that they bore the trace of disuse and had collected a substantial share of the fine white dust which was constantly circulating within the little smoky cottage. Again he thought of the shirt, and, rolling up his sleeves with a stately gesture, he wiped them inside and out till they shone. Then he bent and opened the cupboard. Inside was a quart bottle of pale liquid, obviously untouched. He removed the cork and smelt the contents, pausing for a moment in the act as though to recollect where exactly he had noticed that particular smoky odour before. Then reassured, he rose and poured out with a liberal hand.

'Try that now, sergeant,' he said.

The sergeant, concealing whatever qualms he might have felt at the thought of imbibing illegal whiskey, looked carefully into the cup, sniffed, and glanced up at old Dan.

'It looks good,' he commented.

'It should be.'

'It tastes good, too,' he added.

'Ah, sha,' said Dan, clearly not wishing to praise his own hospitality in his own house, ''tis of no great excellence.'

'You're a good judge, I'd say,' said the sergeant without irony.

'Ever since things became what they are,' said Dan, carefully guarding himself from a too direct reference to the peculiarities of the law administered by his guest, 'liquor is not what it used to be.'

'I have heard that remark made before now,' said the sergeant thoughtfully. 'I have often heard it said by men of wide experience that liquor used to be better in the old days.'

'Liquor,' said the old man, 'is a thing that takes time. There was never a good job done in a hurry.'

''Tis an art in itself.'

'Just so.'

'And an art takes time.'

'And knowledge,' added Dan with emphasis. 'Every art has its secrets, and the secrets of distilling are being lost the way the old songs were lost. When I was a boy there wasn't a man in the barony but had a hundred songs in his head, but with people running here, there and everywhere, the songs were lost. . . . Ever since things became what they are,' he repeated on the same guarded note, 'there's so much running about the secrets are lost.'

'There must have been a power of them.'

'There was. Ask any man to-day that makes liquor do he know how to make it of heather.'

'And was it made of heather?' asked the policeman.

'It was.'

'Did you ever drink it yourself?'

'I did not; but I knew men that drank it. And a purer, sweeter, wholesomer drink never tickled a man's gullet. Babies they used to give it to and growing children.'

'Musha, Dan, I think sometimes 'twas a great mistake of the law to set its hand against it.'

Dan shook his head. His eyes answered for him, but it was not in nature that in his own house a man should criticize the occupation of his guest.

'Maybe so, maybe not,' he said in a non-committal tone.

'But sure, what else have the poor people?'

'Them that makes the laws have their own good reasons.'

'All the same, Dan, all the same, 'tis a hard law.'

The sergeant would not be outdone in generosity. Politeness required him not to yield to the old man's defence of his superiors and their mysterious ways.

'It is the secrets I would be sorry for,' said Dan, summing up. 'Men die, and men are born, and where one man drained another will plough, but a secret lost is lost for ever.'

'True,' said the sergeant mournfully. 'Lost for ever.'

Dan took the policeman's cup, rinsed it in a bucket of clear water beside the door, and cleaned it anew with the aid of the shirt. Then he placed it carefully at the sergeant's elbow. From the dresser he took a jug of milk and a blue bag containing sugar: this he followed up with a slab of country butter and—a sign that his visitor was not altogether unexpected—a round cake of homemade bread, fresh and uncut. The kettle sang and spat, and the dog, shaking his ears, barked at it angrily.

'Go 'way, you brute!' growled Dan, kicking him out of his way.

He made the tea and filled the two cups. The sergeant cut himself a large slice of bread and buttered it thickly.

'It is just like medicines,' said the old man, resuming his theme with the imperturbability of age. 'Every secret there was is lost. And leave no one tell me a doctor is the measure of one that has secrets from old times.'

'How could he?' asked the sergeant with his mouth full.

'The proof of that was seen when there were doctors and wise people there together.'

'It wasn't to the doctors the people went, I'll engage.'

'It was not. And why?' . . . With a sweeping gesture the old man took in the whole world outside his cabin. 'Out there on the hillsides is the sure cure for every disease. Because it is written'—he tapped the table with his thumb—'it is written by the poets "*an galar 'san leigheas go bhfaghair le ceile*" ("wherever you find the disease you will find the cure"). But people walk up the hills and down the hills and all they see is flowers. Flowers! As if God Almighty—honour and praise to Him!—had nothing better to do with His time than be making ould flowers!'

'Things no doctor could cure the wise people cured.'

'Ah musha, 'tis I know it,' said Dan bitterly, ''tis I know it, not in my mind but in my own four bones.'

'Do you tell me the rheumatics do be at you always?'

'They do. . . . Ah, if you were living, Kitty O'Hara, or you, Nora Malley of the Glen, 'tisn't I would be dreading the mountain wind or the sea wind; 'tisn't I'd be creeping down with me misfortunate red ticket for the blue and pink and yellow dribble-drabble of their ignorant dispensary!'

'Why then, indeed,' said the sergeant with sudden determination, 'I'll get you a bottle for that.'

'Ah, there's no bottle ever made will cure me!'

'There is, there is. Don't talk now till you try it. My own mother's brother, it cured him when he was that bad he wanted the carpenter to cut the two legs off him with a hand-saw.'

'I'd give fifty pounds to be rid of it,' said Dan. 'I would and five hundred!'

The sergeant finished his tea in a gulp, blessed himself and struck a match which he then allowed to go out as he answered some question of the old man's. He did the same with a second and third, as though titillating his appetite with delay. At last he succeeded in getting it alight, and then the two men pulled round their chairs, placed their toes side by side in the ashes, and in deep puffs, lively bursts of conversation and long long silences, enjoyed their pipes.

'I hope I'm not keeping you,' said the sergeant, as though struck by the length of his visit.

'Erra, what keep?'

'Tell me if I am. The last thing I'd like to do is to waste a man's time.'

'Och, I'd ask nothing better than to have you here all night.'

'I like a little talk myself,' admitted the policeman.

And again they became lost in conversation. The light grew thick and coloured, and wheeling about the kitchen before it disappeared became tinged with gold; the kitchen itself sank into a cool greyness with cold light upon the cups and the basins and plates upon the dresser. From the ash tree a thrush began to sing. The open hearth gathered brightness till its light was a warm, even splash of crimson in the twilight.

Twilight was also descending without when the sergeant rose to go. He fastened his belt and tunic and carefully brushed his clothes. Then he put on his cap, tilted a little to side and back.

'Well,' he said, 'that was a great talk.'

'It's a pleasure,' said Dan, 'a real pleasure, that's what it is.'

'And I won't forget the bottle'

'Heavy handling from God to you!'

'Good-bye now, Dan.'

'Good-bye and good luck.'

Dan did not offer to accompany the sergeant beyond the door. Then he sat down in his old place by the fire. He took out his pipe once more, blew through it thoughtfully, and just as he leaned forward for a twig to kindle it he heard steps returning to the house. It was the sergeant. He put his head a little way over the half-door.

'Oh, Dan,' he called softly.

'Ay, sergeant,' replied Dan, looking round, but with one hand still reaching for the twig. He could not see the sergeant's face, only hear his voice.

'I suppose you're not thinking of paying that little fine, Dan?'

There was a brief silence. Dan pulled out the lighted twig, rose slowly and shambled towards the door, stuffing it down into the almost empty bowl of the pipe. He leaned over the half-door, while the sergeant with hands in the pockets of his trousers gazed rather in the direction of the laneway, yet taking in a considerable portion of the sea-line.

'The way it is with me, sergeant,' replied Dan unemotionally, 'I am not.'

'I was thinking that, Dan. I was thinking you wouldn't.'

There was a long silence during which the voice of the thrush grew shriller and merrier. The sunken sun lit up islands of purple cloud moored high above the wind.

'In a way,' said the sergeant, 'that was what brought me.'

'I was just thinking so, sergeant, it struck me and you going out the door.'

'If 'twas only the money, I'm sure there's many would be glad to oblige you.'

'I know that, sergeant. No, 'tisn't the money so much as giving that fellow the satisfaction of paying. Because he angered me, sergeant.'

The sergeant made no comment upon this and another long silence ensued.

'They gave me the warrant,' he said at last in a tone which dissociated him from all connexion with the document.

'Ay, begod!' said Dan, without interest.

'So whenever 'twould be convenient to you——'

'Well, now you mention it,' said Dan, by way of throwing out a suggestion for debate, 'I could go with you now.'

'Oh, tut, tut!' protested the sergeant with a wave of his hand, dismissing the idea as the tone required.

'Or I could go to-morrow,' added Dan, warming up to the issue.

'Just as you like now,' replied the sergeant, scaling up his voice accordingly.

'But as a matter of fact,' said the old man emphatically, 'the day that would be most convenient to me would be Friday after dinner, seeing that I have some messages to do in town, and I wouldn't have me jaunt for nothing.'

'Friday will do grand,' said the sergeant with relief that this delicate matter was now practically disposed of. 'You could just walk in yourself and tell them I told you.'

'I'd rather have yourself, if 'twould be no inconvenience, sergeant. As it is, I'd feel a bit shy.'

'You needn't then. There's a man from my own parish there, a warder; one Whelan. You could say you wanted him, and I'll guarantee when he knows you're a friend of mine he'll make you as comfortable as if you were at home by your own fire.'

'I'd like that fine,' said Dan with satisfaction.

'Well, good-bye again now, Dan. I'll have to hurry.'

'Wait now, wait, till I see you to the road!'

Together the two men strolled down the laneway while Dan explained how it was that he, a respectable old man, had had the grave misfortune to open the head of another old man in such a way as to necessitate his being removed to hospital, and why it was that he could not give the old man in question the satisfaction of paying in cash for an injury brought about through the victim's own unmannerly method of argument.

'You see, sergeant,' he said, 'the way it is, he's there now, and he's looking at us as sure as there's a glimmer of sight in his wake, wandering, wathery eyes, and nothing would give him more gratification than for me to pay. But I'll punish him. I'll lie on bare boards for him. I'll suffer for him, sergeant, till he won't be able to rise his head, nor any of his children after him, for the suffering he put on me.'

On the following Friday he made ready his donkey and butt and set out. On his way he collected a number of neighbours who wished to bid him farewell. At the top of the hill he stopped to send them back. An old man, sitting in the sunlight, hastily made his way within doors, and a moment later the door of his cottage was quietly closed.

Having shaken all his friends by the hand, Dan lashed the old donkey, shouted 'hup, there!' and set out alone along the road to prison.

STELLA BENSON
On the Contrary

LEONARD LUMLEY had some very good ideas for keeping cool in the Red Sea. 'Wear *wool* next the skin,' he said, 'and drink nothing but very hot tea. . . . ' He had many such ideas, but no one could be absolutely certain that he practised what he preached. Hot tea was not served, for instance, in the bar, where Leonard spent a good deal of his time, and it seemed that he had lost his only collar-stud, so that his shirt-collar flapped open in defiance of his dictum that Closed Collars were Coolest. However, the very contrariness of his views was impressive, and Leonard himself was a very impressive, though rather stout, young man. Several people trusted him so much that they went about for a day or two in thick Jaegers, looking like kettles boiling over. Miss Dancey admired him so much that she must have lost several pints in weight between Suez and Perim.

Leonard, instinctively aware that all that he could say was safe in Miss Dancey's ear, sat very often at the foot of her deck-chair—indeed partly *on* her feet, since he was of spreading figure—but spiritually, as he knew, their positions were reversed! *His* were the feet that were sat at. He believed that every man should have a profession, he would tell her—but not before he is forty. A man should afford himself leisure while he is young and work when he is old.

'Oh—*oh*, what an eggstrawdinarily interesting idea,' said Miss Dancey.

Leisure is only useful to the young, according to Leonard Lumley; after forty a man should begin to work, having nothing better to do, and should work harder and harder until the age of ninety or so, when death, the supremely full-time job, should interrupt him at his desk or in the pulpit or on his charger riding into battle or at his stethoscope or what not. For, though Mr. Lumley was just over thirty-five and would soon come to the end of his period of leisure, he had not yet decided on the occupation that would most fruitfully employ his declining years.

'Oh—*oh*—a *doctor*,' suggested Miss Dancey. 'Doctors are magnificent, I think—perfect *saints*. . . . '

'On the contrary,' said Leonard, to whose lips this phrase rose almost automatically. 'The doctor's profession is the least noble of any. A stockbroker is more saintly than a doctor.'

'Oh—*oh*—not *really*—do, *do* tell me why. . . .'

'Well, it's to a doctor's interest, you must remember, to live in a sickly world, and also—er—well, if you knew as much about doctors and stockbrokers as I do. . . .'

'Oh—*oh*—' breathed Miss Dancey. 'Then *why* not be a *stockbroker*? Then you'd be both *rich* and *saintly*. . . .'

'On the contrary,' replied Leonard. 'Stockbrokers never make money. Not a penny. They always die in the workhouse.'

'Oh—*oh*—how eggstrawdinary that is. . . . Can you *explain* it to me?'

'Well, you can take it from me,' said Leonard. And she did. Stockbrokers and doctors being thus thrust beyond the pale, she tried soldiers, clergymen, barristers . . . imagining herself the wife of each in turn. But all, it seemed, were not only unsuitable but impossible; soldiers were slaves, clergymen's inhibitions invariably landed them in lunatic asylums, barristers, being always corrupt, finished up in jail.

'*Sailors*, then,' whispered Miss Dancey, a trifle discouraged. 'Such *breezy, healthy darlings*, sailors. . . .'

'On the contrary,' said Leonard. 'I can always see in a sailor's eye that introspective, scarcely sane look that tells of a life spent within unnaturally narrow limits. Show me a sailor and I'll show you a potential homicidal hysteric.'

'Oh, Lord!' said a voice near them.

Leonard looked round, annoyed, to see who this might be that so impertinently appealed from his authority to a Higher Power. He saw Mr. Hospice. s.s. *Meritoria*'s third officer, pausing in a walk round the deck with some unknown fellow-homicidal-hysteric of minor rank.

'Oh—*oh*—Mr. Hospice,' said Miss Dancey. 'I'm learning *such* a *lot* of new things.' (There had been a difference of opinion among the passengers as to whether Miss Dancey ever intended sarcasm. Fortunately for her popularity, however, it was finally proved that she never did.)

'Thplendid,' said Mr. Hospice. 'Thorry I interrupted. I couldn't help overhearing Mithter Lumley'th latht remark, and it thur-prithed me rather. Thorry.' And he and his friend strode away down the deck.

Mr. Lumley, who whole-heartedly despised the thin undersized third officer, was beginning to tell Miss Dancey how perfect an example was this Hospice of all the Lumley theories—when—something happened.

Really, for the first two or three minutes, the passengers could hardly tell what had happened. It was like an earthquake reversed—a sort of lurch from regular movement into stillness. It had the same deeply disturbing effect on the nerves as has an earthquake—gave feet that had learned to trust their foothold a sense of betrayal. The ship, after a futile churning of propellers, was motionless, but listed very slightly. Passengers streamed out of the smoking-room, to ask Leonard what had happened.

The moonlight, which had long been exhibiting a silver panorama of sea to no audience, now attracted general attention. Everybody crowded to the rail, trying, with anxious gimlet eyes, to bore through the curiously substantial silvered air. Every one expected to see—what? A rock? A whale? Some unthinkable menace? Something, at any rate, to write to one's horrified family about from Colombo. Perhaps, even, something that would get into the papers and enable them all to be called Survivors. But there was nothing to be seen except calm sea and, a mile or so away—by the very keen-sighted—very low unobtrusive land.

'*Don't* look over the rail,' rang Leonard's commanding voice. 'In danger, the best thing is *not* to know the worst. Now I propose we all sit down on the deck and play some silly game like Old Maid or something. Better than singing "Nearer My God to Thee", what?'

'Oh—*oh*,' quavered Miss Dancey. 'Then there really *is* danger?'

'Who's got playing-cards on the spot?' asked Leonard. 'Hi, don't go mooning over the rail there, I tell you. Turn your eyes inboard, everybody, and remember you're English.'

'Oh—*oh*—is there anything very *terrible* to be seen over the rail?' asked Miss Dancey hoarsely.

'Cards—cards—cards,' called Leonard gaily.

'Yipp-i-yaddy,' echoed Mr. Hospice, appearing from the direction of the bridge. 'We're aground.'

'Don't make such a fuss, man,' said Leonard sharply. 'You—an officer—ought to know better than to frighten the ladies like that. But we're not going to be frightened, are we?' he added, looking lovingly at his flock—of which Miss Dancey was the bell-wether.

'Not a bit frightened. We're going to play Old Maid sitting on the deck. What a lark!'

'Oh, for the Lord'th thake, don't be tho dam *brave*,' said Mr. Hospice in a low voice. He added more loudly, 'We're aground—on thand—till high tide tomorrow morning. No danger whatever.'

Only a dread of being ridiculous restrained Leonard from strangling Mr. Hospice on the spot. For, unfortunately for the landsman, words spoken from above the brassy buttons of a uniform had a completely soothing effect on the listeners. Nobody even dreamed of playing Old Maid. Everybody went back to interrupted bridge and poker. Everybody in due course went to bed and to sleep—though every one kept, as it were, one ear awake for the sound of a change in the ship's condition.

There was no change. Promenaders before breakfast saw still the same sluggish sea, the same sullen low land. Even the jellyfish looked as if they had been there for generations. Leonard was, by the mercy of his gods, enabled to say at breakfast, 'I told you so. . . . Off at high tide indeed. . . . Didn't I *say* that little shrimp of a third officer didn't know his job?'

Meeting Mr. Hospice on deck after breakfast, he said acidly, 'In spite of your hopeful promise, Mr. Hospice, we're still aground.'

'Why, by jove—*tho* we are!' exclaimed Mr. Hospice blithely.

Leonard had no shyness of asking captains questions. The bluff and buttony spotlessness of captains imposed no humility on him. He felt himself the *moral* captain of every ship he travelled in. Actual captains were sometimes a little irritated by his assumption of a constant right to claim *tête-à-têtes* with them, but Leonard never observed this irritation. The captain of the *Meritoria* admitted, a little fretfully, on being buttonholed by Leonard, that the ship of which they shared the command had taken a firmer seat on the sand than had at first been supposed. 'It'll be a matter of shifting cargo,' said the captain, as he abruptly took flight.

'It'll be a matter of shifting cargo,' retailed Leonard to his flock on deck. 'We shall be here—oh . . . er . . . well . . . quite a time. . . .'

'Oh—*oh*—quite a *time*?' echoed Miss Dancey. 'What would happen if the sea got rough? The ship would break up. Like in *Robinson Crusoe*.'

'On the contrary,' said Leonard. 'The waves would help to jerk us off—but that's a technical question and I won't go into it now. The—er—south-west typhoon isn't due at this time of year. . . .'

Even his hopeful ear detected a flaw in his omniscience here, so he changed the subject. 'What do you all say to my suggestion to the captain that we passengers go ashore for the day? Just to get out of the way while they're shifting cargo.'

'It would be dam hot,' said Bertie Briggs, a slightly mutinous male lamb of his flock, looking at the scarred, heat-dazzled line of land.

'On the contrary,' said Leonard. 'It would be far cooler than in the ship. I've spent years of my life in the tropics and you can take it from me that the way to keep cool in a hot climate is to *keep out* of whatever breeze there is. Directly I take over a house in India, I immediately scrap all punkahs and electric fans. Immediately. "Take the beastly things away," I say to the servants. "I'm not going to sit and catch pneumonia under those fancy gadgets like a callow tourist. . . ."'

A callow tourist! Every tourist within earshot shuddered, shocked at such an idea. For a tourist to behave like a tourist—how degrading! About twenty tourist passengers felt obliged to disprove their shameful tourist-hood by consenting to an expedition to the windless shore, if it could be arranged.

Leonard and Miss Dancey had some difficulty in finding the captain. 'These sailors simply don't know their job,' he said to her as they followed rumours of the captain all over the ship. 'Look at this so-called captain—gets his ship into a hole like this, and then disappears—can't be found, it seems, by any of his subordinates. Why, anything might happen—and yet nobody knows where to lay their hands on the man supposed to be responsible.'

'Oh—*oh*—*might* anything happen?'

They finally ran the captain to earth in the chartroom. 'I'm afraid, Miss Dancey, I can't invite passengers to come and see me here——' he began, but Leonard managed, by talking in a very loud voice, to explain the object of their visit. The captain's attention was caught. 'Well,' he said, on a note of hope, 'I can't think why you should want to go to a burnt-up hole like that, but if you *do* want to—far be it from me. . . . We shall probably spend the day shifting cargo and get off at high tide early to-morrow. You going too, little Miss Dancey? Well, ladies do certainly have some odd fancies. I'll send my third officer, Mr. Hospice, to undertake the expedition.'

'Oh, I'll undertake the expedition all right, captain,' said Leonard.

'God help it, I know you will,' replied the captain with unexpected vigour. 'Let's say, then, that Mr. Hospice will *over*take the *under*taker. . . . Ha-ha. He'll have the boat ready in half an hour's time. I'm afraid I'm busy now. Good-bye. Enjoy yourselves.'

'All ships' captains suffer from a superiority complex,' said Leonard, looking a little ruffled as he helped Miss Dancey down the companion-way. 'They seem to think their authority is supreme.'

'Oh—*oh*—*so* they do. . . . But *isn't* it—on board their own ship?'

'On the contrary. In these days of trade unions, the captain is the slave of the humblest stoker on board.'

'Oh—*oh*—*really*? Then oughtn't we to have gone and asked the humblest stoker on board if we might . . .?'

Really Miss Dancey was almost silly sometimes, thought Leonard.

However, as the boat, bristling with twenty passengers, was rowed to shore, he felt the joy of creation and domination—even though Mr. Hospice was ostensibly in charge—for certainly no other than Leonard Lumley had led out these bleating Israelites from their Egypt—had set the strong machinery of these rowing Lascars' arms in motion.

The most beautiful moment of the expedition was the moment of landing. As the wrinkled sea-bottom, sloping lightly upwards under blue space, stopped being sea-bottom and became Arabia—as the keel of the boat gently grooved the ochre sand, it seemed to all the adventurers that they were about to do something wholly new for the first time. In marking that dazzling virgin beach with their feet, they would print some mystic and undreamt-of-word on the only really blank page their eyes had ever rested on. One by one they jumped out of their boat, murmuring or shrilling their astonishment. The shore—the whole land as far as eye could see—seemed to be newly created by some brusque movement of the earth, like a great nut newly cracked in haphazard fragments. Jagged rocks lay lightly on the sand; nothing was embedded or rooted. The very vegetation was only laid on the sand's surface in the form of large round rolling transparencies of dried tangled shrub—like ogres' thistledowns blown from far roots by some dusty long-dead wind. The uncouth newly-broken rocks were sparsely scattered about the shore, were grouped into a crazy Stonehenge just about high-water mark, and, a little farther inland still, were built into a long ridge which had acted as a kind of dam for the low-blown, shifting, sifting sand from the desert. The horizon, therefore, was very close. The Magnificent Infinities which Leonard had promised his flock were shut away by this wave of rock and sand.

'Oh—*oh*——,' cried Miss Dancey. 'How eggstrawdinarily eggciting it all is. So *dangerous*-looking, kind of. I believe I saw a man's head behind that rock. I suppose this country is *crammed* with *sheiks*.'

'On the contrary,' said Leonard. 'You may take it from me that there isn't a living soul within three hundred miles.'

As he spoke, a young dark boy, almost naked, stepped out from behind a rock where he had been hiding to watch the landing of the strangers.

'—Except, of course,' added Leonard with some presence of mind, 'a few fisher families scattered along the coast.'

'I suppose they're practically savages,' said elderly Mrs. Wilkins, looking dubiously at the morose child.

'On the contrary. Like all simple peoples, they are extremely friendly. They haven't learned to distrust strangers.' He held out his hand with a coin in it. The simple boy seized a rock and threw it at the group—fortunately unskilfully—before he ran away shouting something that, one feared, was an Arabian curse.

'Well, well,' said Leonard, 'boys will be boys all the world over. Now, everybody—let's *enjoy* ourselves. . . . Isn't it *good* to feel the solid earth under our feet again?'

'Yes *and* no,' said Mr. Briggs rather impudently. 'The solid earth is almost burning the soles off my shoes. If you'd told me what we were in for, I'd have brought a pair of stilts along. What's the next move?'

'*My* next move is into the shade of that pile of rocks,' said Mrs. Wilkins, who was rather stout. 'It must be cooler there.'

'On the contrary. . . .' But Leonard's flock, showing a disquieting independence, moved away from him as one lamb, towards the strip of red quivering shadow.

'We'd better have our cool drinkth now or never,' said Mr. Hospice, who had been superintending two cross-looking stewards in the removal of several hampers into the shade. 'The ithed lemonade'll be hot toddy thoon.'

'I strongly disapprove of iced drinks in hot weather,' began Leonard. 'I have often——'

'Oh, thplendid,' said Mr. Hospice. 'Tho much more for the retht of uth.'

There was nothing for Leonard to do but to follow the party to the strip of shade. It was a narrow strip, growing narrower, and they were obliged to sit in a long row to enjoy it. The sand here certainly felt cool in contrast to the baked shore. Mrs. Wilkins said, 'Really, this is quite pleasant,' in a tone of surprise.

'Yes *and* no,' grumbled Mr. Briggs, for at that moment the flies discovered the party.

'I wonder how long we can thtick thith out,' said Mr. Hospice cheerfully.

Nobody answered, but every one—even Leonard—silently wished that it would not seem ridiculous to leave Arabia after a visit of only nine minutes.

'Oh—*oh*—it's an *adventure*, anyway,' said Miss Dancey.

'On the contrary. It is a popular fallacy that adventure is found in wild remote places like this. You can take it from me that there is more chance of adventure in the Strand, London, than in the whole of the Arabian desert.

His luck seemed to be out to-day, for as he finished speaking a startling adventure began happening to them, that certainly would have been unlikely in the Strand. A torrent of dirty and wild-looking men began streaming round from behind the ridge of rocks against which they sat. All were shouting—not apparently to any one in particular—and each carried a naked dagger or a kind of a billhook. They came and stood in front of the long line of seated picnickers— and continued coming—more and more of them—until the travellers' view of the sea was completely shut out. The heat and smell, within this human stockade, became almost unbearable.

'My hat,' said Mr. Hospice, standing up. 'Thethe beggarth don't look any too friendly.'

'On the contrary,' said Leonard, 'they are no doubt friendly fisherfolk, inviting us to visit their village. I see evidences of native industries. Look at the coloured plaited leather round the hilts of their weapons.'

'Look at their toes,' said Bertie Briggs. 'All eaten away.'

Their feet were the easiest part of them to look at, since all the lookers were seated. To stand up against the overhanging boulders, one would have to stand almost nose to nose with the visitors.

'I don't want to look at anything,' said Mrs. Wilkins. 'I shall be sick in a minute.'

Since Mr. Hospice was standing, the Arabs made the mistake of supposing that he was the travellers' mouthpiece, especially as he spoke a little Arabic. So Leonard sat back trying to smile subtly, like a general leaving the drudgery to his aide-de-camp.

'Well, well,' said Mr. Hospice, after a long bellowing talk with the head man, who wore red and sandy striped draperies. 'It theemth thethe beggarth want thome of our good money off uth. No leth than twenty poundth, in fact.'

'Whatever for?' asked Mrs. Wilkins, letting go of her nose for the purpose.

'Well, thtrangely enough, for the privilege of going back on board.'

'Oh—*oh*—are they brigands?' asked Miss Dancey.

'Thomething like it, I'm afraid. But we're perfectly thafe, really. Only I thuppothe there'th nothing for it but to pay up.'

'On the contrary,' began Leonard, but Mr. Briggs interrupted him, 'Can't we knock some of 'em down and run for it? They've got no fire-arms.'

'Oh—*oh*—*don't* talk like that. . . . I'm going to faint,' cried Miss Dancey, and she certainly began to cant alarmingly towards Leonard's shoulder.

'I've got eight and sixpence,' said a desiccated Major. Apart from this sum, no one had more than a shilling or so.

'Well, talk—talk, my dear fellow,' said Leonard to Mr. Hospice. 'Talk, to gain time while I think out a plan of action. *Bargain* with the brutes. Bargaining is the essence of Oriental business.'

'Very pothibly it ith,' agreed Mr. Hospice. 'I've been bargaining like hell. They athked forty firtht—they now conthent to take twenty. No amount of bargaining'll bring 'em down from twenty poundth to theventeen and thixpenthe—which ith all we've got.'

'Let *me* talk to them,' said Leonard, heaving himself to his feet among the crowding draperies of the Arabs. They began laughing coarsely, for some obscure reason expecting entertainment. 'Now then, you scoundrels,' he shouted authoritatively. But he stopped because a lean black hand darted forward and removed his pince-nez from his nose, snapping the little chain that tethered them to his bosom. 'Here—I say—drop it—this is too much—this is robbery.'

But the pince-nez were by now straddling a broad black nose at least twenty noses away from their owner's.

'Better rethink ourthelveth, I'm afraid,' said Mr. Hospice. 'They want me to go back to the ship and get the money, and I think I'd better, on the whole. You'll be quite thafe, ath long ath you don't annoy them. You're *money* to them.'

'So damned ignominious,' said Mr. Briggs.

But Leonard did not feel ignominious, though his eyes, without their glasses, had rather a pink wincing look. 'Yes, go back,' he said haughtily, 'and ask the captain from me to send a party of armed men—all the arms he has, and——'

But Mr. Hospice was hurrying down the beach to where the Lascars—all agog—were waiting in the boat.

'I'd like to see the captain's face when he gets my message,' said Leonard, looking down his line of wilting followers. 'He'll agree with me, of course, that an armed demonstration would be a better course than tamely paying up.'

'Oh—*oh*——' wailed Miss Dancey. 'But if these brigands see men with guns coming, they'll cut our throats—I'm sure of it. They've got us so squeezed up against this cliff.'

'On the contrary,' said Leonard. 'We have a strategic position. An Englishman with his back to the wall is the toughest man to beat on God's earth, you can take it from me.'

'Oh—*oh*—you're so *brave*. . . . I wish I was *brave*. . . .'

'I wish I had a severe cold in the head,' said Mrs. Wilkins.

Now that Mr. Hospice was gone, the robbers seemed to recognize Leonard's leadership, though in no very flattering way. They made him the butt of their simple wit, as he stood among them, trying to trip him up with their sinuous black feet, pushing his hat over his nose, tweaking his coat, putting their hands in his pockets, and even trying to pinch his ear. From above, a shaggy head looking over a split boulder—like holly on the top of a partly eaten plum-pudding—was engaged in spitting assiduously down on to the captives. Leonard haughtily moved out of the range of this marksman.

'Better stand in the shade, Lumley,' said the Major. 'You're the only one of us without a topee or a sunshade.'

'On the contrary,' said Leonard grimly. 'The topee is the cause of more cases of sunstroke than . . . you can take it from me. . . . Oh, *when* is this blasted little sailor coming back? The inefficiency

of sailors is simply——' He covered his burst of petulance with—
'I'm longing to have a dozen armed men behind me and put these
damned niggers in their places. . . . Excuse my language, ladies.'

'Oh—*oh*—you are so *brave*. . . .'

'I can see a boat—no, *two* boats, leaving the ship now,' said Mr.
Briggs.

'Two boats—that means forty men,' said Leonard. 'I knew the
captain would agree with me. Pay up, indeed—what nonsense!'

There was a pause and then Mr. Briggs said, 'The boats are
empty, except for Hospice and the men rowing.'

'On the contrary,' said Leonard, 'the armed men are all crouching
out of sight. Even Hospice would have too much sense to show his
hand too soon.'

'The two boats are separating now,' continued Mr. Briggs. 'One's
going to land right away down the beach. Very mysterious.'

'Not in the least,' said Leonard. 'They understood my suggestions
perfectly. Lord, I wish I could get my glasses back so that I could
see the fun.'

But there was no fun to see. The two boats ran ashore about a
hundred yards apart, and Mr. Hospice alone jumped out of the
nearest one. Even the robbers listened as he began shouting. His
voice reached his friends across the hot air with a brittle, almost
microphonic sound. 'I'm going to walk thlowly up the beach while
you walk thlowly down to that farther boat. I'll thet the pathe. You
mutht all be thafe in the boat by the time I reach the niggerth.'

'Must! Must!' exclaimed Leonard furiously. 'What does he
mean—*must*? Are we to trot about the beach at his orders like a
flock of sheep? I shan't move a step.'

'Well, I shall,' said the Major. 'And I advise the ladies. . . .'

But the ladies needed no advice; they were already gingerly filing
between the bars of their living prison. A few robbers walked with
them, shuffling along packed closely against their victims, treading
on their heels, nudging their ribs, thrusting their chins into their
back hair—meaning no harm, but impelled to this almost lover-like
contiguity by their naïve curiosity.

'Not too fatht,' shrilled Mr. Hospice. 'Keep all together, and
watch me.' He shouted in pidgin Arabic to the robbers. A group of
them left the picnickers and started to meet him, but he at once
retreated towards the boat. The Arabs, understanding the position,

stood still, watching their victims receding, their reward approaching. Leonard stood sullenly against the rock, wondering what gesture of valour and authority remained to him to make.

'Oh—*oh*—Mr. Lumley,' Miss Dancey called back. '*Don't* stay there by yourself. . . . You'll be *killed*.'

'I must stand by Hospice,' said Leonard. This idea occurred to him one second before he put it into words.

The retreat and approach, regulated to synchronize, were slow, but at last the picnickers were safe in the boat and Mr. Hospice reached the robber group.

'Good Lord, Mithter Lumley—you thtill here? Why didn't you go with the otherth?'

'Because I'm a man and not a sheep.'

Mr. Hospice said nothing! He was counting out money into the chief robber's hand. All the Arabs wanted to look at the money; they craned and tiptoed behind each other like excited children. Leonard stood outside the group, trying to keep his looks in keeping with his latest gesture—'Standing By a Fellow Man.' The robbers, finding themselves all bowed by curiosity and avarice to one centre, suddenly awoke to the fact that in the messenger they had another hostage. Why not send Leonard back to the ship for another twenty pounds ransom? And then seize Leonard and send the sailor. What a delightfully easy way of making money, thought the simple fellows. Holding Mr. Hospice by every outlying fold in his clothes, they expounded their idea to him, pointing vigorously to Leonard. But just as Leonard was wondering what this (probably flattering) attention meant, Mr. Hospice, lithe as a fish, burst himself out of his clawed-at coat and kicked the robber chief in the stomach.

'Run for it, Lumley,' he shrieked—and ran.

Mr. Leonard Lumley's legs ran after him, bearing his reluctant body which still throbbed with the thought—'An Englishman never turns his back on danger.' Luckily, his legs knew better. They had never run so fast since they had had the honour of carrying Leonard.

A few of the Arabs, rather half-heartedly, pursued the fugitives, but most of them at once relinquished their too complex plan of seizing alternate hostages and earning ransom after ransom to infinity. They had had a remunerative morning's work, after all. Some of them came, shouting uncertainly, to the sea's edge, but Mr. Hospice and Leonard were being rowed swiftly away. The picnickers were already safe on board the *Meritoria*.

'I thought there'd be trouble,' panted Leonard. 'As it turned out, I was quite right to stay and back you up.'

'Very noble of you, I'm thure.'

'I can't imagine why you didn't bring back a few guns and men as I told you to.'

'My dear thir, thothe bruteth would have cut all your throatth at the firtht shot. They had you penned up like pigth in a thty. Twenty poundth for the lot of you wath only a pound apiethe, after all. Worth that, to get free without bloodshed. Tho the Thkipper thought, at leatht.'

'Pigs in a sty.' Leonard was struck dumb by the outrageous description. What a detestable young man this was! He little knew that the kind Mr. Hospice was suppressing the captain's actual message—'Can't you arrange to pay up nineteen pounds nineteen shillings and elevenpence—and let 'em keep that dam-fool Lumley?'

Leonard and Mr. Hospice, on the deck of the *Meritoria*, found themselves the centre of a frenzied group of ex-picnickers and their friends. 'Oh—*oh*—OH—*what* an adventure.'

'On the contrary——' began Leonard—but his world suddenly played him false. It wavered, whirled, slipped upward, crashed, as he fell flat on the deck in the midst of his flock. Before he became quite unconscious, he heard two voices—good and evil—like the voices described by poets as A Voice and Another Voice.

'Oh—*oh*—poor *darling* Mr. Lumley—he's been so *wonderful*. . . .'

'Sunstroke.' That's what comes of being such a —— fool as not to wear a topee. . . .'

'On the contrary,' gargled Leonard—but he was obliged to reserve his retort for several days. And by that time it was not necessary, for Leonard's convalescence was brightened by the discovery that it was the intention of his flock to present him with a solid silver cigarette-case, in recognition of his splendid behaviour and competent leadership in the hour of danger. Even Mr. Hospice was to be given a pair of enamel cuff-links.

W. SOMERSET MAUGHAM
Jane

I REMEMBER very well the occasion on which I first saw Jane Fowler. It is indeed only because the details of the glimpse I had of her then are so clear that I trust my recollection at all, for, looking back, I must confess that I find it hard to believe that it has not played me a fantastic trick. I had lately returned to London from China and was drinking a dish of tea with Mrs. Tower. Mrs. Tower had been seized with the prevailing passion for decoration; and, with the ruthlessness of her sex, had sacrificed chairs in which she had comfortably sat for years, tables, cabinets, ornaments on which her eyes had dwelt in peace since she was married, pictures that had been familiar to her for a generation; and delivered herself into the hands of an expert. Nothing remained in her drawing-room with which she had any association, or to which any sentiment was attached; and she had invited me that day to see the fashionable glory in which she now lived. Everything that could be pickled was pickled and what couldn't be pickled was painted. Nothing matched, but everything harmonized.

'Do you remember that ridiculous drawing-room suite that I used to have?' asked Mrs. Tower.

The curtains were sumptuous yet severe; the sofa was covered with Italian brocade; the chair on which I sat was in *petit point*. The room was beautiful, opulent without garishness and original without affectation; yet to me it lacked something; and while I praised with my lips I asked myself why I so much preferred the rather shabby chintz of the despised suite, the Victorian watercolours that I had known so long, and the ridiculous Dresden china that had adorned the chimney-piece. I wondered what it was that I missed in all these rooms that the decorators were turning out with a profitable industry. Was it heart? But Mrs. Tower looked about her happily.

'Don't you like my alabaster lamps?' she said. 'They give such a soft light.'

'Personally, I have a weakness for a light that you can see by,' I smiled.

'It's so difficult to combine that with a light that you can't be too much seen by,' laughed Mrs. Tower.

I had no notion what her age was. When I was quite a young man she was a married woman a good deal older than I, but now she treated me as her contemporary. She constantly said that she made no secret of her age, which was forty, and then added with a smile that all women took five years off. She never sought to conceal the fact that she dyed her hair (it was a very pretty brown with reddish tints), and she said she did this because hair was hideous while it was going grey; as soon as hers was white she would cease to dye it.

'Then they'll say what a young face I have.'

Meanwhile it was painted, though with discretion, and her eyes owed not a little of their vivacity to art. She was a handsome woman, exquisitely gowned, and in the sombre glow of the alabaster lamps did not look a day more than the forty she gave herself.

'It is only at my dressing-table that I can suffer the naked brightness of a thirty-two-candle electric bulb,' she added with smiling cynicism. 'There I need it to tell me first the hideous truth and then to enable me to take the necessary steps to correct it.'

We gossiped pleasantly about our common friends and Mrs. Tower brought me up to date in the scandal of the day. After roughing it here and there it was very agreeable to sit in a comfortable chair, the fire burning brightly on the hearth, charming tea-things set out on a charming table, and talk with this amusing, attractive woman. She treated me as a prodigal returned from his husks and was disposed to make much of me. She prided herself on her dinner-parties; she took no less trouble to have her guests suitably assorted than to give them excellent food; and there were few persons who did not look upon it as a treat to be bidden to one of them. Now she fixed a date and asked me whom I would like to meet.

'There's only one thing I must tell you. If Jane Fowler is still here I shall have to put it off.'

'Who is Jane Fowler?' I asked.

Mrs. Tower gave a rueful smile.

'Jane Fowler is my cross.'

'Oh!'

'Do you remember a photograph that I used to have on the piano before I had my room done, of a woman in a tight dress with tight sleeves and a gold locket, with her hair drawn back from a broad forehead and her ears showing and spectacles on a rather blunt nose? Well, that was Jane Fowler.'

'You had so many photographs about the room in your unregenerate days,' I said, vaguely.

'It makes me shudder to think of them. I've made them into a huge brown-paper parcel and hidden them in an attic.'

'Well, who is Jane Fowler?' I asked again, smiling.

'She's my sister-in-law. She was my husband's sister and she married a manufacturer in the North. She's been a widow for many years, and she's very well-to-do.'

'And why is she your cross?'

'She's worthy, she's dowdy, she's provincial. She looks twenty years older than I do and she's quite capable of telling any one she meets that we were at school together. She has an overwhelming sense of family affection and because I am her only living connexion she's devoted to me. When she comes to London it never occurs to her that she should stay anywhere but here—she thinks it would hurt my feelings—and she'll pay me visits of three or four weeks. We sit here and she knits and reads. And sometimes she insists on taking me to dine at Claridge's and she looks like a funny old charwoman and every one I particularly don't want to be seen by is sitting at the next table. When we are driving home she says she loves giving me a little treat. With her own hands she makes me tea-cosies that I am forced to use when she is here and doilies and centrepieces for the dining-room table.'

Mrs. Tower paused to take breath.

'I should have thought a woman of your tact would find a way to deal with a situation like that.'

'Ah, but don't you see, I haven't a chance. She's so immeasurably kind. She has a heart of gold. She bores me to death, but I wouldn't for anything let her suspect it.'

'And when does she arrive?'

'To-morrow.'

But the answer was hardly out of Mrs. Tower's mouth when the bell rang. There were sounds in the hall of a slight commotion and in a minute or two the butler ushered in an elderly lady.

'Mrs. Fowler,' he announced.

'Jane,' cried Mrs. Tower, springing to her feet. 'I wasn't expecting you to-day.'

'So your butler has just told me. I certainly said to-day in my letter.'

Mrs. Tower recovered her wits.

'Well, it doesn't matter. I'm very glad to see you whenever you come. Fortunately, I'm doing nothing this evening.'

'You mustn't let me give you any trouble. If I can have a boiled egg for my dinner that's all I shall want.'

A faint grimace for a moment distorted Mrs. Tower's handsome features. A boiled egg!

'Oh, I think we can do a little better than that.'

I chuckled inwardly when I recollected that the two ladies were contemporaries. Mrs. Fowler looked a good fifty-five. She was a rather big woman; she wore a black straw hat with a wide brim and from it a black lace veil hung over her shoulders, a cloak that oddly combined severity with fussiness, a long black dress, voluminous as though she wore several petticoats under it, and stout boots. She was evidently short-sighted, for she looked at you through large gold-rimmed spectacles.

'Won't you have a cup of tea?' asked Mrs. Tower.

'If it wouldn't be too much trouble. I'll take off my mantle.'

She began by stripping her hands of the black gloves she wore, and then took off her cloak. Round her neck was a solid gold chain from which hung a large gold locket in which I felt certain was a photograph of her deceased husband. Then she took off her hat and placed it neatly with her gloves and cloak on the sofa corner. Mrs. Tower pursed her lips. Certainly those garments did not go very well with the austere but sumptuous beauty of Mrs. Tower's redecorated drawing-room. I wondered where on earth Mrs. Fowler had found the extraordinary clothes she wore. They were not old and the materials were expensive. It was astounding to think that dressmakers still made things that had not been worn for a quarter of a century. Mrs. Fowler's grey hair was very plainly done, showing all her forehead and her ears, with a parting in the middle. It had evidently never known the tongs of Monsieur Marcel. Now her eyes fell on the tea-table with its teapot of Georgian silver and its cups in old Worcester.

'What have you done with the tea-cosy I gave you last time I came up, Marion?' she asked. 'Don't you use it?'

'Yes, I used it every day, Jane,' answered Mrs. Tower glibly.

'Unfortunately we had an accident with it a little while ago. It got burnt.'

'But the last one I gave you got burnt.'

'I'm afraid you'll think us very careless.'

'It doesn't really matter,' smiled Mrs. Fowler. 'I shall enjoy making you another. I'll go to Liberty's to-morrow and buy some silks.'

Mrs. Tower kept her face bravely.

'I don't deserve it, you know. Doesn't your vicar's wife need one?'

'Oh, I've just made her one,' said Mrs. Fowler brightly.

I noticed that when she smiled she showed white, small, and regular teeth. They were a real beauty. Her smile was certainly very sweet.

But I felt it high time for me to leave the two ladies to themselves, so I took my leave.

Early next morning Mrs. Tower rang me up and I heard at once from her voice that she was in high spirits.

'I've got the most wonderful news for you,' she said. 'Jane is going to be married.'

'Nonsense.'

'Her fiancé is coming to dine here to-night to be introduced to me and I want you to come too.'

'Oh, but I shall be in the way.'

'No, you won't. Jane suggested herself that I should ask you. Do come.'

She was bubbling over with laughter.

'Who is he?'

'I don't know. She tells me he's an architect. Can you imagine the sort of man Jane would marry?'

I had nothing to do and I could trust Mrs. Tower to give me a good dinner.

When I arrived Mrs. Tower, very splendid in a tea-gown a little too young for her, was alone.

'Jane is putting the finishing touches to her appearance. I'm longing for you to see her. She's all in a flutter. She says he adores her. His name is Gilbert and when she speaks of him her voice gets all funny and tremulous. It makes me want to laugh.'

'I wonder what he's like.'

'Oh, I'm sure I know. Very big and massive, with a bald head and an immense gold chain across an immense tummy. A large, fat, clean-shaven, red face and a booming voice.'

Mrs. Fowler came in. She wore a very stiff black silk dress with a wide skirt and a train. At the neck it was cut into a timid V and the sleeves came down to the elbows. She wore a necklace of diamonds set in silver. She carried in her hands a long pair of black gloves and a fan of black ostrich feathers. She managed (as so few people do) to look exactly what she was. You could never have thought her anything in the world but the respectable relict of a north-country manufacturer of ample means.

'You've really got quite a pretty neck, Jane,' said Mrs. Tower with a kindly smile.

It was indeed astonishingly young when you compared it with her weather-beaten face. It was smooth and unlined and the skin was white. And I noticed then that her head was very well placed on her shoulders.

'Has Marion told you my news?' she said, turning to me with that really charming smile of hers as if we were already old friends.

'I must congratulate you,' I said.

'Wait to do that till you've seen my young man.'

'I think it's too sweet to hear you talk of your young man,' smiled Mrs. Tower.

Mrs. Fowler's eyes certainly twinkled behind her preposterous spectacles.

'Don't expect any one too old. You wouldn't like me to marry a decrepit old gentleman with one foot in the grave, would you?'

This was the only warning she gave us. Indeed, there was no time for any further discussion, for the butler flung open the door and in a loud voice announced:

'Mr. Gilbert Napier.'

There entered a youth in a very well-cut dinner jacket. He was slight, not very tall, with fair hair in which there was a hint of a natural wave, clean-shaven and blue-eyed. He was not particularly good-looking, but he had a pleasant, amiable face. In ten years he would probably be wizened and sallow; but now, in extreme youth, he was fresh and clean and blooming. For he was certainly not more than twenty-four. My first thought was that this was the son of Jane Fowler's fiancé (I had not known he was a widower) come to say that his father was prevented from dining by a sudden attack of gout. But his eyes fell immediately on Mrs. Fowler, his face lit up, and he went towards her with both hands outstretched. Mrs. Fowler gave him hers, a demure smile on her lips, and turned to her sister-in-law.

'This is my young man, Marion,' she said.

He held out his hand.

'I hope you'll like me, Mrs. Tower,' he said. 'Jane tells me you're the only relation she has in the world.'

Mrs. Tower's face was wonderful to behold. I saw then to admiration how bravely good breeding and social usage could combat the instincts of the natural woman. For the astonishment and then the dismay that for an instant she could not conceal were quickly driven away, and her face assumed an expression of affable welcome. But she was evidently at a loss for words. It was not unnatural if Gilbert felt a certain embarrassment, and I was too busy preventing myself from laughing to think of anything to say. Mrs. Fowler alone kept perfectly calm.

'I know you'll like him, Marion. There's no one enjoys good food more than he does.' She turned to the young man. 'Marion's dinners are famous.'

'I know,' he beamed.

Mrs. Tower made some quick rejoinder and we went downstairs. I shall not soon forget the exquisite comedy of that meal. Mrs. Tower could not make up her mind whether the pair of them were playing a practical joke on her or whether Jane by wilfully concealing her fiancé's age had hoped to make her look foolish. But then Jane never jested and she was incapable of doing a malicious thing. Mrs. Tower was amazed, exasperated, and perplexed. But she had recovered her self-control, and for nothing would she have forgotten that she was a perfect hostess whose duty it was to make her party go. She talked vivaciously; but I wondered if Gilbert Napier saw how hard and vindictive was the expression of her eyes behind the mask of friendliness that she turned to him. She was measuring him. She was seeking to delve into the secret of his soul. I could see that she was in a passion, for under her rouge her cheeks glowed with an angry red.

'You've got a very high colour, Marion,' said Jane, looking at her amiably through her great round spectacles.

'I dressed in a hurry. I dare say I put on too much rouge.'

'Oh, is it rouge? I thought it was natural. Otherwise I shouldn't have mentioned it.' She gave Gilbert a shy little smile. 'You know, Marion and I were at school together. You would never think it to look at us now, would you? But of course I've lived a very quiet life.'

I do not know what she meant by these remarks; it was almost incredible that she made them in complete simplicity; but anyhow they goaded Mrs. Tower to such a fury that she flung her own vanity to the winds. She smiled brightly.

'We shall neither of us see fifty again, Jane,' she said.

If the observation was meant to discomfit the widow it failed.

'Gilbert says I mustn't acknowledge to more than forty-nine for his sake,' she answered blandly.

Mrs. Tower's hands trembled slightly, but she found a retort.

'There is of course a certain disparity of age between you,' she smiled.

'Twenty-seven years,' said Jane. 'Do you think it's too much? Gilbert says I'm very young for my age. I told you I shouldn't like to marry a man with one foot in the grave.'

I was really obliged to laugh and Gilbert laughed too. His laughter was frank and boyish. It looked as though he were amused at everything Jane said. But Mrs. Tower was almost at the end of her tether and I was afraid that unless relief came she would for once forget that she was a woman of the world. I came to the rescue as best I could.

'I suppose you're very busy buying your trousseau,' I said.

'No. I wanted to get my things from the dressmaker in Liverpool I've been to ever since I was first married. But Gilbert won't let me. He's very masterful, and of course he has wonderful taste.'

She looked at him with a little affectionate smile, demurely, as though she were a girl of seventeen.

Mrs. Tower went quite pale under her make-up.

'We're going to Italy for our honeymoon. Gilbert has never had a chance of studying Renaissance architecture and of course it's important for an architect to see things for himself. And we shall stop in Paris on the way and get my clothes there.'

'Do you expect to be away long?'

'Gilbert has arranged with his office to stay away for six months. It will be such a treat for him, won't it? You see, he's never had more than a fortnight's holiday before.'

'Why not?' asked Mrs. Tower in a tone that no effort of will could prevent from being icy.

'He's never been able to afford it, poor dear.'

'Ah!' said Mrs. Tower, and into the exclamation put volumes.

Coffee was served and the ladies went upstairs. Gilbert and I began to talk in the desultory way in which men talk who have nothing whatever to say to one another; but in two minutes a note was brought in to me by the butler. It was from Mrs. Tower and ran as follows:

'Come upstairs quickly and then go as soon as you can. Take him with you. Unless I have it out with Jane at once I shall have a fit.'

I told a facile lie.

'Mrs. Tower has a headache and wants to go to bed. I think if you don't mind we'd better clear out.'

'Certainly,' he answered.

We went upstairs and five minutes later were on the doorstep. I called a taxi and offered the young man a lift.

'No, thanks,' he answered. 'I'll just walk to the corner and jump on a bus.'

Mrs. Tower sprang to the fray as soon as she heard the front-door close behind us.

'Are you crazy, Jane?' she cried.

'Not more than most people who don't habitually live in a lunatic asylum, I trust,' Jane answered blandly.

'May I ask why you're going to marry this young man?' asked Mrs. Tower with formidable politeness.

'Partly because he won't take no for an answer. He's asked me five times. I grew positively tired of refusing him.'

'And why do you think he's so anxious to marry you?'

'I amuse him.'

Mrs. Tower gave an exclamation of annoyance.

'He's an unscrupulous rascal. I very nearly told him so to his face.'

'You would have been wrong, and it wouldn't have been very polite.

'He's penniless and you're rich. You can't be such a besotted fool as not to see that he's marrying you for your money.'

Jane remained perfectly composed. She observed her sister-in-law's agitation with detachment.

'I don't think he is, you know,' she replied. 'I think he's very fond of me.'

'You're an old woman, Jane.'

'I'm the same age as you are, Marion,' she smiled.

'I've never let myself go. I'm very young for my age. No one would think I was more than forty. But even I wouldn't dream of marrying a boy twenty years younger than myself.'

'Twenty-seven,' corrected Jane.

'Do you mean to tell me that you can bring yourself to believe that it's possible for a young man to care for a woman old enough to be his mother?'

'I've lived very much in the country for many years. I dare say there's a great deal about human nature that I don't know. They tell me there's a man called Freud, an Austrian, I believe . . .'

But Mrs. Tower interrupted her without any politeness at all.

'Don't be ridiculous, Jane. It's so undignified. It's so ungraceful. I always thought you were a sensible woman. Really, you're the last person I should ever have thought likely to fall in love with a boy.'

'But I'm not in love with him. I've told him that. Of course I like him very much or I wouldn't think of marrying him. I thought it only fair to tell him quite plainly what my feelings were towards him.'

Mrs. Tower gasped. The blood rushed to her head and her breathing oppressed her. She had no fan, but she seized the evening paper and vigorously fanned herself with it.

'If you're not in love with him why do you want to marry him?'

'I've been a widow a very long time and I've led a very quiet life. I thought I'd like a change.'

'If you want to marry just to be married why don't you marry a man of your own age?'

'No man of my own age has asked me five times. In fact, no man of my own age has asked me at all.'

Jane chuckled as she answered. It drove Mrs. Tower to the final pitch of frenzy.

'Don't laugh, Jane. I won't have it. I don't think you can be right in your mind. It's dreadful.'

It was altogether too much for her and she burst into tears. She knew that at her age it was fatal to cry, her eyes would be swollen for twenty-four hours and she would look a sight. But there was no help for it. She wept. Jane remained perfectly calm. She looked at

Marion through her large spectacles and reflectively smoothed the lap of her black silk dress.

'You're going to be so dreadfully unhappy,' Mrs. Tower sobbed, dabbing her eyes cautiously in the hope that the black on her lashes would not smudge.

'I don't think so, you know,' Jane answered in those equable, mild tones of hers, as if there were a little smile behind the words. 'We've talked it over very thoroughly. I always think I'm a very easy person to live with. I think I shall make Gilbert very happy and comfortable. He's never had any one to look after him properly. We're only marrying after mature consideration. And we've decided that if either of us wants his liberty the other will place no osbstacles in the way of his getting it.'

Mrs. Tower had by now recovered herself sufficiently to make a cutting remark.

'How much has he persuaded you to settle on him?'

'I wanted to settle a thousand a year on him, but he wouldn't hear of it. He was quite upset when I made the suggestion. He says he can earn quite enough for his own needs.'

'He's more cunning than I thought,' said Mrs. Tower acidly.

Jane paused a little and looked at her sister-in-law with kindly but resolute eyes.

'You see, my dear, it's different for you,' she said. 'You've never been so very much a widow, have you?'

Mrs. Tower looked at her. She blushed a little. She even felt slightly uncomfortable. But of course Jane was much too simple to intend an innuendo. Mrs. Tower gathered herself together with dignity.

'I'm so upset that I really must go to bed,' she said. 'We'll resume the conversation to-morrow morning.'

'I'm afraid that won't be very convenient, dear. Gilbert and I are going to get the licence to-morrow morning.'

Mrs. Tower threw up her hands in a gesture of dismay, but she found nothing more to say.

The marriage took place at a registrar's office. Mrs. Tower and I were the witnesses. Gilbert in a smart blue suit looked absurdly young and he was obviously nervous. It is a trying moment for any man. But Jane kept her admirable composure. She might have been in the habit of marrying as frequently as a woman of fashion. Only a slight colour on her cheeks suggested that beneath her calm was some faint excitement. It is a thrilling moment for any woman. She wore a very full dress of silver grey velvet in the cut of which I recognized the hand of the dressmaker in Liverpool (evidently a widow of unimpeachable character), who had made her gowns for so many years; but she had so far succumbed to the frivolity of the occasion as to wear a large picture hat covered with blue ostrich feathers. Her gold-rimmed spectacles made it extraordinarily grotesque. When the ceremony was over the registrar (somewhat taken aback, I thought, by the difference of age between the pair he was marrying) shook hands with her, tendering his strictly official congratulations; and the bridegroom, blushing slightly, kissed her. Mrs. Tower, resigned but implacable, kissed her; and then the bride looked at me expectantly. It was evidently fitting that I should kiss her too. I did. I confess that I felt a little shy as we walked out of the registrar's office past loungers who waited cynically to see the bridal pairs, and it was with relief that I stepped into Mrs. Tower's car. We drove to Victoria Station, for the happy couple were to go over to Paris by the two o'clock train, and Jane had insisted that the wedding-breakfast should be eaten at the station restaurant. She said it always made her nervous not to be on the platform in good time. Mrs. Tower, present only from a strong sense of family duty, was able to do little to make the party go off well; she ate nothing (for which I could not blame her, since the food was execrable, and anyway I hate champagne at luncheon) and talked in a strained voice. But Jane went through the menu conscientiously.

'I always think one should make a hearty meal before starting out on a journey,' she said.

We saw them off, and I drove Mrs. Tower back to her house.

'How long do you give it?' she said. 'Six months?'

'Let's hope for the best,' I smiled.

'Don't be so absurd. There can be no "best". You don't think he's marrying her for anything but her money, do you? Of course it can't last. My only hope is that she won't have to go through as much suffering as she deserves.'

I laughed. The charitable words were spoken in such a tone as to leave me in small doubt of Mrs. Tower's meaning.

'Well, if it doesn't last you'll have the consolation of saying: "I told you so,"' I said.

'I promise you I'll never do that.'

'Then you'll have the satisfaction of congratulating yourself on your self-control in not saying: "I told you so."'

'She's old and dowdy and dull.'

'Are you sure she's dull?' I said. 'It's true she doesn't say very much, but when she says anything it's very much to the point.'

'I've never heard her make a joke in my life.'

I was once more in the Far East when Gilbert and Jane returned from their honeymoon, and this time I remained away for nearly two years. Mrs. Tower was a bad correspondent and though I sent her an occasional picture-postcard I received no news from her. But I met her within a week of my return to London; I was dining out and found that I was seated next to her. It was an immense party, I think we were four-and-twenty, like the blackbirds in the pie, and, arriving somewhat late, I was too confused by the crowd in which I found myself to notice who was there. But when we sat down, looking round the long table I saw that a good many of my fellow guests were well known to the public from their photographs in the illustrated papers. Our hostess had a weakness for the persons technically known as celebrities and this was an unusually brilliant gathering. When Mrs. Tower and I had exchanged the conventional remarks that two people make when they have not seen one another for a couple of years I asked about Jane.

'She's very well,' said Mrs. Tower with a certain dryness.

'How has the marriage turned out?'

Mrs. Tower paused a little and took a salted almond from the dish in front of her.

'It appears to be quite a success.'

'You were wrong then?'

'I said it wouldn't last and I still say it won't last. It's contrary to human nature.'

'Is she happy?'

'They're both happy.'

'I suppose you don't see very much of them.'

'At first I saw quite a lot of them. But now . . .' Mrs. Tower pursed her lips a little. 'Jane is becoming very grand.'

'What *do* you mean?' I laughed.

'I think I should tell you that she's here to-night.'

'Here?'

I was startled. I looked round the table again. Our hostess was a delightful and an entertaining woman, but I could not imagine that she would be likely to invite to a dinner such as this the elderly and dowdy wife of an obscure architect. Mrs. Tower saw my perplexity and was shrewd enough to see what was in my mind. She smiled thinly.

'Look on the left of our host.'

I looked. Oddly enough, the woman who sat there had by her fantastic appearance attracted my attention the moment I was ushered into the crowded drawing-room. I thought I noticed a gleam of recognition in her eye, but to the best of my belief I had never seen her before. She was not a young woman, for her hair was iron-grey; it was cut very short and clustered thickly round her well-shaped head in tight curls. She made no attempt at youth, for she was conspicuous in that gathering by using neither lipstick, rouge, nor powder. Her face, not a particularly handsome one, was red and weather-beaten; but because it owed nothing to artifice had a naturalness that was very pleasing. It contrasted oddly with the whiteness of her shoulders. They were really magnificent. A woman of thirty might have been proud of them. But her dress was extraordinary. I had not seen often anything more audacious. It was cut very low, with short skirts, which were then the fashion, in black and yellow; it had almost the effect of fancy dress and yet so became her that though on any one else it would have been outrageous, on her it had the inevitable simplicity of nature. And to complete the impression of an eccentricity in which there was no pose and of an extravagance in which there was no ostentation she wore, attached by a broad black ribbon, a single eye-glass.

'You're not going to tell me *that* is your sister-in-law,' I gasped.

'That is Jane Napier,' said Mrs. Tower icily.

At that moment she was speaking. Her host was turned towards her with an anticipatory smile. A baldish white-haired man, with a sharp, intelligent face, who sat on her left, was leaning forward eagerly, and the couple who sat opposite, ceasing to talk with one another, listened intently. She said her say and they all, with a sudden movement, threw themselves back in their chairs and burst into vociferous laughter. From the other side of the table a man addressed Mrs. Tower: I recognized a famous statesman.

'Your sister-in-law has made another joke, Mrs. Tower,' he said.

Mrs. Tower smiled.

'She's priceless, isn't she?'

'Let me have a long drink of champagne and then for heaven's sake tell me all about it,' I said.

Well, this is how I gathered it had all happened. At the beginning of their honeymoon Gilbert took Jane to various dressmakers in Paris and he made no objection to her choosing a number of 'gowns' after her own heart; but he persuaded her to have a 'frock' or two made according to his own design. It appeared that he had a knack for that kind of work. He engaged a smart French maid. Jane had never had such a thing before. She did her own mending and when she wanted 'doing up' was in the habit of ringing for the housemaid. The dresses Gilbert had devised were very different from anything she had worn before; but he had been careful not to go too far too quickly, and because it pleased him she persuaded herself, though not without misgivings, to wear them in preference to those she had chosen herself. Of course she could not wear them with the voluminous petticoats she had been in the habit of using, and these, though it cost her an anxious moment, she discarded.

'Now, if you please,' said Mrs. Tower, with something very like a sniff of disapproval, 'she wears nothing but thin silk tights. It's a wonder to me she doesn't catch her death of cold at her age.'

Gilbert and the French maid taught her how to wear her clothes, and, unexpectedly enough, she was very quick at learning. The French maid was in raptures over Madame's arms and shoulders. It was a scandal not to show anything so fine.

'Wait a little, Alphonsine,' said Gilbert. 'The next lot of clothes I design for Madame we'll make the most of her.'

The spectacles of course were dreadful. No one could look really well in gold-rimmed spectacles. Gilbert tried some with tortoise-shell rims. He shook his head.

'They'd look all right on a girl,' he said. 'You're too old to wear spectacles, Jane.' Suddenly he had an inspiration. 'By George, I've got it. You must wear an eye-glass.'

'Oh, Gilbert, I couldn't.'

She looked at him, and his excitement, the excitement of the artist, made her smile. He was so sweet to her she wanted to do what she could to please him.

'I'll try,' she said.

When they went to an optician and, suited with the right size, she placed an eye-glass jauntily in her eye Gilbert clapped his hands. There and then, before the astonished shopman, he kissed her on both cheeks.

'You look wonderful,' he cried.

So they went down to Italy and spent happy months studying Renaissance and Baroque architecture. Jane not only grew accustomed to her changed appearance, but found she liked it. At first she was a little shy when she went into the dining-room of an hotel and people turned round to stare at her, no one had ever raised an eyelid to look at her before, but presently she found that the sensation was not disagreeable. Ladies came up to her and asked her where she got her dress.

'Do you like it?' she answered demurely. 'My husband designed it for me.'

'I should like to copy it if you don't mind.'

Jane had certainly for many years lived a very quiet life, but she was by no means lacking in the normal instincts of her sex. She had her answer ready.

'I'm so sorry, but my husband's very particular and he won't hear of any one copying my frocks. He wants me to be unique.'

She had an idea that people would laugh when she said this, but they didn't; they merely answered:

'Oh, of course I quite understand. You *are* unique.'

But she saw them making mental notes of what she wore, and for some reason this quite 'put her about'. For once in her life that she wasn't wearing what everybody else did, she reflected, she didn't see why everybody else should want to wear what she did.

'Gilbert,' she said, quite sharply for her, 'next time you're designing dresses for me I wish you'd design things that people *can't* copy.'

'The only way to do that is to design things that only you can wear.'

'Can't you do that?'

'Yes, if you'll do something for me.'

'What is it?'

'Cut off your hair.'

I think this was the first time that Jane jibbed. Her hair was long and thick and as a girl she had been quite vain of it; to cut it off was a very drastic proceeding. This really was burning her boats behind her. In her case it was not the first step that cost so much, it was the last; but she took it ('I know Marion will think me a perfect fool, and I shall *never* be able to go to Liverpool again,' she said), and when they passed through Paris on their way home Gilbert led her (she felt quite sick, her heart was beating so fast) to the best hairdresser in the world. She came out of his shop with a jaunty, saucy, impudent head of crisp grey curls. Pygmalion had finished his fantastic masterpiece: Galatea was come to life.

'Yes,' I said, 'but that isn't enough to explain why Jane is here to-night amid this crowd of duchesses, cabinet ministers, and suchlike; nor why she is sitting on one side of her host with an Admiral of the Fleet on the other.'

'Jane is a humorist,' said Mrs. Tower. 'Didn't you see them all laughing at what she said?'

There was no doubt now of the bitterness in Mrs. Tower's heart.

'When Jane wrote and told me they were back from their honeymoon I thought I must ask them both to dinner. I didn't much like the idea, but I felt it had to be done. I knew the party would be deadly and I wasn't going to sacrifice any of the people who really mattered. On the other hand, I didn't want Jane to think I hadn't any nice friends. You know I never have more than eight, but on this occasion I thought it would make things go better if I had twelve. I'd been too busy to see Jane until the evening of the party. She kept us all waiting a little—that was Gilbert's cleverness—and at last she sailed in. You could have knocked me down with a feather. She made the rest of the women look dowdy and provincial. She made me feel like a painted old trollop.'

Mrs. Tower drank a little champagne.

'I wish I could describe the frock to you. It would have been quite impossible on any one else; on her it was perfect. And the eyeglass! I'd known her for thirty-five years and I'd never seen her without spectacles.'

'But you knew she had a good figure.'

'How should I? I'd never seen her except in the clothes you first saw her in. Did *you* think she had a good figure? She seemed not to be unconscious of the sensation she made but to take it as a matter of course. I thought of my dinner and I heaved a sigh of relief. Even if she was a little heavy in hand, with that appearance it didn't so very much matter. She was sitting at the other end of the table and I heard a good deal of laughter, I was glad to think that the other people were playing up well; but after dinner I was a good deal taken aback when no less than three men came up to me and told me that my sister-in-law was priceless, and did I think she would allow them to call on her? I didn't quite know whether I was standing on my head or my heels. Twenty-four hours later our hostess of to-night rang me up and said she had heard my sister-in-law was in London and she was priceless and would I ask her to luncheon to meet her? She has an infallible instinct, that woman: in a month every one was talking about Jane. I am here to-night, not because I've known our hostess for twenty years and have asked her to dinner a hundred times, but because I'm Jane's sister-in-law.'

Poor Mrs. Tower. The position was galling, and though I could not help being amused, for the tables were turned on her with a vengeance, I felt that she deserved my sympathy.

'People never can resist those who make them laugh,' I said, trying to console her.

'She never makes *me* laugh.'

Once more from the top of the table I heard a guffaw and guessed that Jane had said another amusing thing.

'Do you mean to say that you are the only person who doesn't think her funny?' I asked, smiling.

'Had it struck *you* that she was a humorist?'

'I'm bound to say it hadn't.'

'She says just the same things as she's said for the last thirty-five years. I laugh when I see every one else does because I don't want to seem a perfect fool, but I am not amused.'

'Like Queen Victoria,' I said.

It was a foolish jest and Mrs. Tower was quite right sharply to tell me so. I tried another tack.

'Is Gilbert here?' I asked, looking down the table.

'Gilbert was asked because she won't go out without him, but to-night he's at a dinner of the Architects' Institute or whatever it's called.'

'I'm dying to renew my acquaintance with her.'

'Go and talk to her after dinner. She'll ask you to her Tuesdays.'

'Her Tuesdays?'

'She's at home every Tuesday evening. You'll meet there every one you ever heard of. They're the best parties in London. She's done in one year what I've failed to do in twenty.'

'But what you tell me is really miraculous. How has it been done?'

Mrs. Tower shrugged her handsome but adipose shoulders.

'I shall be glad if you'll tell me,' she replied.

After dinner I tried to make my way to the sofa on which Jane was sitting, but I was intercepted and it was not till a little later that my hostess came up to me and said:

'I must introduce you to the star of my party. Do you know Jane Napier? She's priceless. She's much more amusing than your comedies.'

I was taken up to the sofa. The admiral who had been sitting beside her at dinner was with her still. He showed no sign of moving and Jane, shaking hands with me, introduced me to him.

'Do you know Sir Reginald Frobisher?'

We began to chat. It was the same Jane as I had known before, perfectly simple, homely, and unaffected, but her fantastic appearance certainly gave a peculiar savour to what she said. Suddenly I found myself shaking with laughter. She had made a remark, sensible and to the point, but not in the least witty, which her manner of saying and the bland look she gave me through her eye-glass made perfectly irresistible. I felt light-hearted and buoyant. When I left her she said to me:

'If you've got nothing better to do, come and see us on Tuesday evening. Gilbert will be so glad to see you.'

'When he's been a month in London he'll know that he *can* have nothing better to do,' said the admiral.

So, on Tuesday but rather late, I went to Jane's. I confess I was a little surprised at the company. It was quite a remarkable collection of writers, painters, and politicians, actors, great ladies, and great beauties: Mrs. Tower was right, it was a grand party; I had seen nothing like it in London since Stafford House was sold. No particular entertainment was provided. The refreshments were adequate without being luxurious. Jane in her quiet way seemed to be enjoying herself; I could not see that she took a great deal of trouble with her guests, but they seemed to like being there, and the gay, pleasant party did not break up till two in the morning. After that I saw much of her. I not only went often to her house, but seldom went out to luncheon or to dinner without meeting her. I am an amateur of humour and I sought to discover in what lay her peculiar gift. It was impossible to repeat anything she said, for the fun, like certain wines, would not travel. She had no gift for epigram. She never made a brilliant repartee. There was no malice in her remarks nor sting in her rejoinders. There are those who think that

impropriety, rather than brevity, is the soul of wit; but she never
said a thing that could have brought a blush to a Victorian cheek. I
think her humour was unconscious and I am sure it was unpremeditated. It flew like a butterfly from flower to flower, obedient
only to its own caprice and pursuant of neither method nor
intention. It depended on the way she spoke and on the way she
looked. Its subtlety gained by the flaunting and extravagant appearance that Gilbert had achieved for her; but her appearance was
only an element in it. Now of course she was the fashion and people
laughed if she but opened her mouth. They no longer wondered
that Gilbert had married a wife so much older than himself. They
saw that Jane was a woman with whom age did not count. They
thought him a devilish lucky young fellow. The admiral quoted
Shakespeare to me: 'Age cannot wither her, nor custom stale her
infinite variety.' Gilbert was delighted with her success. As I came
to know him better I grew to like him. It was quite evident that he
was neither a rascal nor a fortune-hunter. He was not only
immensely proud of Jane but genuinely devoted to her. His kindness
to her was touching. He was a very unselfish and sweet-tempered
young man.

'Well, what do you think of Jane now?' he said to me once, with
boyish triumph.

'I don't know which of you is more wonderful,' I said. 'You or she.'

'Oh, I'm nothing.'

'Nonsense. You don't think I'm such a fool as not to see that it's
you, and you only, who've made Jane what she is.'

'My only merit is that I saw what was there when it wasn't
obvious to the naked eye,' he answered.

'I can understand your seeing that she had in her the possibility
of that remarkable appearance, but how in the world have you
made her into a humorist?'

'But I always thought the things she said a perfect scream. She
was always a humorist.'

'You're the only person who ever thought so.'

Mrs. Tower, not without magnanimity, acknowledged that she
had been mistaken in Gilbert. She grew quite attached to him. But
notwithstanding appearances she never faltered in her opinion that
the marriage could not last. I was obliged to laugh at her.

'Why, I've never seen such a devoted couple,' I said.

'Gilbert is twenty-seven now. It's just the time for a pretty girl to

come along. Did you notice the other evening at Jane's that pretty
little niece of Sir Reginald's? I thought Jane was looking at them
both with a good deal of attention, and I wondered to myself.'

'I don't believe Jane fears the rivalry of any girl under the sun.'

'Wait and see,' said Mrs. Tower.

'You gave it six months.'

'Well, now I give it three years.'

When any one is very positive in an opinion it is only human nature
to wish him proved wrong. Mrs. Tower was really too cocksure. But
such a satisfaction was not mine, for the end that she had always
and confidently predicted to the ill-assorted match did in point of
fact come. Still, the fates seldom give us what we want in the way
we want it, and though Mrs. Tower could flatter herself that she
had been right, I think after all she would sooner have been wrong.
For things did not happen at all in the way she expected.

One day I received an urgent message from her and fortunately
went to see her at once. When I was shown into the room Mrs.
Tower rose from her chair and came towards me with the stealthy
swiftness of a leopard stalking his prey. I saw that she was excited.

'Jane and Gilbert have separated,' she said.

'Not really? Well, you were right after all.'

Mrs. Tower looked at me with an expression I could not
understand.

'Poor Jane,' I muttered.

'Poor Jane!' she repeated, but in tones of such derision that I was
dumbfounded.

She found some difficulty in telling me exactly what had occurred.

Gilbert had left her a moment before she leaped to the telephone
to summon me. When he entered the room, pale and distraught,
she saw at once that something terrible had happened. She knew
what he was going to say before he said it.

'Marion, Jane has left me.'

She gave him a little smile and took his hand.

'I knew you'd behave like a gentleman. It would have been
dreadful for her for people to think that *you* had left her.'

'I've come to you because I knew I could count on your
sympathy.'

'Oh, I don't blame you, Gilbert,' said Mrs. Tower, very kindly.
'It was bound to happen.'

He sighed.

'I suppose so. I couldn't hope to keep her always. She was too wonderful and I'm a perfectly commonplace fellow.'

Mrs. Tower patted his hand. He was really behaving beautifully.

'And what is going to happen now?'

'Well, she's going to divorce me.'

'Jane always said she'd put no obstacle in your way if ever you wanted to marry a girl.'

'You don't think it's likely I should ever be willing to marry any one else after being Jane's husband,' he answered.

Mrs. Tower was puzzled.

'Of course you mean that *you've* left Jane.'

'I? That's the last thing I should ever do.'

'Then why is she divorcing you?'

'She's going to marry Sir Reginald Frobisher as soon as the decree is made absolute.'

Mrs. Tower positively screamed. Then she felt so faint that she had to get her smelling salts.

'After all you've done for her?'

'I've done nothing for her.'

'Do you mean to say you're going to allow yourself to be made use of like that?'

'We arranged before we married that if either of us wanted his liberty the other should put no hindrance in the way.'

'But that was done on your account. Because you were twenty-seven years younger than she was.'

'Well, it's come in very useful for her,' he answered bitterly.

Mrs. Tower expostulated, argued, and reasoned; but Gilbert insisted that no rules applied to Jane, and he must do exactly what she wanted. He left Mrs. Tower prostrate. It relieved her a good deal to give me a full account of this interview. It pleased her to see that I was as surprised as herself and if I was not so indignant with Jane as she was she ascribed that to the criminal lack of morality incident to my sex. She was still in a state of extreme agitation when the door was opened and the butler showed in—Jane herself. She was dressed in black and white as no doubt befitted her slightly ambiguous position, but in a dress so original and fantastic, in a hat so striking, that I positively gasped at the sight of her. But she was as ever bland and collected. She came forward to kiss Mrs. Tower, but Mrs. Tower withdrew herself with icy dignity.

'Gilbert has been here,' she said.

'Yes, I know,' smiled Jane. 'I told him to come and see you. I'm going to Paris to-night and I want you to be very kind to him while I am away. I'm afraid just at first he'll be rather lonely and I shall feel more comfortable if I can count on your keeping an eye on him.'

Mrs. Tower clasped her hands.

'Gilbert has just told me something that I can hardly bring myself to believe. He tells me that you're going to divorce him to marry Reginald Frobisher.'

'Don't you remember, before I married Gilbert you advised me to marry a man of my own age. The admiral is fifty-three.'

'But, Jane, you owe everything to Gilbert,' said Mrs. Tower indignantly. 'You wouldn't exist without him. Without him to design your clothes, you'll be nothing.'

'Oh, he's promised to go on designing my clothes,' Jane answered blandly.

'No woman could want a better husband. He's always been kindness itself to you.'

'Oh, I know he's been sweet.'

'How *can* you be so heartless?'

'But I was never in love with Gilbert,' said Jane. 'I always told him that. I'm beginning to feel the need of the companionship of a man of my own age. I think I've probably been married to Gilbert long enough. The young have no conversation.' She paused a little and gave us both a charming smile. 'Of course I shan't lose sight of Gilbert. I've arranged that with Reginald. The admiral has a niece that would just suit him. As soon as we're married we'll ask them to stay with us at Malta—you know that the admiral is to have the Mediterranean Command—and I shouldn't be at all surprised if they fell in love with one another.'

Mrs. Tower gave a little sniff.

'And have you arranged with the admiral that if you want your liberty neither should put any hindrance in the way of the other?'

'I suggested it,' Jane answered with composure. 'But the admiral says he knows a good thing when he sees it and he won't want to marry any one else, and if any one wants to marry me—he has eight twelve-inch guns on his flagship and he'll discuss the matter at short range.' She gave us a look through her eye-glass which even the fear of Mrs. Tower's wrath could not prevent me from laughing at. 'I think the admiral's a very passionate man.'

Mrs. Tower indeed gave me an angry frown.

'I never thought you funny, Jane,' she said. 'I never understood why people laughed at the things you said.'

'I never thought I was funny myself, Marion,' smiled Jane, showing her bright, regular teeth. 'I am glad to leave London before too many people come round to our opinion.'

'I wish you'd tell me the secret of your astonishing success,' I said.

She turned to me with that bland, homely look I knew so well.

'You know, when I married Gilbert and settled in London and people began to laugh at what I said no one was more surprised than I was. I'd said the same things for thirty years and no one ever saw anything to laugh at. I thought it must be my clothes or my bobbed hair or my eye-glass. Then I discovered it was because I spoke the truth. It was so unusual that people thought it humorous. One of these days some one else will discover the secret, and when people habitually tell the truth of course there'll be nothing funny in it.'

'And why am I the only person not to think it funny,' asked Mrs. Tower.

Jane hesitated a little as though she were honestly searching for a satisfactory explanation.

'Perhaps you don't know the truth when you see it, Marion dear,' she answered in her mild, good-natured way.

It certainly gave her the last word. I felt that Jane would always have the last word. She *was* priceless.

HUGH WALPOLE

Mr. Oddy

THIS may seem to many people an old-fashioned story; it is perhaps for that reason that I tell it. I can recover here, it may be, for myself something of the world that is already romantic, already beyond one's reach, already precious for the things that one might have got out of it and didn't.

London of but a few years before the war! What a commonplace to point out its difference from the London of to-day and to emphasize the tiny period of time that made that difference!

We were all young and hopeful then, we could all live on a shilling a year and think ourselves well off, we could all sit in front of the lumbering horse buses and chat confidentially with the omniscient driver, we could all see Dan Leno in Pantomime and watch Farren dance at the Empire, we could all rummage among those cobwebby streets at the back of the Strand where Aldwych now flaunts her shining bosom and imagine Pendennis and Warrington, Copperfield and Traddles cheek by jowl with ourselves, we could all wait in the shilling queue for hours to see Ellen Terry in *Captain Brassbound* and Forbes Robertson in *Hamlet*, we could all cross the street without fear of imminent death, and above all we could all sink ourselves into that untidy higgledy-piggledy smoky and beery and gas-lampy London gone utterly and for ever.

But I have no wish to be sentimental about it; there is a new London which is just as interesting to its new citizens as the old London was to myself. It is my age that is the matter; before the war one was so *very* young.

I like, though, to try and recapture that time, and so, as a simple way to do it, I seize upon a young man; Tommy Brown we will call him. I don't know where Tommy Brown may be now; that Tommy Brown who lived as I did in two very small rooms in Glebe Place, Chelsea, who enjoyed hugely the sparse but economical meals provided so elegantly by two charming ladies at 'The Good Intent' down by the river, that charming hostelry whence looking through the bow windows you could see the tubby barges go floating down the river and the thin outline of Whistler's Battersea Bridge, and in the small room itself were surrounded by who knows what geniuses in the lump, geniuses of Art and Letters, of the Stage and of the Law.

For Tommy Brown in those days life was Paradisal.

He had come boldly from Cambridge to throw himself upon London's friendly bosom; despite all warnings to the contrary he was certain that it would be friendly; how could it be otherwise to so charming, so brilliant, so unusually attractive a young man? For Tommy was conceited beyond all that his youth warranted, conceited indeed without any reason at all.

He had, it is true, secured the post of reviewer to one of the London daily papers; this seemed to him when he looked back in later years a kind of miracle, but at the time no miracle at all, simply a just appreciation of his extraordinary talents. There was also reposing in one of the publisher's offices at that moment the manuscript of a novel, a novel that appeared to him of astonishing brilliance, written in the purest English, sparkling with wit, tense with drama.

These things were fine and reassuring enough, but there was more than that; he felt in himself the power to rise to the greatest heights; he could not see how anything could stop him, it was his destiny.

This pride of his might have suffered some severe shocks were it not that he spent all of his time with other young gentlemen quite as conceited as himself. I have heard talk of the present young generation and its agreeable consciousness of its own merits, but I doubt if it is anything in comparison with that little group of fifteen years ago. After all, the war has intervened—however young we may be and however greatly we may pretend this is an unstable world and for the moment heroics have departed from it. But for Tommy Brown and his friends the future was theirs and nobody could prevent it. Something pathetic in that as one looks back.

Tommy was not really so unpleasant a youth as I have described him—to his elders he must have appeared a baby, and his vitality at least they could envy. After all, why check his confidence? Life would do that heavily enough in its own good time.

Tommy, although he had no money and no prospects, was already engaged to a young woman, Miss Alice Smith. Alice Smith was an artist sharing with a girl friend a Chelsea studio, and she was as certain of her future as Tommy was of his.

They had met at a little Chelsea dance, and two days after the meeting they were engaged. She had no parents who mattered, and no money to speak of, so that the engagement was the easiest thing in the world.

Tommy, who had been in love before many times, knew, as he told his friend Jack Robinson so often as to bore that gentleman severely, that this time at last he knew what love was. Alice ordered him about—with her at any rate his conceit fell away—she had read his novel and pronounced it old-fashioned, the severest criticism she could possibly have made, and she thought his reviews amateur. He suffered then a good deal in her company. When he was away from her he told himself and everybody else that her critical judgement was marvellous, her comprehension of all the Arts quite astounding, but he left her sometimes with a miserable suspicion that perhaps after all he was not going to do anything very wonderful and that he would have to work very hard indeed to rise to her astonishing standards.

It was in such a mood of wholesome depression that he came one beautiful spring April day from the A.B.C. shop where he had been giving his Alice luncheon, and found his way to an old bookshop on the river-side round the corner from Oakley Street. This shop was kept by a gentleman called Mr. Burdett Coutts, and the grand associations of his name gave him from the very first a sort of splendour.

It was one of those old shops of which there are, thank God, still many examples surviving in London, in which the room was so small and the books so many that to move a step was to imperil your safety. Books ran in thick, tight rows from floor to ceiling everywhere, were piled in stacks upon the ground, and hung in perilous heaps over chairs and window ledges.

Mr. Burdett Coutts himself, a very stout and grizzled old man enveloped always in a grey shawl, crouched behind his spectacles in a far corner and took apparently no interest in anything save that he would snap the price at you if you brought him a volume and timorously inquired. He was not one of those old booksellers dear to the heart of Anatole France and other great men who would love to discourse to you of the beauties of 'The Golden Ass', the possibility of Homer being a lady, or the virtues of the second Hyperion over the first. Not at all; he ate biscuits which stuck in his grizzly beard, and wrote perpetually in a large moth-eaten ledger which was supposed by his customers to contain all the secrets of the universe.

It was just because Mr. Coutts never interfered with you that Tommy Brown loved his shop so dearly. If he had a true genuine passion that went far deeper than all his little superficial vanities and egotisms, it was his passion for books—books of any kind.

He had at this time no fine taste—all was fish that came to his net. The bundles of Thackeray and Dickens, parts tied up carelessly in coarse string, the old broken-backed volumes of Radcliffe and Barham and Galt, the red and gold Colburn's novelists, all these were exciting to him, just as exciting as though they had been a first Gray's *Elegy* or an original *Robinson Crusoe*.

He had, too, a touching weakness for the piles of fresh and neglected modern novels that lay in their discarded heaps on the dusty floor; young though he was, he was old enough to realize the pathos of these so short a time ago fresh from the bursting presses, so eagerly cherished through months of anxious watching by their fond authors, so swiftly forgotten, dead almost before they were born.

So he browsed, moving like a panting puppy with inquisitive nose from stack to stack with a gesture of excitement, tumbling a whole racket of books about his head, looking then anxiously to see whether the old man would be angry with him, and realizing for the thousandth time that the old man never was.

It was on this day, then, rather sore from the arrogancies of his Alice, that he tried to restore his confidence among these friendly volumes. With a little thrill of excited pleasure he had just discovered a number of the volumes born of those romantic and tragedy-haunted Nineties. Here in little thin volumes were the stories of Crackanthorpe, the poems of Dowson, *The Keynotes* of George Egerton, *The Bishop's Dilemma* of Ella d'Arcy, *The Happy Hypocrite* of Max Beerbohm.

Had he only been wise enough to give there and then for that last whatever the old man had asked him for it he would have been fortunate indeed, but the pennies in his pocket were few—he was not yet a book collector, but rather that less expensive but more precious thing, a book adorer. He had the tiny volume in his hand, when he was aware that some one had entered the shop and was standing looking over his shoulder.

He turned slowly and saw some one who at first sight seemed vaguely familiar, so familiar that he was plunged into confusion at once by the sense that he ought to say 'How do you do?' but could not accurately place him. The gentleman also seemed to know him very well, for he said in a most friendly way, 'Ah, yes, the "Nineties", a very fruitful period.'

Tommy stammered something, put down the Max Beerbohm, moved a little, and pulled about him a sudden shower of volumes. The room was filled with the racket of their tumbling, and a cloud of dust thickened about them, creeping into eyes and mouth and nose.

'I'm terribly sorry,' Tommy stammered, and then, looking up, was sorry the more when he saw how extremely neat and tidy the gentleman was and how terribly the little accident must distress him.

Tommy's friend must have been between sixty and seventy years of age, nearer seventy perhaps than sixty, but his black hair was thick and strong and stood up *en brosse* from a magnificent broad forehead. Indeed, so fine was the forehead and the turn of the head that the face itself was a little disappointing, being so round and chubby and amiable as to be almost babyish. It was not a weak face, however, the eyes being large and fine and the chin strong and determined.

The figure of this gentleman was short and thick-set and inclined to stoutness; he had the body of a prize-fighter now resting on his laurels. He was very beautifully clothed in a black coat and waistcoat, pepper-and-salt trousers, and he stood leaning a little on a thick ebony cane, his legs planted apart, his whole attitude that of one who was accustomed to authority. He had the look of a magistrate, or even of a judge, and had his face been less kindly Tommy would have said good-day, nodded to Mr. Burdett Coutts, and departed, but that was a smile difficult to resist.

'Dear me,' the gentleman said, 'this is a very dusty shop. I have never been here before, but I gather by the way that you knock the books about that it's an old friend of yours.'

Tommy giggled in a silly fashion, shifted from foot to foot, and then, desiring to seem very wise and learned, proved himself only very young and foolish.

'The "Nineties" are becoming quite romantic,' he said in his most authoritative voice, 'now that we're getting a good distance from them.'

'Ah, you think so!' said the gentleman courteously; 'that's interesting. I'm getting to an age now, I'm afraid, when nothing seems romantic but one's own youth and, ah, dear me! that was a very long time ago.'

This was exactly the way that kindly old gentlemen were supposed to talk, and Tommy listened with becoming attention.

'In my young day,' his friend continued, 'George Eliot seemed to everybody a magnificent writer: a little heavy in hand for these days, I'm afraid. Now who is the God of your generation, if it isn't impertinent to inquire?'

Tommy shifted again from foot to foot. Who was the God of his generation? If the truth must be told, in Tommy's set there were no Gods, only young men who might be Gods if they lived long enough.

'Well,' said Tommy awkwardly, 'Hardy, of course—er—it's difficult to say, isn't it?'

'Very difficult,' said the gentleman.

There was a pause then, which Tommy concluded by hinting that he was afraid that he must move forward to a very important engagement.

'May I walk with you a little way?' asked the gentleman very courteously, 'Such a very beautiful afternoon.'

Once outside in the beautiful afternoon air everything was much easier; Tommy regained his self-confidence, and soon was talking with his accustomed ease and freedom. There was nothing very alarming in his friend after all, he seemed so very eager to hear everything that Tommy had to say. He was strangely ignorant too; he seemed to be interested in the Arts, but to know very little about them; certain names that were to Tommy household words were to this gentleman quite unknown. Tommy began to be a little patronizing. They parted at the top of Oakley Street.

'I wonder if you'd mind,' the gentleman said, 'our meeting again? The fact is, that I have very little opportunity of making friends with your generation. There are so many things that you could tell me. I am afraid it may be tiresome for you to spend an hour or two with so ancient a duffer as myself, but it would be very kind of you.'

Tommy was nothing if not generous; he said that he would enjoy another meeting very much. Of course he was very busy and his spare hours were not many, but a walk another afternoon could surely be managed. They made an appointment, they exchanged names; the gentleman's name was Mr. Alfred Oddy.

That evening, in the middle of a hilarious Chelsea party, Tommy suddenly discovered to his surprise that it would please him very much to see Mr. Oddy walk in through the door.

Although it was a hilarious party Tommy was not very happy; for one thing, Spencer Russell, the novelist, was there and showed quite clearly that he didn't think Tommy very interesting. Tommy had been led up and introduced to him, had said one or two things that seemed to himself very striking, but Spencer Russell had turned his back almost at once and entered into eager conversation with somebody else.

This wasn't very pleasant, and then his own beloved Alice was behaving strangely; she seemed to have no eyes nor ears for any one in the room save Spencer Russell, and this was the stranger in that only a week or so before she had in public condemned Spencer Russell's novels, utterly and completely, stating that he was written out, had nothing to say, and was as good as dead. To-night, however, he was not dead at all, and Tommy had the agony of observing her edge her way into the group surrounding him and then listen to him not only as though he were the fount of all wisdom, but an Adonis as well, which last was absurd seeing that he was fat and unwieldy and bald on the top of his head.

After a while Tommy came up to her and suggested that they should go, and received then the shock of his life when she told him that he could go if he liked, but that he was not to bother her. And she told him this in a voice so loud that everybody heard and many people tittered.

He left in a fury and spent then a night that he imagined to be sleepless, although in truth he slept during most of it.

It was with an eagerness that surprised himself that he met Mr. Oddy on the second occasion. He had not seen Alice for two days. He did not intend to be the one to apologize first; besides, he had nothing to apologize for; and yet during these two days there was scarcely a moment that he had not to restrain himself from running round to her studio and making it up.

When he met Mr. Oddy at the corner of Oakley Street he was a very miserable young man. He was so miserable that in five minutes he was pouring out all his woes.

He told Mr. Oddy everything, of his youth, his wonderful promise, and the extraordinary lack of appreciation shown to him by his relatives, of the historical novels that he had written at the age of anything from ten to sixteen and found only the cook for an audience, of his going to Cambridge, and his extraordinary development there so that he became Editor of *The Lion*, that remarkable but very short-lived literary journal, and the President of *The Bats*, the most extraordinary Essay Club that Cambridge had ever known; of how, alas, he took only a third in History owing to the perverseness of examiners; and so on and so on, until he arrived in full flood at the whole history of his love for Alice, of her remarkable talents and beauty, but of her strange temper and arrogance and general feminine perverseness.

Mr. Oddy listened to it all in the kindest way. There's no knowing where they walked that afternoon; they crossed the bridge and adventured into Battersea Park, and finally had tea in a small shop smelling of stale buns and liquorice drops. It was only as they turned homewards that it occurred to Tommy that he had been talking during the whole afternoon. He had the grace to see that an apology was necessary.

'I beg your pardon, sir,' he said, flushing a little, 'I'm afraid I have bored you dreadfully. The fact is, that this last quarrel with Alice has upset me very badly. What would you do if you were in my position?'

Mr. Oddy sighed. 'The trouble is,' he said, 'that I realize only too clearly that I shall never be in your position again. My time for romance is over, or at least I get my romance now in other ways. It wasn't always so; there was a lady once beneath whose windows I stood night after night merely for the pleasure of seeing her candle outlined behind the blind.'

'And did she love you,' Tommy asked eagerly, 'as much as you loved her?'

'Nobody, my dear boy,' Mr. Oddy replied, 'loves you as much as you love them; either they love you more or they love you less. The first of these is often boring, the second always tragic. In the present case I should go and make it up; after all, happiness is always worth having, even at the sacrifice of one's pride. She seems to me a very charming young lady.'

'Oh, she is,' Tommy answered eagerly. 'I'll take your advice, I'll go this very evening; in fact, if you don't mind, I think it would be rather a good time to find her in now.'

Mr. Oddy smiled and agreed; they parted to meet another day.

On the third occasion of their meeting, which was only two days after the second, Tommy cared for his companion enough to wish to find out something about him.

His scene of reconciliation with his beautiful Alice had not been as satisfactory as he had hoped; she had forgiven him, indeed, but given him quite clearly to understand that she would stand none of his nonsense either now or hereafter. The satisfactory thing would have been for Tommy there and then to have left her, never to see her again; he would thus have preserved both his pride and his independence; but, alas, he was in love, terribly in love, and her indignation made her appear only the more magnificent.

And so on this third meeting with his friend he was quite humble and longing for affection.

And then his curiosity was stirred. Who was this handsome old gentleman, with his touching desire for Tommy's companionship? There was an air about him that seemed to suggest that he was some one of importance in his own world; beyond this there was an odd sense that Tommy knew him in some way, had seen him somewhere; so on this third occasion Tommy came out with his questions.

Who was he? Was he married? What was his profession, or was he perhaps retired now? And another question that Tommy would have liked to have asked, and had not the impertinence, was as to why this so late interest in the Arts and combined with this interest this so complete ignorance?

Mr. Oddy seemed to know a great deal about everything else, but in this one direction his questions were childish. He seemed never to have heard of the great Spencer Russell at all (which secretly gave Tommy immense satisfaction), and as for geniuses like Mumpus and Peter Arrogance and Samuel Bird, even when Tommy explained how truly great these men were, Mr. Oddy appeared but little impressed.

'Well, at least,' Tommy burst out indignantly, 'I suppose you've read something by Henry Galleon? Of course he's a back number now, at least he is not modern if you know what I mean, but then he's been writing for centuries. Why, his first book came out when Trollope and George Eliot were still alive. Of course, between ourselves I think *The Roads*, for instance, a pretty fine book, but you should hear Spencer Russell go for it.'

No, Mr. Oddy had never heard of Henry Galleon.

But there followed a most enchanting description by Mr. Oddy of his life when he was a young man and how he once heard Dickens give a reading of *A Christmas Carol*, of how he saw an old lady in a sedan chair at Brighton (she was cracked, of course, and even then a hundred years after her time, but still he had seen it), of how London in his young day was as dark and dirty at night as it had been in Pepys' time, of how crinolines when he was young were so large that it was one of the sights to see a lady getting into a cab, of how in the music-halls there was a chairman who used to sit on the stage with a table in front of him, ring a bell and drink out of a mug of beer, of how he heard Jean de Reszke in *Siegfried* and Ternina in *Tristan*, and of how he had been at the first night when Ellen Terry and Irving had delighted the world with *The Vicar of Wakefield*.

Yes, not only had Mr. Oddy seen and done all these things, but he related the events in so enchanting a way, drew such odd little pictures of such unexpected things and made that old London live so vividly, that at last Tommy burst out in a volley of genuine enthusiasm: 'Why, you ought to be a writer yourself! Why don't you write your reminiscences?'

But Mr. Oddy shook his head gently, there were too many reminiscences, every one was always reminiscing; who wanted to hear these old men talk?

At last when they parted Mr. Oddy had a request—one thing above all things that he would like would be to attend one of these evening gatherings with his young friend to hear these young men and women talk. He promised to sit very quietly in a corner—he wouldn't be in anybody's way.

Of course Tommy consented to take him; there would be one next week, a really good one; but in his heart of hearts he was a little shy. He was shy not only for himself but also for his friend.

During these weeks a strange and most unexpected affection had grown up in his heart for this old man; he really did like him immensely, he was so kind and gentle and considerate.

But he would be rather out of place with Spencer Russell and the others; he would probably say something foolish, and then the others would laugh. They were on the whole a rather ruthless set and were no respecters of persons.

However, the meeting was arranged; the evening came and with
it Mr. Oddy, looking just as he always did, quiet and gentle, but
rather impressive in some way or another. Tommy introduced him
to his hostess, Miss Thelma Bennet, that well-known futuristic
artist, and then carefully settled him down in a corner with Miss
Bennet's aunt, an old lady who appeared occasionally on her niece's
horizon but gave no trouble because she was stone deaf and cared
only for knitting.

It was a lively evening; several of the brighter spirits were there,
and there was a great deal of excellent talk about literature. Every
writer over thirty was completely condemned save for those few
remaining who had passed eighty years of age and ceased to
produce.

Spencer Russell especially was at his best; reputations went down
before his vigorous fist like ninepins. He was so scornful that his
brilliance was, as Alice Smith everywhere proclaimed, 'simply
withering'. Every one came in for his lash, and especially Henry
Galleon. There had been some article in some ancient monthly
written by some ancient idiot suggesting that there was still
something to be said for Galleon and that he had rendered some
service to English literature. How Russell pulled that article to
pieces! He even found a volume of Galleon's among Miss Bennet's
books, took it down from the shelf and read extracts aloud to the
laughing derision of the assembled company.

Then an odd thing occurred. Tommy, who loved to be in the
intellectual swim, nevertheless stood up and defended Galleon. He
defended him rather feebly, it is true, speaking of him as though he
were an old man ready for the almshouse who nevertheless deserved
a little consideration and pity. He flushed as he spoke, and the scorn
with which they greeted his defence altogether silenced him. It
silenced him the more because Alice Smith was the most scornful of
them all; she told him that he knew nothing and never would know
anything, and she imitated his piping excited treble, and then every
one joined in.

How he hated this to happen before Mr. Oddy! How humiliating
after all the things that he had told his friend, the implications that
he was generally considered to be one of England's most interesting
young men, the implication above all that although she might be a
little rough to him at times Alice really adored him and was his
warmest admirer. She did not apparently adore him to-night, and

when he went out at last with Mr Oddy into the wintry, rain-driven
street it was all he could do to keep back tears of rage and
indignation.

Mr. Oddy had, however, apparently enjoyed himself. He put his
hand for a minute on the boy's shoulder.

'Good night, my dear boy,' he said. 'I thought it very gallant of
you to stand up for that older writer as you did: that needed
courage. I wonder,' he went on, 'whether you would allow me to
come and take tea with you one day—just our two selves. It would
be a great pleasure for me.'

And then, having received Tommy's invitation, he vanished into
the darkness.

On the day appointed, Mr. Oddy appeared punctually at
Tommy's rooms. That was not a very grand house in Glebe Place
where Tommy lived, and a very soiled and battered landlady let
Mr. Oddy in. He stumbled up the dark staircase that smelt of all
the cabbage and all the beef and all the mutton ever consumed by
lodgers between these walls, up again two flights of stairs, until at
last there was the weather-beaten door with Tommy's visiting-card
nailed upon it. Inside was Tommy, a plate with little cakes,
raspberry jam, and some very black-looking toast.

Mr. Oddy, however, was appreciative of everything; especially he
looked at the books. 'Why,' he said, 'you've got quite a number of
the novels of that man you defended the other evening. I wonder
you're not ashamed to have them if they're so out of date.'

'To tell you the truth,' said Tommy, speaking freely now that he
was in his own castle, 'I like Henry Galleon awfully. I'm afraid I
pose a good deal when I'm with those other men; perhaps you've
noticed it yourself. Of course Galleon is the greatest novelist we've
got, with Hardy and Meredith, only he's getting old, and everything
that's old is out of favour with our set.'

'Naturally,' said Mr. Oddy, quite approving, 'of course it is.'

'I have got a photograph of Galleon,' said Tommy. 'I cut it out
of a publisher's advertisement, but it was taken years ago.'

He went to his table, searched for a little and produced a small
photograph of a very fierce-looking gentleman with a black beard.

'Dear me,' said Mr. Oddy, 'He does look alarming!'

'Oh, that's ever so old,' said Tommy. 'I expect he's mild and soft
now, but he's a great man all the same; I'd like to see Spencer

Russell write anything as fine as *The Roads* or *The Pattern in the Carpet.*'

They sat down to tea very happy and greatly pleased with one another.

'I do wish,' said Tommy, 'that you'd tell me something about yourself; we're such friends now, and I don't know anything about you at all.'

'I'd rather you didn't,' said Mr. Oddy. 'You'd find it so uninteresting if you did; mystery's a great thing.'

'Yes,' said Tommy, 'I don't want to seem impertinent, and of course if you don't want to tell me anything you needn't, but—I know it sounds silly, but, you see, I like you most awfully. I haven't liked anybody so much for ever so long, except Alice, of course. I don't feel as though you were of another generation or anything; it's just as though we were the same age!'

Mr. Oddy was enchanted. He put his hand on the boy's for a moment and was going to say something, when they were interrupted by a knock on the door, and the terrible-looking landlady appeared in the room. She apologized, but the afternoon post had come and she thought the young gentleman would like to see his letters. He took them, was about to put them down without opening them, when suddenly he blushed. 'Oh, from Alice,' he said. 'Will you forgive me a moment?'

'Of course,' said Mr. Oddy.

The boy opened the letter and read it. It fell from his hand on to the table. He got up gropingly as though he could not see his way, and went to the window and stood there with his back to the room. There was a long silence.

'Not bad news, I hope,' said Mr. Oddy at last.

Tommy turned round. His face was grey and he was biting his lips. 'Yes,' he answered, 'she's—gone off.'

'Gone off?' said Mr. Oddy, rising from the table.

'Yes,' said Tommy, 'with Russell. They were married at a registry office this morning.'

He half turned round to the window, then put his hands as though he would shield himself from some blow, then crumpled up into a chair, his head falling between his arms on the table.

Mr. Oddy waited. At last he said: 'Oh, I'm sorry; that's dreadful for you!'

The boy struggled, trying to raise his head and speak, but the words would not come. Mr. Oddy went behind him and put his hands on his shoulders.

'You know,' he said, 'you mustn't mind me. Of course, I'll go if you like, but if you could think of me for a moment as your oldest friend, old enough to be your father, you know.'

Tommy clutched his sleeve, then, abandoning the struggle altogether, buried his head in Mr. Oddy's beautiful black waistcoat.

Later he poured his heart out. Alice was all that he had; he knew that he wasn't any good as a writer, he was a failure altogether; what he'd done he'd done for Alice, and now that she'd gone——

'Well, there's myself,' said Mr. Oddy. 'What I mean is that you're not without a friend; and as for writing, if you only write to please somebody else, that's no use; you've got to write because you can't help it. There are too many writers in the world already for you to dare to add to their number unless you're simply compelled to. But there—I'm preaching. If it's any comfort to you to know, I went through just this same experience myself once—the lady whose candle I watched behind the blind. If you cared to, would you come and have dinner with me to-night at my home? Only the two of us, you know; but don't if you'd rather be alone.'

Tommy, clutching Mr. Oddy's hand, said he would come.

About half-past seven that evening he had beaten up his pride. Even in the depth of his misery he saw that they would never have got on together, he and Alice. He was quickly working himself into a fine state of hatred of the whole female race, and this helped him—he would be a bachelor all his days, a woman-hater; he would preserve a glorious independence. How much better this freedom than a houseful of children and a bagful of debts.

Only, as he walked to the address that Mr. Oddy had given him he held sharply away from him the memory of those hours that he had spent with Alice, those hours of their early friendship when the world had been so wonderful a place that it had seemed to be made entirely of golden sunlight. He felt that he was an old man indeed as he mounted the steps of Mr. Oddy's house.

It was a fine house in Eaton Square. Mr. Oddy must be rich. He rang the bell, and a door was opened by a footman. He asked for Mr. Oddy.

The footman hesitated a little, and then, smiling, said: 'Oh, yes, sir, will you come in?'

He left his coat in the fine hall, mounted a broad staircase, and then was shown into the finest library that he had ever seen. Books! Shelf upon shelf of books, and glorious books, editions de luxe and, as he could see with half an eye, rare first editions and those lovely bindings in white parchment and vellum that he so longed one day himself to possess. On the broad writing-table there was a large photograph of Meredith; it was signed in sprawling letters, 'George Meredith, 1887'. What could this mean? Mr. Oddy, who knew nothing about literature, had been given a photograph by George Meredith and had this wonderful library! He stared bewildered about him.

A door at the far end of the library opened and an elegant young man appeared. 'Mr. Galleon,' he said, 'will be with you in a moment. Won't you sit down?'

Mr. Galleon! Henry Galleon! Instantly he saw it, remembered with horrid confusion his own ridiculous conceited talk, the abusive nonsense of Russell and the rest. 'My God!' he whispered aloud, 'what he must be thinking!'

The door opened again and Mr. Oddy appeared. Tommy Brown, his face crimson, stammered: 'It was a shame—if I'd only known!' and then, trying to stand up for himself, 'but I had that photograph and there was the beard.'

Mr. Oddy laughed. 'The beard went long ago,' he said; 'I suppose it *was* a shame, but I was hemmed in here in my castle; I had to find out what you young people were like. I get tired of all this sometimes; nobody tells me the truth here. I have to go to you and your friends for that.'

So they went down to dinner together.

Yes, this is an old story. Its principal interest, perhaps, is that it's true. I was, you see, myself Tommy Brown.

DYLAN THOMAS
A Visit to Grandpa's

In the middle of the night I woke from a dream full of whips and lariats as long as serpents, and runaway coaches on mountain passes, and wide, windy gallops over cactus fields, and I heard the old man in the next room crying, 'Gee-up!' and 'Whoa!' and trotting his tongue on the roof of his mouth.

It was the first time I had stayed in grandpa's house. The floorboards had squeaked like mice as I climbed into bed, and the mice between the walls had creaked like wood as though another visitor was walking on them. It was a mild summer night, but curtains had flapped and branches beaten against the window. I had pulled the sheets over my head, and soon was roaring and riding in a book.

'Whoa there, my beauties!' cried grandpa. His voice sounded very young and loud, and his tongue had powerful hooves, and he made his bedroom into a great meadow. I thought I would see if he was ill, or had set his bedclothes on fire, for my mother had said that he lit his pipe under the blankets, and had warned me to run to his help if I smelt smoke in the night. I went on tiptoe through the darkness to his bedroom door, brushing against the furniture and upsetting a candle-stick with a thump. When I saw there was a light in the room I felt frightened, and as I opened the door I heard grandpa shout, 'Gee-up!' as loudly as a bull with a megaphone.

He was sitting straight up in bed and rocking from side to side as though the bed were on a rough road; the knotted edges of the counterpane were his reins; his invisible horses stood in a shadow beyond the bedside candle. Over a white flannel nightshirt he was wearing a red waistcoat with walnut-sized brass buttons. The over-filled bowl of his pipe smouldered among his whiskers like a little, burning hayrick on a stick. At the sight of me, his hands dropped from the reins and lay blue and quiet, the bed stopped still on a level road, he muffled his tongue into silence, and the horses drew softly up.

'Is there anything the matter, grandpa?' I asked, though the clothes were not on fire. His face in the candlelight looked like a ragged quilt pinned upright on the black air and patched all over with goat-beards.

He stared at me mildly. Then he blew down his pipe, scattering the sparks and making a high, wet dog-whistle of the stem, and shouted: 'Ask no questions.'

After a pause, he said slyly: 'Do you ever have nightmares, boy?'

I said: 'No.'

'Oh, yes, you do,' he said.

I said I was woken by a voice that was shouting to horses.

'What did I tell you?' he said. 'You eat too much. Who ever heard of horses in a bedroom?'

He fumbled under his pillow, brought out a small, tinkling bag, and carefully untied its strings. He put a sovereign in my hand, and said: 'Buy a cake.' I thanked him and wished him good night.

As I closed my bedroom door, I heard his voice crying loudly and gaily, 'Gee-up! gee-up!' and the rocking of the travelling bed.

In the morning I woke from a dream of fiery horses on a plain that was littered with furniture, and of large, cloudy men who rode six horses at a time and whipped them with burning bed-clothes. Grandpa was at breakfast, dressed in deep black. After breakfast he said, 'There was a terrible loud wind last night,' and sat in his arm-chair by the hearth to make clay balls for the fire. Later in the morning he took me for a walk, through Johnstown village and into the fields on the Llanstephan road.

A man with a whippet said, 'There's a nice morning, Mr. Thomas,' and when he had gone, leanly as his dog, into the short-treed green wood he should not have entered because of the notices, grandpa said: 'There, do you hear what he called you? Mister!'

We passed by small cottages, and all the men who leant on the gates congratulated grandpa on the fine morning. We passed through the wood full of pigeons, and their wings broke the branches as they rushed to the tops of the trees. Among the soft, contented voices and the loud, timid flying, grandpa said, like a man calling across a field: 'If you heard those old birds in the night, you'd wake me up and say there were horses in the trees.'

We walked back slowly, for he was tired, and the lean man stalked out of the forbidden wood with a rabbit held as gently over his arm as a girl's arm in a warm sleeve.

On the last day but one of my visit I was taken to Llanstephan in a governess cart pulled by a short, weak pony. Grandpa might have been driving a bison, so tightly he held the reins, so ferociously cracked the long whip, so blasphemously shouted warning to boys who played in the road, so stoutly stood with his gaitered legs apart and cursed the demon strength and wilfulness of his tottering pony.

'Look out, boy!' he cried when we came to each corner, and pulled and tugged and jerked and sweated and waved his whip like a rubber sword. And when the pony had crept miserably round each corner, grandpa turned to me with a sighing smile: 'We weathered that one, boy.'

When we came to Llanstephan village at the top of the hill, he left the cart by the 'Edwinsford Arms' and patted the pony's muzzle and gave it sugar, saying: 'You're a weak little pony, Jim, to pull big men like us.'

He had strong beer and I had lemonade, and he paid Mrs. Edwinsford with a sovereign out of the tinkling bag; she inquired after his health, and he said that Llangadock was better for the tubes. We went to look at the churchyard and the sea, and sat in the wood called the Sticks, and stood on the concert platform in the middle of the wood where visitors sang on midsummer nights and, year by year, the innocent of the village was elected mayor. Grandpa paused at the churchyard and pointed over the iron gate at the angelic headstones and the poor wooden crosses. 'There's no sense in lying there,' he said.

We journeyed back furiously: Jim was a bison again.

I woke late on my last morning, out of dreams where the Llanstephan sea carried bright sailing-boats as long as liners; and heavenly choirs in the Sticks, dressed in bards' robes and brass-buttoned waistcoats, sang in a strange Welsh to the departing sailors. Grandpa was not at breakfast; he rose early. I walked in the fields with a new sling, and shot at the Towy gulls and the rooks in the parsonage trees. A warm wind blew from the summer points of the weather; a morning mist climbed from the ground and floated among the trees and hid the noisy birds; in the mist and the wind my pebbles flew lightly up like hailstones in a world on its head. The morning passed without a bird falling.

I broke my sling and returned for the midday meal through the parson's orchard. Once, grandpa told me, the parson had bought three ducks at Carmarthen Fair and made a pond for them in the centre of the garden; but they waddled to the gutter under the crumbling doorsteps of the house, and swam and quacked there.

When I reached the end of the orchard path, I looked through a hole in the hedge and saw that the parson had made a tunnel through the rockery that was between the gutter and the pond and had set up a notice in plain writing: 'This way to the pond.'

The ducks were still swimming under the steps.

Grandpa was not in the cottage. I went into the garden, but grandpa was not staring at the fruit-trees. I called across to a man who leant on a spade in the field beyond the garden hedge: 'Have you seen my grandpa this morning?'

He did not stop digging, and answered over his shoulder: 'I seen him in his fancy waistcoat.'

Griff, the barber, lived in the next cottage. I called to him through the open door: 'Mr. Griff, have you seen my grandpa?'

The barber came out in his shirtsleeves.

I said: 'He's wearing his best waistcoat.' I did not know if it was important, but grandpa wore his waistcoat only in the night.

'Has grandpa been to Llanstephan?' asked Mr. Griff anxiously.

'We went there yesterday in a little trap,' I said.

He hurried indoors and I heard him talking in Welsh, and he came out again with his white coat on, and he carried a striped and coloured walking-stick. He strode down the village street and I ran by his side.

When we stopped at the tailor's shop, he cried out, 'Dan!' and Dan Tailor stepped from his window like an Indian priest but wearing a derby hat. 'Dai Thomas has got his waistcoat on,' said Mr. Griff, 'and he's been to Llanstephan.'

As Dan Tailor searched for his overcoat, Mr. Griff was striding on. 'Will Evans,' he called outside the carpenter's shop, 'Dai Thomas has been to Llanstephan, and he's got his waistcoat on.'

'I'll tell Morgan now,' said the carpenter's wife out of the hammering, sawing darkness of the shop.

We called at the butcher's shop and Mr. Price's house, and Mr. Griff repeated his message like a town crier.

We gathered together in Johnstown square. Dan Tailor had his bicycle, Mr. Price his pony trap. Mr. Griff, the butcher, Morgan Carpenter, and I climbed into the shaking trap, and we trotted off towards Carmarthen town. The tailor led the way, ringing his bell as though there were a fire or a robbery, and an old woman by the gate of a cottage at the end of the street ran inside like a pelted hen. Another woman waved a bright handkerchief.

'Where are we going?' I asked.

Grandpa's neighbours were as solemn as old men with black hats and jackets on the outskirts of a fair. Mr. Griff shook his head and mourned: 'I didn't expect this again from Dai Thomas.'

'Not after last time,' said Mr. Price sadly.

We trotted on, we crept up Constitution Hill, we rattled down into Lammas Street, and the tailor still rang his bell and a dog ran, squealing, in front of his wheels. As we clip-clopped over the cobbles that led down to the Towy bridge, I remembered grandpa's nightly noisy journeys that rocked the bed and shook the walls, and I saw his gay waistcoat in a vision and his patchwork head tufted and smiling in the candlelight. The tailor before us turned round on his saddle, his bicycle wobbled and skidded. 'I see Dai Thomas!' he cried.

The trap rattled on to the bridge. And I saw grandpa there; the buttons of his waistcoat shone in the sun, he wore his tight, black Sunday trousers and a tall, dusty hat I had seen in a cupboard in the attic, and he carried an ancient bag. He bowed to us. 'Good morning, Mr. Price,' he said, 'and Mr. Griff and Mr. Morgan and Mr. Evans.' To me, he said: 'Good morning, boy.'

Mr. Griff pointed his coloured stick at him.

'And what do you think you are doing on Carmarthen bridge in the middle of the afternoon,' he said sternly, 'with your best waistcoat and your old hat?'

Grandpa did not answer, but inclined his face to the river wind, so that his beard was set dancing and wagging as though he talked, and watched the coracle men move, like turtles, on the shore.

Mr. Griff raised his stunted barber's pole. 'And where do you think you are going,' he said, 'with your old black bag?'

Grandpa said: 'I am going to Llangadock to be buried.' And he watched the coracle shells slip into the water lightly, and the gulls complain over the fish-filled water as bitterly as Mr. Price complained:

'But you aren't dead yet, Dai Thomas.'

For a moment grandpa reflected, then: 'There's no sense in lying dead in Llanstephan,' he said. 'The ground is comfy in Llangadock; you can twitch your legs without putting them in the sea.'

His neighbours moved close to him. They said: 'You aren't dead, Mr. Thomas.'

'How can you be buried, then?'

'Nobody's going to bury you in Llanstephan.'

'Come on home, Mr. Thomas.'

'There's strong beer for tea.'

'And cake.'

But grandpa stood firmly on the bridge, and clutched his bag to his side, and stared at the flowing river and the sky, like a prophet who has no doubt.

WALTER DE LA MARE
Seaton's Aunt

I HAD heard rumours of Seaton's aunt long before I actually encountered her. Seaton, in the hush of confidence, or at any little show of toleration on our part, would remark, 'My aunt,' or 'My old aunt, you know', as if his relative might be a kind of cement to an *entente cordiale*.

He had an unusual quantity of pocket-money; or, at any rate, it was bestowed on him in unusually large amounts; and he spent it freely, though none of us would have described him as an 'awfully generous chap'. 'Hullo, Seaton,' we would say, 'the old Begum?' At the beginning of term, too, he used to bring back surprising and exotic dainties in a box with a trick padlock that accompanied him from his first appearance at Gummidge's in a billycock hat to the rather abrupt conclusion of his schooldays.

From a boy's point of view he looked distastefully foreign with his yellowish skin, slow chocolate-coloured eyes, and lean weak figure. Merely for his looks, he was treated by most of us true-blue Englishmen with condescension, hostility, or contempt. We used to call him 'Pongo', but without any much better excuse for the nickname than his skin. He was, that is, in one sense of the term what he assuredly was not in the other sense, a sport.

Seaton and I, as I may say, were never in any sense intimate at school; our orbits only intersected in class. I kept deliberately aloof from him. I felt vaguely he was a sneak, and remained quite unmollified by advances on his side, which, in a boy's barbarous fashion, unless it suited me to be magnanimous, I haughtily ignored.

We were both of us quick-footed, and at Prisoner's Base used occasionally to hide together. And so I best remember Seaton—his narrow watchful face in the dusk of a summer evening; his peculiar crouch, and his inarticulate whisperings and mumblings. Otherwise he played all games slackly and limply; used to stand and feed at his locker with a crony or two until his 'tuck' gave out; or waste his money on some outlandish fancy or other. He bought, for instance, a silver bangle, which he wore above his left elbow, until some of the fellows showed their masterly contempt of the practice by dropping it nearly red-hot down his neck.

It needed, therefore, a rather peculiar taste, and a rather rare kind of schoolboy courage and indifference to criticism, to be much associated with him. And I had neither the taste, nor, probably, the courage. None the less, he did make advances, and on one memorable occasion went to the length of bestowing on me a whole pot of some outlandish mulberry-coloured jelly that had been duplicated in his term's supplies. In the exuberance of my gratitude, I promised to spend the next half-term holiday with him at his aunt's house.

I had clean forgotten my promise when, two or three days before the holiday, he came up and triumphantly reminded me of it.

'Well, to tell you the honest truth, Seaton, old chap——' I began graciously: but he cut me short.

'My aunt expects you,' he said; 'she is very glad you are coming. She's sure to be quite decent to *you*, Withers.'

I looked at him in sheer astonishment; the emphasis was so uncalled for. It seemed to suggest an aunt not hitherto hinted at, and a friendly feeling on Seaton's side that was far more disconcerting than welcome.

We reached his aunt's house, partly by train, partly by a lift in an empty farm-cart, and partly by walking. It was a whole-day holiday, and we were to sleep the night; he lent me extraordinary night-gear, I remember. The village street was unusually wide, and was fed from a green by two converging roads, with an inn and a high green sign at the corner. About a hundred yards down the street was a chemist's shop—a Mr. Tanner's. We descended the two steps into his dusky and odorous interior to buy, I remember, some rat poison. A little beyond the chemist's was the forge. You then walked along a very narrow path, under a fairly high wall, nodding here and there with weeds and tufts of grass, and so came to the iron garden-gates, and saw the high flat house behind its huge sycamore. A coach-house stood on the left of the house, and on the right a gate led into a kind of rambling orchard. The lawn lay away over to the left again, and at the bottom (for the whole garden sloped gently to a sluggish and rushy pond-like stream) was a meadow.

We arrived at noon, and entered the gates out of the hot dust beneath the glitter of the dark-curtained windows. Seaton led me at once through the little garden-gate to show me his tadpole pond, swarming with what (being myself not in the least interested in low life) seemed to me the most horrible creatures—of all shapes, consistencies, and sizes, but with which Seaton was obviously on the most intimate of terms. I can see his absorbed face now as, squatting on his heels, he fished the slimy things out in his sallow palms. Wearying at last of these pets, we loitered about awhile in an aimless fashion. Seaton seemed to be listening, or at any rate waiting, for something to happen or for someone to come. But nothing did happen and no one came.

That was just like Seaton. Anyhow, the first view I got of his aunt was when, at the summons of a distant gong, we turned from the garden, very hungry and thirsty, to go into luncheon. We were approaching the house, when Seaton suddenly came to a standstill. Indeed, I have always had the impression that he plucked at my sleeve. Something, at least, seemed to catch me back, as it were, as he cried, 'Look out, there she is!'

She was standing at an upper window which opened wide on a hinge, and at first sight she looked an excessively tall and over-whelming figure. This, however, was mainly because the window reached all but to the floor of her bedroom. She was in reality rather an undersized woman, in spite of her long face and big head. She must have stood, I think, unusually still, with eyes fixed on us, though this impression may be due to Seaton's sudden warning and to my consciousness of the cautious and subdued air that had fallen on him at sight of her. I know that without the least reason in the world I felt a kind of guiltiness, as if I had been 'caught'. There was a silvery star pattern sprinkled on her black silk dress, and even from the ground I could see the immense coils of her hair and the rings on her left hand which was held fingering the small jet buttons of her bodice. She watched our united advance without stirring, until, imperceptibly, her eyes raised and lost themselves in the distance, so that it was out of an assumed reverie that she appeared suddenly to awaken to our presence beneath her when we drew close to the house.

'So this is your friend, Mr. Smithers, I suppose?' she said, bobbing to me.

'Withers, aunt,' said Seaton.

'It's much the same,' she said, with eyes fixed to me. 'Come in, Mr. Withers, and bring him along with you.'

She continued to gaze at me—at least, I think she did so. I know that the fixity of her scrutiny and her ironical 'Mr.' made me feel peculiarly uncomfortable. None the less she was extremely kind and attentive to me, though, no doubt, her kindness and attention showed up more vividly against her complete neglect of Seaton. Only one remark that I have any recollection of she made to him: 'When I look on my nephew, Mr. Smithers, I realize that dust we are, and dust shall become. You are hot, dirty, and incorrigible, Arthur.'

She sat at the head of the table, Seaton at the foot, and I, before a wide waste of damask tablecloth, between them. It was an old and rather close dining-room, with windows thrown wide to the green garden and a wonderful cascade of fading roses. Miss Seaton's great chair faced this window, so that its rose-reflected light shone full on her yellowish face, and on just such chocolate eyes as my schoolfellow's, except that hers were more than half covered by unusually long and heavy lids.

There she sat, steadily eating, with those sluggish eyes fixed for the most part on my face; above them stood the deep-lined fork between her eyebrows; and above that the wide expanse of a remarkable brow beneath its strange steep bank of hair. The lunch was copious, and consisted, I remember, of all such dishes as are generally considered too rich and too good for the schoolboy digestion—lobster mayonnaise, cold game sausages, an immense veal and ham pie farced with eggs, truffles, and numberless delicious flavours; besides kickshaws, creams and sweetmeats. We even had a wine, a half-glass of old darkish sherry each.

Miss Seaton enjoyed and indulged an enormous appetite. Her example and a natural schoolboy voracity soon overcame my nervousness of her, even to the extent of allowing me to enjoy to the best of my bent so rare a spread. Seaton was singularly modest; the greater part of his meal consisted of almonds and raisins, which he nibbled surreptitiously and as if he found difficulty in swallowing them.

I don't mean that Miss Seaton 'conversed' with me. She merely scattered trenchant remarks and now and then twinkled a baited question over my head. But her face was like a dense and involved accompaniment to her talk. She presently dropped the 'Mr.', to my intense relief, and called me now Withers, or Wither, now Smithers, and even once towards the end of the meal distinctly Johnson, though how on earth my name suggested it, or whose face mine had reanimated in memory, I cannot conceive.

'And is Arthur a good boy at school, Mr. Wither?' was one of her many questions. 'Does he please his masters? Is he first in his class? What does the reverend Dr. Gummidge think of him, eh?'

I knew she was jeering at him, but her face was adamant against the least flicker of sarcasm or facetiousness. I gazed fixedly at a blushing crescent of lobster.

'I think you're eighth, aren't you, Seaton?'

Seaton moved his small pupils towards his aunt. But she continued to gaze with a kind of concentrated detachment at me.

'Arthur will never make a brilliant scholar, I fear,' she said, lifting a dexterously burdened fork to her wide mouth. . . .

After luncheon she preceded me up to my bedroom. It was a jolly little bedroom, with a brass fender and rugs and a polished floor, on which it was possible, I afterwards found, to play 'snow-shoes'. Over the washstand was a little black-framed water-colour drawing, depicting a large eye with an extremely fishlike intensity in the spark of light on the dark pupil; and in 'illuminated' lettering beneath was printed very minutely, 'Thou God Seest ME', followed by a long looped monogram, 'S.S.', in the corner. The other pictures were all of the sea; brigs on blue water; a schooner overtopping chalk cliffs; a rocky island of prodigious steepness, with two tiny sailors dragging a monstrous boat up a shelf of beach.

'This is the room, Withers, my poor dear brother William died in when a boy. Admire the view!'

I looked out of the window across the tree-tops. It was a day hot with sunshine over the green fields, and the cattle were standing swishing their tails in the shallow water. But the view at the moment was no doubt made more vividly impressive by the apprehension that she would presently enquire after my luggage, and I had brought not even a toothbrush. I need have had no fear. Hers was not that highly civilized type of mind that is stuffed with sharp, material details. Nor could her ample presence be described as in the least motherly.

'I would never consent to question a schoolfellow behind my nephew's back,' she said, standing in the middle of the room, 'but tell me, Smithers, why is Arthur so unpopular? You, I understand, are his only close friend.' She stood in a dazzle of sun, and out of it her eyes regarded me with such leaden penetration beneath their

thick lids that I doubt if my face concealed the least thought from
her. 'But there, there,' she added very suavely, stooping her head a
little, 'don't trouble to answer me. I never extort an answer. Boys
are queer fish. Brains might perhaps have suggested his washing his
hands before luncheon; but—not my choice, Smithers. God forbid!
And now, perhaps, you would like to go into the garden again. I
cannot actually see from here, but I should not be surprised if
Arthur is now skulking behind that hedge.'

He was. I saw his head come out and take a rapid glance at the
windows.

'Join him, Mr. Smithers; we shall meet again, I hope, at the tea-
table. The afternoon I spend in retirement.'

Whether or not, Seaton and I had not been long engaged with
the aid of two green switches in riding round and round a lumbering
old grey horse we found in the meadow, before a rather bunched-
up figure appeared, walking along the field-path on the other side
of the water, with a magenta parasol studiously lowered in our
direction throughout her slow progress, as if that were the magnetic
needle and we the fixed Pole. Seaton at once lost all nerve and
interest. At the next lurch of the old mare's heels he toppled over
into the grass, and I slid off the sleek broad back to join him where
he stood, rubbing his shoulder and sourly watching the rather
pompous figure till it was out of sight.

'Was that your aunt, Seaton?' I enquired; but not till then.

He nodded.

'Why didn't she take any notice of us, then?'

'She never does.'

'Why not?'

'Oh, she knows all right, without; that's the damn awful part of it.'
Seaton was one of the very few fellows at Gummidge's who had the
ostentation to use bad language. He had suffered for it too. But it
wasn't I think, bravado. I believe he really felt certain things more
intensely than most of the other fellows, and they were generally
things that fortunate and average people do not feel at all—the
peculiar quality, for instance, of the British schoolboy's imagination.

'I tell you, Withers,' he went on moodily, slinking across the
meadow with his hands covered up in his pockets, 'she sees
everything. And what she doesn't see she knows without.'

'But how?' I said, not because I was much interested, but because
the afternoon was so hot and tiresome and purposeless, and it

seemed more of a bore to remain silent. Seaton turned gloomily and spoke in a very low voice.

'Don't appear to be talking of her, if you wouldn't mind. It's—because she's in league with the Devil.' He nodded his head and stooped to pick up a round, flat pebble. 'I tell you,' he said, still stooping, 'you fellows don't realize what it is. I know I'm a bit close and all that. But so would you be if you had that old hag listening to every thought you think.'

I looked at him, then turned and surveyed one by one the windows of the house.

'Where's your *pater*?' I said awkwardly.

'Dead, ages and ages ago, and my mother too. She's not my aunt even by rights.'

'What is she, then?'

'I mean, she's not my mother's sister, because my grandmother married twice; and she's one of the first lot. I don't know what you call her, but anyhow she's not my real aunt.'

'She gives you plenty of pocket-money.'

Seaton looked steadfastly at me out of his flat eyes. 'She can't give me what's mine. When I come of age half of the whole lot will be mine; and what's more'—he turned his back on the house—'I'll make her hand over every blessed shilling of it.'

I put my hands in my pockets and stared at Seaton; 'Is it much?'
He nodded.

'Who told you?' He got suddenly very angry; a darkish red came into his cheeks, his eyes glistened, but he made no answer, and we loitered listlessly about the garden until it was time for tea. . . .

Seaton's aunt was wearing an extraordinary kind of lace jacket when we sidled sheepishly into the drawing-room together. She greeted me with a heavy and protracted smile, and bade me bring a chair close to the little table.

'I hope Arthur has made you feel at home,' she said as she handed me my cup in her crooked hand. 'He don't talk much to me; but then I'm an old woman. You must come again, Wither, and draw him out of his shell. You old snail!' She wagged her head at Seaton, who sat munching cake and watching her intently.

'And we must correspond, perhaps.' She nearly shut her eyes at me. 'You must write and tell me everything behind the creature's back.' I confess I found her rather disquieting company. The evening drew on. Lamps were brought in by a man with a nondescript face and very quiet footsteps. Seaton was told to bring out the chess-men. And we played a game, she and I, with her big chin thrust over the board at every move as she gloated over the pieces and occasionally croaked 'Check!'—after which she would sit back inscrutably staring at me. But the game was never finished. She simply hemmed me in with a gathering cloud of pieces that held me impotent, and yet one and all refused to administer to my poor flustered old king a merciful *coup de grâce*.

'There,' she said, as the clock struck ten—'a drawn game, Withers. We are very evenly matched. A very creditable defence, Withers. You know your room. There's supper on a tray in the dining-room. Don't let the creature over-eat himself. The gong will sound three-quarters of an hour *before* a punctual breakfast.' She held out her cheek to Seaton, and he kissed it with obvious perfunctoriness. With me she shook hands.

'An excellent game,' she said cordially, 'but my memory is poor, and'—she swept the pieces helter-skelter into the box—'the result will never be known.' She raised her great head far back. 'Eh?'

It was a kind of challenge, and I could only murmur: 'Oh, I was absolutely in a hole, you know!' when she burst out laughing and waved us both out of the room.

Seaton and I stood and ate our supper, with one candlestick to light us, in a corner of the dining-room. 'Well, and how would you like it?' he said very softly, after cautiously poking his head round the doorway.

'Like what?'

'Being spied on—every blessed thing you do and think?'

'I shouldn't like it at all,' I said, 'if she does.'

'And yet you let her smash you up at chess!'

'I didn't let her!' I said indignantly.

'Well, you funked it, then.'

'And I didn't funk it either,' I said; 'she's so jolly clever with her knights.' Seaton stared at the candle. 'Knights,' he said slowly. 'You wait, that's all.' And we went upstairs to bed.

I had not been long in bed, I think, when I was cautiously awakened by a touch on my shoulder. And there was Seaton's face in the candlelight—and his eyes looking into mine.

'What's up?' I said, lurching on to my elbow.

'*Ssh!* Don't scurry,' he whispered. 'She'll hear. I'm sorry for waking you, but I didn't think you'd be asleep so soon.'

'Why, what's the time, then?' Seaton wore, what was then rather unusual, a night-suit, and he hauled his big silver watch out of the pocket in his jacket.

'It's a quarter to twelve. I never get to sleep before twelve—not here.'

'What do you do, then?'

'Oh, I read: and listen.'

'Listen?'

Seaton stared into his candle-flame as if he were listening even then. 'You can't guess what it is. All you read in ghost stories, that's all rot. You can't see much, Withers, but you know all the same.'

'Know what?'

'Why, that they're there.'

'Who's there?' I asked fretfully, glancing at the door.

'Why in the house. It swarms with 'em. Just you stand still and listen outside my bedroom door in the middle of the night. I have, dozens of times; they're all over the place.'

'Look here, Seaton,' I said, 'you asked me to come here, and I didn't mind chucking up a leave just to oblige you and because I'd promised; but don't get talking a lot of rot, that's all, or you'll know the difference when we get back.'

'Don't fret,' he said coldly, turning away. 'I shan't be at school long. And what's more, you're here now, and there isn't anybody else to talk to. I'll chance the other.'

'Look here, Seaton,' I said, 'you may think you're going to scare me with a lot of stuff about voices and all that. But I'll just thank you to clear out; and you may please yourself about pottering about all night.'

He made no answer; he was standing by the dressing table looking across his candle into the looking-glass; he turned and stared slowly round the walls.

'Even this room's nothing more than a coffin. I suppose she told you—"It's all exactly the same as when my brother William died"—trust her for that! And good luck to him, say I. Look at that.' He raised his candle close to the little water-colour I have mentioned. 'There's hundreds of eyes like that in this house; and even if God does see you, He takes precious good care you don't see

Him. And it's just the same with them. I tell you what, Withers, I'm getting sick of all this. I shan't stand it much longer.'

The house was silent within and without, and even in the yellowish radiance of the candle a faint silver showed through the open window on my blind. I slipped off the bedclothes, wide awake, and sat irresolute on the bedside.

'I know you're only guying me,' I said angrily, 'but why is the house full of—what you say? Why do you hear—what you *do* hear. Tell me that, you silly fool!'

Seaton sat down on a chair and rested his candlestick on his knee. He blinked at me calmly. 'She brings them,' he said, with lifted eyebrows.

'Who? Your aunt?'

He nodded.

'How?'

'I told you,' he answered pettishly. 'She's in league. You don't know. She as good as killed my mother; I know that. But it's not only her by a long chalk. She just sucks you dry. I know. And that's what she'll do for me; because I'm like her—like my mother I mean. She simply hates to see me alive. I wouldn't be like that old she-wolf for a million pounds. And so'—he broke off, with a comprehensive wave of his candlestick—'they're always here. Ah, my boy, wait till she's dead! She'll hear something then, I can tell you. It's all very well now, but wait till then! I wouldn't be in her shoes when she has to clear out—for something. Don't you go and believe I care for ghosts, or whatever you like to call them. We're all in the same box. We're all under her thumb.'

He was looking almost nonchalantly at the ceiling at the moment, when I saw his face change, saw his eyes suddenly drop like shot birds and fix themselves on the cranny of the door he had left just ajar. Even from where I sat I could see his cheek change colour; it went greenish. He crouched without stirring, like an animal. And I, scarcely daring to breathe, sat with creeping skin, sourly watching him. His hands relaxed, and he gave a kind of sigh.

'Was *that* one?' I whispered, with a timid show of jauntiness. He looked round, opened his mouth, and nodded. 'What?' I said. He jerked his thumb with meaningful eyes, and I knew that he meant that his aunt had been there listening at our door cranny.

'Look here, Seaton,' I said once more, wriggling to my feet. 'You may think I'm a jolly noodle; just as you please. But your aunt has

been civil to me and all that, and I don't believe a word you say
about her, that's all, and never did. Every fellow's a bit off his pluck
at night, and you may think it a fine sport to try your rubbish on
me. I heard your aunt come upstairs before I fell asleep. And I'll
bet you a level tanner she's in bed now. What's more, you can keep
your blessed ghosts to yourself. It's a guilty conscience, I should
think.'

Seaton looked at me intently, without answering for a moment.
'I'm not a liar, Withers; but I'm not going to quarrel either. You're
the only chap I care a button for; or, at any rate, you're the only
chap that's ever come here; and it's something to tell a fellow what
you feel. I don't care a fig for fifty thousand ghosts, although I
swear on my solemn oath that I know they're here. But she'—he
turned deliberately—'you laid a tanner she's in bed, Withers; well,
I know different. She's never in bed much of the night, and I'll
prove it too, just to show you I'm not such a nolly as you think I
am. Come on!'

'Come on where?'

'Why, to see.'

I hesitated. He opened a large cupboard and took out a small
dark dressing-gown and a kind of shawl-jacket. He threw the jacket
on the bed and put on the gown. His dusky face was colourless, and
I could see by the way he fumbled at the sleeves he was shivering.
But it was no good showing the white feather now. So I threw the
tasselled shawl over my shoulders and, leaving our candle brightly
burning on the chair, we went out together and stood in the
corridor.

'Now then, listen!' Seaton whispered.

We stood leaning over the staircase. It was like leaning over a
well, so still and chill the air was all around us. But presently, as I
suppose happens in most old houses, began to echo and answer in
my ears a medley of infinite small stirrings and whisperings. Now
out of the distance an old timber would relax its fibres, or a scurry
die away behind the perishing wainscot. But amid and behind such
sounds as these I seemed to begin to be conscious, as it were, of the
lightest of footfalls, sounds as faint as the vanishing remembrance
of voices in a dream. Seaton was all in obscurity except his face; out
of that his eyes gleamed darkly, watching me.

'You'd hear, too, in time, my fine soldier,' he muttered. 'Come
on!'

He descended the stairs, slipping his lean fingers lightly along the balusters. He turned to the right at the loop, and I followed him barefooted along a thickly-carpeted corridor. At the end stood a door ajar. And from here we very stealthily and in complete blackness ascended five narrow stairs. Seaton, with immense caution, slowly pushed open a door, and we stood together, looking into a great pool of duskiness, out of which, lit by the feeble clearness of a night-light, rose a vast bed. A heap of clothes lay on the floor; beside them two slippers dozed, with noses each to each, a foot or two apart. Somewhere a little clock ticked huskily. There was a close smell; lavender and eau-de-Cologne, mingled with the fragrance of ancient sachets, soap, and drugs. Yet it was a scent even more peculiarly compounded than that.

And the bed! I stared warily in; it was mounded gigantically, and it was empty.

Seaton turned a vague pale face, all shadows: 'What did I say?' he muttered. 'Who's—who's the fool now, I say? How are we going to get back without meeting her, I say? Answer me that! Oh, I wish to God you hadn't come here, Withers.'

He stood audibly shivering in his skimpy gown, and could hardly speak for his teeth chattering. And very distinctly, in the hush that followed his whisper, I heard approaching a faint unhurried voluminous rustle. Seaton clutched my arm, dragged me to the right across the room to a large cupboard, and drew the door close to on us. And, presently, as with bursting lungs I peeped out into the long, low, curtained bedroom, waddled in that wonderful great head and body. I can see her now, all patched and lined with shadow, her tied-up hair (she must have had enormous quantities of it for so old a woman), her heavy lids above those flat, slow, vigilant eyes. She just passed across my ken in the vague dusk; but the bed was out of sight;.

We waited on and on, listening to the clock's muffled ticking. Not the ghost of a sound rose up from the great bed. Either she lay archly listening or slept a sleep serener than an infant's. And when, it seemed, we had been hours in hiding and were cramped, chilled, and half suffocated, we crept out on all fours, with terror knocking at our ribs, and so down the five narrow stairs and back to the little candle-lit blue-and-gold bedroom.

Once there, Seaton gave in. He sat livid on a chair with closed eyes.

'Here,' I said, shaking his arm, 'I'm going to bed; I've had enough of this foolery; I'm going to bed.' His lips quivered, but he made no answer. I poured out some water into my basin and, with that cold pictured azure eye fixed on us, bespattered Seaton's sallow face and forehead and dabbled his hair. He presently sighed and opened fish-like eyes.

'Come on!' I said. 'Don't get shamming, there's a good chap. Get on my back, if you like, and I'll carry you into your bedroom.'

He waved me away and stood up. So, with my candle in one hand, I took him under the arm and walked him along according to his direction down the corridor. His was a much dingier room than mine, and littered with boxes, paper, cages, and clothes. I huddled him into bed and turned to go. And suddenly, I can hardly explain it now, a kind of cold and deadly terror swept over me. I almost ran out of the room, with eyes fixed rigidly in front of me, blew out my candle, and buried my head under the bedclothes.

When I awoke, roused not by a gong, but by a long-continued tapping at my door, sunlight was raying in on cornice and bedpost, and birds were singing in the garden. I got up, ashamed of the night's folly, dressed quickly, and went downstairs. The breakfast room was sweet with flowers and fruit and honey. Seaton's aunt was standing in the garden beside the open french window, feeding a great flutter of birds. I watched her for a moment, unseen. Her face was set in a deep reverie beneath the shadow of a big loose sunhat. It was deeply lined, crooked, and, in a way I can't describe, fixedly vacant and strange. I coughed politely, and she turned with a prodigious, smiling grimace to ask how I had slept. And in that mysterious fashion by which we learn each other's secret thoughts without a syllable said, I knew that she had followed every word and movement of the night before, and was triumphing over my affected innocence and ridiculing my friendly and too easy advances.

We returned to school, Seaton and I, lavishly laden, and by rail all the way. I made no reference to the obscure talk we had had, and resolutely refused to meet his eyes or to take up the hints he let fall. I was relieved—and yet I was sorry—to be going back, and strode on as fast as I could from the station, with Seaton almost trotting at my heels. But he insisted on buying more fruit and sweets—my share of which I accepted with a very bad grace. It was uncomfortably like a bribe; and, after all, I had no quarrel with his rum old aunt, and hadn't really believed half the stuff he had told me.

I saw as little of him as I could after that. He never referred to our visit or resumed his confidences, though in class I would sometimes catch his eye fixed on mine, full of a mute understanding, which I easily affected not to understand. He left Gummidge's, as I have said, rather abruptly, though I never heard of anything to his discredit. And I did not see him or have any news of him again till by chance we met one summer afternoon in the Strand.

He was dressed rather oddly in a coat too large for him and a bright silky tie. But we instantly recognized one another under the awning of a cheap jeweller's shop. He immediately attached himself to me and dragged me off, not too cheerfully, to lunch with him at an Indian restaurant near by. He chattered about our old school, which he remembered only with dislike and disgust; told me cold-bloodedly of the disastrous fate of one or two of the older fellows who had been among his chief tormentors; insisted on an expensive wine and the whole gamut of the foreign menu; and finally informed me, with a good deal of niggling, that he had come up to town to buy an engagement-ring.

And of course: 'How is your aunt?' I enquired at last.

He seemed to have been awaiting the question. It fell like a stone into a deep pool, so many expressions flitted across his long, sad, sallow, un-English face.

'She's aged a good deal,' he said softly, and broke off.

'She's been very decent,' he continued presently after, and paused again. 'In a way.' He eyed me fleetingly. 'I dare say you heard that—she—that is, that we—had lost a good deal of money.'

'No,' I said.

'Oh, yes!' said Seaton, and paused again.

And somehow, poor fellow, I knew in the clink and clatter of glass and voices that he had lied to me; that he did not possess, and never had possessed, a penny beyond what his aunt had squandered on his too ample allowance of pocket-money.

'And the ghosts?' I enquired quizzically.

He grew instantly solemn, and, though it may have been my fancy, slightly yellowed. But 'You are making game of me, Withers,' was all he said.

He asked for my address, and I rather reluctantly gave him my card.

'Look here, Withers,' he said, as we stood together in the sunlight on the kerb, saying good-bye, 'here I am, and—and it's all very well. I'm not perhaps as fanciful as I was. But you are practically the only friend I have on earth—except Alice. . . . And there—to make a clean breast of it, I'm not sure that my aunt cares much about my getting married. She doesn't say so, of course. You know her well enough for that.' He looked sidelong at the rattling gaudy traffic.

'What I was going to say is this: Would you mind coming down? You needn't stay the night unless you please, though, of course, you know you would be awfully welcome. But I should like you to meet my—to meet Alice; and then, perhaps you might tell me your honest opinion of—of the other too.'

I vaguely demurred. He pressed me. And we parted with a half promise that I would come. He waved his ball-topped cane at me and ran off in his long jacket after a bus.

A letter arrived soon after, in his small weak handwriting, giving me full particulars regarding route and trains. And without the least curiosity, even perhaps with some little annoyance that chance should have thrown us together again, I accepted his invitation and arrived one hazy midday at his out-of-the-way station to find him sitting on a low seat under a clump of 'double' hollyhocks, awaiting me.

He looked preoccupied and singularly listless; but seemed, none the less, to be pleased to see me.

We walked up the village street, past the little dingy apothecary's and the empty forge, and, as on my first visit, skirted the house together, and, instead of entering by the front door, made our way down the green path into the garden at the back. A pale haze of cloud muffled the sun; the garden lay in a grey shimmer—its old trees, its snap-dragoned faintly glittering walls. But now there was an air of slovenliness where before all had been neat and methodical. In a patch of shallowly dug soil stood a worn-down spade leaning against a tree. There was an old decayed wheelbarrow. The roses had run to leaf and briar; the fruit-trees were unpruned. The goddess of neglect had made it her secret resort.

'You ain't much of a gardener, Seaton,' I said at last, with a sigh of relief.

'I think, do you know, I like it best like this,' said Seaton. 'We haven't any man now, of course. Can't afford it.' He stood staring at his little dark oblong of freshly turned earth. 'And it always seems to me,' he went on ruminatingly, 'that, after all, we are all nothing better than interlopers on the earth, disfiguring and staining wherever we go. It may sound shocking blasphemy to say so; but then it's different here, you see. We are further away.'

'To tell you the truth, Seaton, I *don't* quite see,' I said; 'but it isn't a new philosophy, is it? Anyhow it's a precious beastly one.'

'It's only what I think,' he replied, with all his odd old stubborn meekness. 'And one thinks as one *is*.'

We wandered on together, talking little, and still with that expression of uneasy vigilance on Seaton's face. He pulled out his watch as we stood gazing idly over the green meadows and the dark motionless bulrushes.

'I think, perhaps, it's nearly time for lunch,' he said. 'Would you like to come in?'

We turned and walked slowly towards the house, across whose windows I confess my own eyes, too, went restlessly meandering in search of its rather disconcerting inmate. There was a pathetic look of bedraggledness, of want of means and care, rust and overgrowth and faded paint. Seaton's aunt, a little to my relief, did not share our meal. So he carved the cold meat, and dispatched a heaped-up plate by an elderly servant for his aunt's private consumption. We talked little and in half-suppressed tones, and sipped some Madeira which Seaton after listening for a moment or two fetched out of the great mahogany sideboard.

I played him a dull and effortless game of chess, yawning between the moves he himself made almost at haphazard, and with attention elsewhere engaged. Towards five o'clock came the sound of a distant ring, and Seaton jumped up, overturning the board, and so ended a game that else might have fatuously continued to this day. He effusively excused himself, and after some little while returned with a slim, dark, pale-faced girl of about nineteen, in a white gown and hat, to whom I was presented with some little nervousness as his 'dear old friend and schoolfellow'.

We talked on in the golden afternoon light, still, as it seemed to me, and even in spite of our efforts to be lively and gay, in a half-suppressed, lack-lustre fashion. We all seemed, if it were not my fancy, to be expectant, to be almost anxiously awaiting an arrival, the appearance of someone whose image filled our collective consciousness. Seaton talked least of all, and in a restless interjectory way, as he continually fidgeted from chair to chair. At last he

proposed a stroll in the garden before the sun should have quite
gone down.

Alice walked between us. Her hair and eyes were conspicuously
dark against the whiteness of her gown. She carried herself not
ungracefully, and yet with peculiarly little movement of her arms
and body, and answered us both without turning her head. There
was a curious provocative reserve in that impassive melancholy
face. It seemed to be haunted by some tragic influence of which she
herself was unaware.

And yet somehow I knew—I believe we all knew—that this walk,
this discussion of their future plans was a futility. I had nothing to
base such scepticism on, except only a vague sense of oppression, a
foreboding consciousness of some inert invincible power in the
background, to whom optimistic plans and love-making and youth
are as chaff and thistledown. We came back, silent, in the last light.
Seaton's aunt was there—under an old brass lamp. Her hair was as
barbarously massed and curled as ever. Her eyelids, I think, hung
even a little heavier in age over their slow-moving, inscrutable
pupils. We filed in softly out of the evening, and I made my bow.

'In this short interval, Mr. Withers,' she remarked amiably, 'you
have put off youth, put on the man. Dear me, how sad it is to see
the young days vanishing! Sit down. My nephew tells me you met
by chance—or act of Providence, shall we call it?—and in my
beloved Strand! You, I understand, are to be best man—yes, best
man! Or am I divulging secrets?' She surveyed Arthur and Alice
with overwhelming graciousness. They sat apart on two low chairs
and smiled in return.

'And Arthur—how do you think Arthur is looking?'

'I think he looks very much in need of a change,' I said.

'A change! Indeed?' She all but shut her eyes at me and with an
exaggerated sentimentality shook her head. 'My dear Mr. Withers!
Are we not all in need of a change in this fleeting, fleeting world?'
She mused over the remark like a connoisseur. 'And you,' she
continued, turning abruptly to Alice, 'I hope you pointed out to
Mr. Withers all my pretty bits?'

'We only walked round the garden,' the girl replied; then,
glancing at Seaton, added almost inaudibly, 'it's a very beautiful
evening.'

'Is it?' said the old lady, starting up violently. 'Then on this very

beautiful evening we will go in to supper. Mr. Withers, your arm;
Arthur, bring in your bride.'

We were a queer quartet, I thought to myself, as I solemnly led
the way into the faded, chilly dining-room, with this indefinable old
creature leaning wooingly on my arm—the large flat bracelet on
the yellow-laced wrist. She fumed a little, breathing heavily, but as
if with an effort of the mind rather than of the body; for she had
grown much stouter and yet little more proportionate. And to talk
into that great white face, so close to mine, was a queer experience
in the dim light of the corridor, and even in the twinkling crystal of
the candles. She was naïve—appallingly naïve; she was crafty and
challenging; she was even arch; and all these in the brief, rather
puffy passage from one room to the other, with these two tongue-
tied children bringing up the rear. The meal was tremendous. I
have never seen such a monstrous salad. But the dishes were greasy
and over-spiced, and were indifferently cooked. One thing only was
quite unchanged—my hostess's appetite was as Gargantuan as
ever. The heavy candelabra that lighted us stood before her high-
backed chair. Seaton sat a little removed, his plate almost in
darkness.

And throughout this prodigious meal his aunt talked, mainly to
me, mainly *at* him, but with an occasional satirical sally at Alice
and muttered explosions of reprimand to the servant. She had aged,
and yet, if it be not nonsense to say so, seemed no older. I suppose
to the Pyramids a decade is but as the rustling down of a handful of
dust. And she reminded me of some such unshakable prehistoricism.
She certainly was an amazing talker—rapid, egregious, with a
delivery that was perfectly overwhelming. As for Seaton—her
flashes of silence were for him. On her enormous volubility would
suddenly fall a hush: acid sarcasm would be left implied; and she
would sit softly moving her great head, with eyes fixed full in a
dreamy smile; but with her whole attention, one could see, slowly,
joyously absorbing his mute discomfiture.

She confided in us her views on a theme vaguely occupying at the
moment, I suppose, all our minds. 'We have barbarous institutions,
and so must put up, I suppose, with a never-ending procession of
fools—of fools *ad infinitum*. Marriage, Mr. Withers, was instituted in
the privacy of a garden; *sub rosa*, as it were. Civilization flaunts it in
the glare of day. The dull marry the poor; the rich the effete; and so
our New Jerusalem is peopled with naturals, plain and coloured, at

either end. I detest folly; I detest still more (if I must be frank, dear Arthur) mere cleverness. Mankind has simply become a tailless host of uninstinctive animals. We should never have taken to Evolution, Mr. Withers. "Natural Selection!"—little gods and fishes!—the deaf for the dumb. We should have used our brains—intellectual pride, the ecclesiastics call it. And by brains I mean—what do I mean Alice?—I mean, my dear child,' and she laid two gross fingers on Alice's narrow sleeve, 'I mean courage. Consider it, Arthur. I read that the scientific world is once more beginning to be afraid of spiritual agencies. Spiritual agencies that tap, and actually float, bless their hearts! I think just one more of those mulberries—thank you.

'They talk about "blind Love",' she ran on derisively as she helped herself, her eyes roving over the dish, 'but why blind? I think, Mr. Withers from weeping over its rickets. After all, it is we plain women that triumph, is it not so—beyond the mockery of time. Alice, now! Fleeting, fleeting is youth, my child. What's that you were confiding to your plate, Arthur. Satirical boy. He laughs at his old aunt: nay, but thou didst laugh. He detests all sentiment. He whispers the most acid asides. Come, my love, we will leave these cynics; we will go and commiserate with each other on our sex. The choice of two evils, Mr. Smithers!' I opened the door, and she swept out as if borne on a torrent of unintelligible indignation; and Arthur and I were left in the clear four-flamed light alone.

For a while we sat in silence. He shook his head at my cigarette-case, and I lit a cigarette. Presently he fidgeted in his chair and poked his head forward into the light. He paused to rise, and shut again the shut door.

'How long will you be?' he asked me.

I laughed.

'Oh, it's not that!' he said, in some confusion. 'Of course, I like to be with her. But it's not that. The truth is, Withers, I don't care about leaving her too long with my aunt.'

I hesitated. He looked at me questioningly.

'Look here, Seaton,' I said, 'you know well enough that I don't want to interfere in your affairs, or to offer advice where it is not wanted. But don't you think perhaps you may not treat your aunt quite in the right way? As one gets old, you know, a little give and take. I have an old godmother, or something of the kind. She's a bit

queer too. . . . . A little allowance; it does no harm. But hang it all,
I'm no preacher.'

He sat down with his hands in his pockets and still with his eyes
fixed almost incredulously on mine. 'How?' he said.

'Well, my dear fellow, if I'm any judge—mind, I don't say that I
am—but I can't help thinking she thinks you don't care for her;
and perhaps takes your silence for—for bad temper. She has been
very decent to you, hasn't she?'

'"Decent"? My God!' said Seaton.

I smoked on in silence; but he continued to look at me with that
peculiar concentration I remembered of old.

'I don't think, perhaps, Withers,' he began presently, 'I don't
think you quite understand. Perhaps you are not quite our kind.
You always did, just like the other fellows, guy me at school. You
laughed at me that night you came to stay here—about the voices
and all that. But I don't mind being laughed at—because I know.'

'Know what?' It was the same old system of dull question and
evasive answer.

'I mean I know that what we see and hear is only the smallest
fraction of what is. I know she lives quite out of this. She *talks* to
you; but it's all make-believe. It's all a "parlour game". She's not
really with you; only pitting her outside wits against yours and
enjoying the fooling. She's living on inside on what you're rotten
without. That's what it is—a cannibal feast. She's a spider. It
doesn't much matter what you call it. It means the same kind of
thing. I tell you, Withers, she hates me; and you can scarcely dream
what that hatred means. I used to think I had an inkling of the
reason. It's oceans deeper than that. It just lies behind: herself
against myself. Why, after all, how much do we really understand
of anything? We don't even know our own histories, and not a
tenth, not a tenth of the reasons. What has life been to me?—
nothing but a trap. And when one sets oneself free for a while, it
only begins again. I thought you might understand; but you are on
a different level: that's all.'

'What on earth are you talking about?' I said contemptuously, in
spite of myself.

'I mean what I say,' he said gutturally. 'All this outside's only
make-believe—but there! what's the good of talking? So far as this
is concerned I'm as good as done. You wait.'

Seaton blew out three of the candles and, leaving the vacant room in semi-darkness, we groped our way along the corridor to the drawing-room. There a full moon stood shining in at the long garden windows. Alice sat stooping at the door, with her hands clasped in her lap, looking out, alone.

'Where is she?' Seaton asked in a low tone.

She looked up; and their eyes met in a glance of instantaneous understanding, and the door immediately afterwards opened behind us.

'*Such* a moon!' said a voice, that once heard, remained unforgettably on the ear. 'A night for lovers, Mr. Withers, if ever there was one. Get a shawl, my dear Arthur, and take Alice for a little promenade. I dare say we old cronies will manage to keep awake. Hasten, hasten, Romeo! My poor, poor Alice, how laggard a lover!'

Seaton returned with a shawl. They drifted out into the moonlight. My companion gazed after them till they were out of hearing, turned to me gravely, and suddenly twisted her white face into such a convulsion of contemptuous amusement that I could only stare blankly in reply.

'Dear innocent children!' she said, with inimitable unctuousness. 'Well, well, Mr. Withers, we poor seasoned old creatures must move with the times. Do you sing?'

I scouted the idea.

'Then you must listen to my playing. Chess'—she clasped her forehead with both cramped hands—'chess is now completely beyond my poor wits.'

She sat down at the piano and ran her fingers in a flourish over the keys. 'What shall it be? How shall we capture them, those passionate hearts? That first fine careless rapture? Poetry itself.' She gazed softly into the garden a moment, and presently, with a shake of her body, began to play the opening bars of Beethoven's 'Moonlight' Sonata. The piano was old and woolly. She played without music. The lamplight was rather dim. The moonbeams from the window lay across the keys. Her head was in shadow. And whether it was simply due to her personality or to some really occult skill in her playing I cannot say; I only know that she gravely and deliberately set herself to satirize the beautiful music. It brooded on the air, disillusioned, charged with mockery and bitterness. I stood at the window; far down the path I could see the white figure glimmering in that pool of colourless light. A few faint stars shone, and still that amazing woman behind me dragged out of the

unwilling keys her wonderful grotesquerie of youth and love and
beauty. It came to an end. I knew the player was watching me.
'Please, please, go on!' I murmured, without turning. '*Please* go on
playing, Miss Seaton.'

No answer was returned to this honeyed sarcasm, but I realized
in some vague fashion that I was being acutely scrutinized, when
suddenly there followed a procession of quiet, plaintive chords
which broke at last softly into the hymn, 'A Few More Years Shall
Roll.'

I confess it held me spellbound. There is a wistful, strained
plangent pathos in the tune; but beneath those masterly old hands
it cried softly and bitterly the solitude and desperate estrangement
of the world. Arthur and his lady-love vanished from my thoughts.
No one could put into so hackneyed an old hymn tune such an
appeal who had never known the meaning of the words. Their
meaning, anyhow, isn't commonplace.

I turned a fraction of an inch to glance at the musician. She was
leaning forward a little over the keys, so that at the approach of my
silent scrutiny she had but to turn her face into the thin flood of
moonlight for every feature to become distinctly visible. And so,
with the tune abruptly terminated, we steadfastly regarded one
another; and she broke into a prolonged chuckle of laughter.

'Not quite so seasoned as I supposed, Mr. Withers. I see you are
a real lover of music. To me it is too painful. It evokes too much
thought. . . .'

I could scarcely see her little glittering eyes under their penthouse
lids.

'And now,' she broke off crisply, 'tell me, as a man of the world,
what do you think of my new niece?'

I was not a man of the world, nor was I much flattered in my stiff
and dullish way of looking at things by being called one; and I
could answer her without the least hesitation:

'I don't think, Miss Seaton, I'm much of a judge of character.
She's very charming.'

'A brunette?'

'I think I prefer dark women.'

'And why? Consider, Mr. Withers; dark hair, dark eyes, dark
cloud, dark night, dark vision, dark death, dark grave, dark DARK!'

Perhaps the climax would have rather thrilled Seaton, but I was too thick-skinned. 'I don't know much about all that,' I answered rather pompously. 'Broad daylight's difficult enough for most of us.'

'Ah,' she said with a sly, inward burst of satirical laughter.

'And I suppose,' I went on, perhaps a little nettled, 'it isn't the actual darkness one admires, it's the contrast of the skin, and the colour of the eyes, and—and their shining. Just as,' I went blundering on, too late to turn back, 'just as you only see the stars in the dark. It would be a long day without any evening. As for death and the grave, I don't suppose we shall much notice that.' Arthur and his sweetheart were slowly returning along the dewy path. 'I believe in making the best of things.'

'How very interesting!' came the smooth answer. 'I see you are a philosopher, Mr. Withers. H'm! "As for death and the grave, I don't suppose we shall much notice that." Very interesting. . . . And I'm sure,' she added in a particularly suave voice, 'I profoundly hope so.' She rose slowly from her stool. 'You will take pity on me again, I hope. You and I would get on famously—kindred spirits— elective affinities. And, of course, now that my nephew's going to leave me, now that his affections are centred on another, I shall be a very lonely old woman. . . . Shall I not, Arthur!'

Seaton blinked stupidly. 'I didn't hear what you said, aunt.'

'I was telling our old friend, Arthur, that when you are gone I shall be a very lonely old woman.'

'Oh, I don't think so;' he said in a strange voice.

'He means, Mr. Withers, he means, my dear child,' she said, sweeping her eyes over Alice, 'he means that I shall have memory for company—heavenly memory—the ghosts of other days. Sentimental boy! And did you enjoy our music, Alice? Did I really stir that youthful heart? . . . O, O, O,' continued the horrible old creature, 'you billers and cooers, I have been listening to such flatteries, such confessions! Beware, beware, Arthur, there's many a slip.' She rolled her little eyes at me, she shrugged her shoulders at Alice, and gazed an instant stonily into her nephew's face.

I held out my hand. 'Good night, good night!' she cried. 'He that fights and runs away. Ah, good night, Mr. Withers; come again soon!' She thrust out her cheek at Alice, and we all three filed slowly out of the room.

Black shadow darkened the porch and half the spreading sycamore. We walked without speaking up the dusty village street. Here and there a crimson window glowed. At the fork of the high-road I said good-bye. But I had taken hardly more than a dozen paces when a sudden impulse seized me.

'Seaton!' I called.

He turned in the cool stealth of the moonlight.

'You have my address; if by any chance, you know, you should care to spend a week or two in town between this and the—the Day, we should be delighted to see you.'

'Thank you, Withers, thank you,' he said in a low voice.

'I dare say'—I waved my stick gallantly at Alice—'I dare say you will be doing some shopping; we could all meet,' I added, laughing.

'Thank you, thank you Withers—immensely,' he repeated.

And so we parted.

But they were out of the jog-trot of my prosaic life. And being of a stolid and incurious nature, I left Seaton and his marriage, and even his aunt, to themselves in my memory, and scarcely gave a thought to them until one day I was walking up the Strand again, and passed the flashing gloaming of the second-rate jeweller's shop where I had accidentally encountered my old schoolfellow in the summer. It was one of those stagnant autumnal days after a night of rain. I cannot say why, but a vivid recollection returned to my mind of our meeting and of how suppressed Seaton had seemed, and of how vainly he had endeavoured to appear assured and eager. He must be married by now, and had doubtless returned from his honeymoon. And I had clean forgotten my manners, had sent not a word of congratulation, nor—as I might very well have done, and as I knew he would have been pleased at my doing—even the ghost of a wedding present. It was just as of old.

On the other hand, I pleaded with myself, I had had no invitation. I paused at the corner of Trafalgar Square, and at the bidding of one of those caprices that seize occasionally on even an unimaginative mind, I found myself pelting after a green bus, and actually bound on a visit I had not in the least intended or foreseen.

The colours of autumn were over the village when I arrived. A beautiful late afternoon sunlight bathed thatch and meadow. But it was close and hot. A child, two dogs, a very old woman with a heavy basket I encountered. One or two incurious tradesmen looked idly up as I passed by. It was all so rural and remote, my whimsical impulse had so much flagged, that for a while I hesitated to venture under the shadow of the sycamore-tree to enquire after the happy pair. Indeed, I first passed by the faint-blue gates and continued my walk under the high, green and tufted wall. Hollyhocks had attained their topmost bud and seeded in the little cottage gardens beyond; the Michaelmas daises were in flower; a sweet warm aromatic smell of fading leaves was in the air. Beyond the cottages lay a field where cattle were grazing, and beyond that I came to a little churchyard. Then the road wound on, pathless and houseless, among gorse and bracken. I turned impatiently and walked quickly back to the house and rang the bell.

The rather colourless elderly woman who answered my enquiry informed me that Miss Seaton was at home, as if only taciturnity forbade her adding, 'But she doesn't want to see *you*.'

'Might I, do you think, have Mr. Arthur's address?' I said.

She looked at me with quiet astonishment, as if waiting for an explanation. Not the faintest of smiles came into her thin face.

'I will tell Miss Seaton,' she said after a pause. 'Please walk in.'

She showed me into the dingy undusted drawing-room, filled with evening sunshine and with the green-dyed light that penetrated the leaves overhanging the long french windows. I sat down and waited on and on, occasionally aware of a creaking footfall overhead. At last the door opened a little, and the great face I had once known peered round at me. For it was enormously changed; mainly, I think, because the aged eyes had rather suddenly failed, and so a kind of stillness and darkness lay over its calm and wrinkled pallor.

'Who is it?' she asked.

I explained myself and told her the occasion of my visit.

She came in, shut the door carefully after her, and, though the fumbling was scarcely perceptible, groped her way to a chair. She had on an old dressing-gown, like a cassock, of a patterned cinnamon colour.

'What is it you want?' she said, seating herself and lifting her blank face to mine.

'Might I just have Arthur's address?' I said deferentially. 'I am so sorry to have disturbed you.'

'H'm. You have come to see my nephew?'

'Not necessarily to see him, only to hear how he is, and, of course, Mrs. Seaton, too. I am afraid my silence must have appeared . . .'

'He hasn't noticed your silence,' croaked the old voice out of the great mask; 'besides, there isn't any Mrs. Seaton.'

'Ah, then,' I answered, after a momentary pause, 'I have not seemed so black as I painted myself! And how is Miss Outram?'

'She's gone into Yorkshire,' answered Seaton's aunt.

'And Arthur too?'

She did not reply, but simply sat blinking at me with lifted chin, as if listening, but certainly not for what I might have to say. I began to feel rather at a loss.

'You were no close friend of my nephew's, Mr. Smithers?' she said presently.

'No,' I answered, welcoming the cue, 'and yet, do you know, Miss Seaton, he is one of the very few of my old school-fellows I have come across in the last few years, and I suppose as one gets older one begins to value old associations. . . .' My voice seemed to trail off into a vacuum. 'I thought Miss Outram', I hastily began again, 'a particularly charming girl. I hope they are both quite well.'

Still the old face solemnly blinked at me in silence.

'You must find it very lonely, Miss Seaton, with Arthur away?'

'I was never lonely in my life,' she said sourly. 'I don't look to flesh and blood for my company. When you've got to be my age, Mr. Smithers (which God forbid), you'll find life a very different affair from what you seem to think it is now. You won't seek company then, I'll be bound. It's thrust on you.' Her face edged round into the clear green light, and her eyes groped, as it were, over my vacant disconcerted face. 'I dare say, now,' she said, composing her mouth, 'I dare say my nephew told you a good many tarradiddles in his time. Oh, yes, a good many, eh? He was always a liar. What, now, did he say of me? Tell me, now.' She leant forward as far as she could, trembling, with an ingratiating smile.

'I think he is rather superstitious,' I said coldly, 'but, honestly, I have a very poor memory, Miss Seaton.'

'Why?' she said. '*I* haven't.'

'The engagement hasn't been broken off, I hope.'

'Well, between you and me,' she said, shrinking up and with an immensely confidential grimace, 'it has.'

'I'm sure I'm very sorry to hear it. And where is Arthur?'

'Eh?'

'Where is Arthur?'

We faced each other mutely among the dead old bygone furniture. Past all my analysis was that large, flat, grey, cryptic countenance.

And then, suddenly, our eyes for the first time really met. In some indescribable way out of that thick-lidded obscurity a far small something stooped and looked out at me for a mere instant of time that seemed of almost intolerable protraction. Involuntarily I blinked and shook my head. She muttered something with great rapidity, but quite inarticulately; rose and hobbled to the door. I thought I heard, mingled in broken mutterings, something about tea.

'Please, please don't trouble,' I began, but could say no more, for the door was already shut between us. I stood and looked out on the long-neglected garden. I could just see the bright weedy greenness of Seaton's tadpole pond. I wandered about the room. Dusk began to gather, the last birds in that dense shadowiness of trees had ceased to sing. And not a sound was to be heard in the house. I waited on and on, vainly speculating. I even attempted to ring the bell; but the wire was broken, and only jangled loosely at my efforts.

I hesitated, unwilling to call or to venture out, and yet more unwilling to linger on, waiting for a tea that promised to be an exceedingly comfortless supper. And as darkness drew down, a feeling of the utmost unease and disquietude came over me. All my talks with Seaton returned on me with a suddenly enriched meaning. I recalled again his face as we had stood hanging over the staircase, listening in the small hours to the inexplicable stirrings of the night. There were no candles in the room; every minute the autumnal darkness deepened. I cautiously opened the door and listened, and with some little dismay withdrew, for I was uncertain of my way out. I even tried the garden, but was confronted under a veritable thicket of foliage by a padlocked gate. It would be a little too ignominious to be caught scaling a friend's garden fence!

Cautiously returning into the still and musty drawing-room, I took out my watch, and gave the incredible old woman ten minutes in which to reappear. And when that tedious ten minutes had ticked by I could scarcely distinguish its hands. I determined to wait no longer, drew open the door and, trusting to my sense of direction, groped my way through the corridor that I vaguely remembered led to the front of the house.

I mounted three or four stairs and, lifting a heavy curtain, found myself facing the starry fanlight of the porch. From here I glanced into the gloom of the dining-room. My fingers were on the latch of the outer door when I heard a faint stirring in the darkness above the hall. I looked up and became conscious of, rather than saw, the huddled old figure looking down on me.

There was an immense hushed pause. Then, 'Arthur, Arthur,' whispered an inexpressibly peevish rasping voice, 'is that you? Is that you, Arthur?'

I can scarcely say why, but the question horribly startled me. No conceivable answer occurred to me. With head craned back, hand clenched on my umbrella, I continued to stare up into the gloom, in this fatuous confrontation.

'Oh, oh,' the voice croaked. 'It is *you*, is it? *That* disgusting man! . . . Go away out. Go away out.'

At this dismissal, I wrenched open the door and, rudely slamming it behind me, ran out into the garden, under the gigantic old sycamore, and so out at the open gate.

I found myself half up the village street before I stopped running. The local butcher was sitting in his shop reading a piece of newspaper by the light of a small oil-lamp. I crossed the road and enquired the way to the station. And after he had with minute and needless care directed me, I asked casually if Mr. Arthur Seaton still lived with his aunt at the big house just beyond the village. He poked his head in at the little parlour door.

'Here's a gentleman enquiring after young Mr. Seaton, Millie,' he said. 'He's dead, ain't he?'

'Why, yes, bless you,' replied a cheerful voice from within. 'Dead and buried these three months or more—young Mr. Seaton. And just before he was to be married, don't you remember, Bob?'

I saw a fair young woman's face peer over the muslin of the little door at me.

'Thank you,' I replied, 'then I go straight on?'

'That's it, sir; past the pond, bear up the hill a bit to the left, and then there's the station lights before your eyes.'

We looked intelligently into each other's faces in the beam of the smoky lamp. But not one of the many questions in my mind could I put into words.

And again I paused irresolutely a few paces further on. It was not, I fancy, merely a foolish apprehension of what the raw-boned butcher might 'think' that prevented my going back to see if I could find Seaton's grave in the benighted churchyard. There was precious little use in pottering about in the muddy dark merely to discover where he was buried. And yet I felt a little uneasy. My rather horrible thought was that, so far as I was concerned—one of his extremely few friends—he had never been much better than 'buried' in my mind.

ELIZABETH BOWEN
Ivy Gripped the Steps

IVY gripped and sucked at the flight of steps, down which with such
a deceptive wildness it seemed to be flowing like a cascade. Ivy
matted the door at the top and amassed in bushes above and below
the porch. More, it has covered, or one might feel consumed, one
entire half of the high double-fronted house, from the basement up
to a spiked gable: it had attained about half-way up to the girth and
more than the density of a tree, and was sagging outward under its
own weight. One was left to guess at the size and the number of
windows hidden by looking at those in the other side. But these,
though in sight, had been made effectively sightless: sheets of some
dark composition that looked like metal were sealed closely into
their frames. The house, not old, was of dull red brick with stone
trimmings.

To crown all, the ivy was now in fruit, clustered over with fleshy
pale green berries. There was something brutal about its fecundity.
It was hard to credit that such a harvest could have been nourished
only on brick and stone. Had not reason insisted that the lost
windows must, like their fellows, have been made fast, so that the
suckers for all their seeking voracity could not enter, one could have
convinced oneself that the ivy must be feeding on something inside
the house.

The process of strangulation could be felt: one wondered how
many more years of war would be necessary for this to complete
itself. And, the conventionality of the house, the remains, at least,
of ordering its surroundings made what was happening more and
more an anomaly. Mrs. Nicholson's house had always enjoyed
distinction—that of being detached, while its neighbours, though
equally 'good', had been erected in couples or even in blocks of four;
that of being the last in the avenue; that of having on one hand as
neighbour the theatre, to whose façade its front was at right angles.
The theatre, set back behind shallow semi-circular gardens, at once
crowned and terminated the avenue, which ran from it to the
Promenade overhanging the sea. And the house, apart from the
prestige of standing just where it stood, had the air of reserving

something quite of its own. It was thus perhaps just, or not unfitting, that it should have been singled out for this gothic fate.

This was, or had been, one of the best residential avenues in Southstone, into which private hotels intruded only with the most breathless, costly discretion: if it was not that now it was nothing else, for there was nothing else for it to be. Lines of chestnut trees had been planted along the pavements, along the railed strip of lawn that divided the avenue down the centre—now, the railings were, with all other ironwork, gone; and where the lawn was very long, rusty grass grew up into the tangles of rusty barbed wire. On to this, as on to the concrete pyramids—which, in the course of four years of waiting to be pushed out to obstruct the invader, had sunk some inches into the soil—the chestnuts were now dropping their leaves.

The decline dated from the exodus of the summer of 1940, when Southstone had been declared to be in the front line. The houses at the sea end of the avenue had, like those on the Promenade, been requisitioned; but some of those at the theatre end stayed empty. Here and there portions of porches or balustrades had fallen into front gardens, crushing their overgrowth; but there were no complete ruins; no bomb or shell had arrived immediately here, and effects of blast, though common to all of Southstone, were less evident than desuetude and decay. It was now the September of 1944; and, for some reason, the turn of the tide of war, the accumulation of the Invasion victories, gave Southstone its final air of defeat. The withdrawal of most of the soldiers, during the summer, had drained off adventitious vitality. The A.A. batteries, this month, were on the move to another part of the coast. And, within the very last few days, the silencing of the guns across the Channel had ended the tentative love affair with death: Southstone's life, no longer kept to at least a pitch by shelling warnings, now had nothing but an etiolated slowness. In the shuttered shopping streets, along the Promenade, in the intersecting avenues, squares and crescents, vacuum mounted up. The lifting of the ban on the area had, so far, brought few visitors in.

This afternoon, for minutes together, not a soul, not even a soldier crossed the avenue: Gavin Doddington stood to regard the ivy in what was, virtually, solitude. The sky being clouded, though not dark, a timeless flat light fell on to everything. Outside the theatre a very few soldiers stood grouped about; some moodily, some in no

more than apathy. The theatre gardens had been cemented over to
make a lorry park; and the engine of one of the lorries was being
run.

Mrs. Nicholson could not be blamed for the ivy: *her* absence from
Southstone was of long standing, for she had died in 1912—two
years before the outbreak of what Gavin still thought of as Admiral
Concannon's war. After her death, the house had been put up for
auction by her executors: since then, it might well have changed
hands two or three times. Probably few of the residents dislodged in
1940 had so much as heard Mrs. Nicholson's name. In its condition,
today, the house was a paradox: having been closed and sealed up
with extreme care, it had been abandoned in a manner no less
extreme. It had been nobody's business to check the ivy. Nor
apparently, has there been anybody to authorize a patriotic sacrifice
of the railings—Gavin Doddington, prodding between the strands
of ivy, confirmed his impression that that iron lacework still topped
the parapet of the front garden. He could pursue with his finger,
though not see, the pattern that with other details of the house,
outside and in, had long ago been branded into his memory.
Looking up at the windows on the exposed half he saw, still in
position along the sills, miniature reproductions of this pattern, for
the support of window boxes. Those, which were gone, had been
flowery in her day.

The assumption was that, as lately as 1940, Mrs. Nicholson's
house *had* belonged to someone, but that it belonged to nobody now.
The late owner's death in some other part of England must have
given effect to a will not brought up to date, by which the property
passed to an heir who could not be found—to somebody not heard
of since Singapore fell or not yet reported anything more than
'missing' after a raid on London or a battle abroad. Legal hold-ups
dotted the world-wide mess. . . . So reasoning, Gavin Doddington
gave rein to what had been his infant and was now his infantile
passion for explanation. But also he attached himself to the story as
to something that had nothing to do with him; and did so with the
intensity of a person who must think lest he should begin to feel.

His passion for explanation had been, when he knew Mrs.
Nicholson, raised by her power of silently baulking it into the
principal reason for suffering. It had been among the stigmata of
his extreme youth—he had been eight when he met her, ten when

she died. He had not been back to Southstone since his last stay with her.

Now, the lifting of the official ban on the area had had the effect of bringing him straight back—why? When what one has refused is put out of reach, when what one had avoided becomes forbidden, some lessening of the inhibition may well occur. The ban had so acted on his reluctance that, when the one was removed, the other came away with it—as a scab, adhering, comes off with a wad of lint. The transmutation, due to the fall of France, of his '*I* cannot go back to Southstone' into '*One* cannot go there' must have been salutary, or, at least, exteriorizing. It so happened that when the ban came off he had been due for a few days' leave from the Ministry. He had at once booked a room at one of the few hotels that remained at the visitor's disposition.

Arriving at Southstone yesterday evening, he had confined his stroll in the hazy marine dusk to the cracked, vacant and wire-looped Promenade—from which he returned with little more than the wish that he had, after all, brought somebody down here with him. Amorist since his teens, he had not often set off on a holiday uncompanioned. The idea of this as a pilgrimage revolted him: he remained in the bar till it closed. This morning he had no more than stalked the house, approaching it in wavering circles closing through the vaguer Southstone areas of association. He had fixed for the actual confrontation that hour, deadline for feeling, immediately after lunch.

The story originated in a friendship between two young girls in their Dresden finishing year. Edith and Lilian had kept in touch throughout later lives that ran very widely apart—their letters, regularly exchanged, were perhaps more confidential than their infrequent meetings. Edith had married a country gentleman, Lilian a business man. Jimmie Nicholson had bought the Southstone house for his wife in 1907, not long before his death, which had been the result of a stroke. He had been her senior by about fifteen years: their one child, a daughter, had died at birth.

Edith Doddington, who had never been quite at ease on the subject of Lilian's marriage, came to stay more often now her friend was a widow, but still could not come as often as both would have liked. Edith's own married life was one of contrivance and of anxiety. After money, the most pressing of Edith's worries centred round the health of her second son: Gavin had been from birth a delicate little boy. The damp of his native county, inland and low-lying, did not suit him: there was the constant question of change of air—till his health stabilized, he could not go away to school. It was natural that Lilian, upon discovering this, should write inviting Gavin to stay at Southstone—ideally, of course, let his mother bring him; but if Edith could not be free, let him come alone. Mrs. Nicholson hoped he and she, who had not yet met, would not, or would not for long, be shy of each other. Her maid Rockham was, at any rate, good with children.

Gavin had heard of Southstone as the scene of his mother's only exotic pleasure. The maid Rockham was sent to London to meet him: the two concluded their journey with the absurdly short drive, in an open victoria, from the station to Mrs. Nicholson's house. It was early in what was a blazing June; the awnings over the windows rippled, the marguerites in the window boxes undulated, in a hot breeze coming down the avenue from the sea. From the awnings the rooms inside took a tense bright dusk. In the sea-blue drawing-room, up whose walls reared mirrors framed in ivory brackets, Gavin was left to await Mrs. Nicholson. He had time to marvel at the variety of the bric-à-brac crowding brackets and tables, the multitude of cut crystal vases, the earliness of the purple and white sweet pea—at the Doddingtons' sweet peas did not flower before July. Mrs. Nicholson then entered: to his surprise she did not kiss him.

Instead, she stood looking down at him—she was tall—with a glittering charming air of uncertainty. Her head bent a little lower, during consideration not so much of Gavin as of the moment. Her coiffure was like spun sugar: that its crisp upward waves should seem to have been splashed with silvery powder added, only, marquise-like glowing youth to her face.

The summery light-like fullness of her dress was accentuated by the taut belt with coral-inlaid clasp; from that small start the skirts flowed down to dissipate and spread where they touched the floor. Tentatively she extended her right hand, which he, without again raising his eyes, shook. 'Well . . . Gavin,' she said, 'I hope you had a good journey? I am so very glad you could come.'

He said: 'And my mother sends you her love.'

'Does she?' Sitting down, sinking an elbow into the sofa cushions, she added: 'How *is* Edith—how is your mother?'

'Oh, she is very well.'

She vaguely glanced round her drawing-room, as though seeing it from his angle, and, therefore herself seeing it for the first time. The alternatives it offered could be distracting: she soon asked him her first intimate question—'Where do you think you would like to sit?'

Not that afternoon, nor, indeed, until some way on into this first visit did Gavin distinguish at all sharply between Mrs. Nicholson and her life. Not till the knife of love gained sufficient edge could he cut out her figure from its surroundings. Southstone was, for the poor landowner's son, the first glimpse of the enchanted existence of the *rentier*. Everything was effortless; and, to him, consequently, seemed stamped with style. This society gained by smallness: it could be comprehended. People here, the company that she kept, commanded everything they desired, were charged with nothing they did not. The expenditure of their incomes—expenditure calculated so long ago and so nicely that it could now seem artless— occupied them. What there was to show for it showed at every turn; though at no turn too much, for it was not too much. Such light, lofty, smooth-running houses were to be found, quite likely, in no capital city. A word to the livery stables brought an imposing carriage to any door: in the afternoons one drove, in a little party, to reflect on a Roman ruin or to admire a village church. In the Promenade's glare, at the end of the shaded avenue, parasols passed and repassed in a rhythm of leisure. Just inland were the attentive shops. There were meetings for good causes in cool drawing-rooms, afternoon concerts in the hotel ball-rooms; and there was always the theatre, where applause continued long after Gavin had gone to bed. Best of all, there were no poor to be seen.

The plan of this part of Southstone (a plateau backed by the downs and overhanging the sea) was masterful. Its architecture was ostentatious, fiddling, bulky and mixed. Gavin was happy enough to be at an age to admire the one, to be unaware of the other—he was elated, rather than not, by this exhibition of gimcrack size; and bows, bays, balustrades, glazed-in balconies and French-type mansardes not slowly took up their parts in the fairy tale. As strongly was he impressed by the strong raying out, from such points as station and theatre, of avenues; each of which crossed obliquely, just less wide residential roads. Lavishness appeared in the public flowers, the municipal seats with their sofa-like curving backs, the flagpoles, cliff grottoes, perspectives of lawn. There was a climate here that change from season to season, the roughest Channel gale blowing, could not disturb. This town without function fascinated him—outside it, down to the port or into the fishing quarter, 'old Southstone', he did not attempt to stray. Such tameness might have been found odd in a little boy: Mrs. Nicholson never thought of it twice.

Gavin's estimation of Southstone—as he understood much later—coincided with that of a dead man. When Jimmie Nicholson bought the house for his wife here, Southstone was the high dream of his particular world. It was as Lilian's husband he made the choice: alone, he might not have felt capable of this polished leisure. His death left it uncertain whether, even *as* Lilian's husband, he could have made the grade. The golf course had been his object: failing that he was not, perhaps, so badly placed in the cemetery, which was also outside the town. For, for Southstone, dividends kept their mystic origin: they were as punctual as Divine grace, as unmentioned as children still in wombs. Thick-set Jimmie, with his pursuant reek of the City, could have been a distasteful reminder of money's source.

Gavin, like his dead host, beheld Southstone with all the ardour of an outsider. His own family had a touch of the brutishness that comes from any dependence upon land. Mr. and Mrs. Doddington were constantly in wet clothes, constantly fatigued, constantly depressed. Nothing new appeared in the squire's home; and what was old had acquired a sort of fog from being ignored. An austere, religious idea of their own standing not so much inspired as preyed upon Gavin's parents. Caps touched to them in the village could not console them for the letters they got from their bank. Money for them was like a spring in a marsh, feebly thrusting its way up to be absorbed again: any profit forced from the home farm, any rents received for outlying lands, went back again into upkeep, rates, gates, hedging, draining, repairs to cottages and renewal of stock. There was nothing, no nothing ever, to show. In the society round them they played no part to which their position did not compel them: they were poor gentry, in fact, at a period when poverty could not be laughed away. Their lot was less enviable than that of any of their employees or tenants, whose faces, naked in their dejection, and voices pitched to complaints they could at least utter, had disconcerted Gavin since babyhood, at the Hall door. Had the

Doddingtons been told that their kind would die out, they would have expressed little more than surprise that such complicated troubles could end so simply.

Always towards the end of a stay at Southstone Gavin's senses began to be haunted by the anticipation of going back. So much so that to tread the heat-softened asphalt was to feel once more the suck of a sticky lane. *Here*, day and night he breathed with ease that was still a subconscious joy: the thought of the Midlands made his lungs contract and deaden—such was the old cold air, sequestered by musty baize doors, of the corridors all the way to his room at home.

His room *here* was on the second floor, in front, looking on to the avenue. It had a frieze of violets knotted along a ribbon: as dusk deepened, these turned gradually black. Later, a lamp from the avenue cast a tree's shifting shadow on to the ceiling above his bed; and the same light pierced the Swiss skirts of the dressing-table. Mrs. Nicholson, on the first occasion when she came as far as his door to say good-night, deprecated the 'silliness' of this little room. Rockham, it seemed, had thought it suitable for his age—she, Rockham, had her quarters on the same floor—Mrs. Nicholson, though she did not say so, seemed to feel it to be unsuitable for his sex. 'Because I don't suppose,' she said, 'that you really ever *are* lonely in the night?'

Propped upright against his pillows, gripping his glass of milk, he replied: 'I am never frightened.'

'But, lonely—what makes you lonely, then?'

'I don't know. I suppose, thoughts.'

'Oh, but why,' she said, 'don't you like them?'

'When I am here the night seems a sort of waste, and I don't like to think what a waste it is.'

Mrs. Nicholson, who was on her way out to dinner, paused in the act of looping a gauze scarf over her hair and once again round her throat. 'Only tell me,' she said, 'that you're not more lonely, Gavin, because I am going out? Up here, you don't know if I am in the house or not.'

'I do know.'

'Perhaps,' she suggested humbly, 'you'll go to sleep? They all say it is right for you, going to bed so early, but I wish it did not make days so short—I must go.'

'The carriage hasn't come round yet.'

'No, it won't; it hasn't been ordered. It is so lovely this evening, I thought I would like to walk.' She spoke, though, as though the project were spoiled for her: she could not help seeing, as much as he did, the unkindness of leaving him with this picture. She came, even, further into the room to adjust her scarf at his mirror, for it was not yet dark. 'Just once, one evening perhaps, you could stay up late. Do you think it would matter? I'll ask Rockham.'

Rockham remained the arbiter: it was she who was left to exercise anything so nearly harsh as authority. In, even, the affairs of her own house Mrs. Nicholson was not heard giving an order: what could not be thought to be conjured into existence must be part of the clockwork wound up at the start by Jimmie and showing no sign of beginning to run down yet. The dishes that came to table seemed to surprise her as much, and as pleasingly, as they did Gavin. Yet the effect she gave was not of idleness but of preoccupation: what she did with her days Gavin did not ask himself—when he did ask himself, later, it was too late. They continued to take her colour—those days she did nothing with.

It was Rockham who worked out the daily programme, devised to keep the little boy out of Madam's way. 'Because Madam,' she said, 'is not accustomed to children.' It was by Rockham that, every morning, he was taken down to play by the sea: the beach, undulations of orange shingle, was fine-combed with breakwaters, against one of which sat Rockham, reading a magazine. Now and then she would look up, now and then she would call. These relegations to Rockham sent Gavin to angry extremes of infantilism: he tried to drape seaweed streamers around her hat; he plagued to have pebbles taken out of his shoe. There was a literal feeling of degradation about this descent from the plateau to the cliff's foot. From close up, the sea, with its heaving mackerel vacancy, bored him—most of the time he stood with his back to it, shading his eyes and staring up at the heights. From right down here, though Southstone could not be seen—any more than objects set back on a high shelf can be seen by somebody standing immediately underneath it—its illusion, its magical artificiality, was to be savoured as from nowhere else. Tiny, the flags of the Promenade's edge, the figures leaning along the railings, stood out against a dazzle of sky. And he never looked up at these looking down without an interrupted heartbeat—might she not be among them?

The rule was that they, Rockham and Gavin, walked zigzag down by the cliff path, but travelled up in the lift. But one day fate made Rockham forget her purse. They had therefore to undertake the ascent. The path's artful gradients, handrailed, were broken by flights of steps and by niched seats, upon every one of which Rockham plumped herself down to regain breath. The heat of midday, the glare from the flowered cliff beat up Gavin into a sort of fever. As though a dropped plummet had struck him between the eyes he looked up, to see Mrs. Nicholson's face above him against the blue. The face, its colour rendered transparent by the transparent silk of a parasol, was inclined forward: he had the experience of seeing straight up into eyes that did not see him. Her look was pitched into space: she was not only not seeing him, she was seeing nothing. She was listening, but not attending, while someone talked.

Gavin, gripping the handrail, bracing his spine against it, leaned out backwards over the handrail into the void, in the hopes of intercepting her line of view. But in vain. He tore off clumps of sea pinks and cast the too-light flowers outwards into the air, but her pupils never once flickered down. Despair, the idea that his doom must be never, never to reach her, not only now but ever, gripped him and gripped his limbs as he took the rest of the path—the two more bends and few more steps to the top. He clawed his way up the rail, which shook in its socket.

The path, when it landed Gavin on to the Promenade, did so some yards from where Mrs. Nicholson and her companion stood. Her companion was Admiral Concannon. 'Hello, hello,' said the Admiral, stepping back to see clear of the parasol. 'Where have *you* sprung from?'

'Oh, but Gavin,' exclaimed Mrs. Nicholson, also turning, 'why not come up in the lift? I thought you liked it.'

'Lift?' said the Admiral. 'Lift, at his age? What, has the boy got a dicky heart?'

'No, indeed!' she said, and looked at Gavin so proudly that he became the image of health and strength.

'In that case,' said the Admiral, 'do him good.' There was something, in the main, not unflattering about this co-equal masculine brusqueness. Mrs. Nicholson, looking over the railings, perceived the labouring top of her maid's hat. 'It's poor Rockham,' she said, 'that I am thinking about; she hasn't got a heart but she has attacks.—How hazy it is,' she said, indicating the horizon with a gloved hand. 'It seems to be days since we saw France. I don't believe Gavin believes it is really there.'

'It is there all right,' said the Admiral, frowning slightly.

'Why, Rockham,' she interposed, 'you look hot. Whatever made you walk up on a day like this?'

'Well, I cannot fly, can I, Madam; and I overlooked my purse.'

'Admiral Concannon says we may all be flying. What are you waiting for?'

'I was waiting for Master Gavin to come along.'

'I don't see why he should, really—which would you rather, Gavin?'

Admiral Concannon's expression did not easily change, and did not change now. His features were severely clear cut; his figure was nervy and spare; and he had an air of eating himself—due, possibly, to his retirement. His manners of walking, talking and standing, though all to be recognized at a distance, were vehemently impersonal. When in anything that could be called repose he usually kept his hands in his pockets—the abrupt extraction of one hand, for the purpose of clicking thumb and finger together, was the nearest thing to a gesture he ever made. His voice and step had become familiar, among the few nocturnal sounds of the avenue, some time before Gavin had seen his face, for he escorted Mrs. Nicholson home from parties to which she had been wilful enough to walk. Looking out one night, after the hall door shut, Gavin had seen the head of a cigarette, immobile, pulsating sharply under the dark trees. The Concannons had settled at Southstone for Mrs. Concannon's health's sake: their two daughters attended one of the schools.

Liberated into this blue height, Gavin could afford to look down in triumph at the sea by whose edge he had lately stood. But the Admiral said: 'Another short turn, perhaps?'—since they were to *be* three, they had better be three in motion. Mrs. Nicholson raised her parasol, and the three moved off down the Promenade with the dignified aimlessness of swans. Ahead, the distance dissolved, the asphalt quivered in heat; and she, by walking between her two companions, produced a democracy of masculine trouble into which age did not enter at all. As they passed the bandstand she said to Gavin: 'Admiral Concannon has just been saying that there is going to be a war.'

Gavin glanced across at the Admiral, who remained in profile. Unassisted and puzzled, he said: 'Why?'

'Why, indeed?' she agreed. 'There!' she said to the Admiral. 'It's no good trying to tease me, because I never believe you.' She glanced around her and added: 'After all, we live in the present day! History is quite far back; it is sad, of course, but it does seem silly. I never even cared for history at school; I was glad when we came to the end of it.'

'And when, my dear, did you come to the end of history?'

'The year I put up my hair. It had begun to be not so bad from the time we started catching up with the present; and I was glad I had stayed at school long enough to be sure that it had all ended happily. But oh, those unfortunate people in the past! It seems unkind to say so, but can it have been their faults? They can have been no more like us than cats and dogs. I suppose there *is* one reason for learning history—one sees how long it has taken to make the world nice. Who on earth could want to upset things now?—No one could want to,' she said to the Admiral. 'You forget the way we behave now, and there's no other way. Civilized countries are polite to each other, just as you and I are to the people we know, and uncivilized countries are put down—but, if one thinks, there are beautifully few of those. Even savages really prefer wearing hats and coats. Once people wear hats and coats and can turn on electric light, they would no more want to be silly than you or I do. Or *do* you want to be silly?' she said to the Admiral.

He said: 'I did not mean to upset you.'

'You don't,' she said. 'I should not dream of suspecting *any* civilized country!'

'Which civilized country?' said Gavin. 'France?'

'For your information,' said the Admiral coldly, 'it is Germany we should be preparing to fight, for the reason that she is preparing to fight us.'

'I have never been happier anywhere,' said Mrs. Nicholson, more near definitely than usual. 'Why,' she added, turning to Gavin, 'if it were not for Germany, now I come to think of it, you would not be here!'

The Admiral, meanwhile, had become intent on spearing on the tip of his cane a straying fragment of paper, two inches torn off a letter, that was defiling the Promenade. Lips compressed, he crossed to a litter basket (which had till then stood empty, there being no litter) and knocked the fragment into it off his cane. He burst out:

'I should like to know what this place is coming to—we shall have trippers next!'

This concern his beautiful friend *could* share—and did so share that harmony was restored. Gavin, left to stare out to sea, reflected on one point in the conversation: he could never forget that the Admiral had called Mrs. Nicholson 'My dear'.

Also, under what provocation had the Admiral threatened Mrs. Nicholson with war? . . . Back at Gavin's home again, once more with his parents, nothing was, after all, so impossible: this was outside the zone of electric light. As late summer wore slowly over the Midlands, the elms in the Doddingtons' park casting lifeless slate-coloured shadows over sorrel, dung, thistles and tufted grass, it was borne in on Gavin that this existence belonged, by its nature, to *any* century. It was unprogressive. It had stayed as it was while, elsewhere, history jerked itself painfully off the spool; it could hardly be more depressed by the fateful passage of armies than by the flooding of tillage or the failure of crops; it was hardly capable, really, of being depressed further. It was an existence mortgaged to necessity; it was an inheritance of uneasiness, tension and suspicion. One could pre-assume the enmity of weather, prices, mankind, cattle. It was this dead weight of existence that had supplied to history not so much the violence or the futility that had been, as she said, apparent to Mrs. Nicholson, but its repetitive harshness and its power to scar. This existence had no volition, but could not stop; and its never stopping, because it could not, made history's ever stopping the less likely. No signs of, even, an agreeable pause were to be seen round Doddington Hall. Nor could one, at such a distance from Southstone, agree that time had laboured to make the world nice.

Gavin now saw his mother as Mrs. Nicholson's friend. Indeed, the best of the gowns in which Edith went out to dinner, when forced to go out to dinner, had been Lilian's once, and once or twice worn by her. Worn by Edith, they still had the exoticism of gifts, and dispelled from their folds not only the giver's sachets but the easy pitiful lovingness of the giver's mood. In them, Gavin's mother's thin figure assumed a grace whose pathos was lost to him at the time. While the brown-yellow upward light of the table oil lamp unkindly sharpened the hollows in Mrs. Doddington's face and throat, Gavin, thrown sideways out of his bed, fingered the mousseline or caressed the satin of the skirts with an adoring

absorption that made his mother uneasy—for fetichism is, still, to
be apprehended by those for whom it has never had any name. She
would venture: 'You like, then, to see me in pretty clothes?' . . . It
was, too, in the first of these intermissions between his visits to
Southstone that he, for the first time, took stock of himself, of his
assets—the evident pleasingness of his manner; his looks—he could
take in better and better part his elder brother's jibes at his pretty-
prettiness—his quickness of mind, which at times made even his
father smile; and his masculinity, which, now he tried it out, gave
him unexpected command of small situations. At home, nights were
not a waste: he attached himself to his thoughts, which took him,
by seven-league strides, onward to his next visit. He rehearsed,
using his mother, all sorts of little gratuities of behaviour, till she
exclaimed: 'Why, Lilian has made quite a little page of you!' At her
heels round the garden or damp extensive offices of the Hall, at her
elbow as she peered through her letters or resignedly settled to her
accounts, he reiterated: 'Tell me about Germany.'

'Why Germany?'

'I mean, the year you were there.'

A gale tore the slates from the Hall stables, brought one tree
down on to a fence and another to block the drive, the night before
Gavin left for Southstone. This time he travelled alone. At Southstone, dull shingly roaring thumps from the beach travelled as far
inland as the railway station; from the Promenade—on which,
someone said, it was all but impossible to stand upright—there
came a whistling strain down the avenues. It was early January.
Rockham was kept to the house by a nasty cold; so it was Mrs.
Nicholson who, with brilliantly heightened colour, holding her muff
to the cheek on which the wind blew, was on the station platform to
meet Gavin. A porter, tucking the two of them into the waiting
carriage, replaced the footwarmer under the fur rug. She said: 'How
different this is from when you were with me last. Or do you like
winter?'

'I like anything, really.'

'I remember one thing you don't like: you said you didn't like
thoughts.' As they drove past a lighted house from which music
came to be torn about by the wind, she remembered: 'You've been
invited to several parties.'

He was wary: 'Shall you be going to them?'

'Why, yes; I'm sure I *could* go,' she said.

Her house was hermetic against the storm: in the drawing-room, heat drew out the smell of violets. She dropped her muff on the sofa, and Gavin stroked it—'It's like a cat,' he said quickly, as she turned round. 'Shall I have a cat?' she said. 'Would you like me to have a cat?' All the other rooms, as they went upstairs, were tawny with fires that did not smoke.

Next morning, the wind had dropped; the sky reflected on everything in its mild brightness; trees, houses and pavements glistened like washed glass. Rockham, puffy and with a glazed upper lip, said: 'Baster Gavid, you've brought us better weather.' Having blown her nose with what she seemed to hope was exhaustive thoroughness, she concealed her handkerchief in her bosom as guiltily as though it had been a dagger. 'Badam,' she said, 'doesn't like be to have a cold. Poor Bisses Codcadded,' she added, 'has been laid up agaid.'

Mrs. Concannon's recovery must be timed for the little dinner party that they were giving. Her friends agreed that she ought to reserve her strength. On the morning of what was to be the day it was, therefore, the Admiral whom one met out shopping: Gavin and Mrs. Nicholson came on him moodily selecting flowers and fruit. Delayed late autumn and forced early spring flowers blazed, under artificial light, against the milder daylight outside the florist's plate glass. 'For tonight, for the party?' exclaimed Mrs. Nicholson. 'Oh, let us have carnations, scarlet carnations!'

The Admiral hesitated. 'I think Constance spoke of chrysanthemums, white chrysanthemums.'

'Oh, but these are so washy, so like funerals. They will do poor Constance no good, if she still feels ill.'

Gavin, who had examined the prices closely, in parentheses said: 'Carnations are more expensive.'

'No, wait!' cried Mrs. Nicholson, gathering from their buckets all the scarlet carnations that were in reach, and gaily shaking the water from their stems. 'You must let me send these to Constance, because I am so much looking forward to tonight. It will be delightful.'

'I hope so,' the Admiral said. 'But I'm sorry to say we shall be an uneven number: we have just heard that poor Massingham has dropped out. Influenza.'

'Bachelors shouldn't have influenza, should they? But then, why not ask somebody else?'

'So very much at the last moment, that might seem a bit—informal.'

'Dear me,' she teased, 'have you really got *no* old friend?'

'Constance does not feel . . .'

Mrs. Nicholson's eyebrows rose: she looked at the Admiral over the carnations. This was one of the moments when the Admiral could be heard to click his finger and thumb. 'What a pity,' she said. 'I don't care for lopsided parties. *I* have one friend who is not touchy—invite Gavin!'

To a suggestion so completely outrageous, who was to think of any reply? It was a *coup*. She completed, swiftly: 'Tonight, then? We shall be with you at about eight.'

Gavin's squiring of Mrs. Nicholson to the Concannons' party symptomized this phase of their intimacy; without being, necessarily, its highest point. Rockham's cold had imperilled Rockham's prestige: as intervener or arbiter she could be counted out. There being no more talk of these odious drops to the beach, Gavin exercised over Mrs. Nicholson's mornings what seemed a conqueror's rights to a terrain; while with regard to her afternoons she showed a flattering indecision as to what might not please him or what he could not share. At her tea table, his position was made subtly manifest to her guests. His bedtime was becoming later and later; in vain did Rockham stand and cough in the hall; more than once or twice he had dined downstairs. When the curtains were drawn, it was he who lit the piano candles, then stood beside her as she played—ostensibly to turn over the music, but forgetting the score to watch her hands. At the same time, he envisaged their two figures as they would appear to someone—his other self—standing out there in the cold dark of the avenue, looking between the curtains into the glowing room. One evening, she sang, 'Two eyes of grey that used to be so bright'.

At the end, he said: 'But that's supposed to be a song sung by a man to a woman.'

Turning on the piano stool, she said: 'Then you must learn it.'

He objected: 'But your eyes are not grey.'

Indeed they were never neutral eyes. Their sapphire darkness, with that of the sapphire pendant she was wearing, was struck into by the Concannons' electric light. That round fitment on pulleys, with a red silk frill, had been so adjusted above the dinner table as to cast down a vivid circle, in which the guests sat. The stare and sheen of the cloth directly under the light appeared supernatural. The centrepiece was a silver or plated pheasant, around whose base the carnations—slightly but strikingly 'off' the red of the shade, but pre-eminently flattering in their contrast to Mrs. Nicholson's orchid *glacé* gown—were bunched in four silver cornets. This was a party of eight: if the Concannons had insisted on stressing its 'littleness', it was, still, the largest that they could hope to give. The evident choiceness of the guests, the glitter and the mathematical placing of the silver and glass, the prompt, meticulous service of the dishes by maids whose suspended breath could be heard—all, all bespoke art and care. Gavin and Mrs. Nicholson were so placed as to face one another across the table: her glance contained him, from time to time, in its leisurely, not quite attentive play. He wondered whether she felt, and supposed she must, how great had been the effrontery of their entrance.

For this dinner party lost all point if it were not *de rigueur*. The Concannon daughters, even (big girls, but with hair still down their backs) had, as not qualified for it, been sent out for the evening. It, the party, had been balanced up and up on itself like a house of cards: built, it remained as precarious. Now the structure trembled, down to its base, from one contemptuous flip at its top story—Mrs. Nicholson's caprice of bringing a little boy. Gavin perceived that night what he was not to forget: the helplessness, in the last resort, of society—which he was never, later, to be able to think of as a force. The pianola-like play of the conversation did not drown the nervousness round the table.

At the head of the table the Admiral leaned just forward, as though pedalling the pianola. At the far end, an irrepressible cough from time to time shook Mrs. Concannon's decoltage and the crystal *pince-nez* which, balanced high on her face, gave her a sensitive blankness. She had the *devote* air of some sailors' wives, and was heroic in pale blue without a wrap—arguably, nothing could make her iller. The Admiral's pride in his wife's courage passed a current over the silver pheasant. For Mrs. Concannon, joy in sustaining all this for his sake, and confidence in him, provided a light armour: she possibly did not feel what was felt for her. To Gavin she could not have been kinder; to Mrs. Nicholson she had only and mildly said: 'He will not be shy, I hope, if he does not sit beside you?'

Rearrangement of the table at the last moment could not but have disappointed one or other of the two gentlemen who had expected to sit, and were now sitting, at Mrs. Nicholson's right and left hand. More and more, as course followed course, these two showed how highly they rated their good fortune—indeed, the censure around the rest of the table only acted for them, like heat drawing out scent, to heighten the headiness of her immediate aura. Like the quick stuff of her dress her delinquency, even, gave out a sort of shimmer: while she, neither arch nor indolent, turned from one to the other her look—if you like, melting; for it dissolved her pupils, which had never been so dilated, dark, as tonight. In this look, as dinner proceeded, the two flies, ceasing to struggle, drowned.

The reckoning would be on the way home. Silent between the flies' wives, hypnotized by the rise and fall of Mrs. Nicholson's pendant, Gavin ate on and on. The ladies' move to the drawing-room sucked him along with it in the wake of the last skirt. It was without a word that, at the end of the evening, the Admiral saw Mrs. Nicholson to her carriage—Gavin, like an afterthought or a monkey, nipping in under his host's arm extended to hold open the carriage door. Light from the porch, as they drove off, fell for a moment longer on that erect form and implacable hatchet face. Mrs. Nicholson seemed to be occupied in gathering up her skirts to make room for Gavin. She then leaned back in her corner, and he in his: not a word broke the tension of the short dark drive home. Not till she had dropped her cloak in front of her drawing-room fire did she remark: 'The Admiral's angry with me.'

'Because of me?'

'Oh dear no; because of her. If I did not think to be angry was very silly, I could almost be a little angry with him.'

'But you meant to make him angry, didn't you?' Gavin said.

'Only because he's silly,' said Mrs. Nicholson. 'If he were not so silly, that poor unfortunate creature would stop coughing: she would either get better or die.' Still standing before her mantelpiece, she studied some freesias in a vase—dispassionately, she pinched off one fading bloom, rolled it into a wax pill between her thumb and finger, then flicked it away to sizzle in the heart of the fire. 'If people,' she said, 'give a party for no other reason but to show off their marriage, what kind of evening can one expect? However, I quite enjoyed myself. I hope you did.'

Gavin said: 'Mrs. Concannon's quite old. But then, so's the Admiral.'

'He quite soon will be, at this rate,' said Mrs. Nicholson. 'That's why he's so anxious to have that war. One would have thought a man could just be a man. What's the matter, Gavin; what are you staring at?'

'That is your most beautiful dress.'

'Yes; that's why I put it on.' Mrs. Nicholson sat down on a low blue velvet chair and drew the chair to the fire: she shivered slightly. 'You say such sweet things, Gavin: what fun we have!' Then, as though the seconds of silence ticked off over her head by the little Dresden clock or her own words had taken effect with her, she turned and, with an impulsive movement, invited him closer to her side. Her arm stayed round him; her short puffed sleeve, disturbed by the movement, rustled down into silence. In the fire a coal fell apart, releasing a seam of gas from which spurted a pale tense quivering flame. 'Aren't you glad we are back?' she said, 'that we are only you and me? Oh, why endure such people when all the time there is the whole world! Why do I stay on and on here; what am I doing? Why don't we go right away somewhere, Gavin; you and I? To Germany, or into the sun? Would that make you happy?'

'That—that flame's so funny,' he said, not shifting his eyes from it.

She dropped her arm and cried, in despair: 'After all, what a child you are!'

'I am not.'

'Anyhow, it's late; you must go to bed.'

She transmuted the rise of another shiver into a slight yawn.

Overcharged and trembling, he gripped his way, flight by flight, up the polished bannister rail, on which his palms left patches of mist; pulling himself away from her up the staircase as he had pulled himself towards her up the face of the cliff.

After that midwinter visit there were two changes: Mrs. Nicholson went abroad, Gavin went to school. He overheard his mother say to his father that Lilian found Southstone this winter really too cold to stay in. 'Or, has made it too hot to stay in?' said Mr. Doddington, from whose disapproval the story of Gavin and the Concannons' party had not been able to be kept. Edith Doddington coloured, loyal, and said no more. During his first term, Gavin received at school one bright picture postcard of Mentone. The carefully chosen small preparatory school confronted him, after all, with fewer trials than his parents had feared and his brother hoped. His protective adaptability worked quickly; he took enough colour, or colourless-ness, from where he was to pass among the others, and along with them—a civil and indifferent little boy. His improved but never quite certain health got him out of some things and secured others—rests from time to time in the sick-room, teas by the matron's fire. This spectacled woman was not quite unlike Rockham; also, she was the most approachable edge of the grown-up ambience that connected him, however remotely, with Mrs. Nicholson. At school, his assets of feeling remained, one would now say, frozen.

His Easter holidays had to be spent at home; his summer holidays exhausted their greater part in the same concession to a supposed attachment. Not until September was he despatched to Southstone, for a week, to be set up before his return to school.

That September was an extension of summer. An admirable company continued its season of light opera at the theatre, in whose gardens salvias blazed. The lawns, shorn to the roots after weeks of mowing, were faintly blond after weeks of heat. Visitors were still many; and residents, after the fastidious retreat of August, were returning—along the Promenade, all day long, parasols, boater hats and light dresses flickered against the dense blue gauze backdrop that seldom let France be seen. In the evenings the head of the pier was a lighted musical box above the not yet cooling sea. Rare was the blade of chill, the too crystal morning or breathlike blur on the distance that announced autumn. Down the avenues the dark green trees hardened but did not change: if a leaf did fall, it was brushed away before anyone woke.

If Rockham remarked that Gavin was now quite a little man, her mistress made no reference to his schoolboy state. She did once ask whether the Norfolk jacket that had succeeded his sailor blouse were not, in this weather, a little hot; but that he might be expected to be more gruff, mum, stand-offish or awkward than formerly did not appear to strike her. The change, if any, was in her. He failed to connect—why should he?—her new languor, her more marked contrarieties and her odd little periods of askance musing with the illness that was to be her death. She only said the summer had been too long. Until the evenings she and Gavin were less alone; for she rose late; and, on their afternoon drives through the country, inland along the coast or towards the downs, they were as often as not accompanied by, of all persons, Mrs. Concannon. On occasions when Mrs. Concannon returned to Mrs. Nicholson's house for tea, the Admiral made it his practice to call for her. The Concannons were very much occupied with preparations for another social event: a Southstone branch of the Awaken Britannia League was to be inaugurated by a drawing-room meeting at their house. The daughters were busy folding and posting leaflets. Mrs. Nicholson, so far, could be pinned down to nothing more than a promise to send cakes from her own, or rather her cook's kitchen.

'But at least,' pleaded Mrs. Concannon, at tea one afternoon, 'you should come if only to hear what it is about.'

By five o'clock, in September, Mrs. Nicholson's house cast its shadow across the avenue on to the houses opposite, which should otherwise have received the descending sun. In revenge, they cast a shadow back through her bow window: everything in the drawing-room seemed to exist in copper-mauve glass, or as though reflected into a tarnished mirror. At this hour, Gavin saw the pale walls, the silver lamp-stems, the transparent frills of the cushions with a prophetic feeling of their impermanence. At her friend's words, Mrs. Nicholson's hand, extended, paused for a moment over the cream-jug. Turning her head she said: 'But I know what it is about; and I don't approve.'

With so little reference to the Admiral were these words spoken that he might not have been there. There, however, he was, standing drawn up above the low tea-table, cup and saucer in hand. For a moment, not speaking, he weighed his cup with a frown that seemed to ponder its exact weight. He then said: 'Then, logically, you should not be sending cakes.'

'Lilian,' said Constance Concannon fondly, 'is never logical with regard to her friends.'

'Aren't I?' said Mrs. Nicholson. 'But cake, don't you think, makes everything so much nicer? You can't offer people nothing but disagreeable ideas.'

'You are too naughty, Lilian. All the League wants is that we should be alert and thoughtful. Perhaps Gavin would like to come?'

Mrs. Nicholson turned on Gavin a considering look from which complicity seemed to be quite absent; she appeared, if anything, to be trying to envisage him as alert and thoughtful. And the Admiral, at the same moment, fixed the candidate with a measuring eye. 'What may come,' he said, 'is bound, before it is done, to be his affair.' Gavin made no reply to the proposition—and it was found, a minute or two later, that the day fixed for the drawing-room meeting was the day fixed for his return home. School began again after that. 'Well, what a pity,' Mrs. Concannon said.

The day approached. The evenings were wholly theirs, for Mrs. Nicholson dined out less. Always, from after tea, when any guests had gone, he began to reign. The apartnesses and frustrations of the preceding hours, and, most of all, the occasional dissonances that those could but produce between him and her, sent him pitching towards the twilight in a fever that rose as the week went on. This fever, every time, was confounded by the sweet pointlessness of the actual hour when it came. The warmth that lingered in the exhausted daylight made it possible for Mrs. Nicholson to extend herself on the *chaise longue* in the bow window. Seated on a stool at the foot of the *chaise longue*, leaning back against the frame of the window, Gavin could see, through the side pane of the glass projection in which they sat, the salvias smouldering in the theatre gardens. As it was towards these that her chair faced, in looking at them he was looking away from her. On the other hand, they were looking at the same thing. So they were on the evening that was his last. At the end of a minute or two of silence she exclaimed: 'No, I don't care, really, for scarlet flowers. You do?'

'Except carnations?'

'I don't care for public flowers. And you look and look at them till I feel quite lonely.'

'I was only thinking, *they* will be here tomorrow.'

'Have you been happy this time, Gavin? I haven't sometimes thought you've been quite so happy. Has it been my fault?'

He turned, but only to finger the fringe of the Kashmir shawl that had been spread by Rockham across her feet. Not looking up, he said, 'I have not seen you so much.'

'There are times,' she said, 'when one seems to be at the other side of a glass. One sees what is going on, but one cannot help it. It may be what one does not like, but one cannot feel.'

'Here, I always feel.'

'Always feel what?' she remotely and idly asked.

'I just mean, here, I feel. I don't feel, anywhere else.'

'And what is "here"?' she said, with tender mocking obtuseness. 'Southstone? What do you mean by "here"?'

'Near you.'

Mrs. Nicholson's attitude, her repose, had not been come at carelessly. Apparently, relaxed, but not supine, she was supported by six or seven cushions—behind her head, at the nape of her neck, between her shoulders, under her elbows and in the small of her back. The slipperiness of this architecture of comfort enjoined stillness—her repose depended on each cushion's staying just where it was. Up to now, she had lain with her wrists crossed on her dress: a random turn of the wrist or flexing of fingers were the nearest things to gestures she permitted herself—and, indeed, these had been enough. *Now,* her beginning to say, 'I wonder if they were right . . .' must, though it sounded nothing more than reflective, have been accompanied by an incautious movement, for a cushion fell with a plump to the ground. Gavin went round, recovered the cushion and stood beside her; they eyed one another with communicative amazement, as though a third person had spoken and they were uncertain if they had heard aright. She arched her waist up and Gavin replaced the cushion. He said: 'If who were right?'

'Rockham . . . The Admiral. She's always hinting, he's always saying, that I'm in some way thoughtless and wrong with you.'

'Oh, him.'

'I know,' she said. 'But you'll say good-bye to him nicely?'

He shrugged. 'I shan't see him again—this time.'

She hesitated. She was about to bring out something that, though slight, must be unacceptable. 'He *is* coming in,' she said 'for a moment, just after dinner, to fetch the cakes.'

'Which cakes?'

'The cakes for tomorrow. I had arranged to send them round in the morning, but that would not do; no, that would not be soon enough. Everything is for the Admiral's meeting to make us ready, so everything must be ready in good time.'

When, at nine o'clock, the Admiral's ring was heard, Mrs. Nicholson, indecisively, put down her coffee cup. A wood fire, lit while they were at dinner, was blazing languidly in the already warm air: it was necessary to sit at a distance from it. While the bell still rang. Gavin rose, as though he had forgotten something, and left the drawing-room. Passing the maid on her way to open the front door, he made a bolt upstairs. In his bedroom, Rockham was in possession: his trunk waited, open, bottom layer packed; her mending basket was on the bureau; she was taking a final look through his things—his departure was to be early tomorrow morning. 'Time flies,' she said. 'You're no sooner come than you're gone.' She continued to count handkerchiefs, to stack up shirts. 'I'd have thought,' she said, 'you'd have wanted to bring your school cap.'

'Why? Anyway, it's a silly beastly old colour.'

'You're too old-fashioned,' she said sharply. 'It was high time somebody went to school. Now you *have* come up, just run down again, there's a good boy, and ask Madam if there's anything for your mother. If it's books, they ought to go in here among your boots.'

'The Admiral's there.'

'Well, my goodness, you know the Admiral!'

Gavin played for time, on the way down, by looking into the rooms on every floor. Their still only partial familiarity, their fullness with objects that, in the half light coming in from the landing, he could only half perceive and did not dare touch, made him feel he was still only at the first chapter of the mystery of the house. He wondered how long it would be before he saw them again. Fear of Rockham's impatience, of her calling down to ask what he was up to, made him tread cautiously on the thickly carpeted stairs: he gained the hall without having made a sound. Here he smelled the fresh-baked cakes, waiting in a hamper on the hall table. The drawing-room door stood ajar, on, for a minute, dead silence. The Admiral must have gone, without the cakes.

But then the Admiral spoke. 'You must see, there is nothing more to be said, I am only sorry I came. I did not expect you to be alone.'

'For once, that is not my fault,' replied Mrs. Nicholson, unsteadily. 'I do not even know where the child is.' In a voice that hardly seemed to be hers she cried out softly: 'Then this is to go on always? What more do you ask? What else am I to be or do?'

'There's nothing more you can do. And all you must be is, happy.'

'How easy,' Mrs. Nicholson said.

'You have always said that that was easy, for you. For my own part, I have never considered happiness. There you misunderstood me, quite from the first.'

'Not quite. Was I wrong in thinking you were a man?'

'I'm a man, yes. But I'm not that sort.'

'That is too subtle for me,' said Mrs. Nicholson.

'On the contrary, it is too simple for you. You ignore the greater part of my life. You cannot be blamed, perhaps; you have only known me since I was cursed with too much time on my hands.

Your—your looks, charm and gaiety, my dear Lilian, I'd have been
a fool not to salute at their full worth. Beyond that, I'm not such a
fool as I may have seemed. Fool?—all things considered, I could
not have been simply that without being something a good deal
viler.'

'I have been nice to Constance,' said Mrs. Nicholson.

'Vile in my own eyes.'

'I know, that is all you think of.'

'I see, now, where you are in your element. You know as well as
I do what your element is; which is why there's nothing more to be
said. Flirtation's always been off my beat—so far off my beat, as a
matter of fact, that I didn't know what it was when I first saw it.
There, no doubt, I was wrong. If you can't live without it, you
cannot, and that is that. If you have to be dangled after, you no
doubt will be. But don't, my dear girl, go for that to the wrong
shop. It would have been enough, where I am concerned, to watch
you making a ninny of that unfortunate boy.'

'Who, poor little funny Gavin?' said Mrs. Nicholson. 'Must I
have nothing?—I have no little dog. You would not like it, even, if
I had a real little dog. And you expect me to think that you do not
care . . .'

The two voices, which intensity more than caution kept pitched
low, ceased. Gavin pushed open the drawing-room door.

The room, as can happen, had elongated. Like figures at the end
of a telescope the Admiral and Mrs. Nicholson were to be seen
standing before the fire. Of this, not a glint had room to appear
between the figures of the antagonists. Mrs. Nicholson, head bent
as though to examine the setting of the diamond, was twisting
round a ring on her raised left hand—a lace-edged handkerchief,
like an abandoned piece of stage property, had been dropped and
lay on the hearthrug near the hem of her skirts. She gave the
impression of having not moved: if they had not, throughout, been
speaking from this distance, the Admiral must have taken a step
forward. But this, on his part, must have been, and must be, all—
his head was averted from her, his shoulders were braced back, and
behind his back he imprisoned one of his own wrists in a handcuff
grip that shifted only to tighten. The heat from the fire must have
made necessary, probably for the Admiral when he came, the
opening of a window behind the curtains; for, as Gavin advanced

into the drawing-room, a burst of applause entered from the theatre, and continued, drowning the music which had begun again.

Not a tremor recorded the moment when Mrs. Nicholson knew Gavin was in the room. Obliquely and vaguely turning her bowed head she extended to him, in an unchanged look, what might have been no more than an invitation to listen, also, to the music. 'Why, Gavin,' she said at last, 'we were wondering where you were.'

Here he was. From outside the theatre, stink still travelled to him from the lorry whose engine was being run. Nothing had changed in the colourless afternoon. Without knowing, he had plucked a leaf of the ivy which now bred and fed upon her house. A soldier, passing behind him to join the others, must have noticed his immobility all the way down the avenue: for the soldier said, out of the side of his mouth: 'Annie doesn't live here any more.' Gavin Doddington, humiliated, affected to study the ivy leaf, whose veins were like arbitrary, vulgar fatelines. He thought he remembered hearing of metal ivy; he knew he had seen ivy carved round monuments to signify fidelity, regret, or the tomb-defying tenaciousness of memory—what you liked. Watched by the soldiers, he did not care to make the gesture that would be involved by throwing the leaf away: instead, he shut his hand on it, as he turned from the house. Should he go straight to the station, straight back to London? Not while the impression remained so strong. On the other hand, it would be a long time before the bars opened.

Another walk round Southstone, this afternoon, was necessary: there must be a decrescendo. From his tour of annihilation, nothing out of the story was to be missed. He walked as though he were carrying a guide-book.

Once or twice he caught sight of the immune downs, on the ascent to whose contours war had halted the villas. The most open view was, still, from the gates of the cemetery, past which he and she had so often driven without a thought. Through those gates, the extended dulling white marble vista said to him, only, that the multiplicity of the new graves, in thirty years, was enough in itself to make the position of hers indifferent—she might, once more, be lying beside her husband. On the return through the town towards the lip of the plateau overhanging the sea, the voidness and the air of concluded meaning about the plan of Southstone seemed to confirm her theory: history, after this last galvanized movement forward, had come, as she expected, to a full stop. It had only not stopped where, or as, she foresaw. Crossing the Promenade obliquely, he made, between wire entanglements, for the railings; to become one more of the spaced-out people who leaned along them, willing to see a convoy or gazing with indifference towards liberated France. The path and steps up the cliff face had been destroyed; the hand rail hung out rotting into the air.

Back into the shopping centre, he turned a quickening step, past the shuttered, boarded or concave windows, towards the corner florists' where Mrs. Nicholson had insisted on the carnations. But this had received a direct hit: the entire corner was gone. When time takes our revenges out of our hands it is, usually, to execute them more slowly: her vindictiveness, more thorough than ours, might satisfy us, if, in the course of her slowness, we did not forget. In this case, however, she had worked in the less than a second of detonation. Gavin Doddington paused where there was no florist— was he not, none the less, entitled to draw a line through this?

Not until after some time back in the bar did it strike him—there had been one omission. He had not yet been to the Concannons'. He pushed his way out: it was about seven o'clock; twenty minutes or so before the black-out. They had lived in a crescent set just back from a less expensive reach of the Promenade. On his way, he passed houses and former hotels occupied by soldiers or A.T.S. who had not yet gone. These, from top to basement, were in a state of naked, hard, lemon-yellow illumination. Interposing dark hulks gave you the feeling of nothing more than their recent military occupation. The front door of the Concannons' crescent opened, on the inland side, into a curved street, which, for some military reason now probably out of date, had been blocked at the near end: Gavin had to go round. Along the pavements under the front door steps there was so much wire that he was thrust out into the road— opposite only one house was there an inviting gap in the loops. Admiral Concannon, having died in the last war, could not have obtained this as a concession—all the same this *was* as the number faintly confirmed, his house. Nobody now but Gavin recognized its identity or its importance. Here had dwelled, and here continued to dwell, the genius of Southstone that now was. Twice over had there been realized the Admiral's alternative to love.

The Concannons' dining-room window, with its high triple sashes, was raised some distance above the street. Gavin, standing

opposite it, looked in at an A.T.S. girl seated at a table. She faced
the window, the dusk and him. From above her head, a naked
electric light bulb, on a flex shortened by being knotted, glared on
the stripped, whitish walls of the room and emphasized the fact that
she was alone. In her khaki shirt, sleeves rolled up, she sat leaning
her bare elbows on the bare table. Her face was abrupt with youth.
She turned one wrist, glanced at the watch on it, then resumed her
steady stare through the window, downwards, at the dusk in which
Gavin stood.

It was thus that, for the second time in his life, he saw straight
up into eyes that did not see him. The intervening years had given
him words for trouble: a phrase, '*l'horreur de mon néant*,' darted across
his mind.

At any minute, the girl would have to approach the window to
do the black-out—for that, along this coast, was still strictly
enforced. It was worth waiting. He lighted a cigarette: she looked at
her watch again. When she did rise it was, first, to unhook from a
peg beside the dining-room door not only her tunic but her cap.
Her being dressed for the street, when she did reach up, and, with
a succession of movements he liked to watch, begin to twitch the
black stuff across the window, made it his object *not* to be seen—
just yet. Light staggered, a moment longer, on the desiccated pods
of the wallflowers that, seeded from the front garden, had sprung
up between the cracks of the pavement, and on the continuous
regular loops or hoops of barbed wire, through all of which, by a
sufficiently long leap, one *could* have projected oneself head foremost,
unhurt. At last she had stopped the last crack of light. She had now
nothing to do but come out.

Coming smartly down the Concannons' steps, she may just have
seen the outline of the civilian waiting, smoking a cigarette. She
swerved impassively, if at all. He said: 'A penny for your thoughts'.
She might not have heard. He fell into step beside her. Next,
appearing to hear what he had not said, she replied: 'No, I'm *not*
going your way.'

'Too bad. But there's only one way out—can't get out, you know,
at the other end. What have *I* got to do, then—stay here all night?'

'*I* don't know, I'm sure.' Unconcernedly humming, she did not
even quicken her light but ringing tramp on the curved street. If he
kept abreast with her, it was casually, and at an unpressing distance:
this, and the widening sky that announced the open end of the

crescent, must have been reassuring. He called across to her: 'That house you came out of, I used to know people who lived there. I was just looking round.'

She turned, for the first time—she could not help it. 'People lived there?' she said. 'Just fancy. I know I'd sooner live in a tomb. And that goes for all this place. Imagine anyone coming here on a holiday!'

'I'm on a holiday.'

'Goodness. What do you do with yourself?'

'Just look round.'

'Well, I wonder how long you stick it out. Here's where we go different ways. Good night.'

'I've got nobody to talk to,' Gavin said, suddenly standing still in the dark. A leaf fluttered by. She was woman enough to halt, to listen, because this had not been said to her. If her, 'Oh yes, we girls have heard that before,' was automatic, it was, still more, wavering. He cast away the end of one cigarette and started lighting another: the flame of the lighter, cupped inside his hands, jumped for a moment over his features. Her first thought was: yes, he's quite old—that went along with his desperate jauntiness. Civilian, yes: too young for the last war, too old for this. A gentleman—they were the clever ones. But he had, she perceived, forgotten about her thoughts—what she saw, in that moment before he snapped down the lighter, stayed on the darkness, puzzling her somewhere outside the compass of her own youth. She had seen the face of somebody dead who was still there—'old' because of the presence, under an icy screen, of a whole stopped mechanism for feeling. Those features had been framed, long ago, for hope. The dints above the nostrils, the lines extending the eyes, the lips' grimacing grip on the cigarette—all completed the picture of someone wolfish. A preyer. But who had said, preyers are preyed upon?

His lower lip came out, thrusting the cigarette up at a debonair angle towards his eyes. 'Not a soul,' he added—this time with calculation, and to her.

'Anyway,' she said sharply, 'I've got a date. Anyway, what made you pick on this dead place? Why not pick on some place where you know someone?'

FRANK O'CONNOR
Peasants

WHEN Michael John Cronin stole the funds of the Carricknabreena Hurling, Football and Temperance Association, commonly called the Club, everyone said 'Divil's cure to him!' ''Tis the price of him!' 'Kind father for him!' 'What did I tell you?' and the rest of the things people say when an acquaintance has got what was coming to him. And not only Michael John but the whole Cronin family, seed, breed and generation, came in for it; there wasn't one of them for twenty miles round or a hundred years back but his deeds and sayings were remembered and examined by the light of this fresh scandal. Michael John's father (the Heavens be his bed!) was a drunkard who beat his wife, and his father before him a land-grabber. Then there was an uncle or grand-uncle who had been a policeman and taken a hand in the bloody work at Mitchelstown long ago, and an unmarried sister of the same whose good name by all accounts it would have needed a regiment of husbands to restore. It was a grand shaking-up the Cronins got altogether, and anyone that had a grudge in for one of them, even if it was no more than a thirty-third cousin, had rare sport, dropping a friendly word about it and saying how sorry he was for the poor mother, till he had the blood lighting in the Cronin eyes.

There was only one thing for them to do with Michael John; that was to send him to America and let the thing blow over, and that, no doubt, is what they would have done but for a certain unpleasant and extraordinary incident.

Father Crowly, the parish priest, was chairman of the committee. He was a remarkable man, even to look at; tall, powerfully built but very stooped, with shrewd loveless eyes that rarely softened except to two or three of the older people. He was a strange man, well on in years, noted for his strong political views which never happened to coincide with those of any party, and as obstinate as the devil himself. Now what should Father Crowley do but try to force it down the necks of the committee that Michael John should be prosecuted?

The committee were all religious men who up to that had never as much as dared to question the judgements of a man of God; yes, faith, and if the priest had been a bully (which to give him his due he wasn't) he might have danced a hornpipe on the backs of the lot of them and there would have been no complaint. Yet, a man has principles, and the like of this had never been heard of in the parish before. What? Put the police on a boy and he in trouble?

One by one the committee-men spoke up and said so. 'But he did wrong,' said Father Crowley, thumping the table. 'He did wrong and he must be punished.'

'Maybe so, father,' replied Con Norton, the vice-chairman, who acted as spokesman. 'Maybe so indeed; but is that any reason his poor mother should be punished too and she a widow-woman?'

'True for you!' chorused the others.

'Serve his mother right!' said the priest shortly. 'There's none of you but knows better than I do the way that young man was brought up. He's a rogue and his mother is a fool. Why didn't she beat Christian principles into him when she had him on her knee?'

'That may be, too,' agreed Norton mildly. 'I wouldn't say but you're right, but is that any reason his uncle Peter should be punished?'

'Or his uncle Dan?' asked another.

'Or his uncle James?' asked a third.

'Or his cousins, the Dwyers that keep the little shop in Lissnacarriga, as decent a living family as there is in the county Cork?' asked a fourth.

'No, father,' said Norton, 'the argument is against you.'

'Is it, indeed?' exclaimed the priest, growing cross. 'Is it so? What the devil has it to do with his uncle Dan or his uncle James? What are ye talking about? What punishment is it to them? Will ye tell me that? Ye'll be telling me next 'tis a punishment to me, and I a child of Adam like himself!'

'And do you mean, father,' asked Norton, ''tis no punishment to them, having one of their own blood made a public show? Erra, is it mad you think we are? Maybe 'tis a thing you'd like done to yourself?'

'There was none of my family ever a thief,' replied Father Crowley sternly.

'We don't know whether there was or not,' snapped a little man called Daly, a hot-tempered character from the hills.

'Aisy now! Aisy, Phil!' said Norton.

'What do you mean by that?' asked Father Crowley, rising and grabbing his hat and stick.

'What I mean,' said Daly, blazing up, 'is that I won't sit here and listen to insinuations about my native place from any foreigner. There are as many rogues and thieves and vagabonds and liars in Cullough as ever there were in Carricknabreena—ay, begod, and more, and bigger! That's what I mean.'

'No, no, no, no,' said Norton soothingly. 'That's not what he means at all, father. We don't want any bad blood. What he means is that the Crowleys may be a fine substantial family in their own country, but that's fifteen long miles away, and this isn't their country, and the Cronins are neighbours of ours since the dawn of history and time, and it would be a queer thing if at this hour of day we handed one of them over to the police. . . . And listen to me, father,' he went on, forgetting that he was supposed to be making a peaceful speech and hitting the table as hard as the rest, 'if a cow of mine got sick in the morning, 'tisn't a Cremin or a Crowley I'd be asking for help, and damn the bit of use 'twould be if I did. And all knows I'm no enemy of the priests but a respectable farmer that pays his dues and goes to his duties regularly.'

'True for you! True for you!' agreed the committee.

'I don't give a button what you are,' replied the priest. 'And now listen to me, Con Norton. I bear young Cronin no grudge, nor his family either, which is more than some of you can say, but I know my duty and I'll do it in spite of the lot of you.'

He stood at the door and looked back. They were gazing blankly at one another. He shook his fist at them.

'Ye all know me,' he said. 'Ye know that all my life I'm fighting the long-tailed families. Now, with the help of God, I'll shorten the tail of one of them.'

Father Crowley's threat frightened them. They knew he was a determined man and had spent his time attacking what he called the 'corruption' of councils and committees, which was all very well as long as it happened outside your own parish. They dared not oppose him openly because he knew too much about them all, and in public at least had a lacerating tongue. The solution they favoured was a tactful one. They formed themselves into a Michael John Cronin Fund Committee, and canvassed the parishioners for subscriptions to pay off Michael John's debt. Regretfully they decided that the priest would hardly countenance a football match for the purpose.

Then with the defaulting treasurer, who wore a suitably contrite air, they marched up to the presbytery. Father Crowley was at his dinner but he told the housekeeper to show them in. He looked up in astonishment as his dining-room filled with the seven committee-men, pushing before them the cowed Michael John.

'Who the blazes are ye?' he asked, glaring at them over the lamp.

'We are the Club Committee, father,' replied Norton.

'Oh, are ye?'

'And this is the threasurer—the ex-threasurer, I should say.'

'I won't pretend I'm glad to see him,' said the priest.

'He came to say he's sorry, father. He's very sorry, true as God, and I'll tell you no lie, he is. . . .' Norton made two steps forward and in a dramatic silence laid a heap of notes and silver on the table.

'What's that?' asked Father Crowley.

'The money, father. 'Tis all paid back now, and you've no call to be black with us any more. Any little crossness there was we'll say no more about it, in the name of God.'

The priest looked at the money and then at Norton.

'Con,' he said, 'you'd better keep the soft word for the judge. Maybe he'll think more of it than I do.'

'The judge, father?' asked Norton stupidly.

'Ay, Con, the judge.'

For close on a minute there was silence. The committee stood there with open mouths in consternation.

'And is that what you're doing to us, father?' asked Norton, his voice trembling. 'Is it yourself is going to show us up before the whole country as a lot of robbers?'

'You foolish creatures, I'm showing up none of you.'

'You are then, father, and every man, woman and child in the parish,' said Norton savagely. 'And mark my words, 'twon't be forgotten for you.'

On the following Sunday Father Crowley spoke of the matter from the altar. He spoke for a full half-hour, without a trace of emotion on his grim old face, but his sermon was one long venomous denunciation of the 'long-tailed families', which, according to him, were the ruination of the country and made a mockery of truth, justice and charity. He was, as his congregation agreed, a shockingly obstinate old man who never knew when he was in the wrong.

After Mass he was visited in his sacristy by the committee. He gave Norton a terrible look from under his shaggy eyebrows which made that respectable farmer flinch.

'Father,' said Norton appealingly, 'we only want one word with you. One word and then we'll be going. You're a hard character, and you said some bitter things to us this morning, things we never deserved from you. But we're quiet, peaceable, poor men and we won't cross you any more.'

Father Crowley made a sound like a snort.

'We came to make a good bargain with you, father.'

'Well, what is it?'

'We'll say no more about the whole business if you'll do one little thing to oblige us.'

'The bargain?' said the priest impatiently. 'What's the bargain?'

'We'll leave the matter drop for good and all if you'll give the boy a character.'

'Yes, father,' cried the whole committee in chorus. 'Give him a character! Give him a character!'

'Give him a what?' cried the priest.

'Give him a character, father, for the love of God!' said Norton emotionally. 'If you speak up for him, the judge will leave him off, and then there'll be no stain on the parish.'

'Is it out of your minds you are, you half-witted *aindeiseoirs*?' asked the priest, his face suffused with blood, his head trembling. 'Here am I all these long years preaching to ye about decency and justice and truth and ye no more understand me than that wall there! Is it the way ye want me to perjure myself? Is it the way ye want me to tell a damned lie with the name of Almighty God on my lips? Answer me, every one of ye, is it?'

'Ah, what perjure!' said Norton impatiently. 'Sure, can't you say a few words for the boy? There's no one asking you to say much. What harm will it do you to tell the judge he's an honest, good-living, upright lad, and that he took the money without meaning any harm?'

'My God!' muttered the priest, running his hands distractedly through his grey hair. 'There's no talking to ye, no talking to ye, ye lot of sheep.'

* * *

When he was gone the committee-men turned and looked at one
another.

'He's an awful trial,' said one.

'He's a tyrant,' said Daly, vindictively.

'He is indeed,' sighed Norton, scratching his head. 'But in God's
holy name, boys, before we do anything, we'll give him one more
chance.'

That evening while the priest was having his tea the committee-
men called again. This time they looked very spruce and business-
like and independent. Father Crowley glared at them.

'Are ye back?' he asked bitterly. 'Somehow I was thinking ye
would be, and I declare to goodness I'm sick of ye and yeer old
committee, and I'm sorry to the Lord I ever joined it or had
anything to do with it. Because, let me tell ye, it has my peace of
mind destroyed.'

'Oh, we're not the committee, father,' said Norton stiffly.

'Oh, aren't ye?'

'No, we are not.'

'Well, all I have to say is ye look mighty like it. And if I'm not
being impertinent, who the deuce are ye?'

'We're a deputation.'

'Oh! A deputation! Fancy that now! And a deputation from
what?'

'A deputation from the parish. . . . So, now maybe you'll listen to
us?'

'Oh, go on! I'm listening, I'm listening.'

'Well, now 'tis like this, father,' said Norton suddenly dropping
his airs and graces and leaning against the table. ''Tis about that
little business this morning. Now, father, maybe you didn't understand us and we didn't understand you. But we're quiet, simple,
poor men that want to do the best we can by everybody, and a few
words or a few pounds wouldn't stand in our way. Do you follow
me now?'

'I declare,' said Father Crowley, resting his elbows on the table.
'I don't know whether I do or not.'

'Well, 'tis like this. We don't want any blame on the parish and
on the Cronins, and you're the one man that can save us. Now all
we ask of you is to give the boy a character——'

'Yes, father,' interrupted the others in chorus. 'Give him a character! Give him a character!'

'Give him a character, father, and you'll never be troubled with him again. Don't say no to me now till you hear me out! We won't ask you to go next, nigh or near the court. You have pen and ink there beside you, and one couple of lines is all we'll ask of you. The day he walks out of the court you can hand him his ticket to America and tell him never again to show his face in Carrickna-breena. There's the price of it, father,' added Norton, clapping a bundle of notes on the table. 'Put the money in your pocket, and we've his mother's word and his own word that he'll go there when you bid him.'

'He can go to pot!' retorted the priest. 'What is it to me where he goes?'

'Now, now, father, just a minute! Just a minute! Sure, we know well 'tis no advantage to you or the parish, and that's the very thing we came to talk about. Now supposing—just supposing for the sake of argument, you do what we're suggesting, there's a few of us here, and between us we might be able to raise whatever little contribu-tion to the building fund you'd think would be reasonable to cover the expense and trouble to yourself? Do you follow me now?'

'Con Norton,' said the priest, rising and holding the edge of the table with his hands, 'I follow you. This morning it was perjury, and now it's bribery, and the Lord knows what 'twill be next. I see I've been wasting my breath. . . . And I see, too,' he added savagely, leaning across the table towards them, 'a pedigree bull would be more use to ye than a priest.'

'What do you mean, father?' asked Norton in a quiet voice.

'What I say.'

'And that's a saying that will be remembered for you the longest day you live,' hissed Norton, leaning towards him till they were facing one another across the table.

'A bull,' gasped Father Crowley. 'Not a priest.'

''Twill be remembered!'

'Will it? Then remember this too. I'm an old man now. I'm forty years a priest, and I'm not a priest for the money or power or glory of it, like others I know. I gave the best that was in me—maybe 'twasn't much, but 'twas more than many a better man would give, and at the end of my days . . .' Lowering his voice to a whisper he searched them with his terrible eyes, '. . . at the end of my days, if I did a wrong thing, or a bad thing, or an unjust thing, there isn't man or woman in this parish that would brave me to my face and call me a villain, and isn't that a poor story for an old man that tried to be a good priest?' His voice changed again, and he raised his head. 'Now get out before I kick you out!'

And true to his word and character not one word did he say in Michael John's favour the day of the trial, no more than if he was a heathen. Three months Michael John got and by all accounts he got off lightly.

When he came out of gaol he was a changed man. Downcast he was and dark in himself. There was no one but was sorry for him; people who had never spoken to him before spoke to him now, and to all he said, 'I'm very grateful to you, friend, for overlooking my misfortune.' He refused to go to America, so Norton and the committee made another whip-round, and between this and the money they had collected previously and what the Cronins had made up to send him to America, he found himself with enough to open a small shop. Then he secured a job on the County Council and an agency for some shipping company, and at last he was able to buy a public-house.

As for Father Crowley, till he was shifted, twelve months later, he never did a day's good in the parish. The dues went down and the presents went down, and people who had money to spend on Masses took it fifty miles away rather than leave it to him. They said it broke his heart.

He has left unpleasant memories behind him. Only for him, the people say, Michael John Cronin would be in America today. Only for him he would never have married a girl with a fortune, or had it to lend to poor people in the hard times, or ever sucked the blood of Christians. For as an old man said to me of him, 'A robber he is and was, and a grabber like his grandfather before him, and an enemy of the people like his uncle, the policeman; and though some say he'll dip his hand where he dipped it before, for myself I have no hope unless the mercy of God sends us another Moses or Brian Boru to cast him down and hammer him in the dust.'

SOMERSET MAUGHAM
Episode

It was quite a small party because our hostess liked general conversation; we never sat down to dinner more than eight, and generally only six, and after dinner when we went up to the drawing-room the chairs were so arranged that it was impossible for two persons to go into a huddle in a corner and so break things up. I was glad on arriving to find that I knew everyone. There were two nice clever women besides our hostess and two men besides myself. One was my friend Ned Preston. Our hostess made it a point never to ask wives with their husbands, because she said each cramped the other's style and if they didn't like to come separately they needn't come at all. But since her food and her wine were good and the talk almost always entertaining they generally came. People sometimes accused her of asking husbands more often than wives, but she defended herself by saying that she couldn't possibly help it because more men were husbands than women were wives.

Ned Preston was a Scot, a good-humoured, merry soul, with a gift for telling a story, sometimes too lengthily for he was uncommonly loquacious, but with dramatic intensity. He was a bachelor with a small income which sufficed for his modest needs, and in this he was lucky since he suffered from that form of chronic tuberculosis which may last for years without killing, but which prevents you from working for your living. Now and then he would be ill enough to stay in bed for two or three weeks, but then he would get better and be as gay, cheerful and talkative as ever. I doubt whether he had enough money to live in an expensive sanatorium and he certainly hadn't the temperament to suit himself to its life. He was worldly. When he was well he liked to go out, out to lunch, out to dinner, and he liked to sit up late into the night smoking his pipe and drinking a good deal of whisky. If he had been content to live the life of an invalid he might have been alive now, but he wasn't; and who can blame him? He died at the age of fifty-five of a haemorrhage which he had one night after coming home from some house where, he may well have flattered himself, he was the success of the party.

He had that febrile vitality that some consumptives have, and was always looking for an occupation to satisfy his desire for activity. I don't know how he heard that at Wormwood Scrubs they were in want of prison visitors, but the idea took his fancy, so he went to the Home Office and saw the official in charge of prisons to offer his services. The job is unpaid, and though a number of persons are willing to undertake it, either from compassion or curiosity, they are apt to grow tired of it, or find it takes up too much time, and the prisoners whose problems, interests and future they have been concerned with are left somewhat in the lurch. The Home Office people consequently are wary of taking on anyone who does not look as if he would persevere, and they make careful inquiries into the applicant's antecedents, character and general suitability. Then he is given a trial, is discreetly watched, and if the impression is unfavourable is politely thanked and told that his services are no longer required. But Ned Preston satisfied the dour and shrewd official who interviewed him that he was in every way reliable, and from the beginning he got on well with the governor, the warders and the prisoners. He was entirely lacking in class consciousness, so prisoners, whatever their station in life, felt at ease with him. He neither preached nor moralised. He had never done a criminal, or even a mean, thing in his life, but he treated the crime of the prisoners he had to deal with as though it were an illness like his own tuberculosis which was a nuisance you had to put up with, but which it did no good to talk about.

Wormwood Scrubs is a first offenders' prison and it is a building, grim and cold, of forbidding appearance. Ned took me over it once and I had goose-flesh as the gates were unlocked for us and we went in. We passed through the halls in which the men were working.

'If you see any pals of yours take no notice of them,' Ned said to me. 'They don't like it.'

'Am I likely to see any pals of mine?' I asked drily.

'You never can tell. I shouldn't be surprised if you had had friends who'd passed bad cheques once too often or were caught in a compromising situation in one of the parks. You'd be surprised how often I run across chaps I've met out at dinner.'

One of Ned's duties was to see prisoners through the first difficult days of their confinement. They were often badly shaken by their trial and sentence; and when, after the preliminary proceedings they had to go through on entering the jail, the stripping, the bath, the medical examination and the questioning, the getting into prison clothes, they were led into a cell and locked up, they were apt to break down. Sometimes they cried hysterically; sometimes they could neither eat nor sleep. Ned's business then was to cheer them, and his breezy manner, his natural kindliness, often worked wonders. If they were anxious about their wives and children he would go to see them and if they were destitute provide them with money. He brought them news so that they might get over the awful feeling that they were shut away from the common interests of their fellow men. He read the sporting papers to be able to tell them what horse had won an important race or whether the champion had won his fight. He would advise them about their future, and when the time approached for their release see what jobs they were fitted for and then persuade employers to give them a chance to make good.

Since everyone is interested in crime it was inevitable that sooner or later, with Ned there, the conversation should turn upon it. It was after dinner and we were sitting comfortably in the drawing-room with drinks in our hands.

'Had any interesting cases at the Scrubs lately, Ned?' I asked him.

'No, nothing much.'

He had a high, rasping voice and his laugh was a raucous cackle. He broke into it now.

'I went to see an old girl today who was a packet of fun. Her husband's a burglar. The police have known about him for years, but they've never been able to get him till just now. Before he did a job he and his wife concocted an alibi, and though he's been arrested three or four times and sent up for trial, the police have never been able to break it and he's always got off. Well, he was arrested again a little while ago, but he wasn't upset, the alibi he and his wife had made up was perfect and he expected to be acquitted as he'd been before. His wife went into the witness-box and to his utter amazement she didn't give the alibi and he was convicted. I went to see him. He wasn't so much worried at being in jail as puzzled by his wife not having spoken up, and he asked me to go and see her and ask what the game was. Well, I went, and d'you know what she said to me? She said: "Well, sir, it's like this; it was such a beautiful alibi I just couldn't bear to waste it."'

Of course we all laughed. The story-teller likes an appreciative audience, and Ned Preston was never disinclined to hold the floor.

He narrated two or three more anecdotes. They tended to prove a point he was fond of making, that in what till we all got democratic in England were called the lower orders there was more passion, more romance, more disregard of consequences than could ever be found in the well-to-do and presumably educated classes, whom prudence has made timid and convention inhibited.

'Because the working man doesn't read much,' he said, 'because he has no great gift for expressing himself, you think he has no imagination. You're wrong. He's extravagantly imaginative. Because he's a great husky brute you think he has no nerves. You're wrong again. He's a bundle of nerves.'

Then he told us a story which I shall tell as best I can in my own words.

Fred Manson was a good-looking fellow, tall, well-made, with blue eyes, good features and a friendly, agreeable smile, but what made him remarkable so that people turned round in the streets to stare at him was that he had a thick head of hair, with a great wave in it, of a deep rich red. It was really a great beauty. Perhaps it was this that gave him so sensual a look. His maleness was like a heady perfume. His eyebrows were thick, only a little lighter than his hair, and he was lucky enough not to have the ugly skin that so often disfigures redheads. His was a smooth olive. His eyes were bold, and when he smiled or laughed, which in the healthy vitality of his youth he did constantly, his expression was wonderfully alluring. He was twenty-two and he gave you the rather pleasant impression of just loving to be alive. It was inevitable that with such looks and above all with that troubling sexuality he should have success with women. He was charming, tender and passionate, but immensely promiscuous. He was not exactly callous or brazen, he had a kindly nature, but somehow or other he made it quite clear to the objects of his passing fancy that all he wanted was a little bit of fun and that it was impossible for him to remain faithful to anyone.

Fred was a postman. He worked in Brixton. It is a densely populated part of London, and has the curious reputation of harbouring more criminals than any other suburb because trams run to it from across the river all night long, so that when a man has done a job of housebreaking in the West End he can be sure of getting home without difficulty. Fred liked his job. Brixton is a district of innumerable streets lined with little houses inhabited by the people who work in the neighbourhood and also by clerks, shop-assistants, skilled workers of one sort or another whose jobs take them every day across the river. He was strong and healthy and it was a pleasure to him to walk from street to street delivering the letters. Sometimes there would be a postal packet to hand in or a registered letter that had to be signed for, and then he would have the opportunity of seeing people. He was a sociable creature. It was never long before he was well known on whatever round he was assigned to. After a time his job was changed. His duty then was to go to the red pillar-boxes into which the letters were put, empty them, and take the contents to the main post office of the district. His bag would be pretty heavy sometimes by the time he was through, but he was proud of his strength and the weight only made him laugh.

One day he was emptying a box in one of the better streets, a street of semi-detached houses, and had just closed his bag when a girl came running along.

'Postman,' she cried, 'take this letter, will you. I want it to go by this post most particularly.'

He gave her his good-natured smile.

'I never mind obliging a lady,' he said, putting down his bag and opening it.

'I wouldn't trouble you, only it's urgent,' she said as she handed him the letter she had in her hand.

'Who is it to—a feller?' he grinned.

'None of your business.'

'All right, be haughty. But I tell you this, he's no good. Don't you trust him.'

'You've got a nerve,' she said.

'So they tell me.'

He took off his cap and ran his hand through his mop of curling red hair. The sight of it made her gasp.

'Where d'you get your perm?' she asked with a giggle.

'I'll show you one of these days if you like.'

He was looking down at her with his amused eyes, and there was something about him that gave her a funny little feeling in the pit of her stomach.

'Well, I must be on my way,' he said. 'If I don't get on with the job pretty damn quick I don't know what'll happen to the country.'

'I'm not detaining you,' she said coolly.

'That's where you make a mistake,' he answered.

He gave her a look that made her heart beat nineteen to the dozen and she felt herself blushing all over. She turned away and ran back to the house. Fred noticed it was four doors away from the pillar-box. He had to pass it and as he did so he looked up. He saw the net curtains twitch and knew she was watching. He felt pleased with himself. During the next few days he looked at the house whenever he passed it, but never caught a glimpse of the girl. One afternoon he ran across her by chance just as he was entering the street in which she lived.

'Hulloa,' he said, stopping.

'Hulloa.'

She blushed scarlet.

'Haven't seen you about lately.'

'You haven't missed much.'

'That's what you think.'

She was prettier than he remembered, dark-haired, dark-eyed, rather tall, slight, with a good figure, a pale skin and very white teeth.

'What about coming to the pictures with me one evening?'

'Taking a lot for granted, aren't you?'

'It pays,' he said with his impudent, charming grin.

She couldn't help laughing.

'Not with me, it doesn't.'

'Oh, come on. One's only young once.'

There was something so attractive in him that she couldn't bring herself to give him a saucy answer.

'I couldn't really. My people wouldn't like me going out with a fellow I don't know. You see, I'm the only one they have and they think a rare lot of me. Why, I don't even know your name.'

'Well, I can tell you, can't I? Fred. Fred Manson. Can't you say you're going to the pictures with a girl friend?'

She had never felt before what she was feeling then. She didn't know if it was pain or pleasure. She was strangely breathless.

'I suppose I could do that.'

They fixed the night, the time and the place. Fred was waiting for her and they went in, but when the picture started and he put his arm round her waist, without a word, her eyes fixed on the screen, she quietly took it away. He took hold of her hand, but she withdrew it. He was surprised. That wasn't the way girls usually behaved. He didn't know what one went to the pictures for if it wasn't to have a bit of a cuddle. He walked home with her after the show. She told him her name. Grace Carter. Her father had a shop of his own in the Brixton Road, he was a draper and he had four assistants.

'He must be doing well,' said Fred.

'He doesn't complain.'

Gracie was a student at London University. When she got her degree she was going to be a school teacher.

'What d'you want to do that for when there's a good business waiting for you?'

'Pa doesn't want me to have anything to do with the shop—not after the education he's given me. He wants me to better myself, if you know what I mean.'

Her father had started life as an errand-boy, then become a draper's assistant and because he was hard-working, honest and intelligent was now owner of a prosperous little business. Success had given him grand ideas for his only child. He didn't want her to have anything to do with trade. He hoped she'd marry a professional man perhaps, or at least someone in the City. Then he'd sell the business and retire, and Gracie would be quite the lady.

When they reached the corner of her street Gracie held out her hand.

'You'd better not come to the door,' she said.

'Aren't you going to kiss me good-night?'

'I am not.'

'Why?'

'Because I don't want to.'

'You'll come to the pictures again, won't you?'

'I think I'd better not.'

'Oh, come on.'

There was such a warm urgency in his voice that she felt as though her knees would give way.

'Will you behave if I do?' He nodded. 'Promise?'

'Swop me bob.'

He scratched his head when he left her. Funny girl. He'd never met anyone quite like her. Superior, there was no doubt about that. There was something in her voice that got you. It was warm and soft. He tried to think what it was like. It was like as if the words kissed you. Sounded silly, that did, but that's just what it was like.

From then on they went to the pictures once or twice a week. After a while she allowed him to put his arm round her waist and to hold her hand, but she never let him go farther than that.

'Have you ever been kissed by a fellow?' he asked her once.

'No, I haven't,' she said simply. 'My ma's funny, she says you've got to keep a man's respect.'

'I'd give anything in the world just to kiss you, Gracie.'

'Don't be so silly.'

'Won't you let me just once?' She shook her head. 'Why not?'

'Because I like you too much,' she said hoarsely, and then walked quickly away from him.

It gave him quite a turn. He wanted her as he'd never wanted a woman before. What she'd said finished him. He'd been thinking of her a lot, and he'd looked forward to the evenings they spent together as he'd never looked forward to anything in his life. For the first time he was uncertain of himself. She was above him in every way, what with her father making money hand over fist and her education and everything, and him only a postman. They had made a date for the following Friday night and he was in a fever of anxiety lest she shouldn't come. He repeated to himself over and over again what she'd said: perhaps it meant that she'd made up her mind to drop him. When at last he saw her walking along the street he almost sobbed with relief. That evening he neither put his arm round her nor took her hand and when he walked her home he never said a word.

'You're very quiet tonight, Fred,' she said at last. 'What's the matter with you?'

He walked a few steps before he answered.

'I don't like to tell you.'

She stopped suddenly and looked up at him. There was terror on her face.

'Tell me whatever it is,' she said unsteadily.

'I'm gone, I can't help myself, I'm so stuck on you I can't see straight. I didn't know what it was to love like I love you.'

'Oh, is that all? You gave me such a fright. I thought you were going to say you were going to be married.'

'Me? Who d'you take me for? It's you I want to marry.'

'Well, what's to prevent you, silly?'

'Gracie! D'you mean it?'

He flung his arms round her and kissed her full on the mouth.

She didn't resist. She returned his kiss and he felt in her a passion as eager as his own.

They arranged that Gracie should tell her parents that she was engaged to him and that on the Sunday he should come and be introduced to them. Since the shop stayed open late on Saturday and by the time Mr. Carter got home he was tired out, it was not till after dinner on Sunday that Gracie broke her news. George Carter was a brisk, not very tall man, but sturdy, with a high colour, who with increasing prosperity had put on weight. He was more than rather bald and he had a bristle of grey moustache. Like many another employer who has risen from the working class he was a slave-driver and he got as much work out of his assistants for as little money as was possible. He had an eye for everything and he wouldn't put up with any nonsense, but he was reasonable and even kindly, so that they did not dislike him. Mrs. Carter was a quiet, nice woman, with a pleasant face and the remains of good looks. They were both in the early fifties, for they had married late after 'walking out' for nearly ten years.

They were very much surprised when Gracie told them what she had to tell, but not displeased.

'You are a sly one,' said her father. 'Why, I never suspected for a minute you'd taken up with anyone. Well, I suppose it had to come sooner or later. What's his name?'

'Fred Manson.'

'A fellow you met at college?'

'No. You must have seen him about. He clears our pillar-box. He's a postman.'

'Oh, Gracie,' cried Mrs. Carter, 'you can't mean it. You can't marry a common postman, not after all the education we've given you.'

For an instant Mr. Carter was speechless. He got redder in the face than ever.

'Your ma's right, my girl,' he burst out now. 'You can't throw yourself away like that. Why, it's ridiculous.'

'I'm not throwing myself away. You wait till you see him.'

Mrs. Carter began to cry.

'It's such a come-down. It's such a humiliation. I shall never be able to hold up my head again.'

'Oh, ma, don't talk like that. He's a nice fellow and he's got a good job.'

'You don't understand,' she moaned.

'How d'you get to know him?' Mr. Carter interrupted. 'What sort of a family's he got?'

'His pa drives one of the post office vans,' Gracie answered defiantly.

'Working-class people.'

'Well, what of it? His pa's worked twenty-four years for the post office and they think a lot of him.'

Mrs. Carter was biting the corner of her handkerchief.

'Gracie, I want to tell you something. Before your pa and me got married I was in domestic service. He wouldn't ever let me tell you because he didn't want you to be ashamed of me. That's why we was engaged all those years. The lady I was with said she'd leave me something in her will if I stayed with her till she passed away.'

'It was that money that gave me my start,' Mr. Carter broke in. 'Except for that I'd never have been where I am today. And I don't mind telling you your ma's the best wife a man ever had.'

'I never had a proper education,' Mrs. Carter went on, 'but I always was ambitious. The proudest moment of my life was when your pa said we could afford a girl to help me and he said then: "The time'll come when you have a cook *and* a house-maid," and he's been as good as his word, and now you're going back to what I come from. I'd set my heart on your marrying a gentleman.'

She began crying again. Gracie loved her parents and couldn't bear to see them so distressed.

'I'm sorry, ma, I knew it would be a disappointment to you, but I can't help it, I can't really. I love him so, I love him so terribly. I'm sure you'll like him when you see him. We're going for a walk on the Common this afternoon. Can't I bring him back to supper?'

Mrs. Carter gave her husband a harassed look. He sighed.

'I don't like it and it's no good pretending I do, but I suppose we'd better have a look at him.'

Supper passed off better than might have been expected. Fred wasn't shy and he talked to Gracie's parents as though he had known them all his life. If to be waited on by a maid, if to sup in a dining-room furnished in solid mahogany and afterwards to sit in a drawing-room that had a grand piano in it was new to him, he showed no embarrassment. After he had gone and they were alone in their bedroom Mr. and Mrs. Carter talked him over.

'He is handsome, you can't deny that,' she said.

'Handsome is as handsome does. D'you think he's after her money?'

'Well, he must know that you've got a tidy little bit tucked away somewhere, but he's in love with her all right.'

'Oh, what makes you think that?'

'Why, you've only got to see the way he looks at her.'

'Well, that's something at all events.'

In the end the Carters withdrew their opposition on the condition that the young things shouldn't marry until Gracie had taken her degree. That would give them a year, and at the back of their minds was the hope that by then she would have changed her mind. They saw a good deal of Fred after that. He spent every Sunday with them. Little by little they began quite to like him. He was so easy, so gay, so full of high spirits, and above all so obviously head over ears in love with Gracie, that Mrs. Carter soon succumbed to his charm, and after a while even Mr. Carter was prepared to admit that he didn't seem a bad fellow. Fred and Gracie were happy. She went to London every day to attend lectures and worked hard. They spent blissful evenings together. He gave her a very nice engagement ring and often took her out to dinner in the West End and to a play. On fine Sundays he drove her out into the country in a car that he said a friend had lent him. When she asked him if he could afford all the money he spent on her he laughed, and said a chap had given him a tip on an outsider and he'd made a packet. They talked interminably of the little flat they would have when they were married and the fun it would be to furnish it. They were more in love with one another than ever.

Then the blow fell. Fred was arrested for stealing money from the letters he collected. Many people, to save themselves the trouble of buying postal orders, put notes in their envelopes, and it wasn't difficult to tell that they were there. Fred went up for trial, pleaded guilty, and was sentenced to two years' hard labour. Gracie went to the trial. Up to the last moment she had hoped that he would be able to prove his innocence. It was a dreadful shock to her when he pleaded guilty. She was not allowed to see him. He went straight from the dock to the prison van. She went home, and locking herself up in her bedroom, threw herself on the bed and wept. When Mr. Carter came back from the shop Gracie's mother went up to her room.

'Gracie, you're to come downstairs,' she said. 'Your father wants to speak to you.'

Gracie got up and went down. She did not trouble to dry her eyes.

'Seen the paper?' he said, holding out to her the *Evening News*.

She didn't answer.

'Well, that's the end of that young man,' he went on harshly.

They too, Gracie's parents, had been shocked when Fred was arrested, but she was so distressed, she was so convinced that everything could be explained, that they hadn't had the heart to tell her that she must have nothing more to do with him. But now they felt it time to have things out with her.

'So that's where the money came from for those dinners and theatres. And the car. I thought it funny he should have a friend who'd lend him a car on Sundays when he'd be wanting it himself. He hired it, didn't he?'

'I suppose so,' she answered miserably. 'I just believed what he told me.'

'You've had a lucky escape, my girl, that's all I can say.'

'He only did it because he wanted to give me a good time. He didn't want me to think I couldn't have everything as nice when I was with him as what I've been used to at home.'

'You're not going to make excuses for him, I hope. He's a thief, that's what he is.'

'I don't care,' she said sullenly.

'You don't care? What d'you mean by that?'

'Exactly what I say. I'm going to wait for him and the moment he comes out I'm going to marry him.'

Mrs. Carter gave a gasp of horror.

'Gracie, you can't do a thing like that,' she cried. 'Think of the disgrace. And what about us? We've always held our heads high. He's a thief, and once a thief always a thief.'

'Don't go on calling him a thief,' Gracie shrieked, stamping her foot with rage. 'What he did he did just because he loved me. I don't care if he is a thief. I love him more than ever I loved him. You don't know what love is. You waited ten years to marry pa just so as an old woman should leave you some money. D'you call that love?'

'You leave your ma out of this,' Mr. Carter shouted. Then an idea occurred to him and he gave her a piercing glance. 'Have you *got* to marry the feller?'

Gracie blushed furiously.

'No. There's never been anything of that sort. And not through any fault of mine either. He loved me too much. He didn't want to do anything perhaps he'd regret afterwards.'

Often on summer evenings in the country when they'd been lying in a field in one another's arms, mouth to mouth, her desire had been as intense as his. She knew how much he wanted her and she was ready to give him what he asked. But when things got too desperate he'd suddenly jump up and say:

'Come on, let's walk.'

He'd drag her to her feet. She knew what was in his mind. He wanted to wait till they were married. His love had given him a delicacy of sentiment that he'd never known before. He couldn't make it out himself, but he had a funny sort of feeling about her, he felt that if he had her before marriage it would spoil things. Because she guessed what was in his heart she loved him all the more.

'I don't know what's come over you,' moaned Mrs. Carter. 'You was always such a good girl. You've never given us a day's uneasiness.'

'Stop it, ma,' said Mr. Carter violently. 'We've got to get this straight once and for all. You've got to give up this man, see? I've got me own position to think of and if you think I'm going to have a jail-bird for a son-in-law you'd better think again. I've had enough of this nonsense. You've got to promise me that you'll have nothing more to do with the feller ever.'

'D'you think I'm going to give him up now? How often d'you want me to tell you I'm going to marry him the moment he gets out?'

'All right, then you can get out of my house and get out pretty damn quick. And stay out.'

'Pa!' cried Mrs. Carter.

'Shut up.'

'I'll be glad to go,' said Gracie.

'Oh, will you? And how d'you think you're going to live?'

'I can work, can't I? I can get a job at Payne & Perkins. They'll be glad to have me.'

'Oh, Gracie, you couldn't go and work in a shop. You can't demean yourself like that,' said Mrs. Carter.

'Will you shut up, ma,' shouted Mr. Carter, beside himself now with rage. 'Work, will you? You that's never done a stroke of work in your life except that tomfoolery at the college. Bright idea it was of your ma's to give you an education. Fat lot of good it'll be to you when you've got to stand on your feet for hours and got to be civil and pleasant to a lot of old trouts who just try and give you all the trouble they can just to show how superior they are. I bet you'll like it when you're bawled out by the manageress because you're not bright and snappy. All right, marry your jail-bird. I suppose you know you'll have to keep him too. You don't think anyone's going to give him a job, do you, not with his record. Get out, get out, get out.'

He had worked himself up to such a pitch of fury that he sank panting into a chair. Mrs. Carter, frightened, poured out a glass of water and gave him some to drink. Gracie slipped out of the room.

Next day, when her father had gone to work and her mother was out shopping, she left the house with such effects as she could get into a suitcase. Payne & Perkins was a large department store in the Brixton Road, and with her good appearance and pleasant manner she found no difficulty in getting taken on. She was put in the ladies' lingerie. For a few days she stayed at the Y.W.C.A. and then arranged to share a room with one of the girls who worked with her.

Ned Preston saw Fred in the evening of the day he went to jail. He found him shattered, but only because of Gracie. He took his thieving very lightly.

'I had to do the right thing by her, didn't I? Her people, they didn't think I was good enough for her; I wanted to show them I was just as good as they were. When we went up to the West End I couldn't give her a sandwich and half of bitter in a pub, why, she's never been in a pub in her life, I *had* to take her to a restaurant. If people are such fools as to put money in letters, well, they're just asking for it.'

But he was frightened. He wasn't sure that Gracie would see it like that.

'I've got to know what she's going to do. If she chucks me now— well, it's the end of everything for me, see? I'll find some way of doing meself in, I swear to God I will.'

He told Ned the whole story of his love for Gracie.

'I could have had her over and over again if I'd wanted to. And I did want to, and so did she. I knew that. But I respected her, see? She's not like other girls. She's one in a thousand, I tell you.'

He talked and talked. He stormed, he wept. From that confused torrent of words emerged one thing very clearly. A passionate, a frenzied love. Ned promised that he would see the girl.

'Tell her I love her, tell her that what I did I just did because I wanted her to have the best of everything, and tell her I just can't live without her.'

As soon as he could find time Ned Preston went to the Carters' house, but when he asked for Gracie the maid who opened the door told him that she didn't live there any more. Then he asked to see her mother.

'I'll go and see if she's in.'

He gave the maid his card, thinking the name of his club engraved in the corner would impress Mrs. Carter enough to make her willing to see him. The maid left him at the door, but in a minute or two asked him to come in. He was shown into the stiff and little-used sitting-room. Mrs. Carter kept him waiting for some time and when she came in, holding his card in the tips of her fingers, he guessed it was because she had thought fit to change her dress. The black silk she wore was evidently a dress for occasions. He told her his connection with Wormwood Scrubs and said that he had to do with a man named Frederick Manson. The moment he mentioned the name Mrs. Carter assumed a hostile attitude.

'Don't speak to me of that man,' she cried. 'A thief, that's what he is. The trouble he's caused us. They ought to have given him five years, they ought.'

'I'm sorry he's caused you trouble,' said Ned mildly. 'Perhaps if you'd give me a few facts I might help to straighten things out.'

Ned Preston certainly had a way with him. Perhaps Mrs. Carter was impressed because he was a gentleman. 'Class he is,' she probably said to herself. Anyhow it was not long before she was telling him the whole story. She grew upset as she told it and began to cry.

'And now she's gone and left us. Run away. I don't know how she could bring herself to do a thing like that. God knows, we love her. She's all we've got and we done everything in the world for her. Her pa never meant it when he told her to get out of the house. Only she was so obstinate. He got in a temper, he always was a quick-tempered man, he was just as upset as I was when we found

she'd gone. And d'you know what she's been and gone and done?
Got herself a job at Payne & Perkins. Mr. Carter can't abide them.
Cutting prices all the time they are. Unfair competition, he calls it.
And to think of our Gracie working with a lot of shop-girls—oh, it's
so humiliating.'

Ned made a mental note of the store's name. He hadn't been at
all sure of getting Gracie's address out of Mrs. Carter.

'Have you seen her since she left you?' he asked.

'Of course I have. I knew they'd jump at her at Payne & Perkins,
a superior girl like that, and I went there, and there she was sure
enough—in the ladies' lingerie. I waited outside till closing time
and then I spoke to her. I asked her to come home. I said her pa
was willing to let bygones be bygones. And d'you know what she
said? She said she'd come home if we never said a word against
Fred and if we was prepared to have her marry him as soon as ever
he got out. Of course I had to tell her pa. I never saw him in such a
state, I thought he was going to have a fit, he said he'd rather see
her dead at his feet than married to that jail-bird.'

Mrs. Carter again burst into tears and as soon as he could Ned
Preston left her. He went to the department store, up to the ladies'
lingerie, and asked for Grace Carter. She was pointed out to him
and he went up to her.

'Can I speak to you for a minute? I've come from Fred Manson.'

She went deathly white. For a moment it seemed that she could
not utter a word.

'Follow me, please.'

She took him into a passage smelling of disinfectants which
seemed to lead to the lavatories. They were alone. She stared at him
anxiously.

'He sends you his love. He's worried about you. He's afraid
you're awfully unhappy. What he wants to know really is if you're
going to chuck him.'

'Me?' Her eyes filled with tears, but on her face was a look of
ecstasy. 'Tell him that nothing matters to me as long as he loves
me. Tell him I'd wait twenty years for him if I had to. Tell him I'm
counting the days till he gets out so as we can get married.'

For fear of the manageress, she couldn't stay away from her work
for more than a minute or two. She gave Ned all the loving messages
she could get into the time to give Fred Manson. Ned didn't get to
the Scrubs till nearly six. The prisoners are allowed to put down

their tools at five-thirty, and Fred had just put his down. When Ned entered the cell he turned pale and sank on to the bed as though his anxiety was such that he didn't trust his legs. But when Ned told him his news he gave a gasp of relief. For a while he couldn't trust himself to speak.

'I knew you'd seen her the moment you came in. I smelt her.'

He sniffed as though the smell of her body were strong in his nostrils, and his face was as it were a mask of desire. His features on a sudden seemed strangely blurred.

'You know, it made me feel quite uncomfortable so that I had to look the other way,' said Ned Preston when he told us this, with a cackle of his shrill laughter. 'It was sex in its nakedness all right.'

Fred was an exemplary prisoner. He worked well, he gave no trouble. Ned suggested books for him to read and he took them out of the library, but that was about as far as he got.

'I can't get on well with them somehow,' he said. 'I start reading and then I begin thinking of Gracie. You know, when she kisses you ordinary like—oh, it's so sweet, but when she kisses you really, my God, it's lovely.'

Fred was allowed to see Gracie once a month, but their meetings, with a glass screen between, under the eyes of a warder, were so painful that after several visits they agreed it would be better if she didn't come any more. A year passed. Owing to his good behaviour he could count on a remittance of his sentence and so would be free in another six months. Gracie had saved every penny she could out of her wages, and now as the time approached for Fred's release she set about getting a home ready for him. She took two rooms in a house and furnished them on the hire purchase system. One room of course was to be their bedroom and the other the living-room and kitchen. There was an old-fashioned range in it and this she had taken out and replaced by a gas-stove. She wanted everything to be nice and new and clean and comfortable. She took pains to make the two little rooms bright and pretty. To do all this she had to go without all but the barest necessities of existence and she grew thin and pale. Ned suspected that she was starving herself and when he went to see her took a box of chocolates or a cake so that she should have at least something to eat. He brought the prisoner news of what Gracie was doing and she made him promise to give him accurate accounts of every article she bought. He took fond, more than fond, passionate messages from one to the other. He was convinced that Fred would go straight in future and he got him a job as a commissionaire from a firm that had a chain of restaurants in London. The wages were good and by calling taxis or fetching cars he would be able to make money on the side. He was to start work as soon as he came out of jail. Gracie took the necessary steps so that they could get married at once. The eighteen months of Fred's imprisonment were drawing to an end. Gracie was in a fever of excitement.

It happened then that Ned Preston had one of his periodical bouts of illness and was unable to go to the prison for three weeks. It bothered him, for he didn't like to abandon his prisoners, so as soon as he could get out of bed he went to the Scrubs. The chief warder told him that Manson had been asking for him.

'I think you'd better go and see him. I don't know what's the matter with him. He's been acting rather funny since you've been away.'

It was just a fortnight before Fred was due to be released. Ned Preston went to his cell.

'Well, Fred, how are you?' he asked. 'Sorry I haven't been able to come and see you. I've been ill, and I haven't been able to see Gracie either. She must be all of a dither by now.'

'Well, I want you to go and see her.'

His manner was so surly that Ned was taken aback. It was unlike him to be anything but pleasant and civil.

'Of course I will.'

'I want you to tell her that I'm not going to marry her.'

Ned was so astounded that for a minute he could only stare blankly at Fred Manson.

'What on earth d'you mean?'

'Exactly what I say.'

'You can't let her down now. Her people have thrown her out. She's been working all this time to get a home ready for you. She's got the licence and everything.'

'I don't care. I'm not going to marry her.'

'But why, why, why?'

Ned was flabbergasted. Fred Manson was silent for a bit. His face was dark and sullen.

'I'll tell you. I've thought about her night and day for eighteen months, and now I'm sick to death of her.'

When Ned Preston reached this point of his story our hostess and our fellow guests broke into loud laughter. He was plainly taken aback. There was some little talk after that and the party broke up. Ned and I, having to go in the same direction, walked along Piccadilly together. For a time we walked in silence.

'I noticed you didn't laugh with the others,' he said abruptly.

'I didn't think it funny.'

'What d'you make of it?'

'Well, I can see his point, you know. Imagination's an odd thing, it dries up; I suppose, thinking of her incessantly all that time he'd exhausted every emotion she could give him, and I think it was quite literally true, he'd just got sick to death of her. He'd squeezed the lemon dry and there was nothing to do but throw away the rind.'

'I didn't think it funny either. That's why I didn't tell them the rest of the story. I wouldn't accept it at first. I thought it was just hysteria or something. I went to see him two or three days running. I argued with him. I really did my damnedest. I thought if he'd only see her it would be all right, but he wouldn't even do that. He said he hated the sight of her. I couldn't move him. At last I had to go and tell her.'

We walked on a little longer in silence.

'I saw her in that beastly, stinking corridor. She saw at once that there was something the matter and she went awfully white. She wasn't a girl to show much emotion. There was something gracious and rather noble about her face. Tranquil. Her lips quivered a bit when I told her and she didn't say anything for a minute. When she spoke it was quite calmly, as though—well, as though she'd just missed a bus and would have to wait for another. As though it was a nuisance, you know, but nothing to make a song and dance about. "There's nothing for me to do now but put my head in the gas-oven," she said.

'And she did.'

EVELYN WAUGH
Mr. Loveday's Little Outing

I

'You will not find your father greatly changed,' remarked Lady Moping, as the car turned into the gates of the County Asylum.

'Will he be wearing a uniform?' asked Angela.

'No, dear, of course not. He is receiving the very best attention.'

It was Angela's first visit and it was being made at her own suggestion.

Ten years had passed since the showery day in late summer when Lord Moping had been taken away; a day of confused but bitter memories for her; the day of Lady Moping's annual garden party, always bitter, confused that day by the caprice of the weather which, remaining clear and brilliant with promise until the arrival of the first guests, had suddenly blackened into a squall. There had been a scuttle for cover; the marquee had capsized; a frantic carrying of cushions and chairs; a table-cloth lofted to the boughs of the monkey-puzzler, fluttering in the rain; a bright period and the cautious emergence of guests on to the soggy lawns; another squall; another twenty minutes of sunshine. It had been an abominable afternoon, culminating at about six o'clock in her father's attempted suicide.

Lord Moping habitually threatened suicide on the occasion of the garden party; that year he had been found black in the face, hanging by his braces in the orangery; some neighbours, who were sheltering there from the rain, set him on his feet again, and before dinner a van had called for him. Since then Lady Moping had paid seasonal calls at the asylum and returned in time for tea, rather reticent of her experience.

Many of her neighbours were inclined to be critical of Lord Moping's accommodation. He was not, of course, an ordinary inmate. He lived in a separate wing of the asylum, specially devoted to the segregation of wealthier lunatics. These were given every consideration which their foibles permitted. They might choose their own clothes (many indulged in the liveliest fancies), smoke the most expensive brands of cigars and, on the anniversaries of their certification, entertain any other inmates for whom they had an attachment to private dinner parties.

The fact remained, however, that it was far from being the most expensive kind of institution; the uncompromising address, 'COUNTY HOME FOR MENTAL DEFECTIVES,' stamped across the notepaper, worked on the uniforms of their attendants, painted, even, upon a prominent hoarding at the main entrance, suggested the lowest associations. From time to time, with less or more tact, her friends attempted to bring to Lady Moping's notice particulars of seaside nursing homes, of 'qualified practitioners with large private grounds suitable for the charge of nervous or difficult cases', but she accepted them lightly; when her son came of age he might make any changes that he thought fit; meanwhile, she felt no inclination to relax her economical régime; her husband had betrayed her basely on the one day in the year when she looked for loyal support, and was far better off than he deserved.

A few lonely figures in great-coats were shuffling and loping about the park.

'Those are the lower-class lunatics,' observed Lady Moping. 'There is a very nice little flower garden for people like your father. I sent them some cuttings last year.'

They drove past the blank, yellow brick façade to the doctor's private entrance and were received by him in the 'visitors' room', set aside for interviews of this kind. The window was protected on the inside by bars and wire netting; there was no fireplace; when Angela nervously attempted to move her chair further from the radiator, she found that it was screwed to the floor.

'Lord Moping is quite ready to see you,' said the doctor.

'How is he?'

'Oh, very well, very well indeed, I'm glad to say. He had rather a nasty cold some time ago, but apart from that his condition is excellent. He spends a lot of his time in writing.'

They heard a shuffling, skipping sound approaching along the flagged passage. Outside the door a high peevish voice, which Angela recognized as her father's, said: 'I haven't the time, I tell you. Let them come back later.'

A gentler tone, with a slight rural burr, replied, 'Now come along.

It is a purely formal audience. You need stay no longer than you like.'

Then the door was pushed open (it had no lock or fastening) and Lord Moping came into the room. He was attended by an elderly little man with full white hair and an expression of great kindness.

'That is Mr. Loveday who acts as Lord Moping's attendant.'

'Secretary,' said Lord Moping. He moved with a jogging gait and shook hands with his wife.

'This is Angela. You remember Angela, don't you?'

'No, I can't say that I do. What does she want?'

'We just came to see you.'

'Well, you have come at an exceedingly inconvenient time. I am very busy. Have you typed out that letter to the Pope yet, Loveday?'

'No, my lord. If you remember, you asked me to look up the figures about the Newfoundland fisheries first?'

'So I did. Well, it is fortunate, as I think the whole letter will have to be redrafted. A great deal of new information has come to light since luncheon. A great deal. . . . You see, my dear, I am fully occupied.' He turned his restless, quizzical eyes upon Angela. 'I suppose you have come about the Danube. Well, you must come again later. Tell them it will be all right, quite all right, but I have not had time to give my full attention to it. Tell them that.'

'Very well, Papa.'

'Anyway,' said Lord Moping rather petulantly, 'it is a matter of secondary importance. There is the Elbe and the Amazon and the Tigris to be dealt with first, eh, Loveday? . . . *Danube* indeed. Nasty little river. I'd only call it a stream myself. Well, can't stop, nice of you to come. I would do more for you if I could, but you see how I'm fixed. Write to me about it. That's it. *Put it in black and white.*'

And with that he left the room.

'You see,' said the doctor, 'he is in excellent condition. He is putting on weight, eating and sleeping excellently. In fact, the whole tone of his system is above reproach.'

The door opened and Loveday returned.

'Forgive my coming back, sir, but I was afraid that the young lady might be upset at his Lordship's not knowing her. You mustn't mind him, miss. Next time he'll be very pleased to see you. It's only to-day he's put out on account of being behindhand with his work. You see, sir, all this week I've been helping in the library and I haven't been able to get all his Lordship's reports typed out. And he's got muddled with his card index. That's all it is. He doesn't mean any harm.'

'What a nice man,' said Angela, when Loveday had gone back to his charge.

'Yes. I don't know what we should do without old Loveday. Everybody loves him, staff and patients alike.'

'I remember him well. It's a great comfort to know that you are able to get such good warders,' said Lady Moping; 'people who don't know, say such foolish things about asylums.'

'Oh, but Loveday isn't a warder,' said the doctor.

'You don't mean he's cuckoo, too?' said Angela.

The doctor corrected her.

'He is an *inmate*. It is rather an interesting case. He has been here for thirty-five years.'

'But I've never seen anyone saner,' said Angela.

'He certainly has that air,' said the doctor, 'and in the last twenty years we have treated him as such. He is the life and soul of the place. Of course he is not one of the private patients, but we allow him to mix freely with them. He plays billiards excellently, does conjuring tricks at the concert, mends their gramophones, valets them, helps them in their crossword puzzles and various—er— hobbies. We allow them to give him small tips for services rendered, and he must by now have amassed quite a little fortune. He has a way with even the most troublesome of them. An invaluable man about the place.'

'Yes, but why is he here?'

'Well, it is rather sad. When he was a very young man he killed somebody—a young woman quite unknown to him, whom he knocked off her bicycle and then throttled. He gave himself up immediately afterwards and has been here ever since.'

'But surely he is perfectly safe now. Why is he not let out?'

'Well, I suppose if it was to anyone's interest, he would be. He has no relatives except a step-sister who lives in Plymouth. She used to visit him at one time, but she hasn't been for years now. He's perfectly happy here and I can assure you *we* aren't going to take the first steps in turning him out. He's far too useful to us.'

'But it doesn't seem fair,' said Angela.

'Look at your father,' said the doctor. 'He'd be quite lost without Loveday to act as his secretary.'

'It doesn't seem fair.'

2

Angela left the asylum, oppressed by a sense of injustice. Her mother was unsympathetic.

'Think of being locked up in a looney bin all one's life.'

'He attempted to hang himself in the orangery,' replied Lady Moping, '*in front of the Chester-Martins.*'

'I don't mean Papa. I mean Mr. Loveday.'

'I don't think I know him.'

'Yes, the looney they have put to look after Papa.'

'Your father's secretary. A very decent sort of man, I thought, and eminently suited to his work.'

Angela left the question for the time, but returned to it again at luncheon on the following day.

'Mums, what does one have to do to get people out of the bin?'

'The bin? Good gracious, child, I hope that you do not anticipate your father's return *here*.'

'No, no. Mr. Loveday.'

'Angela, you seem to me to be totally bemused. I see it was a mistake to take you with me on our little visit yesterday.'

After luncheon Angela disappeared to the library and was soon immersed in the lunacy laws as represented in the encylopaedia.

She did not reopen the subject with her mother, but a fortnight later, when there was a question of taking some pheasants over to her father for his eleventh Certification Party she showed an unusual willingness to run over with them. Her mother was occupied with other interests and noticed nothing suspicious.

Angela drove her small car to the asylum and, after delivering the game, asked for Mr. Loveday. He was busy at the time making a crown for one of his companions who expected hourly to be annointed Emperor of Brazil, but he left his work and enjoyed several minutes' conversation with her. They spoke about her father's health and spirits. After a time Angela remarked, 'Don't you ever want to get away?'

Mr. Loveday looked at her with his gentle, blue-grey eyes. 'I've got very well used to the life, miss. I'm fond of the poor people here, and I think that several of them are quite fond of me. At least, I think they would miss me if I were to go.'

'But don't you ever think of being free again?'

'Oh yes, miss, I think of it—almost all the time I think of it.'

'What would you do if you got out? There must be *something* you would sooner do than stay here.'

The old man fidgeted uneasily. 'Well, miss, it sounds ungrateful, but I can't deny I should welcome a little outing, once, before I get too old to enjoy it. I expect we all have our secret ambitions, and there *is* one thing I often wish I could do. You mustn't ask me what. . . . It wouldn't take long. But I do feel that if I had done it, just for a day, an afternoon even, then I would die quiet. I could settle down again easier, and devote myself to the poor crazed people here with a better heart. Yes, I do feel that.'

There were tears in Angela's eyes that afternoon as she drove away. 'He *shall* have his little outing, bless him,' she said.

3

From that day onwards for many weeks Angela had a new purpose in life. She moved about the ordinary routine of her home with an abstracted air and an unfamiliar, reserved courtesy which greatly disconcerted Lady Moping.

'I believe the child's in love. I only pray that it isn't that uncouth Egbertson boy.'

She read a great deal in the library, she cross-examined any guests who had pretensions to legal or medical knowledge, she showed extreme goodwill to old Sir Roderick Lane-Foscote, their Member. The names 'alienist,' 'barrister' or 'government official' now had for her the glamour that formerly surrounded film actors and professional wrestlers. She was a woman with a cause, and before the end of the hunting season she had triumphed. Mr. Loveday achieved his liberty.

The doctor at the asylum showed reluctance but no real opposition. Sir Roderick wrote to the Home Office. The necessary papers were signed, and at last the day came when Mr. Loveday took leave of the home where he had spent such long and useful years.

His departure was marked by some ceremony. Angela and Sir Roderick Lane-Foscote sat with the doctors on the stage of the gymnasium. Below them were assembled everyone in the institution who was thought to be stable enough to endure the excitement.

Lord Moping, with a few suitable expressions of regret, presented Mr. Loveday on behalf of the wealthier lunatics with a gold cigarette case; those who supposed themselves to be emperors showered him with decorations and titles of honour. The warders gave him a silver watch and many of the non-paying inmates were in tears on the day of the presentation.

The doctor made the main speech of the afternoon. 'Remember,' he remarked, 'that you leave behind you nothing but our warmest good wishes. You are bound to us by ties that none will forget. Time will only deepen our sense of debt to you. If at any time in the future you should grow tired of your life in the world, there will always be a welcome for you here. Your post will be open.'

A dozen or so variously afflicted lunatics hopped and skipped after him down the drive until the iron gates opened and Mr. Loveday stepped into his freedom. His small trunk had already gone to the station; he elected to walk. He had been reticent about his plans, but he was well provided with money, and the general impression was that he would go to London and enjoy himself a little before visiting his step-sister.

It was to the surprise of all that he returned within two hours of his liberation. He was smiling whimsically, a gentle, self-regarding smile of reminiscence.

'I have come back,' he informed the doctor. 'I think that now I shall be here for good.'

'But, Loveday, what a short holiday. I'm afraid that you have hardly enjoyed yourself at all.'

'Oh yes, sir, thank you, sir, I've enjoyed myself *very much*. I'd been promising myself one little treat all these years. It was short, sir, but *most* enjoyable. Now I shall be able to settle down again to my work here without any regrets.'

Half a mile up the road from the asylum gates, they later discovered an abandoned bicycle. It was a lady's machine of some antiquity. Quite near it in the ditch lay the strangled body of a young woman, who, riding home to her tea, had chanced to overtake Mr. Loveday, as he strode along, musing on his opportunities.

ANGUS WILSON
Realpolitik

JOHN HOBDAY sat on the edge of his desk and swung his left leg
with characteristic boyishness. He waited for the staff to get settled
in their seats and then spoke with careful informality.

'I know how frightfully busy you are. As a matter of fact I am
myself,' he said with the half-humorous urchin smile that he used
for such jokes. Only his secretary, Veronica, gave the helpful laugh
he expected. It was not going to be an easy meeting, he decided 'So
I'm not going to waste your time with a lot of talk' he went on 'I
just thought . . .' He paused and beat with his pencil against the
desk whilst Mrs. Scrutton moved her chair fussily out of the
sunlight. 'Ready?' he asked with an over-elaborate smile 'Right.
Then we'll start again. As I was saying, we're all very busy, but all
the same I thought it was time we had a little meeting. I've been
here a week now and although I've had some very helpful chats
with each of you in turn, we've never had a chance to get together
and outline our plans'. None of the three who formed his audience
made any response. Veronica, who remembered him taking over
new departments at the Ministry during the war, thought he hasn't
got the right tone, he doesn't realize that he's coming up against
deeper loyalties with these people, loyalties to scholarship and ideas.
She almost felt like letting him fend for himself, but old habits were
too strong.

'I'm sure it's what everybody's been wanting' she said in her
deep voice. She had gauged rightly, his moment of uncertainty had
gone, her faithful bark had guided him at the crucial moment. Mrs.
Scrutton tried to discomfort him. She rustled the papers on her lap
and whispered audibly to Major Sarson 'Our plans. *His* plans for
us would be more honest'. But it was too late, she had missed her
chance. John merely frowned at the interruption and it was Mrs.
Scrutton who was left with burning cheeks, hiding her embarrassment by lighting a fresh cigarette.

'As you know' John went on, and Veronica could tell by the loud,
trumpeting, rhetorical note of his voice that he was once more the
confident salesman lost in the dream world of the grandiose schemes

he was putting before them 'I've got some very big ideas for the Gallery. I'm not an expert in any way as you people are, but I think that's possibly why Sir Harold's executors chose me for the job. They felt the Gallery had already got its full weight of scholars and experts, what it needed was a man with administrative experience, whose training had led him to take an over all view of things, to think, shall I say, widely rather than deeply. That's why they got me in. But I'm going to be absolutely frank with you' tossing a lock of brown, wavy hair from his forehead, he stared at his audience with a wide-eyed appeal 'I need *your* help, without my staff I can get nowhere.'

Major Sarson winced slightly. All this theatricality and the loud pitch of John's voice got on his nerves, besides he could feel a draught round his legs. It's like some damned Methodist preacher fellow, he thought.

'You've been grand in this first week' John went on 'absolutely grand. I don't mind telling you now that when I arrived I was dead scared. You'd all been here for years, you knew the collections backwards, you had your own ways of running the place, and above all you'd had the inestimable advantage of knowing Sir Harold, of hearing exactly what was in his mind when he bought this picture or that object, of knowing what his ideals were in giving the public the benefit of his taste and experience. I felt sure you were bound to resent me as an outsider, and I knew I'd have done the same in your place'.

The faces in front of him were quite unresponsive. He isn't going to get anywhere with sentimental appeals, thought Veronica, these people are idealists, there's nothing more hardboiled. The damned fools, thought John, they have the chance of turning this tin pot, cranky provincial gallery into a national institution and they won't play ball. Well if they can't see which way their own chances lie, they're not getting in the way of mine. They'll have to come to heel or go. His voice became a little sharper, a shade less ingenuous and friendly.

'You've all told me your views in our various little chats. Sometimes we've agreed, sometimes we haven't. You've inclined to the feeling that all is for the best in the best of all possible worlds, I've felt that some changes were needed, that the scope of the work here wanted broadening, that the organization wanted, let's face it, bringing up to date a bit, and in all this the Board has agreed with me'.

Tony Parnell's baby face had grown steadily more pouting and scowling as John had been speaking. To think of this mountebank in charge of the Gallery, a professional careerist, who understood nothing of Sir Harold's ideas and aims, who had even laughed when he'd spoken to him of the metaphysical aspects of technique in painting. He had banked so much on becoming Curator. Sir Harold had spoken so often of him as 'my torchbearer, the youngest member of our staff', and now these awful business men who had got control of the estate had put this creature in. Major Sarson and Mrs. Scrutton were too old to fight these changes, he had promised before the meeting that *he* would make the challenge. Now was his opportunity. Red in the face, he opened his mouth, but in his nervousness his voice emerged a high falsetto. John smiled across at Veronica.

'The Board haven't had much opportunity of agreeing with us since they haven't heard our views' Tony squeaked.

'My dear Parnell' said John, and his tone was purposely patronizing and offensive. The old ones he regarded without rancour as dead wood to be cleared away, but Tony he disliked personally for his assumptions of scholarly disinterestedness and moral superiority. 'Don't let that worry you. As soon as you've got your ideas clear come along and push them at the Board as much as you like. I shouldn't use too much of your favourite art jargon if I was you; the Board are anxious to help but they're only ordinary business men and they might not understand. If you follow my advice you'll come down to earth a bit, but of course that's entirely your affair'.

Mrs. Scrutton fingered the buttons on her checked tweed coat nervously. 'There's no need to bully Mr. Parnell' she said.

'Oh, come' said John jocosely 'if Parnell's going to have the ladies on his side I shall have to surrender'. To his delight he saw that Tony was frowning with annoyance.

'Do let me deal with this in my own way' he said to Mrs. Scrutton, whose lip began to tremble.

So that severe grey bobbed hair and man's collar and tie could dissolve early into tears, thought John, so much the better.

'Mrs. Scrutton was only trying to help you, Parnell' said Major Sarson 'Don't let us forget our manners, please'.

John yawned slightly 'When the little civil war's over' he said 'I'd

just like to outline our main functions. As I see them they're these:
Relations with the Public, that's you, Parnell; Display, Mrs. Scrutton; Research, Major Sarson. Miss Clay' he indicated Veronica 'is
maid of all work. And I, well, I'm the Aunt Sally, ready to stop the
bricks and pass on the bouquets'.

Major Sarson looked at his watch impatiently. 'I quite agree,
with you, Major' said John. 'The sooner we get finished the better.
No true gentlemen continue to hold meetings after opening time'.
The old man's face twitched violently, no one before had referred
overtly to his notorious weakness.

'I'd like to take the public first' said John. 'You've done a first-
rate job, Parnell—within its limits. But you haven't gone far
enough. You've got real enthusiasm and that's half the battle—but
only half. You give the public first-rate value in lectures and
catalogues when they get here, but you don't try to get them to
come. I know what you're going to say "They'll come if they're
interested." But aren't you being a bit hard on the poor, tired,
pushed around public of today? They've got to be told about the
place. You've got to compete with the cinema, the football team *and*
the fireside radio. In short you've got to advertise and you can't do
that unless you have figures.' Here John paused and picked up a
file of papers.

'You have all the figures there' said Tony sulkily.

'I know' said John 'but don't you think they're just a bit too
general? "So many people visited the Gallery on August 5th; so
many on November 3rd" But what sort of people? Who are we
catering for? Were they Chinamen, shop-girls, farmers, or just plain
deaf-mutes? To tell us anything these figures want breaking down
into groups—so many foreigners, so many over-forties, so many
under-twenties. That's the way to build up a picture. Now supposing you run over these figures in the way that I suggest and we'll
talk again.'

Tony was about to protest that this task was impossible, but John
held up his hand. 'No, no, time's very short and there's one more
point I want to raise before we pass on to display'. Mrs. Scrutton
drew her coat tightly round her. 'It's about the lecture-room. Sir
Louis Crippen was saying something at the last Board meeting
about its not being free for his archaeological society when he
needed it. Do you know anything about that?'

Tony Parnell hesitated. 'Well, actually' he said 'Mrs. Scrutton makes all the lecture hall arrangements'.

'But isn't it the P.R.O.'s pigeon?' asked John.

'Yes' said Tony. 'But . . . well . . . Mrs. Scrutton . . .'

'I see' said John coldly. 'Perhaps you'd enlighten me, then, Mrs. Scrutton.'

The grey bob shook as she answered, an involuntary shake that was to prove the prelude to age's palsy. 'Sir Louis asked for Tuesday and Tuesdays are always booked by Miss Copley' she said.

'Miss Copley?'

Mrs. Scrutton guessed that he knew the answer and her reply attempted a rebuke. 'Miss Copley is an old and true friend to the Gallery' she said. 'She's been giving her lectures to Schools on Tuesdays for many years.'

'No doubt' said John 'but I still think Sir Louis should have preference'.

'I don't agree at all' said Major Sarson 'it would be most unfair'.

'Yes, why should Sir Louis receive special treatment?' asked Mrs. Scrutton.

'Well, frankly' replied John 'because although Miss Copley maybe a very old friend, Sir Louis is a very influential one and the Gallery needs influential friends.'

Before Mrs. Scrutton there floated Sir Harold's features, like Erasmus she had thought him, the last of the humanists. Major Sarson too, remembered his old friend's handshake and his firm clear voice 'Sarson' he had said 'this money came to me through false standards, false distinctions. There shall be no distinctions in its use but those of scholarship'. The eyes of both these old people filled with tears.

John turned to Veronica. 'You've nothing to do, Miss Clay' he said. 'In future you will take on the lecture hall arrangements. Anything important you'll refer to me.' Mrs. Scrutton made a gesture of protest. 'No, no' said John. 'I'm not going to let you wear yourself out on these minor details, you're far too valuable to the Gallery. Besides, you've got more than a full time job with Display if it's properly carried out.'

Tony Parnell half rose from his chair 'I thought the Lecture Hall arrangements came under Public Relations?'

'So did I' said John 'until you disillusioned me.'

'Next we come to Display. I suppose no side of our work has been more revolutionized in recent years. The Philadelphia report, you know, and the Canadian Association series' he went on, smiling at Mrs. Scrutton. She suddenly felt very tired, she had seen these documents but had never been able to bring herself to read them. 'But there's no need for me to mention these things to you' John continued. 'Your arrangement of the miniature collection . . .' and he sighed in wonder. 'Well, I'm going to pay you a great compliment there. Your arrangement of the miniatures not only makes one want to look at them, it makes it impossible for one not to look at them. I'm sure, Mrs. Scrutton, you'll agree with my wish that some other sides of the collection had the same advantages as the miniatures— the jewellery, for instance, and the armour. But that's not your fault. There's just too much for one person, that's all there is to it. The same applies to the research. I'm not going to embarrass Major Sarson by talking about his position as a scholar' he waved his hand towards the old man who went red round the ears 'suffice it to say what we all know, that the Gallery is honoured by the presence of the world's greatest authority on the Dutch school, and a great scholar of painting generally. Though I doubt, by the way, whether the Major's exactly fond of the moderns. I sometimes wish that the Gallery possessed only paintings, I'm sure Major Sarson does. Unfortunately that isn't the case. I fully sympathized with him when he spoke to me as he did of "those wretched pots and pans,"' here John laughed patronizingly 'but I doubt if a ceramics man would. Frankly' he said, turning to Major Sarson 'I consider it disgraceful that a scholar of your calibre should be taken off your real work in this way. Now how, you may ask, do I suppose to remedy the situation? Well the answer is that I propose to treble the staff. From next month new staff will begin to arrive—some students from the Universities, some more experienced men from other galleries and museums.'

There was silence for a minute, then Mrs. Scrutton spoke. 'Does the Board know of this?'

'Yes' said John 'they fully approve the scheme'.

'Do they realize the expense involved?' asked Tony, the practical man.

'The Board are business men' said John 'they know that outlay must precede returns'. He looked round at their faces. 'Well, I think that's all' he said. 'I know you will give the new members of the staff the same co-operation you have given me, whether it is a question of instructing and training them, or in some cases of working under them'. His tone was openly sarcastic.

'Do I understand that people will be put over us?' asked Mrs. Scrutton.

'In cases where experts are brought in, it may be necessary to make revisions in seniority' said John.

'You realize, of course, that in such an eventuality we should resign' said Major Sarson.

'That would be a great loss to the Gallery, but we could not, of course, control your decisions,' replied John, and opening the door, he bowed them out.

'Golly' said Veronica 'you do tell some lies, don't you? Or have the Board ratified your staff changes?'

'How many more times must I tell you, Veronica, that truth is relative' said John.

Veronica looked down for a minute 'I'll make you some coffee' she said.

'Yes' said John 'Victory always makes me thirsty. I cannot help being satisfied when I think of the well-merited unpleasant few weeks those three are going to have. The punishment of incompetence is always satisfactory.'

'Mmm' said Veronica doubtfully.

'What's that mean? You've not fallen for this sentimental stuff about Sir Harold, have you?'

'Good Lord, no' said Veronica. 'It's not those misfits I'm worrying about, it's you.'

'Me?' said John. 'Why?'

'You're getting too fond of bullying' said Veronica 'it interferes with your charm, and charm's essential for your success'. She went out to make the coffee.

What Veronica said was very true, thought John, and he made a note to be more detached in his attitude. All the same these criticisms were bad for his self-esteem. For all her loyalty Veronica knew him too well, got too near home. Charm was important to success, but self-esteem was more so. His imagination began to envisage further staff changes, perhaps a graduate secretary would really be more suitable now.

JOYCE CARY
Umaru

It had been raining for two days, the drizzling mountain rain of the Cameroons. The detachment, on special duty behind the German lines, was under strict orders not to be noticed. That was its duty as well as its only security. Fires could not be lit except in brightest day. No tents were carried. But the subaltern in charge, young Corner, had brought a tent-fly with him; an old fly looted from some German camp. Camouflage had not yet reached these remote parts, except in practice, but this big oblong of canvas, once green, had withered to shades of dun and olive which matched perfectly the sparse northern bush.

At sundown the drizzle only became more varied in texture. The wind was rising and the sky, till that moment one weeping bank of water-grey mist, so low that at a little distance it could be seen tangled in the thorns, began to break into enormous clouds, or not yet clouds, shapeless drifts. Corner looking at his men, huddled in their cloaks while they ate their cold porridge, and feeling the rain trickle down his own back, thought that no creature in the world could be more miserable than a wet soldier. He called the old Sergeant. 'We'll sleep under the fly, Sergeant. There's room for all of us with our feet in the middle.'

Sergeant Umaru, thirty-year veteran, called often Father Umaru by the men, heard with customary wooden disdain; and answered only with a sketchy war-salute. But the men were shy. When the party went to bed, in a well-drained sandy hollow among low scrub, Corner and the Sergeant found themselves alone at one edge, while the men's heads, pretty close together, stuck out on the other three sides.

The arrangement, no doubt, would have looked comic to an observer in a balloon; it would have seemed like a vast family bed with one white and nineteen black faces sticking out all round a large patchwork quilt. But it did not strike the family as comic. The clouds, as they were lifted higher on the strong wind and rolled into thicker lumps, let fall a much thicker rain, in splashes as if from buckets carelessly tipped about. The family was glad of its cover.

The men murmured together in their high voices, very like sleepy children. Corner, with his head on a rolled macintosh, tried to sleep, but he kept on being waked by some bit of talk in a familiar voice, as a man, even asleep, catches anything said by one of his own household. A certain Salé, a thin gangling lad with a balky eye, remarked that for his part he'd rather be a horseboy. And Corner's ear noted, That was meant for me. So Salé has ambitions—he wants to be in the horselines, and I thought he was hostile. That eye probably meant only that he was wondering how to make an approach. A moment later he was brought awake again by the deeper voice of one Adamu, a tall and powerful river pagan, renowned for his savage temper, who was talking about his village. 'A good place—good land—plenty of water. You never saw such onions. And the fish—aiee! Women too. Now up here women are no good. The north is bad for women. In the sun they burn up and go hard. You want to come down our way for women. But it's what they always say. Women and fish, if good you would wish, seek where shady groves by rivers flourish. Yes, a moist folk.' All this in a soft chant like a man repeating someone else's poem. 'Yes, a good land in all ways—we have a lovely place—aiee!'

'A rotten place. I know it well.' This was from a little bandy-legged hill pagan, called officially Moma Gombe, and unofficially shoot-Monkey. 'Now Kano—that is the place—a real city.'

'No, it isn't very good, perhaps,' Adamu agreed unexpectedly in the same dreamy voice. 'Yes, it has its faults—too many floods—too far from the big markets——'

One of the others suddenly uttered a loud yawn and exclaimed, 'Ow, my bottom,' and the young Corporal at the top left-hand corner reproved him, 'Shut up. You'll wake Three-Eyes.'

Three-Eyes was Corner, who was therefore obliged to lie still and try to sleep. In a few minutes he was actually going to sleep, but at the last moment of half-consciousness, just as he was congratulating himself, I really am nearly asleep, he came so instantly and feverishly awake that it was hopeless even to think of sleeping. His legs ached, every nerve twitched, lights jumped in front of his shut eyes, and all the cells in his brain seemed to be darting about and banging together like bubbles in soda water.

The men were already asleep. There were snores and grunts. One of them muttered a few words, 'But it's so high—I don't——'

Corner gave it up; he could no longer stand the commotion

inside. The rain had stopped some time before, abruptly, after five minutes' quick fire; he turned on his back and opened his eyes, to be startled by a commotion overhead even more wild and much more grand. There were now at least three levels of cloud all moving in different directions. The old round clouds, now once more joined in masses, but masses of enormous size and sharp outline, moved slowly with a vast piled dignity almost due east; a second layer much lower, was made up of fantastic torn shapes, swimming fast like the debris of a flood. One saw something like a drowned bullock, swollen and limp, with twisted body and its legs pointing opposite ways, and a haycock just breaking up into wafts of straw. Or it was more like the ruins of some immense jigsaw map— Germany, France, Italy, England, Scotland, with their jagged coastlines and frontiers, caught up in some furious gale of time, and being stretched, squeezed, joined and divided in the process; not by sudden jerks, but by a smooth, continuous deformation, which was much more expressive of the powers at work.

And below all, moving faster still, as fast as a horse could gallop, and in a third direction, white fragments, wisps trailing their filmy skirts not much higher than the trees, seemed like ghosts of clouds, lost benighted creatures rushing through the dark transparent space below the tumult in the desperate anxious hurry of all lost creatures trying to find out where they are, and what they are, and where they ought to be.

A sudden movement beside him made Corner turn his head. Old Umaru, also on his back, with open eyes, had just scratched the calf of one leg with the toe-nails of the other. Corner spoke without meditation. It was as if the vivacity of his nerves was glad to find tongue, 'How would you like to be back in Bauchi, Sargy, in a nice warm house?'

Umaru said in his driest tone, 'I don't live in Bauchi.'

'Then why are you called Umaru Bauchi?'

'That's just a Company name.'

'Where do you come from then?'

'Nowhere. I don't belong anywhere.'

'But where were you born?'

'On war.' He used the word used by the old Emirs to mean an army in being, on the move. 'I go where the Company goes,' and he added severely, as if instructing a small boy, 'that's the best way.'

'But the Company has a home; it was stationed at Bauchi. That's where it has its wives and its friends.'

'Friends. I don't have friends. Friends are no good.'

Corner was now quite content to lie awake and to enjoy the sky and the talk. He was extremely awake, but the commotion inside had suddenly vanished, as if drawn out of him by that of the sky, that was, the lower sky. For in the upper layer, that region of cold majestic forms, the moon, which had for a long time, itself out of sight, been throwing a brilliant greenish light on the precipices of the top clouds, as on a range of Himalayas, was now very slowly projecting one edge of itself into a small triangle of blue already so full of white glitter that it was scarcely blue at all.

Suddenly in a different tone, abrupt and reluctant, but undoubtedly curious, such as Corner had never before heard from the old man, he asked, 'In your country, Caftin, among the water, do you keep friends?'

'Of course, plenty.'

The Sergeant pondered. At last he exclaimed, 'Plenty. I have friends too—like that.' His tone abolished this promiscuous relation as something casual and frivolous. But his voice ended on a high note; it seemed that he was about to make further confidences. The young man waited with an expectation which seemed to have occupied all the place of those restless cells, a feeling not only of curiosity but discovery. He had taken the Sergeant for a good stolid Hausa, a sun-dried old soldier without an idea beyond his trade, and now it seemed that he had reflections of his own. He had always liked Umaru for his honesty and his courage, but now he felt, especially at the point where his elbow touched the old man's back, a warmth of sympathy.

The moon, but half disclosed, was cut off as by a shutter. A vast black cloud below, a ragged tormented thing shaped like Greece, but with an immensely stretched-out isthmus at Corinth, had come rushing across the middle darkness. It was hustled by in a few minutes, but as its distorted Peloponnese was dragged away by the neck, a volley of big rain, cold heavy drops, widely spaced, came smacking down as out of clear space. They made a quite surprisingly loud report on the hollow canvas and stung the face. But the young man did not pull in his head. He was still preoccupied with Umaru's last remark.

'But Umaru, it isn't good for a man to be lonely.'

'Yes, it is, very good.' This was with great conviction. Umaru was lying rigid with his little grey beard aimed truculently at the moon, now once more in sight, and with her full face. She had proceeded at least another half-inch upon her way during that interruption. 'Very, very good. That's the way to live—like a Haji.' A Haji is a pilgrim.

'Ah then, God is your friend.'

'No—no, no—no,' with all the explosive violence of the Hausa negative. 'God is——' he paused, trying to find an adequate word. Then he said in a mild tone, 'He is our great One.'

'Yes, that's true.' The young man certainly felt the greatness at that moment, but not with any reverence, only elation. Simply because he began to admire the scene as beauty, it seemed to him more extraordinary. He said to Umaru, carrying on the conversation, 'it's a grand night now—look at those clouds.'

'A bad night,' Umaru said. 'Very bad. More storms coming. A bad, bad night. God help us.'

'But good to look at.'

'To look at.' Umaru said this with wondering contempt. Again there was a long silence. Then suddenly he muttered in a grumbling tone, 'Time for sleep—God bless you with it.'

'And you, Father.'

'And health.'

'And much health.'

'God prolong us,' in a growl. He turned on his side. But the young man lay on his back for another hour, and still at the place where his elbow touched Umaru's back he was aware of a certain activity of feeling at work as if by itself; an affectionate concern which did not stop. At least, it was still there when he noticed it some time later. It was laughing, too, by itself, but not at Umaru. It was quite independent, a serene enjoyment.

WILLIAM SANSOM
The Girl on the Bus

SINCE to love is better than to be loved, unrequited love may be the finest love of all. If this is so, then the less requited the finer. And it follows that the most refined passion possible for us must finally be for those to whom we have never even spoken, whom we have never met. The passing face, the anguish of a vision of a face, a face sitting alone in front of you so endearing and so moving and so beautiful that you are torn and sick inside with hope and despair, instant despair . . . for it is hopelessly plain that no word can ever be spoken, those eyes will never greet yours, in a few minutes the bell will ring, the bus will shudder to a stop, and down some impersonal side street she will be gone. Never to be seen again. Gone even is the pain of listening to where she will book for—a fourpenny, or a threehalfpence ticket?

It is due to such an encounter that I find engaging the story of my friend Harry. Only Harry's girl was not on a bus, she passed on skis.

It was one late January afternoon when Harry was walking out at Haga. The snow lay thick, and everywhere over the fine rolling park groups of Stockholmers had sought out the best slopes for an afternoon's ski-ing. The sun was already low and yellow over the firs, it sent a cold tired dusk across the snow—and one could feel the pleasantly weary, flushed trudge of the skiers making their last climb before nightfall. Harry walked about tasting this air of a winter's day ending, enjoying the rich smell of birchwood burning, watching the first yellow lights square in the cream-coloured palace, tasting his own frosted breath. Up on the highest ridge stood the line of cavalry barracks, the fantastic line of false medieval war-tents—their great carved wooden folds were draped to the snow, a last glint of the sun flashed the gold emblems on their snow-domed roofs. From such an elegant extravagance it must have been fine to see the blue-cloaked cavalry ride forth steaming and jangling onto snowy hills. But now it was a ghost-house: and as if in evocation of its ghosts, every so often through the tall erect firs black-crouched skiers would glide, swift as shadows, like trees themselves flickering downward home.

It was some time then, in this bright half-light, that Harry turned and saw on the path behind him the figure of a girl trudging up on skis. He walked down towards her, enjoying the precision of her slender erect shape slide-stepping along towards him. Skiers walk with a beautifully controlled motion, feet always close together on the long hickory, pressing so lightly forward in long strides, pausing it seems invisibly between each forward motion, listening to a music playing somewhere in their shoulders—and always in firm endeavour, as on some enviable purposed unhurried quest pondering seriously forward.

Harry was looking down at her skis as she came up, taking pleasure from the movement and the slimness of her stride. So that not until she was nearly parallel with him and about to pass did he glance up at her face.

What he saw then took his breath away, he drew in a deep astounded breath and this then disappeared, so that there was nothing inside him at all.

Poor Harry did not have even a bus-ride's worth, not a three-ha'pence worth. He had the length of two long ski-strides' worth. But that, he said, was in its expanded way enough. Not as much as he wanted—that would have amounted to a lifetime—but enough to provoke the indelible impression such passing visions may leave for a lifetime.

It would be useless to describe her. When Harry told me he talked of 'beauty' and of a colour of hair and a grace of cheekbone and an expression of lips. But what he said did not amount to a concrete image, and particularly she did not necessarily fit the blueprint of my own imagined vision, should such a one ever chance to pass. Each to his own. Suffice it that this woman's face and manner and whatever she evoked was for Harry perfection: was beyond what he thought might be perfection: was absolute.

He was so shocked he nearly stopped, he certainly hesitated and half turned his body—heavily coated and thus making what must have been a most noticeable movement to follow his wide-eyed worshipping glance. But in the same short time, perhaps on her second stride forward, she suddenly turned her face to him. Terrified, he looked away. He never knew whether she saw him staring, or saw him at all, or looked past or through him—he only felt a surge of embarrassment out of all proportion to the occasion. He felt small, despairing, hopeless, and above all horrified that she might have caught his eye and thought it the eye of an intruder.

She passed. It was a long time before Harry could bring himself to turn round. But by then she was a black speck among others in the lengthening snow, she was irretrievable.

For the next minutes Harry walked on and out of the park, elated in spite of his distress. He was elated in the way a man is when he has suddenly come face to face with a giddying good work of art. The feeling was universal—it made to say: 'Good, good—so there are still such things in the world!' It was a feeling of hope.

But of no practical hope. He knew that he would never see the girl again. However, she had sent his spirits up . . . but soon it was apparent, too far. For once outside the park, her park, the world proclaimed itself again. And it looked exceedingly bare and dull. The tram-ride home, among skiers now wet and drab in the electric light, was lowering. His hotel, white-walled as a sanatorium, primed with red corridor lights and reticent switches, appalled him with its sterile gloom. He took a glass of aquavit and telephoned a friend for dinner.

They went to a large old-fashioned restaurant. There were many hundreds of people, an orchestra of twenty players blared music to the farthest microphoned corner, waiters bobbed and slid like black dolphins in the white sea of tablecloth, and all around and up to the roof, high as an exhibition hall, the gilded ornament twisted and plushly glittered. There were palms, flowers, flags and chandeliers.

But here also Strindberg had kept his private dining-room: and it was with something of the same pessimist eye that Harry now allowed his spirits to sink below the level of the nightfaring populace about. A tarnish shadowed the gilt, a dull propriety seemed to stuff the people. The band played ballad music of the 'nineties—and he felt no nostalgia, but a vehement disgust at the stuffed rose-love-garden pomp the song pictured for him. The diners, sitting too erect and quiet and uncomfortably unlaughing, began to look like the awkward guests at a staff-dinner. Two Salvation Army lasses, in fur bonnets, threaded their way through the tables. When the band began suddenly to play a gay Spanish march it was no better, it sounded too slow. And there were too many fiddles.

Now if you knew Harry as I know Harry, you would know that Harry then began to worry. He began to theorize. 'The sight of that girl,' he told himself, 'has coloured my whole life. By a hundredth chance I was in Stockholm, by a hundredth chance I went to Haga, by another hundredth I happened to be passing that path at that moment—and I had to see *her*. Now forever I am left with a standard of beauty which my world will always slightly fail. My relationships with women will never seem quite so keen, all other pursuits will seem henceforth without quite so much purpose. Of course, I shall enjoy myself in degree. But perfection has been trifled with. This kind of thing goes deeper than one thinks. . . . Oh why in hell did I go to Haga? And it is not as if I was as young as I was.'

He was still considering her on the train next morning at Malmö: 'The woman was always destined to be unattainable—and it is significant that I am leaving the city today. I suppose this will result in a fixation on Stockholm for the rest of my life. God knows how many superior contracts in other towns I shall discard for the subconscious opportunity of getting back to this blasted place.'

The train drew into Norrköping and lunch was served. It was difficult, sitting wedged with three other men, to know how much of each small dish to take for himself, so he took too little of each. But rather much of the one he liked most. In guilty despondence, he looked out at the short orange trams circling the Norrköping neatnesses. How plain life could be! And these men eating in front and to the side of him were so large and well-conditioned! He felt himself smaller against their giant, businessy, grey-suited size. None of them spoke. They exchanged the dishes with little bows, and then relapsed into their erect selves. But as the train drew slowly out of Norrköping a group of children waved from behind railings. As one man, the three leaned slightly forward and made small flutterings with their white heavy hands. And without a word re-addressed themselves to their food.

Hell, thought Harry looking down at his own hand and seeing that it had not even the initiative to join in such a dull nice action. Hell, he thought, I shall have to wake myself up. And it was then that he decided on a new course of life, a disciplined course of self-indulgence. He would drink more, seek out more people, spend more money and work less.

The lowlands of Sweden rolled by. The sky hung grey and wet, the mossy turf with its scattering of huge time-smoothed boulders looked very ancient. Sometimes these boulders had been rolled to the edge of a field, but often they were too heavy to be moved, and lay still in the centre proclaiming their great, icy age. It was very difficult for Harry, wedged in now with his coffee, to see how to start on his new programme. It would have been ostentatious, he felt, to order a few brandies. But when one of the men asked for an after-dinner sherry, he did the same. One of these was enough. He felt slightly sick. The business-men, in their hard girth and with their large pale faces, began to look very like boulders.

But at Malmö a difference charged the air. At first this might have passed for the ambrosia of arrival—a search for luggage, the disturbing sea-air, the genial sheds and asphalt of docks. The delight of safe danger. But no—once aboard the ferry what had come upon people was evident. A glance into the smoke-room told much of the tale. Already, five minutes after the train had arrived, they were singing in the smoke-room. Tables were already massing empty bottles. The three silent, kind, well-conditioned, Swedish business men were laughing together and sitting spread and easy. But it was not only a matter of alcohol—although the free dispensation of this, after a severely restricted country, proved in every way intoxicating. It was a broader sense of freedom. A shedding of propriety, of reserve—a change of manners, not from good to bad, but from good to good of another kind. Geniality and tolerance warmed the air.

Waiters hurried up with plates of enormous Danish sandwiches. In the very sandwiches there could be felt the difference between the two countries parted by a mile of water. Gone were the elegant and excellent Swedish confections, here were thick slabs of appetitious meat and fish piled hugely helter-skelter on a token of bread: Smörgåsbord had become Smørrebrød. And when they landed and he walked about the Danish train, Harry noticed immediately how the people had lost height and gained thickness: and how the porters wore dirtier, easier clothes. And standing in the street there was a beggar.

But although at first Harry responded to this interesting new brightness, he soon found he was the only one on the train who had no reason to be elated. He sank into greater gloom. He tried to revive his spirits with a fine meal and a night out in Copenhagen. But even when friendly Copenhageners, seeing him sitting alone, asked him to sit with them, plied him with food and drink, joked and prompted him in every way to enjoy himself—his mood remained. He felt nervous, frustrated, dull.

The next day, a little freshened by the morning, he boarded a midday boat train for Esbjærg and England. After all, he felt, things might be better. He was a fool to have taken a passing emotion so seriously. In fact, it was only an emotion and as such ephemeral and replaceable.

So that when they came to the Great Belt, and the train trundled aboard the ferry that was to take it across that wide flat water— Harry took to regarding his fellow-passengers with more interest. There is always an excitement when a compartmented train turns out its passengers to walk about and make a deckful. One has grown used and even loyal to one's own compartment: one knows the number of the carriage, it seems to be the best number of all! one even feels a sympathetic acquaintanceship with people seen through the glass of adjoining compartments and with those in the corridor. But there, on the boat, one must face a rival world—the world of other carriages. One resents their apparent assumption of equality—yet, inimical or not, it is a source of wonder that here are so many fellow-travellers of whose existence one was ignorant. One notes them with interest. One must watch and sniff.

Almost the first person Harry noted was the girl from Haga.

It could not be, it could, it was. Harry's heart jumped and his stomach sank. He turned furtively away.

He walked twenty yards down the deck, took out a cigarette and pretended that it was necessary to turn to light this against the wind. Then he backed against the cabin wall and, thus hidden, watched her. His emotion beat so strong that he imagined every passenger on the boat must recognize it, there would be a conspiracy aboard to smile about him. And consequently, though in the past days he had reproved himself for not having taken more courageous action at their first encounter—he had imagined all kinds of calm, forceful gallantry—his instinct now was for instant flight. However, common sense and a suspicion of the ridiculous strengthened him. And he was able to compromise by watching her from a distance.

She stood for a few minutes on deck, not watching the wide grey water but engrossed in her bag and some process of putting her coat and scarf and hat in order. These affairs she conducted with a tranquil efficiency. She was detached and sure, removed from all the others. She never raised her eyes to look at other people.

Then she turned and walked along to the luncheon saloon. Carefully Harry followed, pausing and looking away as if in search of somebody or something else, and chose a table about three away from hers. There he munched his enormous pork cutlet and kept her surveyed. Every time he dared to look at her it seemed a stolen, intrusive moment. But he congratulated himself on his discretion. He told himself there was time, she must be going aboard for the Harwich boat. There, with a day and a night to stroll about the large saloons, opportunity would present itself. He stole another glance. With horror he found her looking straight at him, frowning a little. She knew!

He left, and went down the steel staircase to where the train, strangely tall and of such dark heavy metal, stood waiting. He sat smoking and unnerved, alone in the carriage. But in a few minutes the ferry docked, and soon the train was rumbling out onto Jutland and the last stretch to Esbjærg.

The ship, white and clean and smiling with stewardesses, welcomed them from the smoke and cramp of the train. But the weather was beginning to blow, a freshness of pounding black waves echoed in from the North Sea and storm clouds raced ragged across a dark sky. Harry hurried aboard, established his cabin, and went up to watch the other passengers come up the gangway. He waited for half an hour, watched the last arrivals drift in from the lighted sheds across the gritty dark quay. But he had missed her. In some panic, and in her absence growing more self-assured each moment, he searched the ship. Up and down the steep stairways, in and out of strange saloons, into the second class and once, daring all, by intentional mistake into the ladies' rest room. But she was nowhere. And the ship sailed.

Harry saw how he had missed his second chance. He looked back at that hour on the ferry and cursed his ineptitude. He despised himself, as he saw himself independent and adult and assured yet baulking at the evident chance. He swore that if ever again . . . but when she appeared in the lounge after dinner he plunged his hand out for a coloured engineering gazette. All his fears returned. One does not necessarily learn from experience.

The smoking-room was large and furnished with fresh, modern, leather arm-chairs. The tables were ridged: and on that evening the ridges were necessary, and then not always high enough—for it was a very stormy night, and the ship was rolling badly. Glasses and cups slid slowly about like motivated chessmen, and more than once the ship gave a great shuddering lurch that threw everything smashing to the floor. Harry, behind his gazette, prayed that his coffee would not be shot off clownishly across the saloon. He did not think then what a good excuse that might make to smile at her. He only prayed not to look a fool.

For her part, she sat serenely writing a letter. For some reason her glass of brandy never slid an inch. It seemed to borrow composure from her. Harry concentrated on an advertisement for dozers. And, curiously, this calmed him. It seemed so absurd, it showed up the moment: life is so very various, nothing has quite such a unique importance as we give it.

The storm grew in force. High waves smashed themselves with animal force against the windows, and the ship rolled more thunderously than ever. Stewards staggered, the arm-chairs tugged at their floor-chains. Perhaps the smoke-room was half-full when coffee began: but now it was emptying, people who had resisted so far began to feel sick, and for others it had become difficult to read or to talk or, among those tilting tables, to think. As they went swaying and skidding through the doors some laughed like people at a funfair: others dared not open their mouths. And so there came a moment, in spite of the drumming sea-noises outside, when Harry noticed a distinct quiet in the room. He looked round and saw that the room was nearly empty. There had descended the well-kept void dullness, the perceptible silence of a waiting-room. Two business men sat apart reading. Their smallest movement in that polished quiet attracted attention. The girl wrote calmly on. The panic rose again in Harry's chest. It would be so easy to go over and pick a magazine from the case at her side. There were even magazines lying on her own table! With no possibility of offence he could ask her permission to read one.

He knew it was then or never. He began instantly to invent excuses. For the first time he tried to reason. There, Harry said to himself, is this girl whose appearance has knocked me silly. But I know that a hundred to one her personality will never match this illusory loveliness. How do I know she won't be an utter fool? a bitch? A moron? . . . And then I'll have spoiled this—he could almost sigh with romantic detachment—beautiful experience. I have sipped—and that is forever more satisfying than the gross full draught. Then he looked at her again, and the detachment left him.

All right, he groaned, then at least there is the curse of classification. That has not yet disappeared. Suppose she answered me too genteelly? Or too broadly? Or in this accent or that—he heard in his ears those for which he held a deep, illogical antipathy. Then he remembered she was Swedish. It would not happen.

He looked back at the dozers. He saw they were described in refined lettering as 'earth-moving equipment'. He flung the magazine aside and in pale apprehension rose to his feet. The ship gave a lurch. He steadied himself. And then with great difficulty moved towards her.

Half-way across, exactly opposite the door, he who never did began to feel sea-sick. It was as if the paleness he had felt come over his face was spreading through him, and now with every roll of the ship a physical quease turned his stomach. It may have begun as a sickness of apprehension, but it took on all the symptoms of a sickness of sea. He felt weak, wretched and unsure of what next. He turned out through the door and balanced down the stairway to his cabin. In the lower bunk his cabin-companion lay pale and retching. The room smelled richly of sick. Harry added to it.

But only a little later, weak and having forgotten all about the girl, he fell into a deep, unmolested sleep. Twice in the night he woke—once when his heavy suitcase slid thudding from one end of the cabin to the other, once when he himself was nearly rolled out of the bunk. But he was no longer sick.

He woke late, feeling well and hungry. The ship was still pitching as heavily as before. He shaved with difficulty, watching his face swing in and out of the mirror, chasing with his razor the water that rolled in the opposite direction to that chosen by the ship. Then upstairs to breakfast. The whole ship was deserted. Harry looked at his watch, wondering whether he had misread the time and if it was perhaps still early—but his watch and the purser's clock made it already eleven o'clock. The notion smiled through him that the company had taken to the boats in the night, he was in a well-equipped ghost-ship with steam up. And indeed, walking through the deserted saloons, it felt like that. But in the dining-room three waiters were sitting.

During a breakfast that he could only eat by holding his cup in one hand and both cutting and forking his ham with the other, a waiter told him they were having one of the worst crossings he had ever known. Waves, even in such a great modern ship, had smashed plate-glass in the night. A settee had broken its chains, raced across the smoking-lounge and had run over a steward, breaking his leg.

Of course, it was quite safe, but the ship would be about six hours late. They had made no headway at all during the night, they had simply sat rolling in the middle of the North Sea.

Harry wandered out along the passages and into the smoke-room. It was vexing to be so late. He was in no exact hurry, but an empty ship in stormy weather is a most tedious ordeal, and the long tossing day stretched out grey and eventless. One cannot easily write, it is difficult even to read, getting drunk is simpler but as aimless as the crashing glasses. To be sick is dreadful, but to spend a day lurching among lurching things, with never a level moment, is if not unendurable of the deepest, most troublesome tedium.

For a while Harry watched the waves. Some seemed higher than the ship itself, it seemed impossible not to be capsized. A sudden wet wall of grey running water would erect itself high as a housefront over the valley of the smoke-room window: then at the last moment up would go the ship on another unseen wave. All blew cold grey, but there was no mist—a gale wind whipped spray from the waves and tore the dishcloth smoke to pieces. Low clouds scudded too fast to notice the ship, the horizon was no more than a jagged encampment of near waves. Not a bird, not a ship in sight.

Harry's thoughts naturally centred on what was still at the back of his mind. Breakfast over, he brought her foremost. And found to his surprise that he was no longer apprehensive of her. He welcomed the probability of her appearance, he welcomed the emptiness of the ship. She was obviously not the sea-sick type, she was likely to appear. And with an empty ship there would be more opportunity to speak—and at the same time nobody to smile behind his back if she snubbed him. It seemed that his sickness of the night before had proved in all ways cathartic.

He welcomed the luncheon gong, and in his expectant joy remembered with a smile the Swedish word for this: gonggong. But she did not appear at luncheon. And gradually his spirits falling and his stomach swelling, Harry ploughed in these difficult seas through the enormous and exquisite Danish meal.

The afternoon was terrible. Nothing, nothing happened. A few odd men came lurching through. Two young Danish fellows sat for a long time laughing over their drinks. Harry went down to pack, but was forced by the state of his companion to complete this as quickly as possible.

An hour before the ship was due in people began to come up

exhausted or rested from the sanctuary of their cabins. The ship was steaming close against the English littoral, and the seas were much calmer. Disconsolate, Harry rose from his arm-chair, threw aside the paper on which he had been reduced to writing lists of all the vegetables he knew beginning with the letter 'p', and walked round to the little bar for a drink. There she was, bright as a bad penny, perched up on a stool between those two laughing young men.

His heart sank, but he went grimly to the other end of the bar and, with his back turned, ordered a dobbeltsnaps. He could not hear what was said, for between high laughter they spoke in the low intimate voices of people telling anecdotes: but he could watch them in a slice of mirror. And . . . So there! What had he told himself? Hadn't he been right? She was just an ordinary flirt! She hadn't talked to these men until five minutes before, and now she was going it hell-for-leather! Easy as pie, pie-in-the-sky! And that's why (subconsciously of course) he hadn't gone up to her. . . . But through this Harry knew deeply and quite consciously that he envied the young men and deprecated his own drivelling loutish cowardice. He turned and took one last look at her. She was wonderful . . . yes, she was wonderful.

He went downstairs and made ready to leave. In a while the ship docked. He took his bags and shuffled down among the line of passengers to the rail-lined dock. It was a curious relief to feel the land under one's feet, it brought what felt like a light unheard buzzing to the ears. Then the familiar smells and a further shuffle through the customs.

Suddenly, going through the doorway to the platform, he saw her again. She was clutching the arm of a large ugly elderly man. She was stroking this man. Together the two, the elegant fresh young girl and that obscene old figure, passed through the door. Harry believed his eyes and he was disgusted.

He had to pass them. They stood in the wan light of the old-fashioned station, she fingering about in her bag and at every moment flashing her eyes up at him, he bloated, gloat-eyed, mumbling heaven-knew-what salivary intimacies. It crossed Harry's mind how strange was the phenomenon of these shipboard passengers one never sees until the last moment, these cabined mysteries—and it struck him again horribly how this applied to those two, the old slug lying down there in the comfortable depths of the ship with his fair, fresh girl. . . .

The girl looked up and met Harry's eyes. She immediately smiled, it seemed in relief, and came up to him. She spoke excitedly, apologetically in Swedish:

—Oh, please do excuse me . . . but it's funny I remember distinctly I once saw you in Haga, you speak Swedish? You see, my father and I—we've lost our seat reservations. Could you tell me what is best to do? . . . We're new here. . . .

Harry's heart leapt. The lights in the station seemed to turn up, it was suddenly almost sunny. With delight he showed them to the end of the train where he knew there were empty carriages. Together they travelled to London and never stopped talking. He insisted on driving them to their hotel.

Harry and his lady have now been married some seven years. He has never, so far as can be known, regretted the requital.

L. P. HARTLEY
The Killing Bottle

UNLIKE the majority of men, Jimmy Rintoul enjoyed the hour or so's interval between being called and having breakfast; for it was the only part of the day upon which he imposed an order. From nine-fifteen onwards the day imposed its order upon him. The 'bus, the office, the hasty city luncheon; then the office, the 'bus, and the unsatisfactory interval before dinner: such a promising time and yet, do what he would with it, it always seemed to be wasted. If he was going to dine alone at his club, he felt disappointed and neglected; if, as seldom happened, in company, he felt vaguely apprehensive. He expected a good deal from his life, and he never went to bed without the sense of having missed it. Truth to tell, he needed a stimulus, the stimulus of outside interest and appreciation, to get the best out of himself. In a competitive society, with rewards dangled before his eyes, his nature fulfilled itself and throve. How well he had done at school, and even afterwards, while his parents lived to applaud his efforts. Now he was thirty-three; his parents were dead; there was no one close enough to him to care whether he made a success of his life or not. Nor did life hand out to grown-up men incontestable signs of merit and excellence, volumes bound in vellum or silver cups standing proudly on ebony pedestals. No, its awards were far less tangible, and Jimmy, from the shelter of his solicitors' office, sometimes felt glad that its more sensational prizes were passing out of his reach—that he need no longer feel obliged, as he had once felt, to climb the Matterhorn, play the 'Moonlight Sonata,' master the Spanish language, and read the *Critique of Pure Reason* before he died. His ambition was sensibly on the ebb.

But not in the mornings. The early mornings were still untouched by the torpors of middle age. Dressing was for Jimmy a ritual, and like all rituals it looked forward to a culmination. Act followed act in a recognised sequence, each stage contributing its peculiar thrill, opening his mind to a train of stimulating and agreeable thoughts, releasing it, encouraging it. And the culmination: what was it? Only his morning's letters and the newspaper! Not very exciting. But the newspaper might contain one of those helpful, sympathetic articles about marriage, articles that warned the reader not to rush into matrimony, but to await the wisdom that came with the early and still more with the late thirties; articles which, with a few tricks of emphasis, of skipping here and reading between the lines there, demonstrated that Jimmy Rintoul's career, without any effort of his own, was shaping itself on sound, safe lines. The newspaper, then, for reassurance; the letters for surprise! And this morning an interesting letter would be particularly welcome. It would distract his mind from a vexing topic that even the routine of dressing had not quite banished—the question of his holiday, due in a fortnight's time.

Must it be Swannick Fen again? Partly for lack of finding others to take their place, he had cherished the interests of his boyhood, of which butterfly-collecting was the chief. He was solitary and competitive, and the hobby ministered to both these traits. But alas! he had not the patience of the true collector; his interest fell short of the lesser breeds, the irritating varieties of Wainscots and Footmen and whatnots. It embraced only the more sensational insects—the large, the beautiful, and the rare. His desire had fastened itself on the Swallowtail butterfly as representing all these qualities. So he went to Swannick, found the butterfly, bred it, and presently had a whole hutch-full of splendid green caterpillars. Their mere number, the question of what to do with them when they came out, whether to keep them all in their satiating similarity, to give them away, or to sell them; to let them go free so that the species might multiply, to the benefit of all collectors; to kill all but a few, thus enhancing the value of his own—these problems vexed his youthful, ambitious, conscientious mind. Finally he killed them all. But the sight of four setting-boards plastered with forty identical insects destroyed by a surfeit his passion for the Swallow-tail butterfly. He had coaxed it with other baits: the Pine Hawk moth, the Clifden Nonpareil; but it would not respond, would accept no substitute, being, like many passions, monogamous and constant. Every year, in piety, in conservatism, in hope, he still went to Swannick Fen; but with each visit the emotional satisfaction diminished. Soon it would be gone.

However, there on his dressing-table (for some reason) stood the killing bottle—mutely demanding prey. Almost without thinking he released the stopper and snuffed up the almond-breathing fumes. A safe, pleasant smell; he could never understand how anything died of it, or why cyanide of potassium should figure in the chemists' book of poisons. But it did; he had had to put his name against it. Now, since the stuff was reputed to be so deadly, he must add a frail attic to the edifice of dressing and once more wash his hands. In a fortnight's time, he thought, I shall be doing this a dozen times a day.

On the breakfast-table lay a large, shiny blue envelope. He did not recognise the handwriting, nor, when he examined the post-mark, did it convey anything to him. The flap, gummed to the top and very strong, resisted his fingers. He opened it with a knife and read:

'VERDEW CASTLE.

MY DEAR RINTOUL

How did you feel after our little dinner on Saturday? None the worse, I hope. However, I'm not writing to inquire about your health, which seems pretty good, but about your happiness, or what I should like to think would be your happiness. Didn't I hear you mutter (the second time we met, I think it was, at Smallhouse's) something about going for a holiday in the near future? Well, then, couldn't you spend it here with us, at Verdew? Us being my brother Randolph, my wife, and your humble servant. I'm afraid there won't be a party for you; but we could get through the day somehow, and play bridge in the evenings. Randolph and you would make perfect partners, you would be so kind to each other. And didn't you say you collected bugs? Then by all means bring your butterfly-net and your killing bottle and your other engines of destruction and park them here; there are myriads of green-flies, bluebottle-flies, may-flies, dragon-flies, and kindred pests which would be all the better for your attentions. Now don't say no. It would be a pleasure to us, and I'm sure it would amuse you to see ye olde castle and us living in our medieval seclusion. I await the favour of a favourable reply, and will then tell you the best way of reaching the Schloss, as we sometimes call it in our German fashion.

Yours,

ROLLO VERDEW.'

Jimmy stared at this facetious epistle until its purport faded from his mind, leaving only a blurred impression of redundant loops and twirls. Verdew's handwriting was like himself, bold and dashing and unruly. At least, this was the estimate Jimmy had formed of him, on the strength of three meetings. He had been rather taken by the man's bluff, hearty manner, but he did not expect Verdew to like him: they were birds of a different feather. He hadn't felt very well after the dinner, having drunk more than was good for him in the effort to fall in with his host's mood; but apparently he had succeeded better than he thought. Perhaps swashbucklers like Verdew welcomed mildness in others. If not, why the invitation? He considered it. The district might be entomologically rich. Where exactly was Verdew Castle? He had, of course, a general idea of its locality, correct to three counties; he knew it was somewhere near the coast. Further than that, nothing; and directly he began to sift his knowledge he found it to be even less helpful than he imagined. The notepaper gave a choice of stations: wayside stations they must be, they were both unknown to him. The postal, telegraphic, and telephonic addresses all confidently cited different towns—Kirton Tracy, Shrivecross, and Pawlingham—names which seemed to stir memories but never fully awakened recollection. Still, what did it matter? Verdew had promised to tell him the best route, and it was only a question of getting there, after all. He could find his own way back.

Soon his thoughts, exploring the future, encountered an obstacle and stopped short. He was looking ahead as though he had made up his mind to go. Well, hadn't he? The invitation solved his immediate difficulty: the uncertainty as to where he should take his holiday. The charm of Swannick had failed to hold him. And yet, perversely enough, his old hunting-ground chose this very moment to trouble him with its lures: its willows, its alders, the silent clumps of grey rushes with the black water in between. The conservatism of his nature, an almost superstitious loyalty to the preferences of his early life, protested against the abandonment of Swannick— Swannick, where he had always done exactly as he liked, where bridge never intruded, and the politenesses of society were unknown. For Jimmy's mind had run forward again, and envisaged existence at Verdew Castle as divided between holding open the door for Mrs. Rollo Verdew and exchanging compliments and forbearances and commiseration with Rollo's elder (or perhaps younger, he hadn't said) brother Randolph across the bridge-table, with a lot of spare time that wasn't really spare and a lot of being left to himself that really meant being left to everybody.

Jimmy looked at the clock: it was time to go. If it amused his imagination to fashion a mythical Verdew Castle, he neither authorised nor forbade it. He still thought himself free to choose. But when he reached his office his first act was to write his friend a letter of acceptance.

Four days later a second blue envelope appeared on his breakfast-table. It was evidently a two-days' post to Verdew Castle, for Rollo explained that he had that moment received Jimmy's welcome communication. There followed a few references, necessarily brief, to matters of interest to them both. The letter closed with the promised itinerary:

'So we shall hope to see you in ten days' time, complete with lethal chamber and big-game apparatus. I forget whether you have a car; but if you have, I strongly advise you to leave it at home. The road bridge across the estuary has been dicky for a long time. They may close it any day now, since it was felt to wobble the last time the Lord-Lieutenant crossed by it. You would be in a mess if you found it shut and had to go trailing thirty miles to Amplesford (a hellish road, since it's no one's interest to keep it up). If the bridge carried the Lord-Lieutenant it would probably bear you, but I shouldn't like to have your blood on my head! Come, then, by train to Verdew Grove. I recommend the four o'clock; it doesn't get here till after dark, but you can dine on it, and it's almost express part of the way. The morning train is too bloody for anything: you would die of boredom before you arrived, and I should hate that to happen to any of my guests. I'm sorry to present you with such ghastly alternatives, but the Castle was built here to be out of everyone's reach, and by Heaven, it is! Come prepared for a long stay. You must. I'm sure the old office can get on very well without you. You're lucky to be able to go away as a matter of course, like a gentleman. Let us have a line and we'll send to meet you, not my little tin kettle but Randolph's majestic Daimler. Good-bye.

Yours,
ROLLO.'

It was indeed a troublesome, tedious journey, involving changes of train and even of station. More than once the train, having entered a terminus head first, steamed out tail first, with the result that Rintoul lost his sense of direction and had a slight sensation of vertigo whenever, in thought, he tried to recapture it. It was half-past nine and the sun was setting when they crossed the estuary. As always in such places the tide was low, and the sun's level beams illuminated the too rotund and luscious curves of a series of mud-flats. The railway-line approached the estuary from its marshy side, by a steep embankment. Near by, and considerably below, ran the road bridge—an antiquated affair of many arches, but apparently still in use, though there seemed to be no traffic on it. The line curved inwards, and by straining his neck Rintoul could see the train bent like a bow, and the engine approaching a hole, from which a few wisps of smoke still issued, in the ledge of rock that crowned the farther shore. The hole rushed upon him; Rintoul pulled in his head and was at once in darkness. The world never seemed to get light again. After the long tunnel they were among hills that shut out the light that would have come in, and stifled the little that was left behind. It was by the help of the station lantern that he read the name, Verdew Grove, and when they were putting his luggage on the motor he could scarcely distinguish between the porter and the chauffeur. One of them said:

'Did you say it was a rabbit?'

And the other: 'Well, there was a bit of fur stuck to the wheel.'

'You'd better not let the boss see it,' said the first speaker.

'Not likely.' And so saying, the chauffeur, who seemed to be referring to an accident, climbed into the car. As Rollo had said, it was a very comfortable one. Jimmy gave up counting the turns and trying to catch glimpses of the sky over the high hedges, and abandoned himself to drowsiness. He must have dozed, for he did not know whether it was five minutes or fifty before the opening door let in a gust of cool air and warned him that he had arrived.

For a moment he had the hall to himself. It did not seem very large, but to gauge its true extent was difficult, because of the arches and the shadows. Shaded lamps on the tables gave a diffused but very subdued glow; while a few unshaded lights, stuck about in the groining of the vault, consuming their energy in small patches of great brilliancy, dazzled rather than assisted the eye. The fact that the spaces beween the vaulting-ribs were white-washed seemed to increase the glare. It was curious and not altogether happy, the contrast between the brilliance above and the murk below. No trophies of the chase adorned the walls; no stags' heads or antlers, no rifles, javelins, tomahawks, assegais, or krisses. Clearly the

Verdews were not a family of sportsmen. In what did Randolph Verdew's interests lie? Rintoul wondered, and he was walking across to the open grate, in whose large recess a log-fire flickered, when the sound of a footfall startled him. It came close, then died away completely, then still in the same rhythm began again. It was Rollo.

Rollo with his black moustaches, his swaggering gait, his large expansive air, his noisy benevolence. He grasped Jimmy's hand.

But before he could say more than 'Damned glad,' a footman appeared. He came so close to Jimmy and Rollo that the flow of the latter's eloquence was checked.

'Mr. Rintoul is in the Pink Room,' announced the footman.

Rollo put his little finger in his mouth and gently bit it.

'Oh, but I thought I said——'

'Yes, sir,' interrupted the footman. 'But Mr. Verdew thought he might disturb Mr. Rintoul in the Onyx Room, because sometimes when he lies awake at night he has to move about, as you know, sir. And he thought the Pink Room had a better view. So he gave orders for him to be put there, sir.'

The footman finished on a tranquil note and turned to go. But Rollo flushed faintly and seemed put out.

'I thought it would have been company for you having my brother next door,' he said. 'But he's arranged otherwise, so it can't be helped. Shall I take you to the room now, or will you have a drink first? That is, if I can find it,' he muttered. 'They have a monstrous habit of sometimes taking the drinks away when Randolph has gone to bed. And by the way, he asked me to make his excuses to you. He was feeling rather tired. My wife's gone, too. She always turns in early here; she says there's nothing to do at Verdew. But, my God, there's a lot that wants doing, as I often tell her. This way.'

Though they found the whisky and soda in the drawing-room, Rollo still seemed a little crestfallen and depressed; but Jimmy's spirits, which sometimes suffered from the excessive buoyancy of his neighbour's, began to rise. The chair was comfortable; the room, though glimpses of stone showed alongside the tapestries, was more habitable and less ecclesiastical than the hall. In front of him was an uncurtained window through which he could see, swaying their heads as though bent on some ghostly conference, a cluster of white roses. I'm going to enjoy myself here, he thought.

Whatever the charms of the Onyx Room, whatever virtue resided in the proximity of Mr. Randolph Verdew, one thing was certain: the Pink Room had a splendid view. Leaning out of his window the next morning Jimmy feasted his eyes on it. Directly below him was the moat, clear and apparently deep. Below that again was the steep conical hill on which the castle stood, its side intersected by corkscrew paths and level terraces. Below and beyond, undulating ground led the eye onwards and upwards to where, almost on the horizon, glittered and shone the silver of the estuary. Of the castle were visible only the round wall of Jimmy's tower, and a wing of the Tudor period, the gables of which rose to the level of his bedroom window. It was half-past eight and he dressed quickly, meaning to make a little tour of the castle precincts before his hosts appeared.

His intention, however, was only partially fulfilled, for on arriving in the hall he found the great door still shut, and fastened with a variety of locks and bolts, of antique design and as hard to open, it seemed, from within as from without. He had better fortune with a smaller door and found himself on a level oblong stretch of grass, an island of green, bounded by the moat on the east and on the other side by the castle walls. There was a fountain in the middle. The sun shone down through the open end of the quadrangle, making the whole place a cave of light, flushing the warm stone of the Elizabethan wing to orange, and gilding the cold, pale, mediaeval stonework of the rest. Jimmy walked to the moat and tried to find, to right or left, a path leading to other parts of the building. But there was none. He turned round and saw Rollo standing in the doorway.

'Good-morning,' called his host. 'Already thinking out a plan of escape?'

Jimmy coloured slightly. The thought had been present in his mind, though not in the sense that Rollo seemed to mean it.

'You wouldn't find it very easy from here,' remarked Rollo, whose cheerful humour the night seemed to have restored. 'Because even if you swam the moat you couldn't get up the bank: it's too steep and too high.'

Jimmy examined the farther strand and realised that this was true.

'It would be prettier,' Rollo continued, 'and less canal-like, if the water came up to the top; but Randolph prefers it as it used to be. He likes to imagine we're living in a state of siege.'

'He doesn't seem to keep any weapons for our defence,' commented Jimmy. 'No arquebuses or bows and arrows; no vats of molten lead.'

'Oh, he wouldn't hurt anyone for the world,' said Rollo. 'That's one of his little fads. But it amuses him to look across to the river like one of the first Verdews and feel that no one can get in without his leave.'

'Or out either, I suppose,' suggested Jimmy.

'Well,' remarked Rollo, 'some day I'll show you a way of getting out. But now come along and look at the view from the other side; we have to go through the house to see it.'

They walked across the hall, where the servants were laying the breakfast-table, to a door at the end of a long narrow passage. But it was locked. 'Hodgson!' shouted Rollo.

A footman came up.

'Will you open this door, please?' said Rollo. Jimmy expected him to be angry, but there was only a muffled irritation in his voice. At his leisure the footman produced the key and let them through.

'That's what comes of living in someone else's house,' fumed Rollo, once they were out of earshot. 'These lazy devils want waking up. Randolph's a damned sight too easy-going.'

'Shall I see him at breakfast?' Jimmy inquired.

'I doubt it.' Rollo picked up a stone, looked round, for some reason, at the castle, and threw the pebble at a thrush, narrowly missing it. 'He doesn't usually appear till lunch-time. He's interested in all sorts of philanthropical societies. He's always helping them to prevent something. He hasn't prevented you, though, you naughty fellow,' he went on, stooping down and picking up from a stone several fragments of snails' shells. 'This seems to be the thrushes' Tower Hill.'

'He's fond of animals, then?' asked Jimmy.

'Fond, my boy?' repeated Rollo. 'Fond is not the word. But we aren't vegetarians. Some day I'll explain all that. Come and have some bacon and eggs.'

That evening, in his bath, a large wooden structure like a giant's coffin, Jimmy reviewed the day, a delightful day. In the morning he had been taken round the castle; it was not so large as it seemed from outside—it had to be smaller, the walls were so thick. And there were, of course, a great many rooms he wasn't shown, attics, cellars, and dungeons. One dungeon he had seen: but he felt sure that in a fortress of such pretentions there must be more than one. He couldn't quite get the 'lie' of the place at present; he had his own way of finding his room, but he knew it wasn't the shortest way. The hall, which was like a Clapham Junction to the castle's topographical system, still confused him. He knew the way out, because there was only one way, across a modernised drawbridge, and that made it simpler. He had crossed it to get at the woods below the castle, where he had spent the afternoon, hunting for caterpillars. 'They' had really left him alone—even severely alone! Neither of Rollo's wife nor of his brother was there yet any sign. But I shall see them at dinner, he thought, wrapping himself in an immense bath-towel.

The moment he saw Randolph Verdew, standing pensive in the drawing-room, he knew he would like him. He was an etherealized version of Rollo, taller and slighter. His hair was sprinkled with grey and he stooped a little. His cloudy blue eyes met Jimmy's with extraordinary frankness as he held out his hand and apologized for his previous non-appearance.

'It is delightful to have you here,' he added. 'You are a naturalist, I believe?'

His manner was formal but charming, infinitely reassuring.

'I am an entomologist,' said Jimmy, smiling.

'Ah, I love to watch the butterflies fluttering about the flowers— and the moths, too, those big heavy fellows that come in of an evening and knock themselves about against the lights. I have often had to put as many as ten out of the windows, and back they come—the deluded creatures. What a pity that their larvae are harmful and in some cases have to be destroyed! But I expect you prefer to observe the rarer insects?'

'If I can find them,' said Jimmy.

'I'm sure I hope you will,' said Randolph, with much feeling. 'You must get Rollo to help you.'

'Oh,' said Jimmy, 'Rollo——'

'I hope you don't think Rollo indifferent to nature?' asked his brother, with distress in his voice and an engaging simplicity of manner. 'He has had rather a difficult life, as I expect you know. His affairs have kept him a great deal in towns, and he has had little leisure—very little leisure.'

'He must find it restful here,' remarked Jimmy, again with the sense of being more tactful than truthful.

'I'm sure I hope he does. Rollo is a dear fellow; I wish he came here oftener. Unfortunately his wife does not care for the country, and Rollo himself is very much tied by his new employment—the motor business.'

'Hasn't he been with Scorcher and Speedwell long?'

'Oh no; poor Rollo, he is always trying his hand at something new. He ought to have been born a rich man instead of me.' Randolph spread his hands out with a gesture of helplessness. 'He could have done so much, whereas I—ah, here he comes. We were talking about you, Rollo.'

'No scandal, I hope; no hitting a man when he's down?'

'Indeed no. We were saying we hoped you would soon come into a fortune.'

'Where do you think it's coming from?' demanded Rollo, screwing up his eyes as though the smoke from his cigarette had made them smart.

'Perhaps Vera could tell us,' rejoined Randolph mildly, making his way to the table, though his brother's cigarette was still unfinished. 'How is she, Rollo? I hoped she would feel sufficiently restored to make a fourth with us this evening.'

'Still moping,' said her husband. 'Don't waste your pity on her. She'll be all right tomorrow.'

They sat down to dinner.

The next day, or it might have been the day after, Jimmy was coming home to tea from the woods below the castle. On either side of the path was a hayfield. They were mowing the hay. The mower was a new one, painted bright blue; the horse tossed its head up and down; the placid afternoon air was alive with country sounds, whirring, shouts, and clumping footfalls. The scene was full of an energy and gentleness that refreshed the heart. Jimmy reached the white iron fence that divided the plain from the castle mound, and, with a sigh, set his feet upon the zigzag path. For though the hill was only a couple of hundred feet high at most, the climb called for an effort he was never quite prepared to make. He was tramping with lowered head, conscious of each step, when a voice hailed him.

'Mr. Rintoul!'

It was a foreign voice, the i's pronounced like e's. He looked up and saw a woman, rather short and dark, watching him from the path above.

'You see I have come down to meet you,' she said, advancing with short, brisk, but careful and unpractised steps. And she added, as he still continued to stare at her: 'Don't you know? I am Mrs. Verdew.'

By this time she was at his side.

'How could I know?' he asked, laughing and shaking the hand she was already holding out to him. All her gestures seemed to be quick and unpremeditated.

'Let us sit here,' she said, and almost before she had spoken she was sitting, and had made him sit, on the wooden bench beside them. 'I am tired from walking downhill; you will be tired by walking uphill; therefore we both need a rest.'

She decided it all so quickly that Jimmy, whose nature had a streak of obstinacy, wondered if he was really so tired after all.

'And who should I have been, who could I have been, but Mrs. Verdew?' she demanded challengingly.

Jimmy saw that an answer was expected, but couldn't think of anyone who Mrs. Verdew might have been.

'I don't know,' he said feebly.

'Of course you don't, silly,' said Mrs. Verdew. 'How long have you been here?'

'I can't remember. Two or three days, I think,' said Jimmy, who disliked being nailed down to a definite fact.

'Two or three days? Listen to the man, how vague he is!' commented Mrs. Verdew, with a gesture of impatience apostrophizing the horizon. 'Well, whether it's three days or only two, you must have learnt one thing—that no one enters these premises without leave.'

'Premises?' murmured Jimmy.

'Hillside, garden, grounds, premises,' repeated Mrs. Verdew. 'How slow you are! But so are all Englishmen.'

'I don't think Rollo is slow,' remarked Jimmy, hoping to carry the war into her country.

'Sometimes too slow, sometimes too fast, never the right pace,' pronounced his wife. 'Rollo misdirects his life.'

'He married you,' said Jimmy gently.

Mrs. Verdew gave him a quick look. 'That was partly because I wanted him to. But only just now, for instance, he has been foolish.'

'Do you mean he was foolish to come here?'

'I didn't mean that. Though I hate the place, and he does no good here.'

'What good could he do?' asked Jimmy, who was staring vacantly at the sky. 'Except, perhaps, help his brother to look after—to look after——'

'That's just it,' said Mrs. Verdew. 'Randolph doesn't need any help, and if he did he wouldn't let Rollo help him. He wouldn't even have him made a director of the coal-mine!'

'What coal-mine?' Jimmy asked.

'Randolph's. You don't mean to say you didn't know he had a coal-mine? One has to tell you everything!'

'I like you to tell me things!' protested Jimmy.

'As you don't seem to find out anything for yourself, I suppose I must. Well, then: Randolph has a coal-mine, he is very rich, and he spends his money on nothing but charitable societies for contradicting the laws of nature. And he won't give Rollo a penny—not a penny though he is his only brother, his one near relation in the world! He won't even help him to get a job!'

'I thought he had a job,' said Jimmy, in perplexity.

'You thought that! You'd think anything!' exclaimed Mrs. Verdew, her voice rising in exasperation.

'No, but he told me he came here for a holiday,' said Jimmy pacifically.

'Holiday, indeed! A long holiday. I can't think why Rollo told you that. Nor can I think why I bore you with all our private troubles. A man can talk to a woman about anything; but a woman can only talk to a man about what interests him.'

'But who is to decide that?'

'The woman, of course; and I see you're getting restless.'

'No, no. I was so interested. Please go on.'

'Certainly not. I am a Russian, and I often know when a man is bored sooner than he knows himself. Come along,' pulling him from the bench much as a gardener uproots a weed; 'and I will tell you something very interesting. Ah, how fast you walk! Don't you know it's less fatiguing to walk uphill slowly—and you with all those fishing-nets and pill-boxes. And what on earth is that great bottle for?'

'I try to catch butterflies in these,' Jimmy explained. 'And this is my killing bottle.'

'What a horrible name. What is it for?'

'I'm afraid I kill the butterflies with it.'

'Ah, what a barbarian! Give it to me a moment. Yes, there are their corpses, poor darlings. Is that Randolph coming towards us? No, don't take it away. I can carry it quite easily under my shawl. What was I going to tell you when you interrupted me? I remember—it was about the terrace. When I first came here I used to feel frightfully depressed—it was winter and the sun set so early, sometimes before lunch! In the afternoons I used to go down the mound, where I met you, and wait for the sun to dip below that bare hill on the left. And I would begin to walk quite slowly towards the castle, and all the while the sun was balanced on the hilltop like a ball! And the shadow covered the valley and kept lapping my feet, like the oncoming tide! And I would wait till it reached my ankles, and then run up into the light, and be safe for a moment. It was such fun, but I don't expect you'd enjoy it, you're too sophisticated. Ah, here's Randolph. Randolph, I've been showing Mr. Rintoul the way home; he didn't know it—he doesn't know anything! Do you know what he does with this amusing net? He uses it to catch tiny little moths, like the ones that get into your furs. He puts it over them and looks at them, and they're so frightened, they think they can't get out; then they notice the little holes, and out they creep and fly away! Isn't it charming?'

'Charming,' said Randolph, glancing away from the net and towards the ground.

'Now we must go on. We want our tea terribly!' And Mrs. Verdew swept Jimmy up the hill.

With good fortune the morning newspaper arrived at Verdew Castle in time for tea, already a little out of date. Jimmy accorded it, as a rule, the tepid interest with which, when abroad, one contemplates the English journals of two days ago. They seem to emphasize one's remoteness, not lessen it. Never did Jimmy seem farther from London, indeed, farther from civilization, than when he picked up the familiar sheet of *The Times*. It was like a faint rumour of the world that had somehow found its way down hundreds of miles of railway, changed trains and stations, rumbled across the estuary, and threaded the labyrinth of lanes and turnings between Verdew Grove and the castle. Each day its news seemed to grow less important, or at any rate less important to Jimmy. He began to turn over the leaves. Mrs. Verdew had gone to her room, absent-mindedly taking the killing bottle with her. He was alone; there was no sound save the crackle of the sheets. Unusually insipid the news seemed. He turned more rapidly. What was this? In the middle of page fourteen, a hole? No, not a mere hole: a deliberate excision, the result of an operation performed with scissors. What item of news could anyone have found worth reading, much less worth cutting out? To Jimmy's idle mind, the centre of page fourteen assumed a tremendous importance, it became the sun of his curiosity's universe. He rose; with quick cautious fingers he searched about, shifting papers, delving under blotters, even fumbling in the more public-looking pigeon-holes.

Suddenly he heard the click of a door opening, and with a bound he was in the middle of the room. It was only Rollo, whom business of some kind had kept all day away from home.

'Enter the tired bread-winner,' he remarked. 'Like to see the paper? I haven't had time to read it.' He threw something at Jimmy and walked off.

It was *The Times*. With feverish haste Jimmy turned to page fourteen and seemed to have read the paragraph even before he set eyes on it. It was headed: *Mysterious Outbreak at Verdew*.

'The sequestered, little-known village of Verdew-le-Dale has again been the scene of a mysterious outrage, recalling the murders of John Didwell and Thomas Presland in 1910 and 1912, and the occasional killing of animals which has occurred since. In this instance, as in the others, the perpetrator of the crime seems to have been actuated by some vague motive of retributive justice. The victim was a shepherd dog, the property of Mr. J. R. Cross. The dog, which was known to worry cats, had lately killed two belonging to an old woman of the parish. The Bench, of which Mr. Randolph Verdew is chairman, fined Cross and told him to keep the dog under proper control, but did not order its destruction. Two days ago the animal was found dead in a ditch, with its throat cut. The police have no doubt that the wound was made by the same weapon that killed Didwell and Presland, who, it will be remembered, had both been prosecuted by the R.S.P.C.A. for cruelty and negligence resulting in the deaths of domestic animals. At present no evidence has come to light that might lead to the detection of the criminal, though the police are still making investigations.'

'And I don't imagine it will ever come to light,' Jimmy muttered.

'What do you suppose won't come to light?' inquired a voice at his elbow. He looked up. Randolph Verdew was standing by his chair and looking over his shoulder at the newspaper.

Jimmy pointed to the paragraph.

'Any clue to the identity of the man who did this?'

'No,' said Randolph after a perceptible pause. 'I don't suppose there will be.' He hesitated a moment and then added:

'But it would interest me much to know how that paragraph found its way back into the paper.'

Jimmy explained.

'You see,' observed Randolph, 'I always cut out, and paste into a book, any item of news that concerns the neighbourhood, and especially Verdew. In this way I have made an interesting collection.'

'There seem to have been similar occurrences here before,' remarked Jimmy.

'There have, there have,' Randolph Verdew said.

'It's very strange that no one has even been suspected.'

Randolph Verdew answered obliquely:

'Blood calls for blood. The workings of justice are secret and incalculable.'

'Then you sympathize a little with the murderer?' Jimmy inquired.

'I?' muttered Randolph. 'I think I hate cruelty more than anything in the world.'

'But wasn't the murderer cruel?' persisted Jimmy.

'No,' said Randolph Verdew with great decision. 'At least,' he added in a different tone, 'the victims appear to have died with the minimum of suffering. But here comes Vera. We must find a more cheerful topic of conversation. Vera, my dear, you won't disappoint us of our bridge to-night?'

Several days elapsed, days rendered slightly unsatisfactory for Jimmy from a trivial cause. He could not get back his killing bottle from Mrs. Verdew. She had promised it, she had even gone upstairs to fetch it; but she never brought it down. Meanwhile, several fine specimens (in particular a large female emperor moth) languished in match-boxes and other narrow receptacles, damaging their wings and even having to be set at liberty. It was very trying. He began to feel that the retention of the killing bottle was deliberate. In questions of conduct he was often at sea. But in the domain of manners, though he sometimes went astray, he considered that he knew very well which road to take, and the knowledge was a matter of pride to him. The thought of asking Mrs. Verdew a third time to restore his property irked him exceedingly. At last he screwed up his courage. They were walking down the hill together after tea.

'Mrs. Verdew,' he began.

'Don't go on,' she exclaimed. 'I know exactly what you're going to say. Poor darling, he wants to have his killing bottle back. Well, you can't. I need it myself for those horrible hairy moths that come in at night.'

'But Mrs. Verdew——!' he protested.

'And please don't call me Mrs. Verdew. How long have we known each other? Ten days! And soon you've got to go! Surely you could call me Vera!'

Jimmy flushed. He knew that he must go soon, but didn't realise that a term had been set to his stay.

'Listen,' she continued, beginning to lead him down the hill. 'When you're in London I hope you'll often come to see us.'

'I certainly will,' said he.

'Well, then, let's make a date. Will you dine with us on the tenth? That's to-morrow week.'

'I'm not quite sure——' began Jimmy unhappily, looking down on to the rolling plain and feeling that he loved it.

'How long you're going to stay?' broke in Mrs. Verdew, who seemed to be able to read his thoughts. 'Why do you want to stay? There's nothing to do here: think what fun we might have in London. You can't like this place and I don't believe it's good for you; you don't look half as well as you did when you came.'

'But you didn't see me when I came, and I feel very well,' said Jimmy.

'Feeling is nothing,' said Mrs. Verdew. 'Look at me. Do I look well?' She turned up to him her face: it was too large, he thought, and dull and pallid with powder; the features were too marked; but undeniably it had beauty. 'I suppose I do: I feel well. But in this place I believe my life might stop any moment of its own accord! Do you never feel that?'

'No,' said Jimmy, smiling.

'Sit down,' she said suddenly, taking him to a seat as she had done on the occasion of their first meeting, 'and let me have your

hand—not because I love you, but because I'm happier holding
something, and it's a pretty hand.' Jimmy did not resist: he was
slightly stupefied, but somehow not surprised by her behaviour. She
held up his drooping hand by the wrist, level with her eyes, and
surveyed it with a smile, then she laid it, palm upward, in her lap.
The smile vanished from her face: she knitted her brows.

'I don't like it,' she said, a sudden energy in her voice.

'I thought you said it was a pretty hand,' murmured Jimmy.

'I did; you know I don't mean that. It is pretty: but you don't
deserve to have it, nor your eyes, nor your hair; you are idle and
complacent and unresponsive and ease-loving—you only think of
your butterflies and your killing bottle!' She looked at him fondly;
and Jimmy for some reason was rather pleased to hear all this. 'No,
I meant that I see danger in your hand, in the lines.'

'Danger to me?'

'Ah, the conceit of men! Yes, to you.'

'What sort of danger—physical danger?' inquired Jimmy, only
moderately interested.

'*Danger de mort*,' pronounced Mrs. Verdew.

'Come, come,' said Jimmy, bending forward and looking into
Mrs. Verdew's face to see if she was pretending to be serious. 'When
does the danger threaten?'

'Now,' said Mrs. Verdew.

Oh, thought Jimmy, what a tiresome woman! So you think I'm
in danger, do you, Mrs. Verdew, of losing my head at this moment?
God, the conceit of women! He stole a glance at her; she was looking
straight ahead, her lips pursed up and trembling a little as though
she wanted him to kiss her. Shall I? he thought, for compliance was
in his blood and he always wanted to do what was expected of him.
But at that very moment a wave of irritability flooded his mind and
changed it: she had taken his killing bottle, spoilt and stultified
several precious days, and all to gratify her caprice. He turned
away.

'Oh, I'm tougher than you think,' he said.

'Tougher?' she said. 'Do you mean your skin? All Englishmen
have thick skins.' She spoke resentfully; then her voice softened. 'I
was going to tell you——' She uttered the words with difficulty,
and as though against her will. But Jimmy, not noticing her changed
tone and still ridden by his irritation, interrupted her.

'That you'd restore my killing bottle?'

'No, no,' she cried in exasperation, leaping to her feet. 'How you do harp on that wretched old poison bottle! I wish I'd broken it!' She caught her breath, and Jimmy rose too, facing her with distress and contrition in his eyes. But she was too angry to heed his change of mood. 'It was something I wanted you to know—but you make things so difficult for me! I'll fetch you your bottle,' she continued wildly, 'since you're such a child as to want it! No, don't follow me; I'll have it sent to your room.'

He looked up; she was gone, but a faint sound of sobbing disturbed the air behind her.

It was evening, several days later, and they were sitting at dinner. How Jimmy would miss these meals when he got back to London! For a night or two, after the scene with Mrs. Verdew, he had been uneasy under the enforced proximity which the dining-table brought; she looked at him reproachfully, spoke little, and when he sought occasions to apologise to her, she eluded them. She had never been alone with him since. She had, he knew, little control over her emotions, and perhaps her pride suffered. But her pique, or whatever it was, now seemed to have passed away. She looked lovely to-night, and he realised he would miss her. Rollo's voice, when he began to speak, was like a commentary on his thoughts.

'Jimmy says he's got to leave us, Randolph,' he said. 'Back to the jolly old office.'

'That is a great pity,' said Randolph in his soft voice. 'We shall miss him, shan't we, Vera?'

Mrs. Verdew said they would.

'All the same, these unpleasant facts have to be faced,' remarked Rollo. 'That's why we were born. I'm afraid you've had a dull time, Jimmy, though you must have made the local flora and fauna sit up. Have you annexed any prize specimens from your raids upon the countryside?'

'I have got one or two good ones,' said Jimmy with a reluctance that he attributed partially to modesty.

'By the way,' said Rollo, pouring himself out a glass of port, for the servants had left the room, 'I would like you to show Randolph that infernal machine of yours, Jimmy. Anything on the lines of a humane killer bucks the old chap up no end.' He looked across at his brother, the ferocious cast of his features softened into an expression of fraternal solicitude.

After a moment's pause Randolph said: 'I should be much interested to be shown Mr. Rintoul's invention.'

'Oh, it's not my invention,' said Jimmy a little awkwardly.

'You'll forgive me disagreeing with you, Rollo,' Mrs. Verdew, who had not spoken for some minutes, suddenly remarked. 'I don't think it's worth Randolph's while looking at it. I don't think it would interest him a bit.'

'How often have I told you, my darling,' said Rollo, leaning across the corner of the table towards his wife, 'not to contradict me? I keep a record of the times you agree with me. December, 1919, was the last.'

'Sometimes I think that was a mistake,' said Mrs. Verdew, rising in evident agitation, 'for it was then I promised to marry you.' She reached the door before Jimmy could open it for her.

'Ah, these ladies!' moralised Rollo, leaning back and closing his eyes. 'What a dance the dear things lead us, with their temperaments.' And he proceeded to enumerate examples of feminine caprice, until his brother proposed that they should adjourn to the bridge table.

The next morning Jimmy was surprised to find a note accompany his early morning tea.

'DEAR MR. RINTOUL (it began), since I mustn't say "Dear Jimmy." ('I never said she mustn't' Jimmy thought.) I know it isn't easy for any man, most of all an Englishman, to understand moods, but I do beg you to forgive my foolish outburst of a few days ago. I think it must have been the air or the lime in the water that made me *un po' nervosa*, as the Italians say. I know you prefer a life utterly flat and dull and even—it would kill me, but there! I am sorry. You can't expect me to change, *à mon âge!* But anyhow try to forgive me.

Yours

VERA VERDEW.

PS.—I wouldn't trouble to show that bottle to Randolph. He has quite enough silly ideas in his head as it is.'

What a nice letter, thought Jimmy drowsily. He had forgotten the killing bottle. I won't show it to Randolph, Jimmy thought, unless he asks me.

But soon after breakfast a footman brought him a message: Mr. Verdew was in his room and would be glad to see the invention (the man's voice seemed to put the word into inverted commas) at Mr.

Rintoul's convenience. 'Well,' reflected Jimmy, 'if he's to see it working it must have something to work on.' Aimlessly he strolled over the drawbridge and made his way, past blocks of crumbling wall, past grassy hummocks and hollows, to the terraces. They were gay with flowers; and looked at from above, the lateral stripes and bunches of colour, succeeding each other to the bottom of the hill, had a peculiarly brilliant effect. What should he catch? A dozen white butterflies presented themselves for the honour of exhibiting their death-agony to Mr. Randolph Verdew, but Jimmy passed them by. His collector's pride demanded a nobler sacrifice. After twenty minutes' search he was rewarded; his net fell over a slightly battered but still recognisable specimen of the Large Tortoiseshell butterfly. He put it in a pill-box and bore it away to the house. But as he went he was visited by a reluctance, never experienced by him before, to take the butterfly's life in such a public and cold-blooded fashion; it was not a good specimen, one that he could add to his collection; it was just cannon-fodder. The heat of the day, flickering visibly upwards from the turf and flowers, bemused his mind; all around was a buzzing and humming that seemed to liberate his thoughts from contact with the world and give them the intensity of sensations. So vivid was his vision, so flawless the inner quiet from which it sprang, that he came up with a start against his own bedroom door. The substance of his day-dream had been forgotten; but it had left its ambassador behind it—something that whether apprehended by the mind as a colour, a taste, or a local inflammation, spoke with an insistent voice and always to the same purpose: 'Don't show Randolph Verdew the butterfly; let it go, here, out of the window, and send him an apology.'

For a few minutes, such was the force of this inward monitor, Jimmy did contemplate setting the butterfly at liberty. He was prone to sudden irrational scruples and impulses, and if there was nothing definite urging him the other way he often gave in to them. But in this case there was. Manners demanded that he should accede to his host's request; the rules of manners, of all rules in life, were the easiest to recognise and the most satisfactory to act upon. Not to go would clearly be a breach of manners.

'How kind of you,' said Randolph, coming forward and shaking Jimmy's hand, a greeting that, between two members of the same household, struck him as odd. 'You have brought your invention with you?'

Jimmy saw that it was useless to disclaim the honour of its discovery. He unwrapped the bottle and handed it to Randolph.

Randolph carried it straight away to a high window, the sill of which was level with his eyes and above the top of Jimmy's head. He held the bottle up to the light. Oblong in shape and about the size of an ordinary jam jar, it had a deep whitish pavement of plaster, pitted with brown furry holes like an overripe cheese. Resting on the plaster, billowing and coiling up to the glass stopper, stood a fat column of cotton-wool. The most striking thing about the bottle was the word *poison* printed in large, loving characters on a label stuck to the outside.

'May I release the stopper?' asked Randolph at length.

'You may,' said Jimmy, 'but a whiff of the stuff is all you want.'

Randolph stared meditatively into the depths of the bottle. 'A rather agreeable odour,' he said. 'But how small the bottle is. I had figured it to myself as something very much larger.'

'Larger?' echoed Jimmy. 'Oh, no, this is quite big enough for me. I don't need a mausoleum.'

'But I was under the impression,' Randolph Verdew remarked, still fingering the bottle, 'that you used it to destroy pests.'

'If you call butterflies pests,' said Jimmy, smiling.

'I am afraid that some of them must undeniably be included in that category,' pronounced Mr. Verdew, his voice edged with a melancholy decisiveness. 'The cabbage butterfly, for instance. And it is, of course, only the admittedly noxious insects that need to be destroyed.'

'All insects are more or less harmful,' Jimmy said.

Randolph Verdew passed his hand over his brow. The shadow of a painful thought crossed his face, and he murmured uncertainly:

'I think that's a quibble. There are categories . . . I have been at some pains to draw them up. . . . The list of destructive lepidoptera is large, too large. . . . That is why I imagined your lethal chamber would be a vessel of considerable extent, possibly large enough to admit a man, and its use attended by some danger to an unpractised exponent.'

'Well,' said Jimmy, 'there's enough poison here to account for half a town. But let me show you how it works.' And he took the pill-box from his pocket. Shabby, battered and cowed, the butterfly stood motionless, its wings closed and upright.

'Now,' said Jimmy, 'you'll see.'

The butterfly was already between the fingers and halfway to the bottle, when he heard, faint but clear, the sound of a cry. It was two-syllabled, like the interval of the cuckoo's call inverted, and might have been his own name.

'Listen!' he exclaimed. 'What was that? It sounded like Mrs. Verdew's voice.' His swiftly turning head almost collided with his host's chin, so near had the latter drawn to watch the operation, and chased the tail-end of a curious look from Randolph Verdew's face.

'It's nothing,' he said. 'Go on.'

Alas, alas, for the experiment in humane slaughter! The butterfly must have been stronger than it looked; the power of the killing bottle had no doubt declined with frequent usage. Up and down, round and round flew the butterfly; frantic flutterings could be heard through the thick walls of its glass prison. It clung to the cotton-wool, pressed itself into corners, its straining, delicate tongue coiling and uncoiling in the effort to suck in a breath of living air. Now it was weakening. It fell from the cotton-wool and lay with its back on the plaster slab. It jolted itself up and down and, when strength for this movement failed, it clawed the air with its thin legs as though pedalling an imaginary bicycle. Suddenly, with a violent spasm, it gave birth to a thick cluster of yellowish eggs. Its body twitched once or twice and at last lay still.

Jimmy shrugged his shoulders in annoyance and turned to his host. The look of horrified excitement whose vanishing vestige he had seen a moment before, lay full and undisguised upon Randolph Verdew's face. He only said:

'Of what flower or vegetable is that dead butterfly the parasite?'

'Oh, poor thing,' said Jimmy carelessly, 'it's rather a rarity. Its caterpillar may have eaten an elm-leaf or two—nothing more. It's too scarce to be a pest. It's fond of gardens and frequented places, the book says—rather sociable, like a robin.'

'It could not be described as injurious to human life?'

'Oh, no. It's a collector's specimen really. Only this is too damaged to be any good.'

'Thank you for letting me see the invention in operation,' said Randolph Verdew, going to his desk and sitting down. Jimmy found his silence a little embarrassing. He packed up the bottle and made a rather awkward, self-conscious exit.

* * *

The four bedroom candles always stood, their silver flashing agree-
ably, cheek by jowl with the whisky decanter and the hot-water
kettle and the soda. Now, the others having retired, there were only
two, one of which (somewhat wastefully, for he still had a half-
empty glass in his left hand) Rollo was lighting.

'My dear fellow,' he was saying to Jimmy. 'I'm sorry you think
the new model insecticide fell a bit flat. But Randolph's like that,
you know: damned undemonstrative cove, I must say, though he's
my own brother.'

'He wasn't exactly undemonstrative,' answered Jimmy, perplexity written on his face.

'No, rather like an iceberg hitting you amidships,' said his friend.
'Doesn't make a fuss, but you feel it all the same. But don't you
worry, Jimmy; I happen to know that he enjoyed your show. Fact
is, he told me so.' He gulped down some whisky.

'I'm relieved,' said Jimmy, and he obviously spoke the truth.
'I've only one more whole day here, and I should be sorry if I'd
hurt his feelings.'

'Yes, and I'm afraid you'll have to spend it with him alone,' said
Rollo, compunction colouring his voice. 'I was coming to that. Fact
is, Vera and I have unexpectedly got to go away tomorrow for the
day.' He paused; a footman entered and began walking uncertainly
about the room. 'Now, Jimmy,' he went on, 'be a good chap and
stay on a couple of days more. You do keep us from the blues so.
That's all right, William, we don't want anything,' he remarked
parenthetically to the footman's retreating figure. 'I haven't mentioned it to Randolph, but he'd be absolutely charmed if you'd
grace our humble dwelling a little longer. You needn't tell anyone
anything: just stay and we shall be back the day after tomorrow.
It's hellish that we've got to go, but you know this bread-winning
business: it's the early bird that catches the worm. And talking of
that, we have to depart at cock-crow. I may not see you again—
that is, unless you stay, as I hope you will. Just send a wire to the
old blighter who works with you and tell him to go to blazes.'

'Well,' said Jimmy, delighted by the prospect, 'you certainly do
tempt me.'

'Then fall, my lad,' said Rollo, catching him a heavy blow
between the shoulder-blades. 'I shan't say goodbye, but *au revoir*.
Don't go to bed sober; have another drink.'

But Jimmy declined. The flickering candles lighted them across the hall and up the stone stairs.

And it's lucky I have a candle, Jimmy thought, trying in vain the third and last switch, the one on the reading-lamp by the bed. The familiar room seemed to have changed, to be closing hungrily, with a vast black embrace, upon the nimbus of thin clear dusk that shone about the candle. He walked uneasily up and down, drew a curtain and let in a ray of moonlight. But the silver gleam crippled the candlelight without adding any radiance of its own, so he shut it out. This window must be closed, thought Jimmy, that opens on to the parapet, for I really couldn't deal with a stray cat in this localised twilight. He opened instead a window that gave on to the sheer wall. Even after the ritual of tooth-cleaning he was still restless and dissatisfied, so after a turn or two he knelt by the bed and said his prayers—whether from devotion or superstition he couldn't tell: he only knew that he wanted to say them.

'Come in!' he called next morning, in answer to the footman's knock.

'I can't come in, sir,' said a muffled voice. 'The door's locked.'

How on earth had that happened? Then Jimmy remembered. As a child he always locked the door because he didn't like to be surprised saying his prayers. He must have done so last night, unconsciously. How queer! He felt full of self-congratulation—he didn't know why. 'And—oh, William!' he called after the departing footman.

'Yes, sir?'

'The light's fused, or something. It wouldn't go on last night.'

'Very good, sir.'

Jimmy addressed himself to the tea. But what was this? Another note from Mrs. Verdew!

'DEAR JIMMY (he read),

'You will forgive this impertinence, for I've got a piece of good news for you. In future, you won't be able to say that women never help a man in his career! (Jimmy was unaware of having said so.) As you know, Rollo and I have to leave tomorrow morning. I don't suppose he told you why, because it's rather private. But he's embarking on a big undertaking that will mean an enormous amount of litigation and lawyer's fees! Think of that! (Though I don't suppose you think of anything else.) I know he wants you to act for him: but to do so you positively *must* leave Verdew tomorrow. Make any excuse to Randolph; send yourself a telegram if you want to be specially polite: but you must catch the night train to London. It's the chance of a life. You can get through to Rollo on the telephone next morning. Perhaps we could lunch together—or dine? *A bientôt*, therefore.

VERA VERDEW.

'PS.—I shall be furious if you don't come.'

Jimmy pondered Mrs. Verdew's note, trying to read between its lines. One thing was clear: she had fallen in love with him. Jimmy smiled at the ceiling. She wanted to see him again, so soon, so soon! Jimmy smiled once more. She couldn't bear to wait an unnecessary day. How urgent women were! He smiled more indulgently. And, also, how exacting. Here was this cock-and-bull story, all about Rollo's 'undertaking' which would give him, Jimmy, the chance of a life-time! And because she was so impatient she expected him to believe it! Luncheon, indeed! Dinner! How could they meet for dinner, when Rollo was to be back at Verdew that same evening? In her haste she had not even troubled to make her date credible. And then: 'I shall be furious if you don't come.' What an argument! What confidence in her own powers did not that sentence imply! Let her be furious, then, as furious as she liked.

Her voice, just outside his door, interrupted his meditation.

'Only a moment, Rollo, it will only take me a moment!'

And Rollo's reply, spoken in a tone as urgent as hers, but louder: 'I tell you there isn't time: we shall miss the train.'

He seemed to hustle her away downstairs, poor Vera. She had really been kind to Jimmy, in spite of her preposterous claims on his affection. He was glad he would see her again tomorrow. . . . Verdew was so much nicer than London. . . . He began to doze.

On the way back from the woods there was a small low church with a square tower and two bells—the lower one both cracked and flat. You could see up into the belfry through the slats in the windows. Close by the church ran a stream, choked with green scum except where the cattle went down to drink, and crossed by a simple bridge of logs set side by side. Jimmy liked to stand on the bridge and listen to the unmelodious chime. No one heeded it, no one came to church, and it had gone sour and out of tune. It gave Jimmy an exquisite, slightly morbid sense of dereliction and decay, which he liked to savour in solitude; but this afternoon a rustic had got there first.

'Good-day,' he said.

'Good-day,' said Jimmy.

'You're from the castle, I'm thinking?' the countryman surmised.

'Yes.'

'And how do you find Mr. Verdew?'

'Which Mr. Verdew?'

'Why, the squire, of course.'

'I think he's pretty well,' said Jimmy.

'Ah, he may appear to be so,' the labourer observed; 'but them as has eyes to see and ears to hear, knows different.'

'Isn't he a good landlord?' asked Jimmy.

'Yes,' said the old man. 'He's a tolerably good landlord. It isn't that.' He seemed to relish his mysteriousness.

'You like Mr. Rollo Verdew better?' suggested Jimmy.

'I wouldn't care to say that, sir. He's a wild one, Mr. Rollo.'

'Well, anyhow, Mr. Randolph Verdew isn't wild.'

'Don't you be too sure, sir.'

'I've never seen him so.'

'There's not many that have. And those that have—some won't tell what they saw and some can't.'

'Why won't they?'

'Because it's not their interest to.'

'And why can't the others?'

'Because they're dead.'

There was a pause.

'How did they die?' asked Jimmy.

'That's not for me to say,' the old man answered, closing his mouth like a trap. But this gesture, as Jimmy had already learned, was only part of his conversational technique. In a moment he began again:

'Did you ever hear of the Verdew murders?'

'Something.'

'Well, 'twasn't only dogs that was killed.'

'I know.'

'But they were all killed the same way.'

'How?'

'With a knife,' said the old man. 'Like pigs. From ear to ear,' he added, making an explanatory gesture; 'from ear to ear.' His voice became reminiscent. 'Tom Presland was a friend o' mine. I seed him in the evening and he said, he says, "That blamed donkey weren't worth a ten-pound fine." And I said, "You're lucky not to be in prison," for in case you don't know, sir, the Bench here don't mind fellows being a bit hasty with their animals, although Mr. Verdew is the chairman. I felt nigh killing the beast myself sometimes, it was that obstinate. "But, Bill," he says, "I don't feel altogether comfortable when I remember what happened to Jack Didwell." And sure enough he was found next morning in the ditch with his throat gapin' all white at the edges, just like poor old Jack. And the donkey was a contrary beast, that had stood many a knock before, harder than the one what killed him.'

'And why is Mr. Verdew suspected?'

'Why, sir, the servants said he was in the castle all night and must have been, because the bridge was drawed. But how do they know he had to use the bridge? Anyhow, George Wiscombe swears he saw him going through Nape's Spinney the night poor old Tom was done in. And Mr. Verdew has always been cruel fond of animals, that's another reason.'

How easy it is, thought Jimmy, to lose one's reputation in the country!

'Tell me,' he said, 'how does Mr. Verdew satisfy his conscience when he eats animals and chickens, and when he has slugs and snails killed in the garden?'

'Ah, there you've hit it,' said the old man, not at all non plussed. 'But they say Mr. Rollo Verdew has helped him to make a mighty great list of what may be killed and what mayn't, according as it's useful-like to human beings. And anybody kills anything, they persuade him it's harmful and down it goes on the black list. And if he don't see the thing done with his own eyes, or the chap isn't hauled up before the Bench, he doesn't take on about it. And in a week or less it's all gone from his mind. Jack and Tom were both killed within a few days of what they'd done becoming known; so was the collie dog what was found here a fortnight back.'

'Here?' asked Jimmy.

'Close by where you're standing. Poor beast, it won't chase those b——y cats no more. It was a mess. But, as I said, if what you've done's a week old, you're safe, in a manner of speaking.'

'But why, if he's really dangerous,' said Jimmy, impressed in spite of himself by the old man's tacit assumption of Randolph's guilt, 'doesn't Mr. Rollo Verdew get him shut up?' This simple question evoked the longest and most pregnant of his interlocutor's pauses. Surely, thought Jimmy, it will produce a monstrous birth, something to make suspicion itself turn pale.

'Now don't you tell nothing of what I'm saying to you,' said the old man at length. 'But it's my belief that Mr. Rollo don't want his brother shut up; no, nor thought to be mad. And why? Because if people know he's mad, and he goes and does another murder, they'll just pop him in the lunatic asylum and all his money will go to government and charity. But if he does a murder like you or me might, and the circumstances are circumstantial, he'll be hanged for it, and all the money and the castle and the coal-mine will go into the pockets of Mr. Rollo.'

'I see,' said Jimmy. 'It sounds very simple.'

'I'm not swearing there's anything of the sort in Mr. Rollo's mind,' said the old man. 'But that's the way I should look at it if I was him. Now I must be getting along. Good-night, sir.'

'Good-night.'

Of course it wasn't really night, only tea-time, five o'clock; but he and his acquaintance would meet no more that day, so perhaps the man was right to say good-night. Jimmy's thoughts, as he worked his way up the castle mound, were unclear and rather painful. He didn't believe a tithe of what the old man said. It was not even a distortion of the truth; it was ignorant and vulgar slander, and had no relation to the truth except by a kind of contiguity. But it infected his mood and gave a disagreeable direction to his thoughts. He was lonely; Randolph had not appeared at lunch, and he missed Rollo, and even more he missed (though this surprised him) Rollo's wife. He hadn't seen much of them, but suddenly he felt the need of their company. But goodness knows where they are, thought Jimmy; I can't even telephone to them. In the midst of these uneasy reflections he reached his bedroom door. Walking in, he could not for a moment understand why the place looked so strange. Then he realised; it was empty. All his things had been cleared out of it.

'Evidently,' thought Jimmy, 'they've mistaken the day I was going away, and packed me!' An extraordinary sensation of relief surged up into his heart. Since his luggage was nowhere to be seen, it must have been stacked in the hall, ready for his departure by the evening train. Picturing himself at the booking-office of Verdew Grove station buying a ticket for London, Jimmy started for the hall.

William cut short his search.

'Were you looking for your things, sir?' he asked, with a slight smile. 'Because they're in the Onyx Room. We've moved you, sir.'

'Oh,' said Jimmy, following in the footman's wake. 'Why?'

'It was Mr. Verdew's orders, sir. I told him the light was faulty in your bedroom, so he said to move you into the Onyx Room.'

'The room next to his?'

'That's right, sir.'

'Couldn't the fuse be mended?'

'I don't think it was the fuse, sir.'

'Oh, I thought you said it was.'

So this was the Onyx Room—the room, Jimmy suddenly remembered, that Rollo had meant him to have in the beginning. Certainly its colours were dark and lustrous and laid on in layers, but Jimmy didn't care for them. Even the ceiling was parti-coloured. Someone must have been given a free hand here; perhaps Vera had done the decoration. The most beautiful thing in the room was the Chinese screen masking the door that communicated, he supposed, with Randolph's bedroom. What a clatter it would make if it fell, thought Jimmy, studying the heavy, dark, dully-shining panels of the screen. The door opening would knock it over. He heard the footman's voice.

'Is it for one night or more, sir? I've packed up some of your things.'

'I'm not sure yet,' said Jimmy. 'William, will this screen move?'

The footman took hold of the screen with both hands and telescoped it against his chest. There was revealed an ordinary looking door covered with green baize. Jimmy could see the point of a key-head, so the door was probably not very thick.

'This used to be the dressing-room,' William volunteered, as though making a contribution to Jimmy's unspoken thoughts.

'Thank you,' said Jimmy, 'and would you mind putting the screen back? . . . And, William!'

The footman stopped.

'There's still time to send a telegram?'

'Oh yes, sir. There's a form here.'

All through his solitary tea Jimmy debated with himself as to whether he should send the telegram—a telegram of recall, of course, it would be. The message presented no difficulty. 'Wire if Coxford case opens Tuesday.' He knew that it did, but his attendance was not at all necessary. He was undoubtedly suffering from a slight attack of nerves; and nowadays one didn't defy nerves, one yielded to them gracefully. 'I know that if I stay I shall have a bad night,' he thought; 'I might as well spend it in the train.' But of course he hadn't meant to go at all; he had even promised Rollo to stay. He had wanted to stay. To leave abruptly tonight would be doubly rude: rude to Randolph, rude to Rollo. Only Vera would be pleased. Vera, whose clumsy attempt to lure him to London he had so easily seen through. Vera, whose 'I shall be furious if you don't come' rankled whenever he thought of it. Every moment added its quota to the incubus of indecision that paralysed his mind. Manners, duty, wishes, fears, all were contradictory, all pulled in different directions. A gust of apprehension sent him hot-foot to the writing-table. The telegram was ready written when, equally strong, an access of self-respect came and made him tear it up. At last he had an idea. At six o'clock he would send the telegram; the office might still be open. There might still be time to get a reply. If, in spite of his twofold obstacle he had an answer, he would take it as the voice of fate, and leave that night. . . .

At half-past seven William came in to draw the curtains; he also brought a message. Mr. Verdew begged Mr. Rintoul to excuse him, but he felt a little unwell, and was dining in his own room. He hoped to see Mr. Rintoul tomorrow to say goodbye. 'You are going, then, sir?' added the footman.

Jimmy blindfolded his will, and took an answer at random from among the tablets of his mind.

'Yes. And—William!' he called out.

'Sir?'

'I suppose it's too late now for me to get an answer to my telegram?'

'I'm afraid so, sir.'

For a second Jimmy sunned himself in a warm flow of recovered self-esteem. Luck had saved him from a humiliating flight. Now his one regret was that his nerves had cheated him of those few extra days at Verdew. 'If there had been a bolt on my side of the green door,' he said to himself, 'I should never have sent that telegram.'

How like, in some ways, was the last evening to the first. As bedtime approached, he became acutely conscious of his surroundings—of the stone floors, the vaulted passages, the moat, the drawbridge—all those concrete signs which seemed to recall the past and substitute it for the present. He was completely isolated and immured; he could scarcely believe he would be back in the real, living world tomorrow. Another glass of whisky would bring the centuries better into line. It did; and, emboldened by its heady fumes, he inspected, with the aid of his candle (for the ground-floor lights had been turned out) the defences of door and window, and marvelled anew at their parade of clumsy strength. Why all these precautions when the moat remained, a flawless girdle of protection?

But was it flawless? Lying in bed, staring at the painted ceiling, with its squares and triangles and riot of geometrical designs, Jimmy smiled to remember how Rollo had once told him of a secret entrance, known only to him. He had promised to show it to Jimmy, but he had forgotten. A nice fellow Rollo, but he didn't believe they would ever know each other much better. When dissimilar natures come together, the friendship blossoms quickly, and as quickly fades. Rollo and Jimmy just tolerated each other—they didn't share their lives, their secrets, their secret passages. . . .

Jimmy was lying on his back, his head sunk on the brightly lit pillow, his mind drowsier than his digestion. To his departing consciousness the ceiling looked like a great five of diamonds spread over his head; the scarlet lozenges moved on hinges, he knew that quite well, and as they moved they gave a glimpse of black and let in a draught. Soon there would be a head poking through them all, instead of through this near corner one, and that would be more symmetrical. But if I stand on the bed I can shut them; they will close with a click. If only this one wasn't such a weight and didn't stick so. . . .

Jimmy awoke in a sweat, still staring at the ceiling. It heaved and writhed like a half-dead moth on the setting-board. But the walls stood still, so that there was something more than whisky at the back of it. And yet, when he looked again, the ceiling did not budge.

The dream was right; he could touch the ceiling by standing on the bed. But only with the tips of his fingers. What he needed was a bar of some kind with which to prise it open. He looked round the room, and could see nothing suitable but a towel-horse. But there were plenty of walking-sticks downstairs. To light his candle and put on his dressing-gown and slippers was the work of a moment.

He reached the door in less time than it takes to tell. But he got no further, because the door was locked.

Jimmy's heart began to beat violently. Panic bubbled up in him like water in a syphon. He took a wild look around the room, ran to the bed-head, and pressed the bell-button as though he meant to flatten it in its socket. Relief stole in his heart. Already he heard in imagination the quick patter of feet in the corridor, the hurried, whispered explanations, the man's reassuring voice: 'I'll be with you in a moment, sir.' Already he felt slightly ashamed of his precipitate summons, and began to wonder how he should explain it away. The minutes passed, and nothing happened. He need not worry yet; it would take William some time to dress, and no doubt he had a long way to come. But Jimmy's returning anxiety cried out for some distraction, so he left the edge of the bed where he had been sitting, fetched the towel-horse, and, balancing unsteadily on the mattress, began to prod the ceiling. Down came little flakes and pellets of painted plaster; they littered the sheets, and would be very uncomfortable to sleep on. . . . Jimmy stooped to flick them away, and saw from the tail of his eye that since he rang five minutes had gone by. He resumed the muffled tattoo on the ceiling. Suddenly it gave; the red diamond shot upwards and fell back, revealing a patch of black and letting in a rush of cool air.

As, stupefied, Jimmy lowered his eyes, they fell upon the screen. It was moving stealthily outwards, toppling into the room. Already he could see a thin strip of the green door. The screen swayed, paused, seemed to hang by a hair. Then, its leaves collapsing inwards upon each other, it fell with a great crash upon the floor. In the opening stood Randolph, fully dressed; he had a revolver in his right hand, and there was a knife between his teeth. It was curved and shining, and he looked as though he were taking a bite out of the new moon.

The shot missed Jimmy's swaying legs, the knife only grazed his ankle, and he was safe in the darkness of the attic, with the bolt of the trap-door securely shut. He ran trembling in the direction the draught came from and was rewarded first by a sense of decreasing darkness, and then by a glimpse, through a framed opening in the roof, of the stars and the night sky.

The opening was low down, and to climb out was easy. He found himself in a leaden gully, bounded on one side by a shallow parapet two feet high, and on the other, as it seemed, by the slope of the roof. Finding his way along the gully, he was brought up sharp against an octagonal turret, that clearly marked the end of the building. The moat was directly below him. Turning to the left, he encountered another similar turret, and turning to the left again he found himself up against a wall surmounted by tall chimneys. This wall appeared to be scored with projections and indentations— soot-doors he guessed them to be; he hoped to be able to use them to climb the wall, but they were awkwardly spaced, close to the parapet, and if he missed his footing he ran the risk of falling over its edge.

He now felt a curious lightheartedness, as though he had shuffled off every responsibility: responsibility towards his pyjamas, which were torn and dirty, towards his foot, which was bleeding, towards trains, letters, engagements—all the petty and important demands of life. Cold, but not unhappy, he sat down to await daybreak.

The clock had just chimed three-quarters, which three-quarters he did not know, when he heard a scraping sound that seemed to come from the corresponding parapet across the roof. He listened, crouching in the angle between the chimney wall and the battle- ment. His fears told him that the sound was following the track by which he had come; the shuffling grew indistinct, and then, the first turret passed, began to draw nearer. It could only be Randolph, who clearly had some means of access to the roof other than the trap-door in Jimmy's bedroom. He must have, or he could not have reached it to spy on his victim while he was asleep. Now he was turning the last corner. Jimmy acted quickly and with the courage of desperation. At the corner where he crouched there projected above the battlement three sides of an octagonal turret, repeating the design of the true turrets at the end. Grasping the stone as well as he could, he lowered himself into space. It was a terrible moment, but the cautious shuffle of Randolph's approach deadened his fear. His arms almost at their full stretch, he felt the dripstone under- neath his feet. It seemed about six inches wide, with a downward curve, but it sufficed. He changed his grip from the plain stone band of the parapet to the pierced masonry beneath it, which afforded a better purchase, and held his breath. Randolph could not find him unless he leant right over the balustrade. This he did not do. He muttered to himself; he climbed up to the apex of the roof; he examined the flue-doors, or whatever they were. All this Jimmy could clearly see through the quatrefoil to which he was clinging. Randolph muttered, 'I shall find him when the light comes,' and then he disappeared. The clock struck four, four-fifteen, four-thirty, and then a diffused pallor began to show itself in the eastern sky.

The numbness that had taken hold of Jimmy's body began to invade his mind, which grew dull and sleepy under the effort of compelling his tired hands to retain their hold. His back curved outwards, his head sank upon his breast; the changes of which his cramped position admitted were too slight to afford his body relief. So that he could not at once look round when he heard close above his head the sound of an opening door and the sharp rattle of falling mortar. He recognised the figure as it passed him—Rollo's.

Jimmy restrained his impulse to call out. Why had Rollo come back? Why was he swaggering over the roofs of Verdew Castle at daybreak looking as though he owned it? It was not his yet. Rollo turned, and in the same leisurely fashion walked back towards Jimmy's corner. His face was set and pale, but there was triumph in his eyes, and cruelty, and the marks of many passions which his everyday exterior had concealed. Then his eyebrows went up, his chin quivered, and his underlip shot out and seemed to stretch across his face. 'Just five minutes more, five minutes more; I'll give him another five minutes,' he kept muttering to himself. He leaned back against the wall. Jimmy could have touched the laces of his shoes, which were untied and dirty. 'Poor old Jimmy, poor old James!' Rollo suddenly chanted, in a voice that was very distinct, but quite unlike his own. To Jimmy's confused mind he seemed to be speaking of two different people, neither of whom was connected with himself. 'Never mind, Jimmy,' Rollo added in the conciliatory tone of one who, overcome by his better nature, at last gives up teasing. 'Anyhow, it's ten to one against.' He stumbled down the gully and round the bend.

Jimmy never knew how he summoned strength to climb over the parapet. He found himself sprawling in the gully, panting and faint. But he had caught sight of a gaping hole like a buttery hatch amid the tangle of soot-doors, and he began to crawl towards it. He was trying to bring his stiff knee up to his good one when from close by his left ear he heard a terrible scream. It went shooting up, and seemed to make a glittering arc of sound in the half-lit sky. He also thought he heard the words, 'Oh, God, Randolph, it's me!' but of this he was never certain. But through all the windings of Rollo's bolt-hole, until it discharged itself at the base of a ruined newel-staircase among the outbuildings, he still heard the agonised gasping, spasmodic, yet with a horrible rhythm of its own, that followed Rollo's scream. He locked the cracked paintless door with the key that Rollo had left, and found himself among the lanes.

Late in the evening of the same day a policeman asked to see Mrs. Verdew, who was sitting in a bedroom in the King's Head inn at Fremby, a market town ten miles from Verdew Castle. She had been sitting there all day, getting up from time to time to glance at a slip of paper pinned to one of the pillows. It was dated, '7.30 a.m., July 10th,' and said, 'Back in a couple of hours. Have to see a man about a car. Sorry—Rollo.' She wouldn't believe the constable when he said that her husband had met with an accident some time early that morning, probably about five o'clock. 'But look! But look!' she cried. 'See for yourself! It is his own handwriting! He says he went away at half-past seven. Why are all Englishmen so difficult to convince?'

'We have a statement from Mr. Randolph Verdew,' said the policeman gently. 'He said that he . . . he . . . he met Mr. Rollo at the castle in the early hours of the morning.'

'But how can you be so stupid!' cried Mrs. Verdew. 'It wasn't Rollo—it was Mr. Rintoul who . . .'

'What name is that?' asked the policeman, taking out his notebook.

GRAHAM GREENE
When Greek meets Greek

I

WHEN the chemist had shut his shop for the night he went through a door at the back of the hall that served both him and the flats above, and then up two flights and a half of stairs, carrying an offering of a little box of pills. The box was stamped with his name and address: Priskett, 14 New End Street, Oxford. He was a middle-aged man with a thin moustache and scared, evasive eyes: he wore his long white coat even when he was off duty as if it had the power of protecting him like a King's uniform from his enemies. So long as he wore it he was free, as it were, from summary trial and execution.

On the top landing was a window: outside Oxford spread through the spring evening: the peevish noise of innumerable bicycles, the gasworks, the prison, and the grey spires, beyond the bakers and confectioners, like paper frills. A door was marked with a visiting card Mr. Nicholas Fennick, B.A.: the chemist rang three short times.

The man who opened the door was sixty years old at least, with snow-white hair and a pink babyish skin. He wore a mulberry velvet dinner jacket, and his glasses swung on the end of a wide black ribbon. He said with a kind of boisterousness, 'Ah, Priskett, step in, Priskett. I had just sported my oak for a moment. . . .'

'I brought you some more of my pills.'

'Invaluable Priskett. If only you had taken a degree—the Society of Apothecaries would have been enough—I would have appointed you resident medical officer of St. Ambrose's.'

'How's the college doing?'

'Give me your company for a moment in the common-room, and you shall know all.'

Mr. Fennick led the way down a little dark passage cluttered with mackintoshes: Mr. Priskett, feeling his way uneasily from mackintosh to mackintosh, kicked in front of him a pair of girl's shoes. 'One day,' Mr. Fennick said, 'we must build . . .' and he made a broad confident gesture with his glasses that seemed to press back the walls of the common-room: a small round table covered with a landlady's cloth, three or four shiny chairs and a glass-fronted bookcase containing a copy of *Every Man His Own Lawyer*. 'My niece Elisabeth,' Mr. Fennick said, 'my medical adviser.' A very young girl with a lean pretty face nodded perfunctorily from behind a typewriter. 'I am going to train Elisabeth,' Mr. Fennick said, 'to act as bursar. The strain of being both bursar and president of the college is upsetting my stomach. The pills . . . thank you.'

Mr. Priskett said humbly, 'And what do you think of the college, Miss Fennick?'

'My name's Cross,' the girl said. 'I think it's a good idea. I'm surprised my uncle thought of it.'

'In a way it was—partly—my idea.'

'I'm more surprised still,' the girl said firmly.

Mr. Priskett, folding his hands in front of his white coat as though he were pleading before a tribunal, went on: 'You see I said to your uncle that with all these colleges being taken over by the military and the tutors having nothing to do they ought to start teaching by correspondence.'

'A glass of audit ale, Priskett?' Mr. Fennick suggested. He took a bottle of brown ale out of a cupboard and poured out two gaseous glasses.

'Of course,' Mr. Priskett pleaded, 'I hadn't thought of all this— the common-room, I mean, and St. Ambrose's.'

'My niece,' Mr. Fennick said, 'knows very little of the set-up.' He began to move restlessly around the room, touching things with his hand. He was rather like an aged bird of prey inspecting the grim components of its nest.

The girl said briskly, 'As I see it, Uncle is running a swindle called St. Ambrose's College, Oxford.'

'Not a swindle, my dear. The advertisement was very carefully worded.' He knew it by heart: every phrase had been carefully checked with his copy of *Every Man His Own Lawyer* open on the table. He repeated it now in a voice full and husky with bottled brown ale. 'War conditions prevent you going up to Oxford. St. Ambrose's—Tom Brown's old college—has made an important break with tradition. For the period of the war only it will be possible to receive tuition by post wherever you may be, whether defending the empire on the cold rocks of Iceland or on the burning sands of Libya, in the main street of an American town or a cottage in Devonshire. . . .'

'You've overdone it,' the girl said. 'You always do. That hasn't got a cultured ring. It won't catch anybody but saps.'

'There are plenty of saps,' Mr. Fennick said.

'Go on.'

'Well, I'll skip that bit. "Degree-diplomas will be granted at the end of three terms instead of the usual three years."' He explained: 'That gives a quick turnover. One can't wait for money these days. "Gain a real Oxford education at Tom Brown's old college. For full particulars of tuition fees, battels, &c., write to the Bursar."'

'And do you mean to say the University can't stop that?'

'Anybody,' Mr. Fennick said with a kind of pride, 'can start a college anywhere. I've never said it was part of the University.'

'But battels—battels mean board and lodging.'

'In this case,' Mr. Fennick said, 'it's quite a nominal fee—to keep your name in perpetuity on the books of the old firm—I mean, the college.'

'And the tuition . . .'

'Priskett here is the science tutor. I take history and classics. I thought that you, my dear, might tackle—economics?'

'I don't know anything about them.'

'The examinations, of course, have to be rather simple—within the capacity of the tutors. (There is an excellent public library here.) And another thing—the fees are returnable if the diploma-degree is not granted.'

'You mean . . .'

'Nobody will ever fail,' Mr. Priskett brought breathlessly out with scared excitement.

'And are you really getting results?'

'I waited, my dear, until I could see the distinct possibility of at least six hundred a year for the three of us before I wired you. And today—beyond all my expectations—I have received a letter from Lord Driver. He is entering his son at St. Ambrose's.'

'But how can he come here?'

'In his absence, my dear, on his country's service. The Drivers have always been a military family. I looked them up in *Debrett*.'

'What do you think of it?' Mr. Priskett asked with anxiety and triumph.

'I think it's rich. Have you arranged a boat race?'

'There, Priskett,' Mr. Fennick said proudly, raising his glass of audit ale, 'I told you she was a girl of ideas.'

2

Directly he heard his landlady's feet upon the stairs, the elderly man with the grey shaven head began to lay his wet tea-leaves round the base of the aspidistra. When she opened the door he was dabbing the tea-leaves in tenderly with his fingers. 'A lovely plant, my dear.'

But she wasn't going to be softened at once: he could tell that: she waved a letter at him. 'Listen,' she said, 'what's this Lord Driver business?'

'My name, my dear: a good Christian name like Lord George Sanger had.'

'Then why don't they put Mr. Lord Driver on the letter?'

'Ignorance, just ignorance.'

'I don't want any hanky-panky from my house. It's always been honest.'

'Perhaps they didn't know if I was an esquire or just a plain mister, so they left it blank.'

'It's sent from St. Ambrose's College, Oxford: people like that ought to know.'

'It comes, my dear, of your having such a good address. W.1. And all the gentry live in Mewses.' He made a half-hearted snatch at the letter, but the landlady held it out of reach.

'What are the likes of you writing to Oxford College about?'

'My dear,' he said with strained dignity, 'I may have been a little unfortunate: it may even be that I have spent a few years in chokey, but I have the rights of a free man.'

'And a son in quod.'

'Not in quod, my dear. Borstal is quite another institution. It is— a kind of college.'

'Like St. Ambrose's.'

'Perhaps not quite of the same rank.'

He was too much for her: he was usually in the end too much for her. Before his first stay at the Scrubs he had held a number of positions as manservant and even butler: the way he raised his eyebrows he had learned from Lord Charles Manville: he wore his clothes like an eccentric peer, and you might say that he had even learned the best way to pilfer from old Lord Bellew who had a penchant for silver spoons.

'And now, my dear, if you'd just let me have my letter?' He put his hand tentatively forward: he was as daunted by her as she was by him: they sparred endlessly and lost to each other: interminably the battle was never won—they were always afraid. This time it was his victory. She slammed the door. Suddenly, ferociously, when the door had closed, he made a little vulgar noise at the aspidistra. Then he put on his glasses and began to read.

His son had been accepted for St. Ambrose's, Oxford. The great fact stared up at him above the sprawling decorative signature of the President. Never had he been more thankful for the coincidence of his name. 'It will be my great pleasure,' the President wrote, 'to pay personal attention to your son's career at St. Ambrose's. In these days it is an honour to welcome a member of a great military family like yours.' Driver felt an odd mixture of amusement and of genuine pride. He'd put one over on them, but his breast swelled within his waistcoat at the idea that now he had a son at Oxford.

But there were two snags—minor snags when he considered how far he'd got already. It was apparently an old Oxford custom that fees should be paid in advance, and then there were the examinations. His son couldn't do them himself: Borstal would not allow it, and he wouldn't be out for another six months. Besides the whole beauty of the idea was that he should receive the gift of an Oxford Degree as a kind of welcome home. Like a chess-player who is always several moves ahead he was already seeing his way around these difficulties.

The fees he felt sure in his case were only a matter of bluff: a peer could always get credit, and if there was any trouble after the degree had been awarded, he could just tell them to sue and be damned. No Oxford college would like to admit that they'd been imposed on by an old lag. But the examinations. A funny little knowing smile twitched the corners of his mouth: a memory of the Scrubs five years ago and the man they called Daddy, the Reverend Simon Milan. He was a short-time prisoner—they were all short-time prisoners at the Scrubs: no sentence of over three years was ever served there. He remembered the tall lean aristocratic parson with his iron-grey hair and his narrow face like a lawyer's which had gone somehow soft inside with too much love. A prison, when you came to think of it, contained as much knowledge as a University: there were doctors, financiers, clergy. He knew where he could find

Mr. Milan: he was employed in a boarding-house near Euston Square, and for a few drinks he would do most things—he would certainly make out some fine examination papers. 'I can just hear him now,' Driver told himself ecstatically, 'talking Latin to the warders.'

3

It was autumn in Oxford: people coughed in the long queues for sweets and cakes: and the mists from the river seeped into the cinemas past the commissionaires on the lookout for people without gas-masks. A few undergraduates picked their way through the evacuated swarm: they always looked in a hurry: so much had to be got through in so little time before the army claimed them. There were lots of pickings for racketeers, Elisabeth Cross thought, but not much chance for a girl to find a husband: the oldest Oxford racket had been elbowed out by the black markets in Woodbines, toffees, tomatoes.

There had been a few days last spring when she had treated St. Ambrose's as a joke, but when she saw the money actually coming in, the whole thing seemed less amusing. Then for some weeks she was acutely unhappy—until she realized that of all the war-time rackets this was the most harmless. They were not reducing supplies like the Ministry of Food, or destroying confidence like the Ministry of Information: her uncle paid income tax, and they even to some extent educated people. The saps, when they took their diploma-degrees would know several things they hadn't known before.

But that didn't help a girl to find a husband.

She came moodily out of the matinée, carrying a bunch of papers she should have been correcting. There was only one 'student' who showed any intelligence at all, and that was Lord Driver's son. The papers were forwarded from 'somewhere in England' via London by his father: she had nearly found herself caught out several times on points of history, and her uncle she knew was straining his rusty Latin to the limit.

When she got home she knew that there was something in the air: Mr. Priskett was sitting in his white coat on the edge of a chair and her uncle was finishing a stale bottle of beer. When something went wrong he never opened a new bottle: he believed in happy drinking. They watched her come in in silence: Mr. Priskett's silence was gloomy, her uncle's preoccupied. Something had to be got round—it couldn't be the university authorities: they had stopped bothering him long ago—a lawyer's letter, an irascible interview, and their attempt to maintain 'a monopoly of local education'—as Mr. Fennick put it—had ceased.

'Good evening,' Elisabeth said: Mr. Priskett looked at Mr. Fennick and Mr. Fennick frowned.

'Has Mr. Priskett run out of pills?'

Mr. Priskett winced.

'I've been thinking,' Elisabeth said, 'that as we are now in the third term of the academic year, I should like a rise in salary.'

Mr. Priskett drew in his breath sharply, keeping his eyes on Mr. Fennick.

'I should like another three pounds a week.'

Mr. Fennick rose from the table; he glared ferociously into the top of his dark ale; his frown beetled. The chemist scraped his chair a little backward. And then Mr. Fennick spoke.

'We are such stuff as dreams are made on,' he said and hiccupped slightly.

'Kidneys,' Elisabeth said.

'Rounded by a sleep. And these our cloud-capped towers . . .'

'You are misquoting.'

'Vanished into air, into thin air.'

'You've been correcting the English papers.'

'Unless you allow me to think, to think rapidly and deeply, there won't be any more examination papers,' Mr. Fennick said.

'Trouble?'

'I've always been a Republican at heart. I don't see why we want a hereditary peerage.'

'*A la lanterne*,' Elisabeth said.

'This man, Lord Driver: why should a mere accident of birth . . .?'

'He refuses to pay?'

'It isn't that. A man like that expects credit: it's right that he should have credit. But he's written to say that he's coming down to-morrow to see his boy's college. The old fat-headed sentimental fool,' Mr. Fennick said.

'I knew you'd be in trouble sooner or later.'

'That's the sort of damn fool comfortless thing a girl would say.'

'It just needs brain.'

Mr. Fennick picked up a brass ash-tray—and then put it down again carefully.

'It's quite simple as soon as you begin to think.'

'Think.'

Mr. Priskett scraped a chair-leg.

'I'll meet him at the station with a taxi, and take him to—say Balliol. Lead him straight through into the inner quad, and there you'll be, just looking as if you'd come out of the Master's lodging.'

'He'll know it's Balliol.'

'He won't. Anybody who knew Oxford couldn't be sap enough to send his son to St. Ambrose's.'

'Of course it's true. These military families are a bit crass.'

'You'll be in an enormous hurry. Consecration or something. Whip him round the Hall, the chapel, the Library, and hand him back to me outside the Master's. I'll take him out to lunch and see him into his train. It's simple.'

Mr. Fennick said broodingly, 'Sometimes I think you're a terrible girl, terrible. Is there nothing you wouldn't think up?'

'I believe,' Elisabeth said, 'that if you're going to play your own game in a world like this, you've got to play it properly. Of course,' she said, 'if you are going to play a different game you go to a nunnery or to the wall and like it. But I've only got one game to play.'

4

It really went off very smoothly. Driver found Elisabeth at the barrier: she didn't find him because she was expecting something different. Something about him worried her: it wasn't his clothes or the monocle he never seemed to use—it was something subtler than that. It was almost as though he were afraid of her, he was so ready to fall in with her plans. 'I don't want to be any trouble, my dear, any trouble at all. I know how busy the President must be.' When she explained that they would be lunching together in town, he even seemed relieved. 'It's just the bricks of the dear old place,' he said. 'You mustn't mind my being a sentimentalist, my dear.'

'Were you at Oxford?'

'No, no. The Drivers, I'm afraid, have neglected the things of the mind.'

'Well, I suppose a soldier needs brains?'

He took a sharp look at her, and then answered in quite a

different sort of voice: 'We believed so in the Lancers.' Then he strolled beside her to the taxi, twirling his monocle, and all the way up from the station he was silent, taking little quiet sideways peeks at her, appraising, approving.

'So this is St. Ambrose's,' he said in a hearty voice just beside the porter's lodge and she pushed him quickly by, through the first quad towards the Master's house, where on the doorstep with a B.A. gown over his arm stood Mr. Fennick permanently posed like a piece of garden statuary. 'My uncle, the President,' Elisabeth said.

'A charming girl, your niece,' Driver said as soon as they were alone together: he had really only meant to make conversation, but as soon as he had spoken the old two crooked minds began to move in harmony.

'She's very home-loving,' Mr. Fennick said. 'Our famous elms,' he went on, waving his hand skywards. 'St. Ambrose's rooks.'

'Crooks?' Driver said with astonishment.

'Rooks. In the elms. One of our great modern poets wrote about them. "St. Ambrose elms, oh St. Ambrose elms", and about "St. Ambrose rooks calling in wind and rain".'

'Pretty. Very pretty.'

'Nicely turned, I think.'

'I mean your niece.'

'Ah, yes. This way to the Hall. Up these steps. So often trodden, you know, by Tom, Brown.'

'Who was Tom Brown?'

'The great Tom Brown—one of Rugby's famous sons.' He added thoughtfully. 'She'll make a fine wife—and mother.'

'Young men are beginning to realise that the flighty ones are not what they want for a lifetime.'

They stopped by mutual consent on the top step: they nosed towards each other like two old blind sharks who each believes that what stirs the water close to him is tasty meat.

'Whoever wins her,' Mr. Fennick said, 'can feel proud. She'll make a fine hostess . . .' as the future Lady Driver, he thought.

'I and my son,' Driver said, 'have talked seriously about marriage. He takes rather an old-fashioned view. He'll make a good husband. . . .'

They walked into the hall, and Mr. Fennick led the way round the portraits. 'Our founder,' he said, pointing at a full-bottomed wig. He chose it deliberately: he felt it smacked a little of himself. Before Swinburne's portrait he hesitated: then pride in St. Ambrose's conquered caution. 'The great poet Swinburne,' he said. 'We sent him down.'

'Expelled him?'

'Yes. Bad morals.'

'I'm glad you are strict about those.'

'Ah, your son is in safe hands at St. Ambrose's.'

'It makes me very happy,' Driver said. He began to scrutinise the portrait of a nineteenth-century divine. 'Fine brushwork,' he said. 'Now religion—I believe in religion. Basis of the family.' He said with a burst of confidence, 'You know our young people ought to meet.'

Mr. Fennick gleamed happily. 'I agree.'

'If he passes . . .'

'Oh, he'll certainly pass,' Mr. Fennick said.

'He'll be on leave in a week or two. Why shouldn't he take his degree in person?'

'Well, there'd be difficulties.'

'Isn't it the custom?'

'Not for postal graduates. The Vice-Chancellor likes to make a small distinction. . . . But, Lord Driver, in the case of so distinguished an alumnus I suggest that I should be deputed to present the degree to your son in London.'

'I'd like him to see his college.'

'And so he shall in happier days. So much of the college is shut now. I would like him to visit it for the first time when its glory is restored. Allow me and my niece to call on you.'

'We are living very quietly.'

'Not serious financial trouble, I hope?'

'Oh, no, no.'

'I'm so glad. And now let us rejoin the dear girl.'

5

It always seemed to be more convenient to meet at railway stations. The coincidence didn't strike Mr. Fennick who had fortified himself for the journey with a good deal of audit ale, but it struck Elisabeth. The college lately had not been fulfilling expectations, and that was partly due to the laziness of Mr. Fennick: from his conversation lately it almost seemed as though he had begun to regard the college as only a step to something else—what she couldn't quite make out. He was always talking about Lord Driver and his son Frederick and the responsibilities of the peerage. His Republican tendencies had quite lapsed. 'That dear boy,' was the way he referred to Frederick, and he marked him 100 per cent. for Classics. 'It's not often Latin and Greek go with military genius,' he said. 'A remarkable boy.'

'He's not so hot on economics,' Elisabeth said.

'We mustn't demand too much book-learning from a soldier.'

At Paddington Lord Driver waved anxiously to them through the crowd: he wore a very new suit—one shudders to think how many coupons had been gambled away for the occasion. A little behind him was a very young man with a sullen mouth and a scar on his cheek. Mr. Fennick bustled forward: he wore a black raincoat over his shoulders like a cape and carrying his hat in his hand he disclosed his white hair venerably among the porters.

'My son—Frederick,' Lord Driver said. The boy sullenly took off his hat and put it on again quickly: they wore their hair in the army very short.

'St. Ambrose's welcomes her new graduate,' Mr. Fennick said.

Frederick grunted.

The presentation of the degree was made in a private room at Mount Royal. Lord Driver explained that his house had been bombed—a time bomb, he added, a rather necessary explanation since there had been no raids recently. Mr. Fennick was satisfied if Lord Driver was: he had brought up a B.A. gown, a mortar-board and a Bible in his suitcase, and he made quite an imposing little ceremony between the booktable, the sofa and the radiator, reading out a Latin oration and tapping Frederick lightly on the head with the Bible. The degree-diploma had been expensively printed in two colours by an Anglo-Catholic firm. Elisabeth was the only uneasy person there. Could the world, she wondered, really contain two such saps? What was this painful feeling growing up in her that perhaps it contained four?

. After a little light lunch with bottled brown beer—'almost as good, if I may say so, as our audit ale,' Mr. Fennick beamed—the President and Lord Driver made elaborate moves to drive the two young people out together. 'We've got to talk a little business,' Mr. Fennick said, and Lord Driver hinted, 'You've not been to the flickers for a year, Frederick.' They were driven out together into bombed shabby Oxford Street while the old men rang cheerfully down for whisky.

'What's the idea?' Elisabeth said.

He was good-looking: she liked his scar and his sullenness; there was almost too much intelligence and purpose in his eyes. Once he took off his hat and scratched his head: Elisabeth again noticed his short hair. He certainly didn't look a military type. And his suit, like his father's, looked new and ready-made. Hadn't he had any clothes to wear when he came on leave?

'I suppose,' she said, 'they are planning a wedding.'

His eyes lit gleefully up. 'I wouldn't mind,' he said.

'You'd have to get leave from your C.O., wouldn't you?'

'C.O.?' he asked in astonishment, flinching a little like a boy who has been caught out, who hasn't been prepared beforehand with that question. She watched him carefully, remembering all the things that had seemed to her since the beginning odd.

'So you haven't been to the movies for a year,' she said.

'I've been on service.'

'Not even an Ensa show?'

'Oh, I don't count those.'

'It must be awfully like being in prison.'

He grinned weakly, walking faster all the time, so that she might really have been pursuing him through the Hyde Park gates.

'Come clean,' she said. 'Your father's not Lord Driver.'

'Oh yes he is.'

'Any more than my uncle's President of a College.'

'What?' He began to laugh—it was an agreeable laugh, a laugh you couldn't trust but a laugh which made you laugh back and agree that in a crazy world like this all sorts of things didn't matter a hang. 'I'm just out of Borstal,' he said. 'What's yours?'

'Oh, I haven't been in prison yet.'

He said, 'You'll never believe me, but all that ceremony—it looked phoney to me. Of course the Dad swallowed it.'

'And my uncle swallowed you. . . . I couldn't quite.'

'Well the wedding's off. In a way I'm sorry.'

'I'm still free.'

'Well,' he said, 'we might discuss it,' and there in the pale autumn sunlight of the park they did discuss it—from all sorts of angles. There were bigger frauds all round them; officials of the Ministries passed carrying little portfolios: controllers of this and that purred by in motor-cars, and men with the big blank faces of advertisement hoardings strode purposefully in khaki with scarlet tabs down Park Lane from the Dorchester. Their fraud was a small one by the world's standard, and a harmless one: the boy from Borstal and the girl from nowhere at all—from the draper's counter and the semi-detached villa. 'He's got a few hundred stowed away. I'm sure of that,' said Fred. 'He'd make a settlement if he thought he could get the President's niece.'

'I wouldn't be surprised if Uncle had five hundred. He'd put it all down for Lord Driver's son.'

'We'd take over this college business. With a bit of capital we could really make it go. It's just chicken-feed now.'

They fell in love for no reason at all, in the park, on a bench to save twopences, planning their fraud on the old frauds they knew they could outdo. Then they went back, and Elisabeth declared herself before she'd got properly inside the door. 'Frederick and I want to get married.' She almost felt sorry for the old fools as their faces lit suddenly simultaneously up because everything had been so easy, and then darkened with caution as they squinted at each other. 'This is very surprising,' Lord Driver said, and the President said, 'My goodness, young people work fast.'

All night the two old men planned their settlements, and the two young ones sat happily back in a corner, watching the elaborate fence, with the secret knowledge that the world is always open to the young.

JOYCE CARY
A Good Investment

OLD Mrs. Bill of Hunter's Green had three daughters, Daisy, Letty, and Francie, the youngest. Daisy is a spinster of fifty who travels round the world from one friend's house to another on cargo boats, buses, hitchhikes, and has, she says, a gorgeous time. She drinks a good deal when she can get it free, eats enormously, and loves a noise. Letty is married to a lawyer called Gordon Todd with a taste for archaeology which, it is said, has damaged his practice. They have two children, boy and girl, and Letty complains very much of their wildness, of all her housekeeping troubles and expenses. She spends much of her time in bed, and whenever the children or the husband are too much for her nerves, she telephones to her mother for Francie, who duly rushes over and takes charge of house, husband, and children for as long as Letty can keep her, that is, as long as her mother is ready to spare her. This is usually four days at the most.

Letty complains bitterly of her mother's selfishness when she recalls Francie even after a week. 'What does she want with Francie—she has Mrs. Jones, and there's only herself to look after. And after all Mother is a good deal stronger than I am.'

Mrs. Bill says that Letty is a poor spoiled lily and that she preys on Francie. But she does not excuse Francie for deserting her because she blames Francie for having spoiled Letty at the beginning. 'There's no need for Francie to rush away at a word from Letty and it's very bad for Letty. But it's Francie's affair. I never interfere.'

Francie says nothing. She has no time between her various duties of keeping Mrs. Jones the housekeeper in a good temper, managing her mother's parties; and she knows too that anything she said would only irritate Letty and bring from her mother the remark, 'But why all the fuss? I never fuss, life is too short.'

Francie Bill is a very small woman, about thirty-five years of age, with a big round forehead, deeply lined, small grey eyes, and a rather prominent round chin. Her mouth is good and it has a very serious expression, except when she laughs. She laughs with her whole face, causing her eyes to disappear and her wrinkles to deepen.

Some time ago Francie had a love affair, but for months no one even realized it except the lover. He was a widower with a daughter of nine. His name was Catto, aged forty-eight, partner in a printing firm, moderately well off, and, as he considered, good at life. That is to say, he knew how to make a success of most things. His marriage had been successful, but he was not at all afraid, like so many prudent citizens who have had lucky marriages, of taking another chance. He realized vey well how much luck had gone to his first choice—his wife, actually on the honeymoon, had changed into a different woman with exceedingly strong views on such delicate questions as where to live, how to decorate and manage a house, and which of her husband's friends were worth keeping up with. It was pure luck that he had agreed with her.

But he considered that a man of his age and experience would have more foresight in a second choice. He began to look round almost as soon as his wife was buried. He wanted above all a good housekeeper and a companion for his daughter—he was accustomed to good housekeeping and he distrusted nurses, even the most expensive. And he told himself that even from a financial point of view, the plan was justified. 'With wages at their highest and service at its worst, a competent wife is actually a first-class investment.'

And one day, by good luck, as he said afterwards, he met Daisy Bill at Wimbledon. He had barely settled himself on his stool in the morning queue, when a tall brown girl in a man's shirt, about three yards further down the row, called out loudly, 'Bill, Bill,' and then, 'Daisy.'

Catto as a small boy had known the Bill family very well. For three summers running they had shared the same lodgings at the seaside, and he had got on very well with Daisy especially, nearest to him in age. He had even fallen a good deal in love with Daisy at fifteen, during their last holiday together.

He thought, even before he identified the girl, 'Daisy Bill, could it be the old Daisy, and not married? If Daisy really isn't married, then what about her? The right age, too old for babies, I don't want a rival to poor little Jean, and Daisy was really a very nice girl in a very nice way—good-natured, healthy, and she would probably have money too. As far as I can remember all the Bill girls had something coming from the aunt who maried into toothpaste.'

He looked round him, half stood up, and after a moment recognized Daisy. 'She must be that huge red-faced woman with the cigarette-holder shaped like a pipe. She couldn't be anyone else with that nose and those eyes. Yes, there she is waving to her friend.'

He excused himself to the neighbours and edged past them to present himself. Daisy knew him at once. She cried out in a voice to be heard ten yards away, 'Good Lord, Tommy, Tom Cat!' and wrung his fingers in a powerful clasp. 'But how wonderful, you haven't changed a bit. How extraordinary. What a bit of luck. You must join us.' The neighbours in the queue, discreetly interested and pleased, with that almost family feeling which belongs to the Wimbledon queue, made way for his stool, and he joined the Bill party. It consisted now of Daisy, a little thin, sharp woman who turned out to be a celebrated authoress, and the brown girl in the man's shirt who was a tennis star, a county champion.

Catto had been shocked by the change in Daisy's looks, but her greeting reassured him. He was reminded again of his old love, her easy good nature, her freedom from all those airs which in a girl of sixteen he most detested, touchiness and sudden changes of mood. He had told himself then that, with all her charm, she was as reliable a friend as any of the boys at school.

'Good heavens,' Daisy said, breathing tobacco in his face, 'do you remember those walks along the shore? And how you hated the kids for trailing after us?' She gave a loud laugh and then, dropping his hand, turned to the champion and exclaimed in a serious tone, as one who takes up again the more important affairs of life, 'So you don't think much of Seixas' service?'

And the pair continued their tennis gossip with enthusiasm. Catto might not have existed for either of them.

The authoress, having glared at the champion for some time, dismissed Catto with a single glance, and then, with a twist of her little pursed mouth and a droop of her eyelids, fell into a gloomy meditation which made her all at once ten years older and gave her a sad but distinguished beauty.

Catto had no recollection of his jealousy; Daisy seemed to have a more accurate memory of their affair. But he was already sorry that he had so impulsively presented himself. He observed his old friend with a rueful amusement. 'Yes, steady as a boy and now a regular fellow.' He recoiled from this bluff Daisy. It was obvious why she had never married. And neither of her sisters, even if they were unmarried, had ever attracted him. The languid, fragile, lovely Letty, always being rescued from crabs and wrapped up from the cold; the rat-tailed Francie, at six, with her red button of a nose, hurling herself into the seas and making love to the very fishermen.

But just before the party, having obtained its tickets, dispersed for lunch, Daisy recalled her manners and became even more hearty, asked after his family, expressed a manly sympathy for his loss, and told of her own father's death. But her mother was still at the old place, she would so like to see him again. Why not come out next week-end? There was to be quite an amusing party to dinner.

Catto accepted these attentions in their own spirit and resolved not to go to dinner on any account. Why waste time on the Bills if Daisy was not a suitable prospect? He was put out when Mrs. Bill wrote to him. She also expressed her sympathy, a cheerful sympathy: 'These things must happen, one has to take them,' and she pressed him to come to dinner. 'You remember Hunter's? It's just the same, and Daisy tells me so are you. Isn't that nice? It's quite encouraging in these days when everything else seems to get worse and worse, including the people. But poor things, I suppose they can't be blamed for being so flat when the newspapers are so full of bombs. Though I can't imagine why everyone should go off so terribly before the bombs even tick, or whatever they do when they drop.'

And in a postscript she wrote, 'Quite a small party, about eight, don't dress. Mrs. Mair is coming, who lost her husband last year in that plane crash, and the Offer girl who used to be so fond of you.'

Catto seemed to hear a voice, a rattling little voice like a cracked dinner bell. He had not heard it for thirty years, in fact since his last holiday with the Bills, before he had gone to the university and they had gone to Switzerland for Letty's health. He had not paid much attention to it then. Mrs. Bill had not talked much with boys of his age, nor, indeed, with her own children. She had been preoccupied with her handsome husband and the half-dozen other men, much older than herself, who frequented the house. Even at the seaside her life had been a series of parties, chiefly on yachts. The Bills had taken rooms at Clarksfoot, small and remote, unfashionable and even uncouth, with its mining workers, its Welsh Bethels singing hymns on the beach, because of her frined, Lord S., who kept his big yacht there.

S. asked her to his parties in harbour, but did not expect her to
go cruising. Mrs. Bill was a very bad sailor. Her stories of her own
feelings on the sea were among her most amusing. The voice tinkled
with laughter in the background of Catto's mind. But now that it
came back to him in the cadences of the note, so neatly written in a
minute, precise hand, he found, to his surprise, that he liked his
memory of Mrs. Bill, as of someone always gay, lively, good-
tempered, and tolerant. 'Perhaps she did not trouble much with us
children, but she never worried us either. She understood how to
make things pleasant and comfortable. And then this widow, Mrs.
Mair? I know Mrs. Bill was a bit of a match-maker. But why not—
a widow might be the answer for me. She'd know the ropes and
wouldn't have fantastic expectations, and yet she would appreciate
the solid advantages of a husband and being on good terms with
him. And this Offer girl too, she must be somewhere near my age if
she was fond of me thirty years ago.'

He accepted Mrs. Bill's invitation; and it was true that the house
had not changed. But the neighbourhood had. The place had been
a farm, and Theodore Bill had even kept it as a farm, without a
bailiff, losing money every year. Now the farm house with its garden
stood incongruously in a vast new suburb which was actually
named after it, Hunter's Green.

Catto, opening the old wooden gate, a farm gate still, had the
sense of one who finds an unexpected treasure and, at the same
moment sees it fall into the dust, as the bodies of the old saints are
said to do when you dig them up. He had loved Hunter's Green
where he had ridden his first pony, and had his first passionate love,
with the slim, lovely girl who had put him over the jumps. With
Daisy, in short. And where was that Daisy now? She was less than
an existence, for the actual Daisy was already making faint and
unreliable even that sweet memory that had been a vivid existence.
And now Hunter's Green, the old Hunter's Green, the solid bricks,
the immense elms, the coach-house with its dovecot, mysteriously
disintegrated before his very eyes.

Hunter's Green had never pretended to beauty. It had always
been a plain house—square, three-storied, with a slate roof a little
too small, and a long lean-to conservatory.

In the farm among its trees, with the cows grazing opposite the
windows, this plainness had been a charm. It seemed to say, 'I am
the unpretending home of plain country people.' True, Theodore

and Tottie Bill were anything but plain country people. But for that very reason, they had appreciated Hunter's Green, and carefully preserved its honest want of make-up.

But now the rough five-bar gate, the coarse grass in the lawn which was much too small for a paddock, a minute haycock in one corner of it, and the rusty pump at the angle of the wall, looked false, stagy. They had indeed become false by being preserved into a different age.

Catto went in expecting more disappointment of the same kind, relics of the past that spoiled and obscured the past by their meretricious survival. He was delighted, therefore, by Mrs. Bill. The little woman seemed no older. She was the same—pretty, vivacious, with her fine thin nose, her dead white skin, her black eyes that sparkled all the more for the contrast of her cheeks, her cracked voice, her high Edwardian handshake.

'Ah, but this is an occasion—don't you feel the sand between your toes? Don't you smell the stairs on the *Naiad*? I have never been able to use rubber since poor S. died. It makes me cry and it makes me seasick, and those are two things that simply can't go together. Some people drink claret with oysters, yes I know, I met such a man and he wasn't a character part. In fact, it was old Roger Kent.' And turning to another guest, 'Do you remember Roger in *Mrs. Tanqueray*?'

She had turned from Catto, as Daisy had turned from him, to a more responsive audience, and seeing her white curly head from behind, he reflected, 'But she was dark then—she must be seventy. I think she hasn't changed because I've been getting old too. And certainly she's kept her features.'

The dinner was quite good, the company distinguished, if not of the first distinction. A well-known Shakespearian actor, sholarly and earnest like all those who have never been stars; an ugly, amusing old critic with a broken nose, like a boxer's nose; and the vicar, a big red-faced man, full of good stories, and, Catto would have said, old port, a type that he had not met for years, and enjoyed. 'A sensible stout fellow,' he thought, 'and probably a fine preacher. I wish we had more of them in the Church. Good fellows with their feet on the ground.'

Mrs. Mair, a well-known women's editor under her maiden name, arrived late with a new husband, and the Offer girl, a thin pale creature of about seventeen, enthusiastic about ballet, had never even heard of Catto. He remembered that Mrs. Bill was celebrated for her inconsequence. It had been one of her charms and, because it had been a charm, he enjoyed it again.

Francie was the eighth at the table. That is to say, she did not appear till after the soup, when, flushed, hot, with damp hair and red shiny nose, she slipped into her place between the young bridegroom and the critic's wife.

As the vicar sat opposite Mrs. Bill it was impossible to alternate the sexes, and Catto, on her left, sat next to the critic. No one explained Francie, or her sudden appearance. Catto was left to infer, after some reflection, that this thick-set woman, with grey streaks in her hair, must be the youngest Bill daughter, Frank, Frankie, Francie. He could not recognize her at all. But when she disappeared again with the chickens, and came in soon after the ice pudding, he perceived that she was acting as cook. The maid who waited was no doubt a daily woman, possibly a waiter hired only for the party. And when the party moved to the veranda, overlooking the bogus paddock and the decorator's haycock, he noticed that Francie not only arranged her mother's cushions but mixed the vicar's whisky and fetched the actor's pipe from his room.

The actor, Maxton, was staying in the house. He seemed like an old family friend, and when Francie, noticing that he fumbled in his pocket, silently disappeared and brought the pipe, he did not interrupt his description of Bernhardt's absurd masterpiece in *L'Aiglon*, he received the pipe with his fingers as a man at table who has dropped a fork takes a new one from the waiter.

'Or a father from a daughter,' Catto thought. 'But she calls him Mr. Maxton. He can't be so familiar. Yet she knew what he wanted and where to find it.'

And suddenly he had a new recollection of the old Francie, the child of six who had always been so dirty, noisy, always falling into the water, tearing her frocks, so often in the way when he had wanted to be alone with the lovely, so friendly Daisy. He recalled a general cry of 'Frankie, Frankie,' and the small girl with flying tangled hair tearing madly along the corridor; his brain lighted up a snapshot of Mrs. Bill at her prettiest in a white serge frock, standing on the stairs above a group of men and saying with a charming bend of her head, 'But don't bother, I'm absolutely fated to lose things. Frankie will find it for me,' and then again, 'Frankie is the practical one, aren't you, Frankie?'

And again he saw, at forty-eight, an angle of his old friends that, at eighteen, had made only an impression on his memory, none on his observation. Daisy had been so easy, so friendly, yes, and Mrs. Bill's tinkling voice had usually been heard by the children in these cheerful laments. She was always needing something fetched or found. Her good-humour confessed, 'I'm a nuisance, I know, but you'll forgive me because I forgive everyone else.'

And Frankie had been the practical one. Had they given her the character and made her a family slave, was she really fit for nothing else? And looking at the girl's face as she sat, silent as usual, half hidden behind her mother's chair, listening to the actor and the critic discussing Bernhardt, he thought amused by the recollection, 'Yes, how she trailed after me—after anything in trousers. How she would throw herself into my arms and say, "But Tom, you haven't kissed me good night." And I should think she's a real woman still—rather shy and dull perhaps but the tomboy has quite disappeared.' And suddenly he thought, 'Why not Francie, could I do better? A kind soul, modest, simple, pretty capable too if she cooked that dinner. Of course, she's a bit young—she can't be more than thirty-six. There could be a baby, and that's a complication I particularly wanted to avoid. Of course, one could make a bargain—babies barred. It's common enough in second marriages.'

He reflected a moment on this tricky point. But like many steady, careful fellows who look for a fair deal in life, he had also a strong sense of what is fair in dealing with others. 'No,' he thought, "if she wanted a baby I should have to give her one. On the other hand, youth does have some advantages. She'd stand up better to the job.'

He looked again at Francie, and caught her at a plainer moment. The lamp shine on her nose and the prominent forehead, a strand of damp hair, well steamed from the kitchen, was lying limp against her cheek. But Catto rallied. 'Damn it, I'm not a boy. What do looks matter? What I need is a good home-maker—someone to take an interest in Jean—domestic competence and peace.'

He sought some private talk with her, but this was difficult to manage. Rain was falling in thick heavy lines and the cars could not come down to the door because at Hunter's Green, as in a proper farmhouse, there was a little front garden full of old-fashioned flowers, with a narrow brick path to the front porch. The party stood crowded in the hall, looking out disgustedly, while Francie was busy with hats and coats.

When she brought him his coat he turned smiling and said, 'Frances, Frankie, do you remember Clarksfoot?'

But Mrs. Bill interrupted with a remark to the world, 'Dear me, there used to be a carriage umbrella in the hall. But it seems to have lost itself. Everything in this house gets itself lost.'

Francie, still silent, ran for the carriage umbrella in the back passage and escorted the guests to their cars.

Catto, who had come by train and taxi, had a lift in the critic's car. He made one more attempt to speak to Francie from the back window. 'Thank you, Francie, do you remember how you used to go round at bedtime and wish us all good night?'

The girl had turned away at a call from the house. Someone had dropped a scarf. She did not even hear him. But Catto was a determined man. He wrote to Mrs. Bill, thanking her for a delightful evening, and asked her to the theatre 'with my old friend Francie'.

And when Mrs. Bill refused on account of an engagement, he took the train again to Hunter's Green and called.

He was lucky. Mrs. Bill was out, and Frances was weeding the garden. In an old pair of trousers, gardening boots, a plaid shirt, and a handkerchief tied over her hair, she looked like a picture of slave labour in a Soviet camp. But she received Catto with something of Daisy's frankness. 'I'm sorry Mother's out, but she'll be in at six. Do wait. She'll be so upset to miss you.'

'Thanks, I should like to. And how are you, Francie? I didn't really see you last week.'

'Do you mind if I finish this border—I've got so behind with the weeds.'

'No—let me help you.'

'Oh you couldn't—you'll get filthy.'

'I can wash.'

'Are you sure you know which are weeds?'

'I see you're still practical.'

The woman looked at him in surprise. He explained his point, as a joke, but she did not smile. She reflected and said at last, 'I wonder——'

'You were a quaint little thing at six.'

But she was weeding again, he saw only the short broad back.

'You don't remember me at all.'

'Not really.' She stood up again and looked at him intently. She was obviously curious, she felt that his visit had some purpose beyond a mere call.

She shook her head, 'Mother says that you were Daisy's great friend.'

'I liked to think I was yours too. You never let me leave the house without a kiss.'

'Oh well, at six.' She dismissed this carelessly. She was not at all embarrassed, as Catto had expected. She showed no shyness. Indeed now that he had been able to talk to her, he felt that she had grown up with something of the Bill poise. She asked him abruptly, 'What do you do, Mr. Catto? Tell me about yourself.'

'That's a very dull story. I'm a printer, a widower, with a young daughter—forty-eight years old. Really there's nothing more to tell.'

'Is it long since you——' she hesitated.

'Lost my wife? No, eighteen months. But it seems a very long time indeed. We were very happy—I am a lonely man, Francie—a very lonely man. Men like me who have been happily married and then widowed, suffer a very special kind of loneliness.'

The woman looked at him and the wrinkles in her forehead were very noticeable. 'Yes, I can imagine it. I'm sorry. But then you did have all that happiness.'

'It's a danger.'

'Yes, it's a danger. But worth it. Or don't you think so? Perhaps now——'

'Oh yes, tremendously worth it.'

'In fact, in spite of everything, you've been——'

'Yes, I've been lucky. I was always rather lucky. I was lucky to know you when I was a boy.'

'Me——'

'I mean the family as a whole. Yes, you too. You were rather an important part of the experience.'

The woman looked at him and her expression was critical. She was taking a new view of this middle-aged man who made such rapid advances. Then she said that she must really get the weeding done, and set to work. No word was said for twenty minutes and the silence itself was expressive. It said plainly that there was a situation.

'I've been too sudden,' Catto said to himself. 'She doesn't seem shy—at thirty-six, she knows how to manage her feelings. But she's timid and wary.'

The bed finished, they straightened up together face to face, and the girl smiled in a broad and frank manner. Her whole face expressed a personal interest. She had settled something with herself. 'Come Mr. Catto, you need tea, or a drink.'

'Why Mr. Catto?'

'Well, what did I call you?'

'I was Tom to you all.'

'Come, Tom, we'll have tea.' She blushed as she spoke and stooped to gather her basket.

For the moment, Catto was afraid that he had been too enterprising. He did not want to commit himself to the girl before he knew her better. He had, as we have seen, as well as prudence, a strong sense of responsibility.

But the woman at once recovered her practical air. She had placed Catto to her satisfaction as a nice middle-aged man eager to renew his childhood memories. They talked of the days at Clarksfoot, they exchanged news. She told how Mrs. Bill after her husband's death had lost most of her money and sold the land, how Daisy loved travelling and seldom appeared at home, how Letty needed special treatment and how much it cost.

He told her about his marriage, about Jean, and how hard he thought it for a girl of nine to lose her mother. That he had seriously considered marrying again, on her account alone.

'I'm sure you're right,' Francie said, 'if you can find the right person.'

'That's the problem.'

'A widow perhaps, without children, who wanted a child to care for.'

'I'm not so sure. A younger woman might be a better companion.'

'A widow could be quite young. There are lots of young widows. What about war widows?'

'It's the person that matters. I don't see why she need be a widow.'

'Oh no, of course.'

'Or why I shouldn't have another baby if she were young enough.'

There was a pause, and Catto again thought that he had been indiscreet. But the woman was only reflecting. 'You'd have to discuss that with the new wife.' In fact, it was not till three months later, when Catto actually proposed in so many words that Francie understood him.

'You really want to marry me?'

'Yes, yes. I've been trying to tell you so for the last fortnight.'

'Well, I did wonder sometimes but I didn't like to think——'

'But you haven't answered me yet.'

'But don't you see?'

'What?'

'Why I didn't like to think. Why Tom,' and she laughed that tomboyish broad laugh which brought all her wrinkles and made her little eyes disappear, 'of course I'll marry you.'

The laugh disappeared and she looked suddenly very serious. All at once Catto understood that the headlong Francie of thirty years before was still there. He was much startled. He had not expected so passionate a kiss, so eager an embrace.

Mrs. Bill was greatly amused by the news. She congratulated Catto and said, laughing, 'Sir Galahad to the rescue, or is it Perseus? But I'm not really a monster, you know, and Francie loves her chains. She adores a fuss.' Catto, taken by surprise, found himself turning red. He did not know what to answer. But Mrs. Bill had dashed on at once, 'Letty will hate you, but it won't do Letty any harm to take a little exercise.'

He received a most friendly letter from Daisy in Venezuela, who said how glad she was to see that her darling Francie was to get away from home at last and have some life of her own. She wanted Catto to 'keep mother at bay, for Francie's sake, or you'll have no peace'.

The wedding was quiet. Mrs. Bill forgot to provide linen and Francie bought her own wedding dress, but Catto presented his bride with the latest refrigerator, freezer, enamelled stove, and double sink in a completely remodelled kitchen, and all Mrs. Bill's old friends sent autographed copies of their works—published twenty or thirty years before, period sensations now wearing as strange a look as the hats and skirts of that ancient world in which they had achieved their distinction.

Catto had already arranged for a honeymoon in Paris. His first honeymoon had been in Paris. Francie had hoped for Italy, but she enjoyed Paris enormously as a bride. And she was deeply apologetic when the month they had planned was cut a week short because Daisy came back from Jamaica, in a banana boat, with a mysterious

illness called Daisy's fever, and the Cattos had to hurry home to
look after her. But Catto could not complain that Daisy looked
upon his home as a refuge in time of trouble.

Francie nursed her for six weeks before Catto got a hint, from
Mrs. Bill, that Daisy's fever came on only when she was broke.
'Don't let her kill Francie,' she wrote. 'Daisy has always treated
Francie as her private and personal slave. Have you tried the gold
cure for the fever? A cheque, I've found, is far the best prescription.'

Daisy had been complaining every day of all the wonderful
holidays she was missing by this unlucky illness, and Catto now
offered her a loan of twenty pounds to take advantage of an
invitation to Finland. She left the next morning by milk-float to
catch a trawler whose captain was an old Bombay friend. Catto,
relieved, told himself that Daisy would not come very often. But he
protested when Francie confessed that she had engaged herself to
stay three days at Hunter's Green in order to cook for her mother's
traditional Easter party. He wrote to Mrs. Bill suggesting that he
should advertise for a temporary cook. But she answered none was
required.

'Francie seems to think she ought to come, but it's quite unnecessary—Mrs. Jones is quite lazy enough as it is. She does just as
little as she dares.' She addressed the note to Galahad Catto, Esq.,
and signed herself 'the monster'.

Catto took it to Francie and said, 'You see, your mother doesn't
even want you.'

'But it was Mummie told me that Mrs. Jones threatened to give
notice if she asked five people to stay. And now she's asked seven
people. And you know if we lose Mrs. Jones we'll never get another
up to Mummie's standards.'

'Then she'll have to change her standards—like other people.'

Francie was silent, as usual in these arguments. But a certain
obstinate desperation in her forehead and chin seemed to ask,
'How? It's easy to say, but how do you do it?' And she went to the
work—Mrs. Bill's celebrated party was again a great success, for
which she received much praise, even a graceful notice in a Sunday
newspaper. And for three months afterwards she did not send for
Francie; either she did not need her or she had been offended by
Catto's note.

Francie believed that she was offended, and it worried her.

'Mummie is so sensitive about being a nuisance,' she said. 'And of course she'll never tell you when she's hurt.'

'She's no right to be hurt.'

Francie's wrinkles deepened. 'It's not very nice for her, living alone. I should hate it.'

Catto did not answer that Francie was off the point. He told himself that women have their own methods of argument and that, above all, he must not start a quarrel with Francie about her mother. That situation was too foolish as well as too vulgar. How easy for a sensible man to avoid it. And it seemed that Mrs. Bill, hurt or not, meant to leave Francie alone.

Francie's first baby was born in December, a very cold December; and on the day before she got up there was a note from Letty asking if she could take the elder girl to school, she herself had a migraine; and on the day after she got up, Mrs. Bill telephoned. She did not ask for help. Mrs. Bill's claim that she never sought Francie's help, was perfectly justified. Her method was to send news of trouble, as a joke, or to ask advice. This time she did both.

'I've got three people for the week-end and of course Mrs. Jones has sprained her ankle. You can rely on Mrs. Jones's ankle, it's never failed her yet when there's some real work to do. But meanwhile I have to find an experienced daily. Should I advertise? I'm so bad at these things. And I simply must get someone by this evening.'

Catto, running in from the works in the mid-morning, to have a glimpse of his wife, finds her up and dressed. She is at the telephone, nursing the baby through her opened coat and arguing with Letty about school clothes. Jean, with an expression of reserved disapproval which comically reproduces her father's look in the same kind of crisis, stands looking on. Jean, a sensible Catto, is already devoted, in her sensible way, to her stepmother. She knows how to value her practical good nature, and quite agrees with her father about the Bill relations.

'But Letty,' Francie's voice implores her sister to be reasonable. 'She simply must have four face towels. It may be ridiculous but you know there was trouble last time when she went with only two, and it upsets a child so much to be different.'

Catto, furious, tries to take the telephone out of Francie's hands. Startled, she turns crimson and fights him.

'No—what are you doing?'

And he, equally surprised by this strong resistance, gives way. She says hastily to Letty, 'It's all right, darling. Nothing. I'll be round in ten minutes,' and hangs up. She smiles nervously at Catto and says, 'I can do Letty on the way to Mother's. How lucky that I was going anyhow?'

'You're not going to do Letty, or your mother either. This is where we stop. You're not fit.' And seeing the obstinate look in her face, he begins to storm. Her mother and Letty are two of the most selfish people on earth. And has she no consideration for her baby, not to speak of her husband?

Francie, flustered, tries to interrupt. Suddenly she bursts into tears. Catto, alarmed by her violent agitation, sits down beside her and puts an arm around her.

'My darling, you see how it is. Someone has to make a stand. Let me do it for you if you're afraid.'

'But you can't, you can't. No one can.'

'But that's nonsense.'

'You don't understand. Letty would simply let that poor child go off again with all the wrong things, and of course Mother won't get a daily in time for dinner this evening. There isn't a hope. She'll leave everything to settle itself, and Mrs. Jones will limp about and get up a grievance till she gives notice. She loves a real grievance. And if Mother loses Mrs. Jones I'd have to go every day. Either that or Mother would have to live with us. And you'd hate that. Oh dear, there's Gordon in the car.' And still nursing, while her brother-in-law, chattering about Letty's headache, gathers her bag, she hurries out.

Six months later Mrs. Bill did lose Mrs. Jones, and she has failed to keep another housekeeper. She is very cheerful and says that on the whole she prefers to manage without Mrs. Jones, who had no humour.

Francie has her second baby, and she lives a still more distracted life, dashing over three times a week to manage her mother's household. It has been proposed that Mrs. Bill should live with the Cattos, but she absolutely refuses to give up her dear old house, with its glorious memories of William Archer, E. F. Benson, and George Alexander. And as for the proposal that the Cattos should live with her, taking half the house for their separate apartment, which is Mrs. Bill's solution to the problem, Catto can't bring himself to leave his home. He points out that the kitchen was especially designed for Francie's convenience.

So that he too lives a distracted life. See him now at ten o'clock at night waiting at Hunter's Green to take Francie home. It is raining, but he is so angry that he won't leave the car to go into the house. This, of course, is stupid, for Mrs. Bill is always good-natured with him and says, 'My dear Tom, I don't ask Francie to run my show; it's Francie who insists on it. She's so practical—she hates a muddle. Now I don't mind muddle a bit.'

For Mrs. Bill has never suffered from a muddle—Francie sees to that. And Catto thinks bitterly, 'Practical and affectionate—how true that was—and is.'

Suddenly the house door opens and Francie comes running through the rain. He starts the engine, before he realizes that she has neither hat nor coat. She comes to the driver's side, pulls open the door, and puts her arms round his neck. 'Darling, only ten more minutes, I swear.'

'But you're getting wet.'

'Yes, I saw the car from the window and I knew how you were feeling. Only ten more minutes. And then we'll be off. And I am so longing——'

She kisses him again and again, there is a cry from the house, 'Francie,' and she runs.

Catto falls back in his seat. He is excited, his heart is beating fast, there are tears in his eyes. For he adores his wife, it is an agony for him to see Francie used, worn out by people that, to him, are worthless beside her. And it seems that there is no cure. He suffers, he grumbles, he quarrels with the amused Mrs. Bill, he makes a fool of himself, he does not know if he is more happy or more wretched. All he knows is this passionate love, a thing he has never imagined before—that devours him with anxiety, with anger, with despair.

V. S. PRITCHETT
The Aristocrat

It was at two o'clock and after a good lunch that Mr. Murgatroyd
went into the Prince of Denmark and took his stand four-square
and defensive against the bar. The time was seven minutes past two
by the clock above the bottles, but by his gold watch, which he
slipped out of its chamois case, it was two. He remarked upon this
to Mrs. Pierce, the publican, who was leaning with her fat forearms
on the bar, musing like a cat; and she croaked out a long story
about her husband winding up the clock on Saturday nights. The
usual people were on the bench in the small bar, crowded, cheerful,
and comfortable, Mr. Sanders with a red carnation in his button-
hole, squeezing his little legs together with glee, like a house-fly in
the sun, in the midst of three women and not sitting next to his wife.
They all heard the conversation with Mrs. Pierce and they heard
her say:

'Bit of an 'eat wave isn't it, Mr. Murgatroyd?' nodding to the first
flakes of March snow in the street.

To this Mr. Sanders added his news:

'Couple of cases of sunstroke in the Theobald's Road they tell
me.'

The presence of Mr. Murgatroyd brought out Mr. Sanders's wit.
He was a dogged little man with a waxed moustache and tobacco-
stained fingers, one to nudge the ladies in the ribs with his sharp
elbows, a jumping cracker at three-ten a week in the provision
trade. And bald.

Mr. Murgatroyd was wearing a smart, new grey flannel suit. A
pair of yellow gloves drooped in one hand like the most elegant
banana-skins. He was a shy and important man. His eloquence was
in the breadth of his shoulders, in the thick pink of his face after the
first drink, in the full-moon expansion of his stomach under the
smooth waistcoat and in the polish of his shoes. Mrs. Sanders, a
woman pushed to the outskirts of everything and sitting on the
extreme edge of the bench, was ashamed of her wriggling husband
when Mr. Murgatroyd, blue-eyed, shy and impressive, stood with
his lids lowered, gazing at the floor, secure and silent in his

substance. The young Jewess who was always there on Saturday afternoon got up and opened her fur coat when Mr. Murgatroyd came in. She rested one hand on her hip, gave a long look into the mirror and began walking up and down, almost touching Mr. Murgatroyd when she turned. Mr. Murgatroyd lowered his eyes when she came, rolling her hips, humming and laughing towards him.

It was Mr. Sanders's round. Mr. Murgatroyd took a deep drink, faced the eyes of the dancing Jewess for a second, and then, as the beer sank down in him, grew heavy in the head, solid in his silence and vague in his vision.

It was at this moment when they were busy with their glasses, all talking at once, when Mr. Murgatroyd unbuttoned his new coat and was easing out his disclaiming stomach and when the Jewess gave it a tap on the fourth button, with the words: 'What you got in there, Mr. Murgatroyd?'—it was at this moment that a stranger came into the bar. He was a tall, white-haired man and was among them just as Mr. Sanders was pulling the money out of his pocket. Mr. Sanders was bobbing about, standing in his way.

'Jim,' whispered Mrs. Sanders, anxiously leaning across to pull her husband's coat-tails. 'There's a gentleman wants to get past.'

'Excuse me, mister,' said Mr. Sanders, holding a full glass in each hand and abashed by the height of the stranger. A quiet, slightly wavering voice replied and the stranger walked past them to the bar.

'A beer, if you please,' he said. He turned round, and all talk stopped. They saw the old man looking at them, counting them, giving each one of them a fine, quick calculating stab of his eyes. There were wet points of thawed snow on his long shabby green overcoat. Without a word he took his glass and walked slowly over to the mirror and put his glass down on the shelf. They watched him. His clothes were worn but they were carefully kept.

One hand was fidgeting in his overcoat pocket as he stood. He was an old man; he might have been seventy, even seventy-five. He was thin, rigid and austere, a soldierly old man with quick crafty eyes. His lips were pared away to two thin, stiff lines, he carried his chin high like a sentry. His nose was lean and aquiline and he wore a long, carefully clipped moustache which curled with a military flourish. It was the alertness of the grey threadbare eyes of the old man and something supple and gentle in him that silenced everyone.

Mr. Murgatroyd lowered his eyes and studied the old man's clothes. They were old and respectable. Mr. Sanders was silenced by the aristocratic curve, the disciplined richness of that white moustache. Mrs. Tagg jostled her various selves together within her corsets and stared. Mrs. Sanders timidly admired. The Jewess stood yielding, softening her gaiety before his white age.

'Cold day,' said the old man to them all. They were all surprised. Only the Jewess and Mrs. Tagg murmured a reply.

Although he stood still, he was a restless old man. He moved his feet a little as he stood, and one of his hands was continually fingering something hidden in his pocket. Everybody noted this. Then his eyes moved in soft, darting glances at them all, so that they shifted their eyes. By those razor-cut glances he seemed to observe not their faces but things on their persons. Mr. Sanders straightened his carnation after one of these looks and Mrs. Tagg felt for her black beads. When he turned to Mr. Murgatroyd he looked straight into the middle of Mr. Murgatroyd's fine grey flannel stomach. Mr. Murgatroyd leaned back rather more defensively against the bar; then he relented; being a very shy man, he could not resist the chance of a conversation when someone had got over the first difficulties.

'Was it snowing still?' Mr. Murgatroyd asked.

'It was,' said the old man.

Mr. Murgatroyd wagged his head impressively.

'This wind finds out all your weak spots,' said the old man. There was a movement of sympathy; he drew himself up with dignity to repel it.

Then the old man, with some deliberation, opened his overcoat and he was seen to be even thinner than he had at first appeared. His long hand went into the pocket of his carefully darned jacket and he drew out something which amazed them all.

It was a very large green silk handkerchief with a brilliant pattern of red and yellow suns on it, rich, exotic and expensive. Mrs. Tagg reckoned out the price at once. He let the handkerchief fall to its full length and caught it with his other hand. He gave it a small shake and gathered it up, clutching it tightly and watching it spring out and open like a gorgeous flower. Mr. Sanders had expected to see it lifted straight to the beads of foam on the old man's fine moustache; but now he was playing with it, showing it off, conjuring with its brilliant lightness in the snow darkness of the bar. Would it fall to the dirty floor?

But the old man did not let it fall. He lightly touched his moustache with it and put it not into the inner pocket, but into the outside pocket of his overcoat. It hung out and Mr. Murgatroyd looked down his own chest and gave a touch to his own handkerchief in his breast pocket. The old man took one of his economical drinks and then smiled a friendly, faintly triumphant smile.

Mrs. Tagg smiled back at him. She was gazing at the handkerchief hanging far out of the pocket.

'Mind you don't drop that handkerchief of yours,' said Mr. Murgatroyd with great difficulty.

The old man, still smiling, drew back before this friendliness and straightened himself.

'You don't want to lose a nice one like that,' said Mrs. Tagg.

The old man surveyed them all and murmured something impatiently as if resenting interference. Rebuked, they watched. Presently, eyeing them all, he drew out of his other pocket the thing he had been fingering for so long. It was a short smooth stick about a foot long, like a wooden whistle.

It was not a whistle, but merely a stick. He took it out and ran it through his hands, smoothing it and stroking it, and with every touch his thin, stiff hands seemed to become lighter and softer and more pliable. He passed the stick from one hand to the other, sometimes holding it only between the tips of his two forefingers. The Jewess came forward to watch this.

'Nice bit of wood,' said Mr. Murgatroyd enquiringly.

'Uh,' grinned the old man and then with a severe look put the stick back in his pocket. There was disappointment in the wondering eyes of Mrs. Sanders. But the old man was fumbling and muttering:

'Yes, yes,' and went on fumbling.

'Your handkerchief is in the other pocket,' said Mr. Sanders eagerly. The Jewess looked admiringly at Mr. Sanders for being so quick to read her thoughts.

'I know,' said the old man, giving him a severe glance, and still fumbling and frowning now with irritation.

Mr. Murgatroyd expanded and said with amusement:

'Lost something?'

The old man looked round sharply.

'Have you got a sixpence?' he jerked.

Mr. Murgatroyd's smile died in his soul but remained fixed on his face. He coloured. He moved his lips. He concealed a swallow. He leaned farther back against the counter. Everyone was watching the crisis in Mr. Murgatroyd.

'I want a sixpence,' said the old man and appealed to the others. 'A sixpence,' he said quickly. And at the same time he drew out the brilliant handkerchief and caught it with the other hand.

'I'll show you something. I'll show you what I can do with this handkerchief.'

His whole manner had changed. He had become sharp and assertive.

The Jewess saw it at once. Her eyes woke up.

'You are going to do a trick,' she said.

He looked at her with contempt and a smile on the tail of it.

'A conjuring trick?' asked Mr. Murgatroyd, widening his eyes. 'What are you going to do? Sixpence and a handkerchief?' he said deprecatingly.

'You know it?' said the old man.

'Everyone knows it. Everyone sees it. The vanishing sixpence.'

'There's nothing new in that,' laughed Mr. Sanders. 'Eh, ma?' he said.

They all laughed. God, the old man was a conjuror. Mrs. Pierce, without unfolding her arms, slid them farther down the bar. The old man's eyes glittered.

'I'll bet you a tanner,' said the old man, 'you don't see it.' And he stared full and unanswerably at Mr. Murgatroyd. Mr. Murgatroyd stared back with all his might. He entrenched himself against the counter. Mrs. Pierce stepped nearer on her side and he entrenched himself against the support of Mrs. Pierce and the bar. He went very red and a mist came into his eyes.

'You want my sixpence,' he said in a stupor, strenuously defending himself.

'No. I'll make a bet,' the old man said, 'with anyone.' He snapped his fingers at them all. 'You'll get it back,' he said softly, smiling. They were ashamed of their suspicions. They gazed with command at Mr. Murgatroyd hemmed in against the bar. He was obliged to hand the old man a sixpence.

The old man looked at the sixpence on the pink palm of Mr.

Murgatroyd's hand. Very relucantly he took it and held it in his fingers.

'It's a funny thing,' he said, 'but you see all kinds of handkerchief tricks, but no one sees this.'

'Let's see it,' interrupted Mr. Murgatroyd and was frowned on for interrupting.

'Some of these men you see on the halls are quick.' He chattered away and he told them of ways of doing the trick, ways of folding the handkerchief and of concealing the coin.

'There, hold it a minute,' he said, giving the sixpence back to Mr. Murgatroyd to the astonishment of all. And his fingers captivated them with the play of his handkerchief as he illustrated his points.

They all leaned forward.

'Well, let's see it,' said Mr. Murgatroyd from his defence. But the old man went on talking. And then he insisted on Mr. Murgatroyd holding the handkerchief. The Jewess came forward and wanted to hold it too.

'Now watch,' said the old man. And he took back the sixpence and placed it in the handkerchief and began to knot it in. Mr. Murgatroyd held one end of the handkerchief while the old man got to work with both his nimble hands. He folded and knotted. He stopped to explain.

'Get on with it,' said Mr. Sanders.

'Shut up. You watch,' said Mrs. Tagg, sitting vast in nervous judgement.

'Well, there you are,' said the old man. 'The sixpence is in there, isn't it? You saw me put it in.'

'I saw it,' said Mr. Murgatroyd very hot.

'It was his sixpence, he ought to know,' said Mr. Sanders.

The old man smiled along his lips. Mrs. Sanders gazed sadly at her husband. The Jewess watched like a jackdaw for brightness.

'Feel it,' said the old man.

Reluctantly, ashamed of suspicion, Mr. Murgatroyd put out his hand. He could feel the hard round coin.

'It's there,' he said to the others.

'Oh!' said the old man coldly, whipping the handkerchief open.

It was empty. There was no sixpence. The beautiful rich, green handkerchief with the yellow suns on it waved. Mrs. Sanders was glad the poor old gentleman had a beautiful silk handkerchief.

'There!' said Mrs. Pierce gloomily from the bar.

'That's done it,' said Mr. Sanders, screwing up his legs.

Mrs. Tagg made more room for herself on the bench and then breathed deeply.

'A man who can do that,' she frowned, 'is a clever man.'

'He had it in his hand all the time,' said the Jewess.

The old man showed her his empty hands.

'Eh?' said the old man, faintly smiling. He began absently to fold up the handkerchief with his rippling hands which never ceased in their movements.

'Yes,' said Mr. Murgatroyd, rather proud of himself. 'Yes,' he said, shaking his head.

The handkerchief was whipped open again and there was the sixpence in it.

'You see!' Mrs. Pierce murmured miserably.

They all began to talk at once.

The old man put his handkerchief back into his pocket and reached for his drink. He listened to the arguments and explanations.

'Oh, I must give you your sixpence,' he said to Mr. Murgatroyd. But Mr. Murgatroyd recoiled. He was shamed by the sight of his coin. He thickened with generosity, his skin gleamed with admiration and the flush of his second pint. He felt he was the leader of a delegation, the master of ceremonies, the mayor of a town; but too much of a man of the world to show it crudely. He condescended in a knowing, intimate, chatty way with the sparse of speech old man.

'No, that's your sixpence,' said Mr. Murgatroyd casually. 'You won it.'

'Oh . . .' the old man hesitated.

'Yes, go on. You take it. Go on,' said Mrs. Tagg firmly, shaking her head. Mrs. Tagg was proud of being out for justice.

The old man drew the stick from his pocket and began sliding it to and fro and shyly pocketed the sixpence. Mrs. Sanders smiled wistfully and gladly at him when he did this.

'There's nothing in it,' said the old man. 'It's all a swindle. The quickness of the hand deceiving the eye and human nature,' he said. 'Take the stick and tumbler trick.' He picked up an empty glass and rammed the stick several times at the bottom of it. The third or fourth time it appeared to go through.

'Gawd,' said Mr. Sanders with admiration. 'That's clever. See how he done that? Do it again! There now.'

'Dear me. Look at that,' said Mrs. Tagg.

They all saw it. They all felt warm and intimate.

'There's a trick in everything,' said the old man.

'A man with a brain can diddle anyone,' said Mr. Sanders, nodding intimately to the old man, whose eye faintly fluttered and then ignored him.

Somehow a ring had come into the old man's hand. The Jewess was the first to notice it.

'A ring and a stick,' said the old man. 'Get it off without moving your hands.' He slid the ring up and down the stick and then slipped it off.

It was the maddening way of this old man to start a trick and then stop and talk and begin all over again.

Now he was off again and he got Mr. Murgatroyd to hold one end of the stick, while he took out his handkerchief again. He covered the stick up. The ring was on it. The handkerchief in all its colours covered the stick and Mr. Murgatroyd's hand was resting pressed against his waistcoat. The old man kept altering the position of Mr. Murgatroyd's hand, pulling the stick away to show the ring was still on it, and then giving it back again.

'The chair trick now,' he was saying. 'They tie a man up to a chair with his arms behind his back. You can go up and see he's properly knotted, and yet he just steps out of it. What's the explanation? Trick knots.'

'They're not real knots, then?' accused Mr. Sanders.

'He's knotted up,' said the old man.

'But not with real knots,' said the Jewess.

'They're knots all right,' said the old man. 'He's got a couple of tapes up his sleeve coming out in slits in his coat.'

They exclaimed. He was fidgeting all the time, straightening out his handkerchief. He even gave Mr. Murgatroyd a tap in the ribs and said he was sorry. Mr. Murgatroyd smiled pityingly at the poor fussy old conjuror with all his tricks. Suddenly the old man said 'Look!' and whipped off the handkerchief. There was no ring on the stick.

'What are you drinking?' said Mr. Murgatroyd with embarrassment.

The old man hesitated. 'No, thank you,' he said. 'Not before my dinner. I haven't had my dinner yet.'

'Oh, I see,' murmured Mr. Murgatroyd with embarrassment.

No dinner! What did he mean, no dinner? Did he mean he was earning his dinner? They were all very comfortable people with full stomachs. It was embarrassing to sit there full of food while an old man going on for seventy-five stood there empty, a fine old man like that. An aristocratic old man and nothing inside him. Mr. and Mrs. Sanders, they had had a stew. Mrs. Tagg had had a nice bit of crab and a Guinness. Crab didn't agree with the Jewess. 'It isn't that it repeats, but, you know, I know I've had it.' So she had had spaghetti. As for Mr. Murgatroyd, he had been built up on steak and two vegetables and raisin roll. They were diffusing their goodness in him.

All were touched when the old man gave a short bow and murmured in his quavering dignified voice that an old soldier would be grateful for a copper or two. His quick eyes watched their hands.

A handsome old man like that doing this for a living! Mrs. Sanders signalled to her husband. The Jewess opened her handbag.

'An old soldier did you say?' asked Mrs. Tagg on behalf of everyone.

'The East Kents,' said the old man, straightening.

'The Buffs!' she smiled with sudden reminiscent warmth, imperiousness vanishing in a glitter of long-forgotten gaiety.

'Yes, that's it. The Buffs,' the old man repeated mechanically. His thin, long, clever, hungry hands.

'Steady, the Buffs!' exclaimed Mrs Tagg, with a shake of her head and tears of pleasure in her eyes.

'Oh, ah . . .' murmured the old man.

'Chatham?' said Mr. Sanders. 'Nice place. The Bells, Chatham. Know that?'

'Twenty-five years' service,' said the old man. 'Not so young now.'

'I could tell you was an old soldier,' said Mrs. Tagg with pride.

He stood there talking to them as he put the few coppers in his pocket. Mr. Sanders began to remember the good old days at Chatham during the war.

'I was talking about the Boer War,' said the old man.

Mrs. Sanders raised her head high in shame for her husband. She was proud of the heroic old man.

'Well,' he said, after a while. 'I suppose I'd better be moving along to my dinner.'

They were sad. But they understood. They realized he was a hungry old man.

'Good day, and I thank you,' he said.

Mr. Murgatroyd put out his hand. The old man was surprised by this handshake. It was the only time he had been taken aback. Raising his hat, he went slowly out of the bar. The swing door bumped after him and Mrs. Pierce raised herself from the counter and went to the window to see the tall, upright figure walk away. When she came back she said: 'It's snowing hard now.'

They all sat in silence staring into the tops of their glasses. Except the Jewess, who took off her hat and combed her hair by the mirror. There on the mantelpiece was the froth-laced glass the old man had used.

'Well, well,' said Mr. Murgatroyd uncomfortably. He relaxed from the slanting position into which he had recoiled before the old man. 'He gets a living,' said Mr. Murgatroyd.

There was a long silence. The bar seemed to be much darker now that the old man had gone. They were thinking about Mr. Murgatroyd's words. Mr. Murgatroyd was all right, he had a new suit of clothes, gloves in his hand, a fountain-pen in his pocket, a car outside and a new Trilby hat. But everyone had to get a living. Mrs. Sanders moved to the end of the bench and pulled up the collar of her coat with a shiver.

'Hunger,' said Mrs. Sanders in her timid voice. 'That's the worst thing.'

They all looked at her with curiosity and reproof for speaking that word.

And that uncomfortable word reminded Mr. Murgatroyd of something. His shyness and importance were moving inside him. It was his round.

'What's everyone having?' he said at last, looking away up at the clock among the bottles. Mrs. Pierce looked up, too.

'Guinness, ma'am. Time for another, I think. Your clock's fast, Mrs. Pierce. . . .'

And his hand went down his waistcoat for his watch. Down and down it went. And as it went down he seemed to feel a nudge in his stomach and a look of consternation came on his face. The watch was not there. His hand dug in his other pocket.

'Well, I'm . . .' he said aloud. The watch had gone.

His eyes popped wide and hard, his jaw dropped. He went very pale and then flushed to the colour of a beetroot.

'Here,' he blurted out, starting from the counter. 'My watch. It was here. I know it was. It's gone. You saw it, Mrs. Pierce. You saw me take it out. It's gone. That artful old swine has pinched my watch!'

He glared at them all.

'Where is he?' he shouted. 'Which way did he go? Look for him! Of all the thieves . . .'

Unable to do more because of the vast heaving and of his rage, Mr. Murgatroyd looked as though he would burst.

V. S. PRITCHETT
The Scapegoat

THERE were long times when we were at peace and when the world left us alone. We could go down Earl Street and, although we did not like the place and it felt strange to us and the women stared down from the windows and a child here and there might call out a name after us, we just walked on thinking of something else. But we were always more at ease and more ourselves, even in the quietest times of truce, when we had turned the corner by the hop-warehouse and had got back into Terence Street, which was our own. The truth is that you can't live without enemies, and the best enemies are the ones nearest home; and though we sometimes went out to the Green to boo the speakers and some of our lads went after the Yids or joined a procession up West, that was idleness and distraction. The people we hated were not a mile away on the main road where the trams and the buses are and you don't know one man from the next; no, the people we hated were round the corner, next door, in Earl Street. They were, we used to say, a different class of people from ourselves altogether.

I don't know why, but if there was any trouble in the world, we turned out and attacked them. I don't know either how these things began. You would know there was trouble coming when you heard the voices of the children getting shriller and more excited, until their cries became rhythmic like the pulse of native war-cries in the forest. We were, indeed, lost in a *jungle* of streets. Somehow the children would have sticks, old pieces of board and stones in their hands, and they would be rushing in groups to the hop-warehouse and jeering and then scattering back. A similar thing would be happening in Earl Street. Usually this happened in the warm long evenings of the summer. Then, after the children, the thing got hold of the women and they came down from their windows where they had been watching and scratching their arms, very hot and restless, and would stand at their doorsteps and start shouting at their children. A stone would fly up and then the women would be down in the middle of the street.

It might take a day to work up or it might take longer. You would get the Earl Street girls going down our street talking in loud voices daring us, and our young lads would stand by saying nothing until the girls got to the corner. And then those girls would have to bolt. Towards closing time the Gurneys, the fighting family in Earl Street, would be out and we had our Blackers and then it was a question of who came out of the Freemasons and how he came out. But perhaps nothing would happen and we would just go down Earl Street after dark and merely kick their milk-bottles down the basements.

This has been going on ever since the old people can remember. When the war came we knew everyone in Earl Street was a spy or a Hun or a Conchie. The Great War, for us, was between Earl Street and Terence Street. They had a V.C. and we hadn't, though we had a bunch of other stuff and one man who escaped from the Turks and was in the papers; and, though we did our best, the tea we gave was nothing to the tea they did in Earl Street for their V.C. Where they got the money from was the puzzle. Thirty-two pounds. Some of our women said the Earl Street girls must have been on the streets; and at the Freemasons the men said half of Earl Street were nothing but bloody pensioners. The police came in before we had the question settled. But when the war ended, things changed. Half of our lot was out of work and when we went down Earl Street we would see half of their lot out of work too, and Earl Street did not seem quite so strange to us. One street seemed to blend into the other. This made some of our lot think and they gave their steps an extra clean to show there was a difference between Earl Street and Terence Street after all.

In the years that followed, sometimes we were up on Earl Street, sometimes we were down. We were waiting for some big event. It did not come for a long time and a stranger might have thought that the old frontiers had gone and the reign of universal peace was upon us. It was not. The Jubilee came and we saw our chance. Earl Street had collected thirty-two pounds for its V.C.'s tea-party. We reckoned we would top that for the Jubilee. We would collect forty.

There was a red-haired Jew in our street called Lupinsky. He was a tailor. He was round-shouldered from bending over the table and his eyes were weak from working by gas at night. In the rush season he and his family would be up past midnight working. He was a keen man. He came out in pimples—he was so keen. Lupinsky saw everything before any of us. He saw the Jubilee before the King himself. He had got his house full of bunting and streamers and Union Jacks. 'Get in at the early doors,' he said. 'What'll you have?' he used to say to us when we went to his shop. 'Rule Britannia or God Save the King?' 'Who's that?' we said. 'The King of the Jews?' 'Getcha,' said Lupinsky. 'He's dead. Didn't you hear?' He raked in the money. They had another Jew in Earl Street doing the same. 'I say!' called Lupinsky. 'I say!'—we used to call him. 'I-say-what'll-you-have'—'Cohen's sold 120 yards to Earl Street and you've only done 70.' So we doubled. 'I say,' says Lupinsky. 'I say. When you going to start collecting? They got ten quid in Earl Street and you haven't started.'

And this was true. The trouble was we couldn't agree upon who should collect. We had had a nasty experience with the Club a few years back. And then Lupinsky was hot for doing it himself. He'd got the bunting. He'd seen it coming. He'd even got boxes. He'd thought of everything. We had nothing against Lupinsky, but when we saw him raking in the money on his God Saves and Kiss-me-quicks and his flags of all the nations, we thought he was collecting enough as it was. He might mix up the two collections. 'No,' we said to Lupinsky. 'You're doing your bit, we'll do the rest.' 'That's O.K.' Lupinsky said. He never bore resentment, he was too keen. 'But I hear Earl Street's up to twelve ten.' He wasn't upset with us, but he couldn't bear to see us shilly-shallying around while Earl Street walked away with it. 'If you don't trust me,' he said, 'can't you trust yourselves? I don't know what's happened to this street.' And he spat from the top of his doorstep into the gutter.

Lupinsky was wrong about us. We trust each other. There is not a man in Terence Street you cannot trust. In that nasty business we had with the Club, the man was not a Terence Street man. We could trust one another. But we were frightened. Forty pounds! We thought. That's a big sum. We didn't like the handling of it. There wasn't one of us who had seen forty pounds in his life. The Blackers, a good fighting lot, were terrified. Albert Smith and his uncle were the most likely, but they said they were single and didn't like the idea. And we, for some reason, thought a single man wasn't right for the job. And the wives, the married ones, though eagerly wanting their husbands to do it, were so afraid the honour would go to someone else, that they said to give it to a married man was tempting Providence. Lupinsky went down the street almost in tears, saying Earl Street had touched seventeen ten.

Then suddenly we saw the right man had been staring us in the face all the time. He was not single and he was not married. He was a widower, made serious by death: Art Edwards. We chose Art Edwards, and he agreed.

Art Edwards was a man of forty-seven, and the moment he agreed we were proud of him. He was a grey-haired man, not very talkative and of middle height, very patient and looked you straight in the face. He lived with his sister, who looked after his two children, he had a fruit stall in the main road—he had been there for twenty years—and every Sunday he used to go alone with a bunch of flowers for his wife's grave at the cemetery. The women admired him very much for doing this. He never changed. His house was the neatest house in our street and he never seemed to get richer or poorer. He just went on the same.

He had been a widower a good long time, too, and some thought he ought to marry again. The women were curious about him and said you couldn't but respect a man who didn't take a second, and Art was held up as a model. This didn't prevent many of them running after him and spreading the rumour afterwards that his sister was a woman who wouldn't let a man call his soul his own. But the way Art mourned for the dead and kept faithful to The First, the ONE AND ONLY, as the women said, was striking. Some of the men said that being a model wasn't healthy and that if they had been in Art's shoes they would muck around on the quiet. They wondered why the hell he didn't, yet admired him for his restraint. Some of us couldn't have lived with temptation all those years without slipping up.

Art had put a black band on his sleeve when his wife died and had worn it ever since. But when he started collecting for the tea we had the feeling he had put off his mourning and had come alive again. We were pleased about this because, with his modest, retiring ways, we hardly knew him. 'It will bring him out,' we said. He came round with his little red book and his tin and we said, 'What's it now, Art? How we doin'?' Art was slow at adding up, but accurate. He told us. We made a big effort and we touched the ten-pound mark pretty soon.

This woke us up and made us feel good, but Lupinsky came round and said it wasn't any bloody good at all. They'd touched nineteen pounds in Earl Street. So one of the women said they'd help Art. He didn't want this, or his sister didn't. So she joined in, too, to keep the other women off him. They knocked at his door at all hours and stopped him in the street. And when she saw this his sister put on her best hat and coat and went round and stopped their men. The result was everyone was collecting and came round to Art and said:

'Here y'are, Art. One and eight,' or 'Here y'are, Art, eight and six.'

And two of the Blacker girls had a fight because one said the other wasn't collecting fair, but was cheapening herself to get the money. For we touched seventeen and went on to twenty-one.

The night we passed Earl Street some of our girls went out and just walked down Earl Street telling them. They didn't like it. A crowd from Earl Street came round and called 'Down with the Yids' outside Lupinsky's. Then Earl Street picked up and passed us again. We went round to Art and planked down more money. Art got out his book and he couldn't write it down fast enough.

'Where do you keep it, Art?' we said.

He showed us a box in the cupboard. It was a fine sight all that money. His sister said:

'Art's picked up a bit in the High Street.' We looked at him as if he were a hero. ''Slike business,' he said. 'You've got to go out for it.'

We looked with wonder at him. We had chosen the right man. It was bringing him out. And he had ideas too. He got some of the kids to go out at night with tins.

We passed Earl Street and they passed us. Then we passed them again. It was ding-dong all the time. Lupinsky flew in and out with the latest like a wasp and stung us to more. Art Edwards, he said, had no life in him. After this, it became madness. People got out their savings.

There was a funny case at Harry Law's. He was a boozer, a big, heavy man, very particular in the house and very religious. Some nights when he was bad he used to beat his wife and we used to look down into their basement window wondering what would be happening inside, for something usually was happening. There were often shouts and curses and screams coming from that room and then times, which made you uncomfortable, when everything was quiet. Harry Law was often out of a job. Mrs. Law was a timid woman and everyone was sorry for her. She used to go up to the Freemasons and look though the door at him. She was a thin, round-shouldered woman, always anxious about her husband and sorry that he made a fool of himself, for he got pompous when he was drunk and she hated the way people laughed at him. He used to say she had no ambition and he had dragged her out of the gutter. She said, '*Down* into the gutter, you mean.' They used to have guilty arguments like this for hours, each boasting they were better than the other and wondering all the time why they had got into their present situation. Then Harry Law would go to church so as to feel good and find out why, and his wife used to stop at home and think about it too. She would put her arms round him and love him when he came back. And he would be all right for a few days until he got some scheme into his head for making money. When he had the scheme he would go out and get drunk again.

Harry Law wanted to show everyone that he was a man of ideas and ambitions, and better than the rest of us in Terence Street. He used to dress up on Sundays. He used to say he had been better off once and had had a shop. The truth was, as his wife bitterly told everyone, he'd always been the same; up and down all his life. She couldn't bear other people laughing at him, but she used to tear his reputation to bits herself and get great pleasure out of doing it.

It was just at the height of our madness that he came into the Freemasons and, instead of cadging for drinks, began to order freely. A funny thing had happened, he said. And he said, in his lordly voice, 'I want Art Edwards.' It turned out that he had been going across the room while his wife was out and had tripped up on something on the floor. There was a bump in the lino. Being a very inquisitive man who never had anything to do, he knelt down and felt the lump. 'I thought it was dirt,' he said. One of the things he always said about his wife was that she was dirty. He was a very clean man himself. He decided to take up the lino, and underneath he found a lump of money wrapped up in notes. It was his wife's savings.

That was why Harry Law was lording it at the Freemasons. He had hardly given a penny to the Collection, but now, when everyone was present, he was going to make a great gesture and show his greatness. When Art came in, he said, 'Here, Art. Have a fiver.'

We all stared. Harry Law was leaning against the bar with the notes in the tips of his fingers as if they were dirt, like a duke giving a tip.

At that moment his wife came in.

'That's mine,' she screamed. 'It's mine.'

There was a row and Art wouldn't take the money. Everyone said that a man hadn't the right to take his wife's money. But Harry said, 'What!' Wasn't his money as good as anybody's?' and we said, 'Yes, Harry, but that belongs to your missus.' She was crying, and he kept saying, 'Go home. I'll teach you to come round here. It is my money. I earned it.'

This was awkward. Between her tears, with her hands covering her face, Mrs. Law was saying she had saved it. He was always ruining them, so she had to save. Still, if he'd earned it, it was his.

'Take that money,' said Harry, dropping it like a lord on the floor. The notes fell down, we all looked at them and no one moved. Mr. Bell of the Freemasons got a laugh by saying we were littering up his bar with paper. Then Harry turned his back and we picked it up and were going to give it to Mrs. Law, but Harry said in a threatening voice, 'That's Art's. For the Collection. I reckon I got Earl Street knocked silly.'

That part of the statement was irresistible. While we hesitated, Art said:

'Give it here then. I'll look after it.' Lupinsky, who had been sitting there all the time clutching his hands and his eyes starting out of his head with misery at the sight of money lying in the sand, gave a shout.

'That's the boy,' he said. 'We've got 'em.'

We all felt uncomfortable with Harry and we went away in ones and twos and Mrs. Law went out still crying. After she went out Art went too, and when we got down the street Art stopped and told Mrs. Law he wasn't going to take the money and he made her take it back. She clutched it with both hands and looked at him like a dog with gratitude.

That night half the men in Terence Street wanted to take up their lino and sat up late arguing with their wives; but the madness was still in the air, especially when Earl Street, hearing our news, sent all their kids up West and passed us. There was a fight in the High Street between out kids and the Earl Street kids and one of ours lost her box. But there was nothing in it except stones. They put stones in to make a rattle so that people would think they were doing well. If there had been any money in that box there wouldn't have been a pane of glass in Earl Street left.

'They've passed us,' the cry went down our street. In the middle of this Mrs. Law came over to Art and gave him back the money. She made him take it.

'Your husband made you,' says Art.

'Him,' she said scornfully. 'He don't know anything about it. I told him you gave it me back and he said, "A good thing too." He's feeling sorry for himself. I'll teach him to touch my money, I said. If there's going to be any giving in this house, it's me that's got the money. I'm going to teach my husband a lesson,' she said.

This surprised Art, for he had been very sorry for poor Mrs. Law, and had shown it. But I've no doubt she was tired of being pitied. That money was all she had. She was going to show us that the Laws had their pride and she wasn't going to let them down. Only *she* was going to give it.

Her eyes shone and were sharp. They were greenish, miserly grey eyes, yet she was not miserly. Now she was proud and not bedraggled with tears and misery, she looked jubilant and cunning. She had been a gay, quick-tongued woman in her time.

'I kept it under the floor. That was wrong of me,' she said. 'I oughter have put it in the Post Office.'

She said she knew her husband was right. It was not right to hide money.

Everyone in Terence Street had supposed Mrs. Law to be a poor, timid, beaten soul, and Art had always thought the same, he said; but now he said that she had some spirit. She had opened her heart to him because he had been kind to her and now she said, very proudly, that he should come and have a chat with her husband. She took Art triumphantly to her basement just to show her husband there were other men in the world. Old Harry Law saw this at once—he was always on his dignity—so he just talked largely to Art about the shops he had had, the ups and downs, his financial adventures. Investments, he called them. We had all heard of investments, but none of us had ever had any. If he had his life over again, Harry Law said, he'd invest every penny.

'There's a man,' Art said when he went, 'who doesn't practise what he preaches.' But he respected Harry's preaching, though he despised him a bit. And Harry said, 'There's a man who stays the same all his life. Never made a penny, never lost a penny. The only money he's got,' said Harry, 'isn't his—this collection.'

And Harry asked him how much it was. There were some thirty-odd pounds, Art said.

Harry respected him when he heard that and said with a sigh, 'Money makes money.'

When Art got back, his sister was short with him. 'Going after other men's wives,' she said. And she lectured him about Mrs. Law. It had been such a warm, pleasant, friendly evening over at Harry Law's that Art was hurt about this.

'Him and her,' he said, 'has got more brains than you think. They've lived, all right. They've had their ups and downs.'

'He's a boozer.'

'We've all got our faults. He's had his ups and downs.'

And that was the phrase that he kept repeating. It fascinated him. He felt generous. It came to him that he had never felt anything for years. He had just gone on standing in the High Street by the stall. He had never taken a holiday. He had never bought himself anything he wanted. He had never done anything. It startled him—but he suddenly didn't want his wife who was in the grave. The street had chosen him, singled him out above all others, and there he stood naked, nothing. He was shy about his nonentity. He felt a curious longing for ups and downs.

You will say, 'How did we know what Art Edwards thought?' That was the strange thing: we did know. We knew as if he had told us, as if we were inside him. You see, because we had singled him out he was, in a sense, ourselves. We could see him thinking and feeling and doing what we would. He had taken the burden off us. By doing that he had become nearer and more precious to us than any other person.

And there was Terence Street two pounds ahead of Earl Street, drunk with the excitement of it. Art used to get the money out and count it—it was the biggest sum of money he had ever seen—and a sober pride filled him. He had done this. People like Mrs. Law had just thrown in all they had. He had put in his bit cautiously, but everyone had scraped and strained and just wildly thrown in the cash. It made him marvel. He marvelled at us, he marvelled—as his hands trembled over the money—that he had been picked out by us to hold it.

We went round once or twice to look at the money too. What a nest egg, what an investment! Over thirty pounds! We said we wished it was ours. We said we wished we could give more, or double it. We all wanted to double it. We looked at it sadly. 'If that thirty pounds had been on the winner today,' someone said. 'Or on the dogs.'

We laughed uneasily. And we dreamed. The more we looked at that money the more we thought of things you could do with it— mad things like backing a horse or sensible things like starting a business or having a holiday.

When we got up in Art's kitchen and saw him put the money in the cupboard and lock the door, we nodded our heads sadly. It was like burying the dead.

'It's sad it's got to go,' we thought.

And it seemed fitting that Art, who had buried the dead and who was a dour man with iron-grey hair and level-looking eyes, should have the grim task of keeping that money, like some sexton. And we were glad to have him doing it, to have him be responsible instead of us. For some of us had to admit we'd go mad at times with temptation tingling in our fingers and hissing like gas in coal in our hearts.

When we left him we felt a kind of sorrow for Art for bearing our burden, for being the custodian of our victory over Earl Street.

It made us all very friendly to Art. The time went by. We used to stop and have a word with him in the street. And Art became friendly too. But he wasn't at the Freemasons much. He went over to Mrs. Law's. And Harry Law didn't go on the booze. He stayed at home talking largely to Art. Once or twice Art went out in the evenings with Mr. and Mrs. Law. Lupinsky used to see them up at the Pictures.

Lupinsky was our reporter of everything, and gradually, expressing no doubt the instinct of the street, he had become our reporter on Art Edwards. We wanted a friendly eye kept on him not because he was valuable but because he was—well, as you would keep an eye on a sick man, say, a man who might have a heart attack or go dizzy in the street. When Lupinsky came back and said, 'I see Art Edwards getting on a tram,' we used to look up sharply and then, annoyed with ourselves, say 'What of it? What was he doing, having a ride?'

That Jew used to make us tired. And he'd started worrying already about the catering. They'd started arranging about the catering already in Earl Street. 'It's a funny thing,' we said, 'about the Yids. He's only been here fifteen years and you'd think he'd

been here for ever. Anyone'd think he'd been born in the street.
You'd bloody well think it was Jerusalem.'

We had been born there, most of us, and we said:

'It *will* be Jerusalem soon.'

But we would have been nowhere without Lupinsky.

And then one morning he came along and said:

'Seen Art?'

'No,' we said.

'He's not up in the High Street,' said Lupinsky. 'And he's not at
his house.'

'What of it?' we said.

Lupinsky was breathless. All the pimples on his face seemed
about to burst. He had the kind of red hair that is coarse and stands
up on end and thick arched eyebrows which were raised very high
but were now higher for his eyes were starting out of his head.
There were always bits of cotton from tailoring on his clothes and
he was, as I have said, rather hump-backed from leaning all day
over his machine.

'I saw him last night at the station. Nine o'clock. He took a ticket
on the North London and hasn't been back.'

'Smart baby,' we said. But we were thinking of Lupinsky. We
didn't believe him and yet we did believe him. 'What were you
doing up at the station—brother had another fire?' we said.
Lupinsky's brother was always having fires.

But it was true. Art hadn't been home that night and his sister
was very shifty when we went to see her. We never liked Art's sister
and we grinned to think he'd got away from her for a night.

'Art had to go away on business,' she said.

Theirs was a tidy house and Art's sister worked hard in it. The
window-sills were hearth-stoned. That woman never stopped. She
always came to the door with an iron in her hand or a scrubbing-
brush or with something she was cleaning or cooking. She was a
tall, straight-nosed woman and she had the best teeth I've ever
seen, but there was no thickness in her, no give.

She used to say, 'I've never had justice done me.'

And Art used to sigh and say, 'I can never do justice to her.'

'What about it now?' said Lupinsky, who was waiting for us.

'Art can go away if he likes,' we said. 'Why not?'

'Sure, yes, why not?' said Lupinsky. 'What are you worrying
about?'

Later on Lupinsky came and told us Art was still away. His stall was still in the lock-up and he hadn't been down to the market. Lupinsky had a friend who had told him. Then Lupinsky had another friend who said he'd seen Art at Wembley.

'Too many Yids here,' said Albert Blacker. 'You can't move but you catch one in your clothes. What's up with Wembley?'

We went over to Mrs. Law's and called down to her. She was ironing in the light of the window.

'Seen Art Edwards?' we said.

'No,' she said. 'He hasn't been here for two or three days.'

'Oh,' we said.

Then Harry Law got up from his chair by the stove and said: 'Art gone?'

'We're just looking for him. Thought he might be with you?'

Mrs. Law gazed at us and then she looked at her husband. She was one of those women who when anything serious or unexpected happens, when they don't know what to think, when they are bewildered, always turn to their husbands; as if by studying him she would always know the worst about any event in the world and would be prepared. It was like looking up something in a book or gazing into a crystal. And when she had gazed at her husband and thought about him, she said:

'Oh dear.' And she put down her iron and her shoulders hunched up. She looked accusingly at her husband and he lowered his eyes. He knew she could read him like that.

We did not think so at the time, but afterwards we said we had the feeling that when Mrs. Law looked at her husband in that accusing way, she knew something about Art Edwards that we did not know. It turned out that she did not know. I looked out of the window that night when I went to bed. It was a warm night. I work in a fur-warehouse and the air had the close, dead, laid-out smell of ladies' furs. There was a cold hollow lilac light over the roofs from the arc-lamps in the High Street. At night our street is quiet and often you can hear the moan of a ship's siren from the river like the hoarse voice of someone going away. But the commonest sound is the clinking of shunting trucks on the railway—a sound that is meaningless as if someone who couldn't play the piano had struck the keys anyhow, trying to make a tune. It is a sound which makes you think the city has had an attack of nerves. As I stood there on one leg, undoing my boots, I heard quick footsteps coming along. They were Lupinsky's. Lupinsky was always up late.

'I say. I say,' he called up to me. 'Art's come back. I just seen him. He came back and let himself in.'

That night Art Edwards went into the lock-up in his yard and, attaching his braces to a hook in the roof, he hanged himself. The box in the cupboard was empty. He had gone off to Wembley and lost all the money on the dogs.

We went out into the street in the morning and stood outside the house and stared at the windows. The people from Earl Street came too. All the children came and stared and no one said anything in the street. Albert Blacker went into the yard at the back and Lupinsky was there with the police. Mrs. Law would not leave her house, but stood on her doorstep holding the railing tightly, watching from a distance. Harry Law would not come out. He walked up and down the room and called up to his wife to come down. He could not bear being left alone. She was afraid to leave her house and yet, I thought, wanted to be with Art.

'The bloody twister,' we said between our teeth.

'That bloody widower,' we said.

'Takes our money and has a night out. Our savings! Our money!'

'The rotten thief.'

We muttered like this standing in front of the house. We were sorry for the police who had to touch the body of a man like that.

'You wouldn't trust me,' Lupinsky said.

We looked at him. We turned away. We couldn't bear the sight of that man's pimples.

'I'm used to money,' Lupinsky said.

I could not repeat all the things we said. I remember clearly the red, white, and blue streamers drooping over the street and looking dirty, with 'God Save the King' on them. 'God Save Art Edwards,' said Harry Law, coming up. He was tight.

We thought of the spirit of Art Edwards's sister being humbled. All down the street, at all the windows, the women leaned on their bare arms thinking about this. They cuffed their children and the children cried. There was the low murmur of our voices in the street and then the whining voices of children. Presently a couple of women came down, pushed their way through the crowd and went in to help Art's sister. We gaped at them.

And then Lupinsky, who gave the lead to everything and always knew what we were thinking underneath, said:

'They're jeering at us in Earl Street.'

They were. We set our teeth. Kids came round shouting, 'Who swiped the money box! Who swiped the money box!' Our kids did nothing for a long time. Then they couldn't stand it. Our kids went for the Earl Street kids. Some of our women came down to pull their kids off and this drew out the Earl Street women. In half an hour Albert Blacker came out of the Freemasons with his sleeves rolled up, just when the Earl Street men were getting together, and then Harry Law came out roaring. Mrs. Law ran towards him. But it was too late. A stone went and a window crashed and that brought out the rest of the Blacker family. We got it off our chests that night and we crowded into Earl Street. Half their milk-bottles had gone before the police whistles went.

And then it was clear to us. We knew what to do. Lupinsky headed it. Art Edwards was suddenly our hero. We'd kill the man who said anything against Art Edwards. In our hearts we said, it might have been ourselves. Thirty pounds. We remembered the sight of it! We even listened to Harry Law.

'He was trying to double it at the dogs,' he said. 'Investing it. Every man has . . .'

His wife pulled his coat and tried to stop him.

'Every man,' continued Harry Law, 'has his ups and downs.'

And to show Earl Street what we were and to show the world what we thought of Art Edwards, we got up the biggest funeral that has ever been seen in our street. He was ourselves, our hero, our god. He had borne our sins. You couldn't see the hearse for flowers. The street was black with people. The sun shone. We'd been round and got every stall-holder every barrrow-man in the neighbourhood. The procession was a mile long when it got going. There was a Jubilee for you, covered in red, white and blue wreaths. Art Edwards our king. It looked like a wedding. The great white trumpets of the lilies rocked thick on the coffin. Earl Street couldn't touch that. And Lupinsky collected the money.

BIOGRAPHICAL NOTES

BENSON, STELLA (1892–1933). Educated at home. Life largely spent abroad in Switzerland, France, Germany, America, and China. Took a small part in Women Suffrage work 1914. During the War worked for eighteen months in East London, later on the land. Went to America 1918, and lived chiefly in California until 1920. Her published works include: *I Pose*; *This is the End*; *Living Alone*; *The Poor Man*; *The Little World, Sketches of Travel*; *Worlds within Worlds*; *Tobit Transplanted*, and *Hope against Hope*.

BOWEN, ELIZABETH (1899–1973). Born in Dublin and educated at Downe House School in Kent. Her published works include: *The Last September*; *To the North*; *The House in Paris*; *The Death of the Heart*; *Bowen's Court*; *The Heat of the Day*, and *A World of Love*.

CARY, JOYCE (1888–1957). Born in Donegal and educated at Clifton and Trinity College, Oxford. Studied art in Edinburgh. Fought in the Balkan War, 1912–13. Served in Sir Horace Plunkett's Irish Co-operative Organization and in the Nigerian Political Service from 1913 to 1920. Fought with the Nigeria Regiment in the Cameroons 1915–16. Author of many novels, including *Herself Surprised*; *To be a Pilgrim*; *The Horse's Mouth*; *Mr. Johnson*; *A Fearful Joy*; *Prisoner of Grace*; *Except the Lord*, and *Not Honour More*.

DE LA MARE, WALTER (1873–1956). Best known as a poet, but author of stories and novels also. His published works include: *The Return*; *Peacock Pie*; *Memoirs of a Midget*; *The Riddle*; *Broomstick*; *Behold, This Dreamer*; *The Traveller*; *Winged Chariot*, etc.

GALSWORTHY, JOHN (1869–1933). O.M. (1929). Educated at Harrow, and New College, Oxford. Travelled very extensively. Wrote a great number of novels, plays, and short stories, including the series beginning with *The Man of Property*; *The Silver Box*; *Strife*; *Justice*; *The Inn of Tranquillity*; *The Skin Game*; *The Forsyte Saga*; *Loyalties*; *The Forest*; *Maid in Waiting*, and *Flowering Wilderness*.

GREENE, GRAHAM (1904). Educated Berkhamsted and Balliol College, Oxford. Served on staff of *The Times* and the *Spectator*. Foreign Office, 1941–44. Director: Eyre and Spottiswoode Ltd., 1944–8; Bodley Head, 1958–68. His published works include: *It's a*

Battlefield; *England Made Me*; *The Basement Room*; *Brighton Rock*; *The Power and the Glory*; *The Heart of the Matter*; *The End of the Affair*, and *The Quiet American*.

HARTLEY, LESLIE POLES (1895–1972). Educated Harrow and Balliol College, Oxford. His published works include: *The Killing Bottle*; *The Shrimp and the Anemone*; *The Sixth Heaven*; *Eustace and Hilda*; *The Go-Between*, and *A Perfect Woman*.

HUGHES, RICHARD (1900–1976). Educated at Charterhouse, and Oriel College, Oxford. Author and dramatist; contributor to London and American literary journals; co-founder of the Portmadoc Players; Vice-Chairman of the Welsh National Theatre. His published works include: *The Sisters' Tragedy*; *A Comedy of Good and Evil*; *A Moment of Time*; *A High Wind in Jamaica*; *The Spider's Palace*, and *In Hazard*.

JAMES, MONTAGUE RHODES (1862–1936). O.M., Litt.D. Born at Livermere, Suffolk. Educated at Eton, and King's College, Cambridge. Bell Scholar; Craven Scholar; 1st Chancellor's Medallist; Director of Fitzwilliam Museum; Provost of King's College, Cambridge; Schweich Lecturer, British Academy; David Murray Lecturer, Glasgow University, and Provost of Eton. His published works include: *Psalms of Solomon* and *Testament of Abraham*. His writings are very numerous, including much editorial work on ancient MSS. and on stained glass. His works include also: *Ghost Stories of an Antiquary*; *More Ghost Stories of an Antiquary*; *A Thin Ghost and Others*; *The Five Jars*; *A Warning to the Curious*, and *Collected Ghost Stories*.

MAUGHAM, WILLIAM SOMERSET (1874–1965). F.R.S.L., M.R.C.S., L.R.C.P. Educated at King's School, Canterbury, Heidelberg University, and St Thomas's Hospital. Author and dramatist; Officer of the Legion of Honour. His published works include: *Liza of Lambeth*; *Mrs. Craddock*; *The Merry-go-round*; *The Bishop's Apron*; *The Explorer*; *The Magician*; *The Moon and Sixpence*; *The Trembling of a Leaf*; *The Painted Veil*; *Ashenden*; *Cakes and Ale*; and the following plays: *A Man of Honour*; *Lady Frederick*; *Jack Straw*; *Penelope*; *Smith*; *Loaves and Fishes*; *The Land of Promise*; *Love in a Cottage*; *Our Betters*; *East of Suez*; *The Constant Wife*, and *The Breadwinner*.

MERRICK, LEONARD (1864–1939). Born in London. Educated at Brighton College and private schools. His published works include:

A Chair on the Boulevard; Conrad in Quest of his Youth; When Love Flies out o' the Window; The Position of Peggy Harper; The Man who Understood Women; The Quaint Companions; Cynthia; One Man's View; The Worldlings; The Actor-Manager; While Paris Laughed, and *A Woman in the Case.* His work was reissued in 1918 in a collected edition with Introductions by some of the most famous writers of the day.

MITCHISON, NAOMI MARGARET (1897). Born in Edinburgh. Educated at the Dragon School, Oxford, and Oxford University (Home Student). Officier de l'Académie Française; Labour Candidate for Scottish Universities, 1935. Her published works include: *The Conquered; Cloud Cuckoo Land; Black Sparta; Anna Comnena; Barbarian Stories; The Hostages; The Corn King and the Spring Queen; An Outline for Boys and Girls and Their Parents; The Home; We Have Been Warned,* and *The Fourth Pig.* Contributor to *New Statesman, Daily Herald, Clarion,* and *Time and Tide.*

MOSS, GEOFFREY (MAJOR G. MCNEILL-MOSS) (1888). Born in London. Educated at Rugby and R.M.C. Sandhurst. 2nd-Lieut. Grenadier Guards 1905–19; commanded a Battalion of the Gordon Highlanders in France 1915. His published works include: novels: *I face the Stars; Thursby; Sweet Pepper;* modern history: *The Epic of the Alcazar,* 1937; plays: *Sweet Pepper; The Siege;* short stories: *Defeat; The Three Cousins,* and *Wet Afternoon.*

O'CONNOR, FRANK (1903–1966). Born in Cork. Educated by the Christian Brothers. His published works include: *Guests of the Nation* and *Bones of Contention* (stories); *The Saint and Mary Kate* (novel); *The Wild Bird's Nest* and *Lords and Commons* (verse), and *The Big Fellow* (biography).

PRITCHETT, SIR VICTOR SAWDON (1900). Educated at Alleyn's School. Director of *New Statesman* and *Nation.* Holder of various academic posts since 1953. His published works include: *Marching Spain; The Spanish Virgin; Nothing Like Leather; Dead Man Leading; Mr. Beluncle; Collected Short Stories,* and a biography of Turgenev, *The Gentle Barbarian.*

'SAKI' MUNRO, HECTOR HUGH (1870–1916). Born in Burma. Educated at a private school at Exmouth, and later at Bedford. With his elder brother and his sister produced a newspaper. Lived in Normandy and Dresden. Settled in north Devon, and visited

Davos. Joined the Burmese Mounted Police, and after having fever seven times returned to England. His literary talent was recognized by Sir Francis Gould, and he began to write for the *Westminster Gazette* under the name of 'Saki'. In 1902 he went to the Balkans for the *Morning Post* as journalist. In 1905 was correspondent for the *Morning Post* in St. Petersburg, and afterwards in Paris, returning to London in 1908. With great difficulty managed to enlist in the 2nd King Edward's Horse as a trooper, and later exchanged into the 22nd Royal Fusiliers, and rose to the rank of Lance-sergeant, having refused to take a commission. Fell in action at Beaumont-Hamel in 1916. His published works include: *The Chronicles of Clovis*; *The Unbearable Bassington*; *When William Came*, and *The Toys of Peace*.

SANSOM, WILLIAM (1912–76). Educated Uppingham and in Europe. His publications include: *Fireman Flower*; *Something Terrible, Something Lovely*; *The Body*; *The Passionate North*; *The Face of Innocence*, and *A Bed of Roses*.

SAYERS, DOROTHY LEIGH (MRS. FLEMING) (1893–1957). Educated at Somerville College, Oxford. Her published works include: *Clouds of Witness*; *Unnatural Death*; *The Unpleasantness at the Bellona Club*; *Lord Peter views the Body*; *Strong Poison*; *Murder Must Advertise*; *The Nine Tailors*; *Gaudy Night*; *Busman's Honeymoon* (also a play with M. St. Clare Byrne), and *The Zeal of Thy House*. Edited *Great Short Stories of Detection, Mystery and Horror*.

THOMAS, DYLAN (1914–53). Educated Swansea. His published works include: *Deaths and Entrances*; *The Map of Love*; *Portrait of the Artist as a Young Dog*; *Under Milk Wood*; *The Doctor and the Devils*; *Quite Early One Morning*; *Collected Poems*.

WALPOLE, SIR HUGH SEYMOUR (1884–1941). Born in Edinburgh. Educated at King's School, Canterbury, and Emmanuel College, Cambridge. Served with the Russian Red Cross in European War. His published works include: *Mr. Perrin and Mr. Trail*; *Fortitude*; *The Dark Forest*; *The Green Mirror*; *The Secret City*; *The Captives*; *The Cathedral*; *The Old Ladies*; *Portrait of a Man with Red Hair*, and *Harmer John*. He gave the Rede Lecture on the English Novel in 1925.

WAUGH, EVELYN (1903–1966). Educated at Lancing and Hertford College, Oxford. Was in Royal Marines and Royal Horse Guards during 1939–45 War. His publications include: *Decline and Fall*; *Vile*

Bodies; *Black Mischief*; *A Handful of Dust*; *Edmund Campion*; *Brideshead Revisited*; *The Loved One*; *Men at Arms*, and *Officers and Gentlemen*.

WELLS, HERBERT GEORGE (1866–1946). Educated at Midhurst Grammar School, and the Royal College of Science, from which he graduated with first-class honours in Zoology. After teaching Science for some time he took to journalism, and since then devoted himself to writing. The books themselves are so numerous that only the more important can be mentioned. His first efforts in fiction took the form of scientific romances: *The Time Machine*; *The Stolen Bacillus*; *The Invisible Man*; *The Plattner Story*; *The War of the Worlds*; *Tales of Space and Time*, and *The Food of the Gods*; then came a series of genuine novels: *Love and Mr. Lewisham*; *Kipps*, and *The History of Mr. Polly*; after this a series introducing problems of modern society, social, religious, political, and commercial: *Mankind in the Making*; *Tono-Bungay*; *Ann Veronica*; *The New Machiavelli*; *Marriage*; *The World of William Clissold*; and a fourth series with the discursive and dogmatic elements predominant: *Mr. Britling Sees It Through* and *Joan and Peter*. In addition the following should be mentioned: *The Island of Doctor Moreau*; *A Modern Utopia*; *New Worlds for Old*; *The Outline of History*; *A Short History of the World*, and a study of modern educational methods in *The Story of a Great Schoolmaster*; *The Open Conspiracy*; *The Work, Wealth, and Happiness of Mankind*; *The Shape of Things to Come*, and *Experiment in Autobiography*.

WILSON, ANGUS (1913). Educated at Westminster School and Merton College, Oxford. Foreign Office, 1942–6; Deputy Superintendent of Reading Room, British Museum, 1949–55; Lecturer 1963–66, and Professor of English Literature since 1966, at the University of East Anglia. His published works include: *The Wrong Set*; *Such Darling Dodos*; *Emile Zola*; *Hemlock and After*; *Anglo-Saxon Attitudes*; *The Old Men at the Zoo*, and *The World of Charles Dickens*.

ACKNOWLEDGEMENTS

We are grateful for permission to reproduce the following copyright stories:

Elizabeth Bowen: 'Ivy Gripped the Steps.' Copyright 1946 and renewed 1974 by Elizabeth Bowen. Reprinted from *The Demon Lover* by permission of Jonathan Cape Ltd. on behalf of the Estate of Elizabeth Bowen and from *The Collected Stories of Elizabeth Bowen* by permission of Alfred A. Knopf, Inc.

Joyce Cary: 'The Good Investment' and 'Umaru'. Copyright 1950 Joyce Cary. Reprinted by kind permission of Andrew Lownie, Literary Agent.

Walter de la Mare: 'Seaton's Aunt' from *The Best Stories of Walter de la Mare*. Reprinted by permission of The Literary Trustees of Walter de la Mare and The Society of Authors as their representative.

Graham Greene: 'When Greek Meets Greek' from *Collected Stories*, copyright 1947, renewed © 1975 by Graham Greene. All rights reserved. (London: William Heinemann Ltd., and The Bodley Head; New York: Viking.) Reprinted by permission of Laurence Pollinger Ltd., and Viking Penguin, Inc.

L. P. Hartley: 'The Killing Bottle' from *The Travelling Grave* in *The Complete Short Stories of L. P. Hartley*. Copyright © The Executors of the Estate of the late L. P. Hartley. Reprinted by permission of Hamish Hamilton Ltd.

Richard Hughes: 'A Night at a Cottage'. Reprinted by permission of David Higham Associates Ltd.

W. Somerset Maugham: 'Jane' from *Complete Short Stories*. Reprinted by permission of William Heinemann Ltd., and A. P. Watt Ltd., on behalf of the Royal Literary Fund.
'Episode.' Copyright 1946 by Fawcett Publications, Inc. Reprinted from *Creatures of Circumstance* by permission of Doubleday, a division of Bantam, Doubleday, Dell Publishing Group, Inc., and William Heinemann, Ltd.

Leonard Merrick: 'Judgement of Paris.' Reprinted by permission of the National Society for Cancer Relief.

Naomi Mitchison: 'The Hostages.' Reprinted by permission of David Higham Associates Ltd.

Frank O'Connor: 'The Majesty of the Law.' Copyright 1952 by Frank O'Connor. Reprinted from *Collected Stories* by Frank O'Connor, by permission of Alfred A. Knopf, Inc. and from *Stories of Frank O'Connor* (Hamish Hamilton Ltd.) by permission of A. D. Peters & Co. Ltd.
'Peasants'. Copyright 1936 by Frank O'Connor. Reprinted from *Stories of Frank O'Connor* by permision of A. D. Peters & Co. Ltd., and from *Collected Stories* by permission of Alfred A. Knopf, Inc.

V. S. Pritchett: 'The Aristocrat' and 'The Scapegoat'. Reprinted from *You Make Your Own Life* by permission of Chatto & Windus Ltd., and from *Collected Stories* (Random House, Inc.) by permission of A. D. Peters & Co. Ltd.

William Sansom: 'The Girl on the Bus' from *The Passionate North*. Copyright 1950 by William Sansom. Reprinted by permission of Elaine Greene Ltd.

Dorothy L. Sayers: 'The Learned Adventure of the Dragon's Head' from *Lord Peter Views the Body* (NEL). Reprinted by permission of David Higham Asociates Ltd.

Dylan Thomas: 'A Visit to Grandpa's' from *Portrait of the Artist as a Young Dog*. Reprinted by permission of David Higham Associates Ltd.

Sir Hugh Walpole: 'Mr Oddy.' Reprinted by permission of Sir Rupert Hart-Davis.

Evelyn Waugh: 'Mr. Loveday's Little Outing.' Reprinted from *Work Suspended* (London: Chapman & Hall Ltd.) by permission of A. D. Peters & Co. Ltd. Published in the United States in *Mr. Loveday's Little Outing and Other Sad Stories* (Boston: Little, Brown & Co.). US Copyright handled by Harold Matson Literary Agency.

H. G. Wells: 'The Door In The Wall' from *The Short Stories of H. G. Wells*. Reprinted by permission of A. P. Watt Ltd., on behalf of The Literary Executors of the Estate of H. G. Wells.

Angus Wilson: 'Realpolitik' from *The Wrong Set*. Copyright © Angus Wilson 1949. Reprinted by permission of Secker & Warburg Ltd., and Curtis Brown Ltd., London.

Unfortunately we were unable to trace the copyright holder for the following. If contacted we shall be pleased to include correct acknowlegement in any future reprints and/or new editions:

Geoffrey McNeill-Moss: 'Defeat' from *Defeat* (Century Hutchinson).